The Land
of Everlasting Gloom
Napoleon's Vampire Hunters - 3

BY THE SAME AUTHOR

The Land
of Everlasting Gloom
Napoleon's Vampire Hunters - 3

by
Frank Schildiner

A Black Coat Press Book

Acknowledgements: Paul Féval and Brian Stableford.

Copyright © 2020 by Frank Schildiner.
Introduction © 2020 by Jean-Marc Lofficier.
Cover illustration Copyright © 2020 Mariusz Gandzel.

Visit our website at www.blackcoatpress.com

Introduction

In addition to *La Vampire* (1856; tr. as *The Vampire Countess*), whose chief protagonist is swordmaster Jean-Pierre Séverin, already reviewed in our previous volume, Frank Schildiner's *The Land of Everlasting Gloom* draws on and incorporates characters and elements from Paul Féval's *Le Chevalier Ténèbre* (1860; tr. as *Knightshade*)[1] and *La Ville-Vampire* (1867; tr. as *Vampire City*)[2].

In *Knightshade*, the tale of the brothers Ténèbre's exploits as undead monsters, petty criminals and ingenious storytellers is so steadfast in its refusal to decide whether its supernatural apparatus is to be taken literally, metaphorically, or merely as a joke, that the drunken progress and hasty conclusion leave a great many pertinent questions unanswered–but that kind of playfulness is not at all inappropriate to the type of narrative it is, or to the time in which it was written.

It is a story which continually raises questions about the terms on which storytellers may legitimately approach their audiences, and the way in which they manipulate those audiences, all the while exemplifying its own conclusions in its own approaches and manipulations. The narrative is full of nudges and winks, which seek–with a blithe disingenuousness that is actually rather ingenious–to establish that the reader is an active conspirator in the spinning of the story as well as a hapless victim of the spin.

Knightshade displays some of Féval's weaknesses as conspicuously as it displays his main strengths, but it is undoubtedly one of the most interesting works in his vampiric canon, and one whose substance is echoed in many half-

---

[1] Black Coat Press, ISBN 978-0-9740711-4-5.
[2] Black Coat Press, ISBN 978-0-9740711-6-9.

hidden corners of the contemporary popular fiction market-place.

Like it, *Vampire City* is also a mixture of comedy and horror fiction, but whereas *Knightshade* was structured as tales nested within tales, *Vampire City* is a parody of the classic Gothic novel, and appropriates as its heroine the most success-ful of all the authors in that genre, Ann Radcliffe (1764-1823).

At the time of its first publication, the hybrid hor-ror/comedy genre to which both novel belong hardly existed, and Féval may be credited with its invention. It was not a great success in its own day, but now that comic books and movies have made horror/comedy a familiar genre, it is difficult to write "traditional" horror stories–especially those with Gothic elements–without a gloss of satirical humor. The spread of gruesome horror motifs from 18-rated movies to the universal-ly-accessible medium of television has resulted in the restora-tion of a certain calculated coyness to the presentation of Gothic imagery, which is routinely combined with a calculat-edly light note of stylized irony.

With the aid of hindsight, we can easily see in *Vampire City* the ultimate literary ancestor of the popular television show *Buffy the Vampire-Slayer*. Although the fictitious "Anne Radcliffe" is not permitted by her gentlemanly author actually to slay any vampires with her own hand, she is nevertheless the prime mover of the expedition to the Vampire City of Se-lene; she watches with a distinctly proto-feminist fascination as the Irish hero carefully excises the heart from the breast of a comatose vampire.

Jean-Marc Lofficier
& Brian Stableford

Prologue

The great explorer lay dying in his own bed, alone, saddened by the chill that slowly spread up his legs. He knew the end was near and accepted that fact—he merely wished he had just a little more time. An odd feeling, but life was always one filled with opposing feelings and experiences.

The dying man's name was Abraham Hyacinthe Anquetil-Duperron, and his history was one that would make for excellent tales in the penny dreadfuls. Philologist, explorer, occultist, and teacher; Anquetil-Duperron was the first European expert in ancient Indian languages, religions, and history. His work was celebrated by academics throughout the world-especially his hundreds of translations of ancient religious texts.

Once a man of medium height, broad shoulders, a dancer's willow waist, and handsome, dissolute countenance, time had transformed this image. His pale flesh resembled that of an elderly, overfed boar, jiggling and quivering as he walked. His receding hairline and full face now looked like a caricature of wealthy merchant or noble from pre-revolutionary days.

None of which mattered in these final moments. He had once sought an understanding of the nature of life and death, of the ancient truths of the universe. Now, Abraham Hyacinthe Anquetil-Duperron fully comprehended one final truth—death was inevitable, whether you studied religious texts written at the dawn of time or not. One of his teachers, an ancient Zoroastrian priest named Darab, once said that in a famed quote:

"One need not scale the heights of the Heavens, nor travel along the highways of the world, to find God. With puri-

ty of mind and holiness of heart, one can find Him in one's own heart."

Simplistic, brilliant—and quite true. Despite having sought the secrets of life and death throughout India and through texts written before recorded history, life was fleeting. Abraham Hyacinthe Anquetil-Duperron accepted this now, as he lay alone in his cold room.

The front door suddenly swung open, the low creaking of the hinge waking him from his musing. A figure in dark clothing strode inside, a long steel dagger in one hand, a heavy stick in the other. The hidden individual stood in the shadows, face hidden beneath a heavy scarf, body covered in a dark blue boating cloaking.

Anquetil-Duperron opened his mouth, intent on greeting his visitor, but no sound emerged from his cracked, black lips.

The visitor pulled aside a scarf, revealing a smiling face beneath.

"What…?" the dying man said, lips forming words without sounds.

"What do I want?" the other asked and chuckled softly. "I think you already know."

The visitor's woolen-gloved hand pocketed the dagger and reached out towards the quivering flesh beneath Anquetil-Duperron's chin. The fingers gently removed a leather tong from the dying man's neck, revealing a complex brass key.

"No," Abraham Hyacinthe Anquetil-Duperron croaked, his body convulsing slightly under his heavy coverlet. "...ev… il… death…"

He could say no more; the exertion was too much for his failing form. Anquetil-Duperron's vision grew murky and he knew the end was near.

"Evil? Death? Of course, professor, that is why I spent so much time in your company," the other said with a grating snicker. "It was not for your poor wit or ridiculous beliefs. I awaited the day I could quietly discover where you hid the folio. I learned the truth at the ceremony of your intronisation at the Institut de France. My patience is now rewarded,"

Leaning forward, the smiling man met the gaze of Abraham Hyacinthe Anquetil-Duperron.

"When you reach Heaven or Hell, or whatever lies beyond the veil, go with the knowledge that the *asura Raktabīja* shall rise again. Then the demon shall cleanse this world of life and shall start anew. This is your legacy, professor…"

Abraham Hyacinthe Anquetil-Duperron did not reply or even gasp at this revelation, having died partway through the speech.

His visitor frowned with annoyance, robbed of the moment of triumph by the slack face and unseeing eyes.

Glancing at the key and chuckling, the thief headed back into the chilly evening. It would be hours before anyone discovered the corpse. The locked safe was nearby and nobody would miss one ancient, untranslated manuscript.

What is it that the stupid Christians say about the end of the world? the thief thought. *Oh yes, Matthew 24:29, "Immediately after the tribulation of those days, the Sun will be darkened, and the Moon will not give its light, and the stars will fall from Heaven, and the powers of the Heavens will be shaken." That is the truth. When Raktabīja returns, he shall bring the end of all things…*

CHAPTER ONE

September, 1806

The vampire shrieked, extended his claws, and pounced like a cat onto the wooden floor of the warehouse.

Two women followed, landing on his left and right, sinking low as they spat at the intruders.

They were three naked creatures, their hairless bodies glowing bright under the silver moonlight rays that peeked through the holes in the roof.

"Why are they hairless?" a voice asked.

The accented French sounded Germanic in tone, with harsh emphasis on the consonants.

"That is an interesting question," a calm voice answered, in the drawl of a native Parisian. "I asked my second teacher that same question thirty years ago. He had no answer. I still await a reason."

The speakers were an odd pair, unalike in every way. A director in the *Commedia dell'arte* would have happily cast this pair as *Il Dottore* and *Colombine*—the dour head of the household and his sneaky servant.

The first was a tall, rapier-thin man with dark hair which blended in with the darkness of the warehouse. He was handsome in the fashion of a nobleman from the days of ancient knights and kings, despite a jagged scar across his right cheek. However, most who met this man found themselves caught by his light blue eyes. There was an almost lupine air to his gaze, and few met it for longer than a few seconds.

His name was Franz von Karnstein, and he was an Austrian nobleman. His family, one of the oldest in Europe, possessed a somber reputation that many used as a warning against naughty children. "Lock your doors or the Karnsteins will get you," was a saying heard across many locations from Austria and Hungary, all the way to France and Italy.

Dressed in black clothing and bearing a simple metal cross, Franz von Karnstein resembled a Puritan crusader rather than the heir to one of the oldest titles in Europe.

His companion was a solidly built man with a lined, hard face and a sinewy body. His light hair and dark eyes, eerie calm and superhuman control, gave him an air of mystery. Dressed in simple, well-cut clothing from an earlier age, he thought that outward displays of wealth or opulence were unnecessary and ridiculous. Most would have labeled him a revolutionary, like those that had overthrown the Bourbons from the French throne thirteen years earlier. In a sense, they would have been correct, for he was a strict Republican who held deep sympathies for the original beliefs of the Revolution.

His name was Jean-Pierre Séverin, and he was, among other things, a sword master and the head of the Paris Morgue. A confidant of Emperor Napoleon Bonaparte, Séverin was an important, if mostly unknown, member of the Imperial government.

"I think it does not matter," Karnstein said while placing a hand on his sword hilt. "At least, not at the moment."

Séverin nodded once. "Yes, I believe you are correct,"

The lead vampire snarled, revealing rows of serrated, yellow fangs, and a long, lolling black tongue that slithered across his bloodless lips. His red and yellow eyes grew wider and he reared back, like a cat preparing to leap. His female followers moved in the same manner, their motions precisely matching their master's actions.

The lead vampire leaped forward, his snarl rending the air, aiming for Karnstein. The nobleman stepped aside, his sword arm slashing out with a speed nearly as impressive as that of his undead opponent. A heavy cavalry saber appeared in his hand, the sharp steel slashing across the monster's exposed neck.

The vampire shrieked as the blade bit deep within the undead flesh. Black ichor splattered across the creature's skin as viscous bubbles appeared across his oversized mouth.

The vampire shook and then snarled, a liquid sound that evoked images of a drowning animal growling as it fought back. Rearing back a second time, the monster prepared for a second strike, his ragged talons glistening in the spare light.

Nearby, the female vampire on the left leaped towards Séverin, her hairless, emaciated, body resembling a sexless statue carved by a mad, if somewhat talented, artist.

The swordmaster lunged forward, piercing the vampire's right shoulder with a long, silver rapier. The undead woman howled, her head convulsing with inhuman violence. The delicate neck bones cracked and reassembled as the monster shuddered and moved towards the older Frenchman.

Within seconds, she would be upon him, her vicious claws and oversized incisors ripping his flesh.

The third vampire woman sailed above the humans' heads, landing in a low crouch mere feet away from their exposed backs. Pulling her shoulders back, she pointed her skeletal skull towards Karnstein, preparing for another pounce.

The Austrian nobleman slashed the air before the male vampire, missing the undead monster by a foot. The creature stepped forward; his glittering eyes widened as the handsome nobleman's other hand rose into view, a massive musket pistol gripped in his fist, cocked and prepared in advance.

Karnstein said in a phlegmatic tenor, "*In nomine Patris, et Filii, et Spiritus Sancti, Amen.*"

He then pulled the trigger. After a thunderous roar, a tongue of flame, and gray smoke, the vampire's head exploded in an appalling cloud of ichor, bone, and dust. Gore spread across the floor, spattering in a massive, viscous, black pool.

Nearby, Séverin lunged forward with his free hand, a wicked wooden stake held tightly in his scarred fist. The weapon pierced the exposed flesh, sinking between the visible ribs, piercing the heart.

The female vampire moaned softly, quivered once, and fell away, her body crumbling into a fine pale powder.

The third vampire screeched at the death of her sire and sister, and moaned as a wooden shard emerged from her chest.

She toppled forward, her undead existence over before collapsing.

"*Idiota*!" a feminine voice said. "You left your back exposed again!"

"I did not," Karnstein said, "and stop called me an idiot,"

"Then stop acting like one," came the amused reply.

The woman stepping into view was a vision of loveliness, the type used as inspiration by poets and artists since the dawn of time. She was tall for a woman, with a wide, oval face, olive skin, full lips, heavy, dark lashes and straight black hair that she wore in a tight pony tail down her back. Her figure was the classic hourglass, with an astonishingly narrow waist, wide hips and high, full breasts. A battered, outdated tricorn hat sat atop her head, somehow appearing elegant despite being a fashion shunned even by street beggars.

"If there had been another vampire holding my attention," she said, approaching Karnstein while lowering her old crossbow, "that monster would have been consuming you as we speak."

"There were only three," replied the Austrian, pulling out a rag and cleaning his blade. "No others lie within this building or below."

"We were both exposed, Franz," Séverin intervened. "However, I knew the precise location of every item or person in this room. Did you?"

Karnstein shook his head, sheathed his sword and reloaded his musket.

"I did not," he admitted. "But I did know there were only three of these damned creatures in the building,"

The woman, whose name was Sylvia Dardi, exchanged a resigned look with the older swordmaster. Both knew the Austrian baron possessed certain skills and abilities beyond comprehension. He could, after a brief prayer in ancient Sumerian, exorcise demons, and he could spot the world's supernatural beings even from a great distance. The latter talent taxed his mind and body and, they both believed, endangered his very soul.

"Very well," Sylvia said, also sheathing his sword, "but I do not like the risks you take in battle. A saber and a pistol against a vampire? You are completely *pazzesco!*"

The corner of Karnstein's mouth lifted slightly, the closest he often came to a grin.

"But it worked."

Sylvia rounded on him, pushing her face close to his and placing both hands on her hips in obvious annoyance.

"But what if you'd missed, *idiota?*"

Karnstein threw back his cloak, revealing a pair of muskets across his hips.

"The monster would have found me prepared... and stop calling me an idiot."

Sylvia grinned, pulled his face down to hers, and kissed the handsome Austrian for several seconds.

"Then stop acting like one," she said, laughing.

Séverin sighed and shook his head.

"Before you begin alternating between squabbling and embracing," he said patiently, "let us leave this location. These were not the monsters we sought."

Sylvia looped an arm through Karnstein's while nodding.

"You're right, Maestro," she said, "these pathetic creatures were little more than *animali.* They could not steal away women and children unseen in the night."

Séverin nodded and led the pair towards the shattered wall barely visible in the distance.

"Quite so, Sylvia. I would wager that if we searched below this floor, we would find a nest of shattered animal bones. Vampires such as those three are mindless creatures who crave blood from any source. Ending their undead existence was merely an act of mercy."

"We are still no closer to the source of these attacks across Paris," Karnstein said, his words taut with anger.

"Oh, but we are," Sylvia said, grinning in his direction. "The Maestro and I discovered the identity of the pair who terrorize this city."

Karnstein raised an eyebrow quizzically and asked, "Oh? Why was I not made aware of this information?"

"Because my dearest, *idiota fidanzato*, you arrived late at this rendezvous and we had no time for chat," Sylvia replied.

Sensing another lover's quarrel coming, Séverin intervened: "We believe that, based on the available information, the abductions and murders were the acts of a vampire and a ghoul. I know of only one such pairing,"

"The Ténèbre Brothers," Sylvia said, shaking her head and sighing.

"*Ach du lieber Himmel*," Karnstein said and crossed himself.

CHAPTER II

The luxuriant black coach rumbled across the cobble-stoned streets, drowning out the clip-clop from the two gray horses pulling it. The carriage appeared expensive and tasteful, possessing none of the gilt stylings one expected from tasteless wealthy merchants. A gold painted coat of arms, carefully covered by a draped blanket, hung over the left side door, partially peeking into view as the cloth flapped from errant wind gusts.

Seated atop and steering the horses sat a man, a shrunken figure huddling beneath a heavy red cloak, with a long top hat resting on the crown of his hunched head. A scarf held the hat in place, an elaborate and bizarre knot laying beneath his pointed chin. Lashing the horses with a long, thin whip, the coach trotted through the streets, forcing the few pedestrians to step aside.

The carriage's gait slowed as they turned onto the Boulevard du Temple. Normally a bustling, fashionable district frequented by young and old for recreation, the area was surprisingly clear of inhabitants this day. The heavy, frigid winds threw swirling vortices of frost through the air, adding to the desolate, abandoned atmosphere.

The driver stomped his foot down three times as he slowly drove down the lane. A small trapdoor near his feet opened with a dull thud.

"Yes?" asked a voice from below.

"Nobody is about, Jean," the driver said, his voice light and surprisingly cultured. "This is a waste of time,"

"No matter," the hidden speaker said. "We promised Strix three, and we only have two. If necessary, we shall ride all night."

The trapdoor closed with a snap and the driver glanced down before shaking his head violently for a moment. The carriage rattled along with nobody in sight for several minutes.

Eventually, a man appeared around a corner, a hand holding his cap upon his head.

The driver stomped his foot again and spoke after the trapdoor opened again.

"A man, fifty yards ahead. Based on his clothing, he had money, but not now."

A chuckle rose from below.

"Well done, Ange. I knew we would succeed,"

The driver grunted and said, "Next time, you drive."

The only reply from the passenger was a loud guffaw.

The trapdoor slammed shut and the coach picked up speed. The pedestrian wisely moved away from the street, his head down against the chill. He was a tall man with long, bony arms and legs, dressed in a blue suit with fraying cuffs and stains across the lapels. His rectangular face appeared red from the wind and his wispy blond mustache and beard fluttered as the breeze's intensity grew.

Slowing, the carriage's window rolled down with a snap and a dark form filled the space.

"Monsieur," a calm, cultured voice said, "you look chilled to the bone. Please, join me and we shall see you home. Come, come, you shall become ill if you remain outside in such a thin coat!"

The lone pedestrian, whose name was René Gros, glanced at the luxuriant carriage with a suspicious glint in his eyes.

"I'm sorry," he said in a rough, gravely timbre. "Do we know each other?"

"I am Comte de Gercourt," said the passenger. "Perhaps you've heard of me? Perhaps not. However, Christian charity would not allow me to pass a man suffering in this terrible cold."

René Gros frowned, but was unable to admit he never heard of this nobleman. To do so might insult the man, which might mean he would have to walk three more miles in the freezing cold.

"Yes, of course," René Gros finally said, nodding slowly. "I would be grateful. My home is a long way away…"

The passenger could not be seen, as he had slid back. The carriage door opened slowly and a hand beckoned René Gros inside.

"Please, Monsieur, do not be shy. Enter and we shall share a brandy and chase away the chill,"

René Gros, who rarely trusted his fellow man, none-the-less felt the cold worse today than he had in a long time. A gambler and minor thief by profession, he had been suffering from a bad losing streak over the last months.

First, a group of sailors had discovered the special dice he kept up his sleeve after cheating them out of their wages. They had beaten him after taking back their money, tossing him into the Seine and destroying his best suit. Then, Esmée, his wife, had discovered his affair with Catherine and had thrown him out of their hovel.

"My grandmother? You slept with my grandmother? You, vermin!" Esmée had shouted as she had thrown his clothes into the street.

From that day on, René Gros had lost almost every game, with only a few small thefts keeping him fed and living in a garret above his cousin's butcher shop. Just this day, a potential new lover, a seamstress named Odile, had turned him down and returned to her drunken husband.

Perhaps my luck has changed, thought René Gros as he stepped inside, closed the door, and lifted the window into place.

The simple, comfortable carriage interior impressed him, possessing an elegance he had never seen, but heard existed. The leather cushioned walls were not flashy, like those of the coach owned by Oscar Chaput, the Breton brandy smuggler who ran all crime in Ménilmontant. His carriage had gold painted metal, red fabric, and a giant Moor in a turban and a sword riding atop the box.

"Thank you, Monsieur le Comte," he said, happy his teeth were not chattering, "You are a true Christian gentleman and I am in your debt."

The Comte was as tall as René Gros, with dark brown hair, a triangular face that could be anywhere from thirty to sixty, and small lobeless ears. His clothing was dark, but appeared well-cut and, if not new, then well-cared for. He had long, thin fingers that fluttered through the air and resembled pale spiders descending from hidden webs.

"No, no, Monsieur," the Comte said, slowly shaking his head/ "You oblige me by providing me with company on this lonely, cold day. Now, a brandy?"

The Comte's dancing fingers opened a hidden compartment built into the coach wall, revealing a small collection of bottles and two squat silver cups. Pouring a caramel-colored liquid in the two glasses, the Comte handed René Gros one and took the second for himself.

"Please, drink away, Monsieur," he said, raising his cup in salute.

René Gros sipped his brandy, savoring the smooth flavor. The liquor was no better or worse than any he drank when he had funds, which was something of a surprise. He had always imagined the wealthy drank and ate items of better quality than other people.

Or maybe, nobles are so powerful that they choose lesser quality drink for some reason? Rich people are strange, he thought, gulping down the brandy greedily.

The Comte poured him another, and a third a moment later.

"Good, no? A special blend made for my family by a monastery west of Paris. Please, have more if you please."

René Gros grunted a thanks, grateful for the warm feeling that filled his body. This surprised him. Usually, he could down a bottle or more before feeling the effects of alcohol.

"Strong," he slurred after slurping down a fourth.

His eyelids felt heavy and the cup fell from his fumbling fingers. He tried mumbling an apology, but his tongue felt too large for his mouth. Within seconds, René Gros fell forward, snoring and drooling on the carriage floor.

The man who had called himself the Comte de Gercourt pulled a small lever on the side of his seat. Above his head the trapdoor opened, sending a quick blast of frigid air into the coach.

"What now?" came the voice of the driver.

"He is unconscious," the *faux* Comte said. "Let us return to Strix."

"It took long enough. What of the others?"

The *faux* Comte pulled aside the curtains beneath the seats. Beneath the one he sat upon lay a woman of about twenty. Her clothes were expensive, a silken outfit one would expect from a lady of quality. She was unconscious and snoring, a lock of blond hair plastered across her damp face.

Below the second seat lay a boy, probably no older than thirteen, with a youthful face. He was a chubby child, round-faced with pale, soft skin and sugary stains from sweets spread across his chin and chest. Like the woman, and now René Gros, he too lay unconscious.

"All are asleep. Your potion proved perfect, Ange," the *faux* Comte said, leaning back in his seat and crossing his legs.

"Of course, it was, Jean," Ange replied, kicking the trapdoor closed.

A moment later, the carriage picked up speed. Jean, returned the drugged brandy and glasses to the secret compartment. Sighing with contentment, he examined René Gros's exposed neck and shook his head.

"Not much eating there," he said.

He leaned down, examining the unconscious boy while licking his lips with a long, scarlet tongue.

CHAPTER III

"I believe," Jean-Pierre Séverin said as they climbed into a cab and headed off, "that you already know of the Ténèbre Brothers."

The remark appeared directed at Franz von Karnstein, who was busy adjusting his sword so he had both access to it and some comfort. When he did not answer, Sylvia elbowed him in his side while rolling her eyes his direction.

"I was listening," he said, gently elbowing Sylvia back.

Séverin sighed long and loud, knowing the young lovers' chat could easily degenerate into a scene of laughter, teasing, and kissing. Though they were a couple he approved of and encouraged, Sylvia and Franz were at the stage where they became tiresome for outsiders. Before this scene occurred, he stepped in:

"I assumed you were. Please tell me how you know of them."

Franz turned away from Sylvia, focusing his pale eyes upon his teacher.

"I learned of those creatures from my last teacher. He told me that they were brothers who went off to join John Hunyadi in his crusade against the Turks. Their actions were considered heinous, even by standards of that bloody war. While there, they fell under curses, the source of which I am unaware. One, Jean Ténèbre, became an *oupire*, which I believe is what some call a ghoul. The other, Ange Ténèbre, became a vampire. According to my master, they've each died many deaths, but always return to their undead state. That is all I know."

"You know less than I, *mi amore*," Sylvia said, "The Ténèbre Brothers are marauders who love trickery, murder, and rapine. A bishop once described them as the embodied versions of the seven deadly sins."

"The bishop who said that was Theodoric of Novi Sad one hundred and thirty-four years ago," Karnstein said, earning another elbow from Sylvia.

Séverin silently applauded.

"Correct. They are experienced, powerful, intelligent, dangerous, and possibly unkillable. I should sooner face one of Franz's evil ancestors before this pair. We must investigate their actions and determine why they are acting so overtly. The Ténèbre Brothers are often circumspect until the end of their rampages. We shall act both overtly and covertly in our search. Teams of two worked well in Venice. We shall attempt that again,"

"But we are three?" Karnstein pointed out, waving one finger in a circle and encompassing the cab's passengers.

Sylvia giggled and mockingly covered her mouth. With false sincerity, she asked, "Oh, did I forget to mention my dearest Papa arrives tomorrow and shall join us in our search for the evil undead?"

"Yes, you did," Franz said, though his voice sounded mild.

Bartolomeo Dardi, Sylvia's father, was Séverin's oldest friend and a fellow swordmaster of the Italian school of combat. A member of the famed vampire-hunting Dardi clan, he possessed the joyful spirit of a buccaneer with the intensity of a master of the art of swordfight.

"Papa has questions about the wedding. I hope he shall be satisfied with your answers…" Sylvia said.

Karnstein raised a hand, as close to a shrug as he appeared willing to perform with respect to his fiery fiancée. As a noble with connections to the Pope and the Emperor of Austria, he required permission for marriage to Sylvia Dardi. Both important figures could reject the engagement for any reason.

"My grandfather agreed and sent his permission to us and to the Emperor. Now we can only wait and pray," Karnstein said.

Sylvia harrumphed and crossed her arms, tapping one foot in annoyance.

"Same answer every time, *idiota*."

"That is the only answer I have, and stop calling me an idiot."

"Then stop acting like one…"

Séverin glanced skyward, wondering if he and his late wife were so quarrelsome when they were courting.

Probably, yes, he thought, a little indulgently towards his students.

He then said, "I believe all shall go as you hope soon enough. Until then, Franz, we must work more on your opening attack. Your speed was better, but your placement of the initial attack was somewhat offline. Report to the training hall before dawn and we shall exercise before your Matines prayers."

Seeing the grin spreading upon Sylvia's face, Séverin smiled inwardly and decided to act:

"As to you, Mademoiselle Dardi," he said, "I shall expect you by dawn for your training session. Your smallsword work has improved, but your rapier ripostes are not particularly crisp and precise."

With that, the older French swordmaster sat back content with the day's work. His pupils were progressing, and they had an important mission. One thought remained in the back of his mind:

Why are the Ténèbre Brothers acting so openly? Have we made a mistake in our identification? he asked himself as the cab stopped before Sylvia's apartments.

Ignoring the extended farewell between the two lovers, he ran over the problem of the ghoul and the vampire who used the evil name of Ténèbre.

CHAPTER IV

Jean Ténèbre wrapped the chains around the unconscious woman's wrists and ankles, licking his lips at her succulent flesh. He hoped this one at least could be fit for consumption after Strix completed the bloody rites. The last set were completely inedible, tainted with a queer energy that transformed the flesh into mere dust.

"I claim this one," Ange said as he caressed the neck of the young boy. "I smell his blood… untainted and full of youthful life… I must have it…"

Driver's livery gone, Ange Ténèbre was a unique sight. Several heads smaller than his ghoulish brother Jean, he possessed curling blond hair that fell in ringlets about his face. He dressed in the simple cassock of a priest, though the gold, jewel encrusted crucifix on his narrow chest was inverted. His face was not handsome, but pretty and soft, resembling that of a Renaissance painting cherub.

"If that one is not tainted like the last group," Jean said, retracting the black talons that peeked out from his fingertips.

"There shall be none for either of you," Strix said, striding into view.

The figure that had just appeared stood slightly taller than Ange and was covered in a heavy black and red robe. A neatly stitched pentagram lay across the fabric's front and rear, glimmering in the torchlight.

An oversized goat's mask hid Strix's head and face, a bizarre merger of man and beast. The dark lacquered wood mask was intricately carved and its spiraling horns were the actual product of an actual goat or similar animal. Blood-red stones lay in the eye sockets and each glistened in the spare light.

Ange Ténèbre snarled and balled his hands into tight, knuckle popping fists. His small sharp teeth showed as he approached the masked sorcerer.

"I must feed," Ange said. "Not later, now!"

Jean appeared at his brother's side and nodded, his face grave, his shoulders and back taut and ridged.

"We both require sustenance. Animals are an inadequate diet. If this does not occur, we shall revert to an uncontrolled form."

A loud sigh emerged from Strix's mask and the mystic swiveled towards the prone captives.

"I can make do with two, this time. Take the woman, but dispose of her body elsewhere. Now, leave me. I must commune with the powers from beyond the veil."

Ange growled again, opening his mouth and flashing his fangs. Before he spoke, Jean squeezed his brother's shoulder and the vampire glanced up at the taller ghoul. Neither spoke, but their expressions changed as if they held an unspoken conversation.

The vampire then nodded once and the undead brothers turned their attention to Strix.

"Acceptable," Ange said. "But do not make that mistake again,"

Strix's goat mask nodded and the echoing voice within said, "My apologies. My acquaintance with the undead was limited to former denizens of Selene. Your needs remain mysterious to me."

"Those are not vampires, no matter what they call themselves. They are something strange and uncanny," Ange said, turning away.

"They steal lives and exist many years beyond humanity's limitations. They are vampires, according to all texts upon the subject," Strix retorted, moving towards the unconscious boy with slow, methodical steps.

Jean shook his head as he unfastened the bonds holding the girl in place.

"They are not. Ange is a vampire, and we met others in our travels. But those beings from Selene confuse us. They drink blood, but they receive no sustenance from their feast."

Strix did not answer, still examining the boy and René Gros. Jean and Ange lifted the girl's body from her slab and vacated the chamber, heading towards their rooms.

Slicing away René Gros' clothes, Strix raised the bronze blade up and created a complex pattern in the air. The blade then sliced deep into the man's exposed chest, sending a scarlet spray of viscous *vitae* across the goat mask.

"*Abhisaṃśru mayate dānavāri narakasya...*" came the words as the blood and gore spread across the sorcerer's chest and arms.

CHAPTER V

The Englishman and his servant slipped into Paris unnoticed, having hidden in a cart filled with hay. Leaping out at a particularly dark street, they stole through the night. Staying in the shadows of alleys, they found the ruined building they planned to use as their base.

"What is that stench?" Lord Henry Morley said, grabbing his nose in disgust.

"Wolf urine," Ishaani said without inflection.

She pulled Morley's hand from his nose and shook her head.

"Breathe and become accustomed to the smell. Soon it shall be of little notice. This building holds far worse odors if one ventures below this floor,"

The structure in question was a nearly demolished apartment building with vast gouges in the walls, ceilings and floors. A layer of heavy dust and neglect hung over every room, though, oddly, nothing stirred as they explored the first floor. They did not hear the rustle and squeak of rodents, nor the skittering chatter of insects. A choking stillness hung over this location, one that sent waves of disquiet through Henry Morley.

He was a man of middle height, with a square face, a long bony nose, and large dark blue eyes. He wore his blonde hair in a pony tail that fell to his back and he walked with a rolling gait reminiscent of a sailor.

"Why this berth?" he asked, wrinkling his nose again.

"Terrible creatures resided in this place," Ishaani said. "Monsters more beast than man. Many died here and people shun this neighborhood. They know this is a bad place."

"There are many bad places in Paris," Morley said. "This city was once attacked by Ragnar Lodbrok. Why, after these fools overthrew their king, they painted the streets with the blood of their fellow countrymen!"

Ishaani shook her head and righted an overturned chair.

"Few places in the world hold such darkness as this building."

"What does that mean?" Morley asked, as he stepped into her line of vision.

"You name human horrors," Ishaani said as she dusted the chair clean. "The monsters who dwelled in this place were worse. They were cursed creatures, a dreadful merger of man and beast. Their appetites were bottomless, and they lived only for blood, flesh, and pain,"

"Werewolves?" he said, not hiding his incredulity. "Such stuff is nonsense. Peasant superstition!"

Ishaani shook her head slowly as she unpinned her heavy knot of ebony hair from the base of her long, elegant neck.

"Not so, sahib Captain. Most cases of this type are simply sad souls whose minds are lost. A few are insane from the eating of human meat. However, some receive the curse of the beast and become as dangerous as the legends foretold. You should know by now that demons of the dark exist and seek the blood and bones of mankind,"

"I only know that your father made me a promise," Morley said. "If I help you find your pagan papers, you will enrich me with a king's ransom in jewels and gold,"

"We shall do so, sahib Captain," she said as she picked up a second chair and cleaned it with a rag. "You must do your part and discover their location."

"Fine, fine," Morley said, waving a hand and sniffing. "I shall discover what happened to Professor Anquetil-Duperron's effects, and we shall take the beastly pages in a simple boarding action. That is what I do best, after all."

"I doubt it shall be so simplistic, but yes. That is what we require. I shall remain hidden and watch your activities. Should the need arise, I shall kill anyone who threatens our mission," Ishaani said, adding, "Now I shall find an unbroken table and we shall eat. Then I must sacrifice to the Goddess for good fortunes on our mission."

Morley turned away, hiding his revulsion from his servant. Her religion was pagan superstition that he knew was both evil and horrific. Yet, the jewels and gold they offered overcame his misgivings. He had viewed the wealth at their temple hidden in the Indian hills. Their rites horrified and disgusted him, but their gift of three rubies and a bag of gold coins had cleared all the family debts.

The next payment will return my family to its rightful place as leaders of the country. I can accept a pact with pagans for the greater good of the family, he thought as he searched for a clean spot where he could sling a hammock.

CHAPTER VI

"Papa!" Sylvia shrieked as she ran into her father's embrace.

Tears streamed down her face as they spoke in rapid Neapolitan-accented Italian.

Jean-Pierre Séverin and Franz von Karnstein remained a short distance away, unwilling to intrude upon the family reunion.

Bartolomeo Dardi stood about his daughter's height, with a triangular face, a jet-black beard and a mustache clipped close to his face. His huge eyes that almost burst from their sockets. He possessed a wide, almost oversized, grin, perfect white teeth, and the body of a professional acrobat.

Dressed in a bright red silk shirt, dark blue pantaloons, high Hessian style boots, and a battered old cloak that resembled a horse blanket, he cut a comical figure. A well-used smallsword lay strapped across his hip, and he moved with the ease of a dancer.

"Few realize," Séverin said *sotto voce*, "that this man who laughs constantly and performs silly magic tricks for children is probably the best swordsman in Italy, if not all Europe,"

"Better than you?" Karnstein asked, cocking his head to the side in some show of interest.

Séverin performed an elaborate Gallic shrug.

"That depends upon the details. With smallsword, we are roughly equal. My greater reach occasionally surpassed his lightning speed. With rapier and saber, no. I defeat him easily. With rapier and *main gauche* or daggers, he is the master. The differences between master of the art of the sword is sometimes measured in inches."

"An inch is often the difference between life and death," Karnstein approved.

"Correct," Séverin agreed, "which is why you must perfect your sword drawing and follow-up attack. It will represent the difference between life and death for you against men and monsters."

"I do not fully understand your meaning, Maestro," Karnstein said and then flicked his fingers, "but I shall accept your statement as true. I have never heard or read of any system of battle that relies on such attacks. It does not appear like the saber training you taught me shortly after we met."

"You are correct," Séverin said. "How goes your musket and foot fighting training?"

Karnstein frowned at the change of subject, but did not argue.

"The first proceeds well, though I shall never reload with the celerity of your French *Grande Armée*. Those gentlemen reload and fire four times in one minute. I find that quite impressive."

"That is correct," Séverin said. "Though the English riflemen are said to be their equals. In any event, we shall talk again later; Barto and Sylvia are through with their reunion."

Bartolomeo Dardi approached in a bound and embraced Séverin with a loud laugh.

"Gâteloup!" he said, pounding his old friend on the back.

"Barto!" Séverin replied with equal enthusiasm.

"And this is my soon-to-be son-in-law. Why do you make my dearest child wait so long?" Dardi asked, hugging Karnstein with equal enthusiasm.

The Austrian permitted the embrace with as little enthusiasm as possible.

"Not I, sir, but the Pope and Emperor Francis proceed at their own speed," he said as the smaller, powerful man released him. "My grandfather, Count von Karnstein, approved immediately and sent his agreement to the Emperor."

"Ah!" Dardi laughed, pulling a sealed envelope from under his cloak. "I almost forgot! One of *Il Papa*'s Cardinals asked that I give you this message. Read it!"

Karnstein said a brief prayer upon spotting the seal of Pope Pius VII. He broke the wax seal, removed the single page, and scanned the lines.

"His Holiness gives his permission and offers his prayers and congratulations. But he will not intervene with Emperor Francis."

"*Idiota!*" Sylvia said. "Did you think that so great a man would involve himself in something so unimportant?"

"I never asked him to," Karnstein said. "That was Archbishop Genga's way of making clear my unimportance in the Church's hierarchy. And stop calling me an idiot."

"Then stop acting like one," Sylvia said.

She smiled and kissed him quickly.

"Two foes defeated, one more remaining," she said.

"That is a unique phrasing of the situation," Karnstein said. "You are becoming more Karnstein each day."

"Now, that is cruel," Sylvia said, mock pouting.

"Gâteloup," Dardi asked, "are they always this way?"

"No," Séverin said. "This is a sedate version."

"*Madonna!* You must have the patience of a saint!" Dardi replied with a smile and a head shake. "Now, let us eat and plan. Sylvia says we finally face the Ténèbre Brothers. Now, that should prove a true challenge!"

"As opposed to the pestilence demon we battled last summer with you in Naples?" Karnstein asked, as they climbed into a nearby carriage.

"Bah!" Dardi replied. "Demons are simple-minded creatures, without thought or passion. They live for their mission alone. The Ténèbre Brothers are legends who survived battles against the Turks, the Crusaders, vampire hunters and ancient cultists. Fighting this pair is not a duel, but a war against humanity's evil in its purest form. Defeating this pair shall be a triumph as great as any in history."

"Very poetic, Barto," Séverin said, "though I believe your belief is correct to some degree. These monsters are dangerous and clever. Most importantly, they are survivors. Tracking them down shall not be easy. The difficult lays not merely in the battle, but in their reason for such bold actions. I sense there is more to this story than we fully realize."

"*Madonna*, that is bad. When Gâteloup has one of his feelings, life often becomes lethal," Dardi said, grinning madly and shaking his head. "Next, he shall inform us he has a plan in which we can trap the monsters."

Séverin shrugged.

"This is so, my friend. First, we shall repair to a small café and eat and share a bottle of the delightful wine they keep in their cellars. Then, I shall tell you how we shall seek out the vampire and ghoul brothers in high and low places."

Karnstein snorted and followed with Sylvia.

"It does not take a soothsayer to know you and I shall discover that our assignment involves the dirtier, places he refers to as *low*."

"*Mio amante*," Sylvia said, rolling her eyes, "this much was obvious. Tell me something I do not know."

"Easy enough," Karnstein said, "the first place the Maestro shall send us is in search of a satanic cult in the heart of Paris."

"He is correct," Séverin said.

"That is quite a prediction," Sylvia said, looking at him with narrowed eyes. "How did you know?"

"Simple," Karnstein said, "the woman who runs that black circle has said I shall one day father her children. It is a connection the Maestro will utilize for his own purposes."

Sylvia did not reply, but she did grip his arm a little tighter and a low growl exited her taut, tense lips.

CHAPTER VII

"I still do not understand something," Ange Ténèbre said, licking his bright red lips.

Jean Ténèbre gnawed on a finger, spitting aside a tiny bone. He could not remember if this was the tip or the lower bit.

"There is much not to understand on Earth, my brother," he said. "Perhaps you can be more specific?"

The vampire snarled, his pale hands twisting into fists and his sharp incisors adding an inhuman aspect to his pretty face.

"I warn you, Jean. Do not behave as if I am a fool."

Jean Ténèbre raised one hand, his ragged, onyx, talons glistening with unknown fluids as he stared back at his undead sibling.

"And do not threaten me, Ange. I am not so easily overcome."

The two stared at each other for a moment, the vampire's snarl matched by a subsonic growl from the chest of his larger, *oupire* brother. After a full minute, both looked aside, and a hush filled their chamber.

"I do not understand why you tied us to this lunatic, Strix," Ange said, moving to the window and staring down at the Parisians passing through the street below.

"Did you not listen to his goals?" Jean asked, dropping the last finger bone and reaching into the small cauldron for mire bones.

Ange closed his eyes and breathed slowly with deep breaths. He remained silent for several minutes before whispering, "I did not."

"Understandable," the taller ghoul said with a laugh.

He stepped back across the room and clapped his brother on the shoulder. He looked down at the busy thoroughfare and shook his head.

"Come," Jean said. "We must begin the search again for our next victims. I think we shall attend Madame Desmarais salon today. Strix will require at least two noble-born sacrifices soon. We may as well enjoy some talk and good wine as we quest. I shall explain as we travel."

They headed out into the cold streets, unaffected by the elements, but dressed appropriately for the weather. Jean wore a dark, well-tailored, severe suit made from expensive fabrics. Upon one long, bony finger lay a silver signet ring with a faded crest on the surface.

Ange was, in contrast, in a black soutane that fell to his ankles. He held his hands folded before his body and resembled an artistic image of a Catholic saint.

They proceeded down the street.

"You promised me an explanation," Ange said in a low voice. "I would have it now."

"I did, and I shall comply. I am sure you remember something of Strix's schemes. The resurrection of an ancient demon, a being so mighty that it imperiled the very universe," Jean said.

"Yes, I do," Ange said, smiling benignly upon a strolling pair of elderly ladies in black dresses. "But I fail to understand how this benefits us in any manner."

Jean chuckled again and nodded.

"Quite right. The plan is clearly ridiculous and, if true, would consume all life upon this world. However, you did not pay attention to the final portion of that insane sorcerer's words."

Ange nodded and looked away while saying, "That is true. I stopped listening when Strix provided details of the sacrifices and the many reasons for it."

"I assumed as much," Jean said, raising a hand languidly as if brushing aside a curtain. "The critical portion followed that rather repulsive soliloquy. The site of the summonsing."

Stopping in his tracks, the vampire grabbed his ghoulish brother's arm in a grip of iron.

"Stop hinting at things, Jean! Tell me what I missed!"

Jean shook off the hand and stared down at his brother; a slow, mirthless smile spread across his face.

"To complete the summonsing of the ancient demon known as the Raktabīja, the spell must be performed in a place where light has never fallen. It must be beneath the sky, but in total darkness. Our compatriot Strix determined, incorrectly I may add, that it meant one particular location..."

"Selene!" Ange said. "The Sepulchre!"

Jean pantomimed clapping at this revelation and nodded slowly.

"Correct, my brother. Selene, the Vampire City! The place where we fell upon our curses. The one place we sought more than any upon the Earth..."

"And the one place which we are barred from entering. This Strix has a means of admission? Only vampires born of that land may enter the city of black jasper and endless gloom."

"Yes, Strix has a method of entry," Jean said, "though I know not what it is. Now you understand why helping him is essential. How else could we enter the temple of the vampires and enact our revenge?"

"What of Strix? The demon that lunatic spoke of would kill..." Ange stopped speaking at a gesture from Jean.

"You leave Strix to me. Concern yourself with remaining loyal to the sorcerer until we stride through the murky gates of Selene. Once we step into the Sepulchre, Strix is no longer of any use to us, except as food."

Jean laughed long and loud.

A moment later, Ange Ténèbre's low titter joined Jean's booming guffaw. Pedestrians passing the pair along the street smiled at them. A clearly noble gentleman and a man of God sharing a moment of mirth was a pleasure to behold.

CHAPTER VIII

"You never finished your explanation as to why we must live in that stinking cesspit," Lord Henry Morley said as he led Ishaani along the Rue Saint-Denis.

This slum, once known as the *Cour des miracles*, was one of the most dangerous areas of in Paris. It was also perfect for the odd Indian woman's work as well as the start of their search for her nonsense.

Just remember, Henry old lad, Morley thought, *one of their jewels paid off all your creditors and prevented a stay in debtors' prison. Imagine what a pot would do!*

Ishaani, whose face was invisible beneath her heavy dark hood, did not answer for several minutes. Finally, she raised a slim hand a stepped under the eves of a crumbling brick structure.

"I do not have much time, so I shall be brief. All scientists and members of the holy orders divide the world into two sections. Light, which some call good, and dark, which, for lack of another term, is evil. This, you understand?"

"I went to church growing up, and my first captain kept a chaplain aboard his ship. The idiot did not care that the lower deck lads view a holy man as bad luck. Turned into a shot rolling ship by the time we hit the Med. Why?" Morley asked.

Ishaani looked up at him, her shadowy face denoting confusion with his statements.

"Shot rolling ship?" she asked.

Morley sighed and explained, "Sailor's life, woman. When a ship is run by a tyrant, the lower deck boys take the cannonballs and roll them across the decks. This shatters the bones of midshipmen and officers who support the idiot in command."

"I understand less than I did a moment ago," the Indian woman said. Then she waved her hand vigorously. "No matter, I promised you an answer, Morley sahib. As I said, light and darkness, good and evil. On this we agree, yes?"

"Yes."

"Very good. Then, I proceed. The one who stole the pages I seek is a follower of the dark path. They may hold mighty powers. This, they could use to discover our presence in the city and send messengers of darkness against us. Those creatures are deadly to life and we would have difficulty surviving a battle."

Morley snorted and pulled a silver flask from under his cloak.

"Devils and other superstitious rot! I have been aboard ship as man and boy, traveled all over the world, and never saw so much as a mermaid or spook. Why do I listen to your foreign tomfoolery?"

Crossing her arms across her chest, Ishaani looked up at the taller sea captain and said, "For pots of gold and jewels, sahib. I shall complete my explanation and then we shall speak of this no more. We hide from the dark priest who seeks the return of Raktabīja. Only one filled with terrible evil and pain would desire such a terrible act. Now, you shall answer for me and understand better. How do you hide a ship when you seek your enemy?"

Morley looked confused and then shrugged.

"Use fog if you have it and set up a raft with lights. Or change the ship by shifting the mast and other rigging. Why?"

"In other words, disguise, yes?" she asked.

The Englishman nodded and said, "That is a way of stating it, yes."

"Then we have an understanding. We hide in the darkest space of Paris. Even if you do not believe my words, know this… No man, woman, child, or beast shall seek us in that place. We hide in a place of horror," Ishaani said, glancing up at her taller companion.

Morley frowned, but nodded again. "I think I understand. That aside, what's next?"

The smaller Indian woman reached into her voluminous sleeve and removed a long, thin, silken cord. She grasped the line with both hands and pulled it taut.

"Now I shall kill someone and prevent the end of the world for a brief time. Wait here. When I complete my ritual, we shall seek information about the demon worshipper."

Morley sighed as she slipped away, moving as silently as a stalking cat. Over in India, they called Ishaani and her people Thuggee. They were a cult who believed they protected the world by strangling innocent people. There were millions of men, women, and children in those lands, each, good, bad or otherwise. It was a land that was odd to westerners, to say the least. However, having spent time there did render her human in his eyes.

Lord Henry Morley knew that he was better than all Indians; he was white after all. No dark-skinned savage could equal even the lowest European. Among the Indians, there were those he could even consider gentlemen and worthy temporary bedmates. None particularly interested or scared him, other than the sect Ishaani represented. They lived quieter than most groups, their killings performed without cruelty or profit. In fact, as he later learned, she only executed those whom society no longer needed.

A few beggars and dying people are a small price to pay for keeping such a wealthy pack of savages happy, Morley thought as he awaited Ishaani's return.

CHAPTER IX

"Tell me of this woman who desires your children," Sylvia said after sipping her wine wordlessly for several minutes. "This story interests me since this is the first I hear of it," she added in an oddly impassive manner.

This was unlike Sylvia Dardi in every way. She was a woman of strong feelings and temper, reacting fiercely to anything she viewed as a threat. The last time a woman had displayed any interest in Franz von Karnstein, she had addressed her by a host of vicious names. The lady in question, the wife of the head of the Neapolitan street gangs, had challenged Sylvia to a knife fight, which had only ended because of a small army of walking dead approaching their position with murderous intent.

Therefore, a calm and controlled Sylvia was a great deal more frightening. Even her father, a warrior with many duels to his credit, stared at her with something approaching concern.

Karnstein observed her for a moment, then nodded to himself.

"The woman, whose name I do not know, is the mistress of a satanic coven that the Maestro interrupted. They attacked us with a demon, which I sent back to Hell. Frightened, they provided us with some information regarding the vampire who sought the death of the soon-to-be Emperor. Later, she spoke to me on the street... We had a brief exchange..."

"I will have you one day, exorcist. You will father my latest child. I last mated with your kind a century ago. My son was terrible, a monster who destroyed the lives of many humans. But it was prophesized that my next offspring would be a beast who would serve the King of the World when he casts forth the shackles of light..."

40

Now it was Karnstein's turn to laugh. Throwing back his head, he said and wept, nearly falling over in his mirth. "You think... you believe you... me... oh, Lord, protect me, I may expire..."

The female Satanist watched the sniggering Austrian, trying to maintain her dignity. But she did flush red when the giggles continued for several minutes.

"You doubt my pledge?"

Karnstein suddenly stopped cackling, his face freezing. His pale eyes were suddenly filled with rage. "You believe I would soil myself with the Devil's handmaiden? Your physical charms remind me of my ancestor, Mircalla. I ended her undead existence when I was a mere child. She was as lovely to the eye as yourself. And you both possess souls as black as the pits of perdition. Have me? I would sooner mate with a sewer rat."

"I believe," Séverin said, "that she was not false in her words. She may be an ancient being of great power. None-the-less, she is the only resource we have regarding satanic activity in the city."

He did have a secondary source of information, one the swordmaster rarely invoked. He knew the leader of the city's beggars; a woman called the "Antipope" by her followers. She was a dangerous, beautiful woman who may dislike him for actions over the last decade.

I will contact her despite the danger. The Ténèbre Brothers are a degree of danger I cannot underestimate, he thought.

Sylvia listened to the details of the story and nodded slowly.

"I do believe you," she said, narrowing her eyes Karnstein's direction, "though next time, this situation would not arise if you told me of your entanglements before they emerge."

"This was a threat, not a romance," Karnstein said, his face registering a growing anger.

"Then tell me of the threats next time!" Sylvia said

Barto Dardi slapped the table and shouted, "*Basta!* You two would drive a saint of the Church to drink! Quarrel later, preferably when I am back in Naples. I still desire the knowledge of how you exorcise demons in seconds. The shortest I know of requires eight hours!"

"He cannot tell you," Séverin said as the waiter appeared and placed chicken and other dishes upon the table. "None save the Pope and a Cardinal or two know the truth."

"And me," Sylvia added, smiling winningly at the shocked swordmasters.

"You told her? I thought you were under seal by the Pope and the Inquisition..." Séverin asked, tilting his head with surprise.

Karnstein reached for a chicken leg and rolled his eyes.

"Of course, I told her. We are to be married and I would not lie to my future wife."

Dardi snorted and rolled his eyes.

"Gâteloup," he said with a laugh, "do you think she would accept the secrecy?"

Gâteloup, or Spoiler of Wolves, was Séverin's nickname, one acquired in his distant, adventurous past. Dardi used it regularly as part of their long-standing friendship.

Both maestros exchanged a smile as the lovely, young woman ignored them with a haughty silence.

"That aside," Dardi said ,as he picked up a prawn with his fingers, "I should hear Gâteloup's plan for determining the whereabouts of the vampire and *oupire*."

"Simple enough," Sylvia said, "he shall take you to the Paris Morgue, where he still holds the title of Director. There he shall find all terrible deaths and trace them through the streets. *Mio amante* and I shall proceed to the Satanists and confront this *porca puttana* and her devil worshiping fools. Am I correct?"

"You are," Séverin said, chewing his chicken for a moment. "We shall equip ourselves back at my fencing school and proceed on our respective missions. Eat well, for we shall no doubt be in great danger by the time night falls."

"That is not unexpected," Karnstein said. "Our lives are anything but quiet."

This sent both Dardis into gales of laughter, and even Séverin managed a low chuckle. The Austrian continued eating, his lack of reaction neither proud nor confused. There was a disinterested quality to his motions, as if he sat alone. The contrast was marked and caused a few stares of confusion from outsiders.

There are times, Séverin reflected as Karnstein slowly chewed his food without interest in the merriment, *that even I find my pupil disconcerting. Even Kronos never possessed the calm disinterest in humanity that controls this young Baron. I see that same intensity in him that I viewed in Kanga Sakugawa or Hung Hsi-kuan. That could be very good, or incredibly dangerous...*

CHAPTER X

Madame Desmarais's salon was as dreadful as Jean Ténèbre had feared. Filled with the new Napoleonic nobility, the people present were as vapid as the lotus-eaters they'd met in England thirty years ago. London had appeared filled with young epicene dandies dressed in wigs so high they stooped deeply upon entering doorways. Those silly fops, known as *macaronis* by the popular press, were ridiculous creatures whose affected behavior had filled the Ténèbre Brothers with resentful annoyance within moments.

Who was it that wrote about them and said, "It talks without meaning, it smiles without pleasantry, it eats without appetite, it rides without exercise, it wenches without passion?" That fits these creatures, though the men wear no tiny hats above enormous wigs. Despite that, they are the same in so many way, Jean thought as he listened to the flowing conversation.

While the English *macaronis* had pranced, cooed, tittered, and behaved with ludicrous, over affected manners, their current French counterparts were, in many ways, worse.

The horrific side of the men and women who appeared at the fashionable Madame Desmarais's salon was not their external appearance. All present dressed properly, some slightly better than others, none particularly eye-catching. The issue was internal, which was far worse.

"They are tradesmen," Ange said, as he sipped a glass of wine, "jumped up merchants and military men with no family line."

"Yes," Jean said, hiding a frown, "I noticed."

Though resembling men of the times, Jean and Ange Ténèbre possessed some attitudes rooted in their youth. Since that was almost five hundred years ago, their views often conflicted with this new era's social structure.

Nobles were men whose family distinguished themselves and followed ancient traditions. Only those with proper breeding fought the king's enemies or served the church. Now, anyone could rise and become a member of the better class, Jean thought ruefully.

His thoughts formed on this subject months earlier when he had met the legendary Marshal of France, the Emperor's brother-in-law, Joachim Murat. In past days, Murat may have risen to the rank of knight, based on his skill at arms and leadership qualities. This was the correct position for a man whose ancestry included an innkeeper and a postmaster for a father. A commoner, but an exceptional one.

That usurping Corsican does not understand proper social structure, Jean thought, *and makes a common soldier into a noble. Nor merely a baron or even a vicomte, but Prince Murat and Grand Duke of Berg. A travesty!*

"Murat," Ange mumbled, echoing his brother's thoughts.

"Murat," Jean agreed, feeling that standards as those represented by this new French Empire were laughable.

"Ah," Madame Desmarais said, approaching with all the drama of a *grande dame* of the Opera, "here you are, my dears! I wondered where you two were hiding!"

Jean clicked his heels and bowed deeply before the approaching hostess. A woman of middle height with pale hair and a florid complexion, Madame Desmarais was handsome rather than beautiful. Noted for her kindly treatment of artists and musicians, she was one of Caroline Bonaparte's closest friends. Caroline was, of course, the wife of Joachim Murat.

"My dear, this is Baron von Altenheimer and his brother the delightful Bishop of Hermopolis. My lords, have you met Contessa Maria Favrini? She is the new wife of the cousin of the Duke of the former states of Modena and Reggio. Her husband is a staunch supporter of our good Emperor, is he not, Maria?"

"Yes, Madame," the Contessa said.

She was a tiny woman with a thick head of blond curls held in a Psyche knot on the back of her head. Her oval face and large green eyes gave her the appearance of a child's doll brought to life and grown close to adult size. Her accent was not from the Italian peninsula, but of the educated class of Paris itself.

"You are Prussians?" the Contessa asked, blinking her eyes slowly as she examined their faces.

"No, my lady," Ange said, "we are from a region on the border of Austria. A beautiful land of rolling hills and old crusaders' castles. Come, let me tell you of the meadows near where my brother and I spent our childhood..."

Dressed in a cassock and resembling a painting of a holy man, Ange easily lead the attractive young noblewoman aside and towards the veranda. Madame Desmarais, having performed her obligations, gave Jean the sketch of a curtsey and smile and vanished into a knot of other guests.

Jean, having lost sight of his brother and his prey, sighed and shook his head. Ange was easily enticed by attractive women—always had been. That, plus Jean's own greed, had played a part in their downfall centuries earlier.

I did not pay attention to that young woman because she wore no jewelry other than a tiny old chain about her slim neck. Not worth the cost of stealing. Now, that older couple across the room... he thought as he strolled towards a portly man with a yellow silk waistcoat covered with jeweled gold buttons.

"Hello there, my good sir," the man said in a voice filled with bonhomie and loud bluster. "I do not believe we have met. I am Maurice Hatry and this is my wife, Hélène. Perhaps you know of my firm... Hatry & fils, Coachmakers?"

The question was almost plaintive in its urgency. Jean sensed that this man, probably new to wealth and position, felt wracked with fear of his position among these so-called "leaders of society." This was something the *oupire* understood, having witnessed similar scenes with greater regularity as the social order transformed in the modern age. *Nouveau riche* merchants gave parties and associated themselves with the educated, artists, and impoverished nobility, and discovered

46

that they were often the objects of teasing. Some reacted with hostility, others with amused indifference. But many more, like Hatry, toadied to anyone who could deliver them from this form of abuse.

Fortunately for Maurice Hatry, Jean Ténèbre knew his name and his firm's work. The well-equipped vehicle he and Ange used for snatching victims was, in fact, a Hatry conveyance.

"I do, Monsieur," Jean said, nodding his head slowly. "You delivered an impressive vehicle for a friend of mine. A carriage with several clever devices built into the passenger's compartment. Your work is excellent."

Hatry practically wriggled in delight at this information. Smiling broadly, he bowed deeply before Jean, resembling a vast bullock stooping for grass.

"You do me too much honor, Monsieur. Should you ever require a coach of any type, please consider my firm first," he said, ignoring the supercilious sniffs and sneers from the noblemen clustered nearby.

"I shall do so," Jean said, "and I shall recommend your work to my noble friends…"

With that, Jean slipped away, having no need for the man. He and his unspeakingly boring wife were not members of the nobility. This rendered them useless for him.

Possibly Ange shall find a suitable pair, Jean considered, *if he does not claim the woman first as his latest prize…*

Jean Ténèbre the ghoul swept through the room again. He was on the hunt, but not for food. That, he could retrieve from the pauper's graveyard near his dwellings. There was always new, rotting meat available if one had some time and a shovel…

CHAPTER XI

"Now, Gâteloup," Bartomeleo Dardi said as he heard the door close behind his daughter and her beloved baron, "what is our true mission?"

Jean-Pierre Séverin glanced out the window, spotting his students striding away in distance. Based on their postures, they were squabbling again.

They argue and fight constantly, he thought with some amusement, *but the Lord God protect anyone who speak ill of either.*

"My friend? Are you awake?" Dardi asked, checking the weight of a dagger from the weapons rack.

"Yes, yes," Séverin said, "I was considering the danger of speaking ill of Franz to Sylvia, or of Sylvia to Franz."

Dardi threw back his head and howled with laughter. His bulging eyes glistened with tears as he said with laughter at the thought.

"Gâteloup, my friend and brother," he finally said, "I should sooner face another coven of vampire witches than that horror. My daughter turned on me when I once agreed her young *barone* was an *idiota*... even though she calls him that thousands of times each day."

"And Franz once broke the jaw of a sailor who made an improper suggestion towards Sylvia. One punch and the man was unconscious and was incapable of speech for the rest of the voyage," the elder French swordmaster added with a soft chuckle.

Dardi laughed again, picking a knife and a stiletto from the rack.

"I do ask my question again, my friend. What is our true mission? I sensed you have more planned than a simple search."

Séverin sheathed his favorite rapier and reached for an English pocket pistol.

"You know me too well, Barto. Yes, there is more to our mission. I intend a dangerous direction. Have you ever heard of the *Cour des miracles*?"

Dardi tilted his head to the right and blinked several times in thought.

"The court of miracles? No, that is an unfamiliar term."

"It was a terrible slum in Paris," the swordmaster said, "as bad as any in India or China. Life was short and deadly, and diseases ran rampant. Fifty years ago, the royalists cleared the area and demolished the buildings."

"You tell me this, why?" Dardi asked.

Séverin led him down the stairs and towards the back entrance of the building.

"Because like all royalist solutions, their work was incomplete. They cleared the horrific location, but not the actual problem."

"The poor, the sick, the insane…" Dardi said.

"As well as the criminal and those born to such extreme poverty. The disease remained and the royalists did only the barest work for social justice," Séverin agreed.

"What happened? In Naples, there was a king of beggars who protected a portion of the city from intrusion," Dardi said as they turned off the main avenue and into a smaller street.

"What happened to the man? You did not mention him when Franz and I spent time in Naples recently," Séverin swordmaster asked.

"Fra Diavolo and his Camorra found him and poured molten gold down his throat. I believe that was a symbolic act, though the only reference I had to such behavior was when the Parthian captured Crassus."

"The Parthians did that because Crassus thirsted for wealth. Fra Diavolo probably had that performed because it was horrific and amused him," Séverin said, choosing a direction seemingly at random.

"Ah," the Neapolitan swordsman said, shrugging broadly. "No matter, the French hung him recently."

Séverin doubted that was true, having met the man and knowing that he was a master manipulator who would have terrified the Borgias themselves, but he kept these thoughts to himself, knowing that airing such ideas would endanger many lives.

Spotting a beggar he recognized, he stopped and pulled out a small collection of coins from his vest.

"Léo," he said to the man who kept one leg hidden and wore an eye patch over his right eye.

"Maestro," Léo-le-Boîteux, the Lame, replied, his voice surprisingly light in tenor. "I have not seen you here in some time."

"I was away," Séverin said, dropping several coins in the brass pot near the man's single visible foot.

Leo-the-Lame resembled a scarecrow in many ways. He possessed a long, unlined, emaciated face with a stub nose, one visible black eye that looked like a piece of coal, and a thatch of filthy straw-colored hair. Formerly a failing actor, he had lost part of one foot to frostbite and had become a professional beggar. He was popular since he spoke well and regaled passing crowds with passages from Molière, Pascal, Brécourt, and Gringore. His deep, dramatic delivery entertained a wide-range of customers, from wealthy members of society to young children enthralled by his powerful performances.

Touching his forelock to a passing tradesman with a large graying mustache, Léo said, "What he reproves deserves reproof, he's out to save your souls, and all of you must love him, as my son would have you do."

"*Tartuffe*?" Dardi asked after the pedestrian tossed a coin in the bucket and moved off with a smile.

"Quite so," Léo said, grinning and showing his gaping array of brown, rotting teeth. "Quoting the great Molière's plays earn me my best living. What do you want, Maestro?"

"I wish a meeting with the Antipope," the swordmaster said, dropping another coin into the bucket.

The beggar grimaced and appeared pained for a moment. He looked towards his one visible foot and sighed.

"I was afraid that would be your request. This shall not be easy. The Antipope does not wish contact with you. However, it might be possible…"

"Why?" Séverin asked.

Léo looked about for a full moment and said, "In truth, because our guild is under siege. We are the elders of Harfleur and Henry lies at our gate, howling for blood and madness."

"Is this gentleman always so poetic?" Dardi asked, smiling broadly.

"Forgive him, my friend. He was an actor and never lost the need for drama in all things," Séverin said with a shrug.

For his part, Léo chuckled and lifted his filthy hands upward. The position was ridiculous, a plea to God above in supplication. The motions might work better in a church, but even there, the exaggerated actions would have probably appeared comical.

"I shall mention your request to the Antipope. Whether said leader of the beggars' guild agrees to a meeting is entirely out of my hands," Léo said.

Séverin dropped several more coins in the bucket and said, "Thank you," before turning away.

Dardi followed. Behind them, they heard Léo's powerful voice rising in triumphal terms as he harangued the crowds:

"If everyone were clothed with integrity,

"If every heart were just, frank, kindly,

"The other virtues would be well-nigh useless,

"Since their chief purpose is to make us bear with patience

"The injustice of our fellows."

"I believe that is Molière too," Dardi said. "The man would do better if he sang some opera. *Figaro* by that German Mozart for example."

"Mozart was Austrian," Séverin said, but knew his friend was not listening.

"Tutto è tranquillo, e placido, Entrò la bella Venere, Col vago Marte prendere, Nuovo Vulcan del secolo, In rete la potrò!" Dardi sang, his voice strong, but untrained.

"Well done," Séverin said, performing a small, false clapping motion. "I may call upon your operatic talents at our next location."

"Where is that? The Paris Opera? I always dreamed of singing on that grand stage!" Dardi said, grinning.

"Not quite," Séverin said, returning his oldest friend's grin. "Though this is a site of many dramatic performances. Have you ever visited the Paris Morgue?"

CHAPTER XII

"We are here," Franz von Karnstein said as he stopped before a small door on an empty street.

Sylvia Dardi glanced about, confused by his statement. They stood on an old street with a muddy track down the center and a few cobblestones visible beneath the heavy layer of filth. The stench from the unclean avenue was noxious, though she had known worse from the worst parts of Naples. There were no visible streetlights and, though only afternoon, the area already appeared gloomy, silent, and unwelcoming.

No inhabitants appeared, though shadowy figures showed up momentarily in cracked doorways and boarded windows. At least twice, Sylvia spotted the glimmer of a spectral face or a shimmer of a single watery eye as she passed by the decaying tenements. Yet, nobody emerged, not even rats or insects.

"We are where? I would ask if this was a joke on your part, but you do not possess a sense of humor," she said while keeping one gloved hand on her smallsword.

Dressed in knee-high black boots, men's pantaloons, a dark jacket and a blue coat, Sylvia resembled a sporting woman who spent her time riding horses and hunting small game. The tricorn hat she invariably wore, an heirloom from her former secret agent aunt, added to this image, which was her point. Men smiled when they viewed her dressed in this manner, and the criminals did not see her as a possible victim. Women who dressed for sport often proved excellent shots and usually carried a dagger on their person. Even foolish robbers viewed such ladies as dangerous risks and chose weaker members of her sex.

"I have a sense of humor," Karnstein said, removing a large white crystal stone from his jacket.

"You have nothing of the sort," she replied, taking the stone as he retrieved a similar object from under his cloak.

"I do," he insisted. "I keep it locked away in one of my castles in Styria. One day, I shall release it into the world."

Sylvia rolled her eyes and shook her head.

"*Idiota.*"

"I should think that would be you. After all, you accepted my proposal," Karnstein said, chuckling softly.

"I was a young fool," Sylvia said, crossing her arms in a pose of annoyance, "and do not call me an *idiota.*"

"That was mere months ago," he replied, "and stop acting like one."

Their eyes met and they smiled, no words needed. In the same gesture, their hands moved forward and interlocked. Their clasp was tight, their look intense, and an electricity filled the air where they stood.

"*Ti amo,*" Karnstein said.

"*Ich liebe dich,*" Sylvia replied, kissing him softly.

This was something that emerged naturally between them when stating they loved each other. Sylvia's Italian phrases and Franz's German statement somehow, without discussion, were exchanged, and they used these words in private.

"Now," Sylvia said as she stepped several inches away, "you shall explain why we are standing before a building that should be destroyed for the safety of Paris in a neighborhood probably filled with rats and people whose diet includes sleeping children."

"Very poetic," Karnstein said, as he pulled a long metal rod from his cloak, "and false. This structure, though far from noteworthy, is sound. Maestro Séverin and I visited it several times before we left for Naples. Additionally, the inhabitants are unusual, but not cannibals… at least I believe not…"

"You are avoiding the question, Franz von Karnstein," she said.

His eyes narrowed and he glanced in her direction. He then turned his back to the door and pressed the rod into a hidden location in the frame.

Half the metal vanished from sight and he twisted the rod left twice, then right three times before removing the item.

"This is not something worthy of anger."

"How do you know I am annoyed by your evasions?" Sylvia's eyes also narrowed.

"You used my surname. Had you spoken my other names, I would become nervous. If you added my titles, I would probably flee Paris for Switzerland."

He opened the door with a gentle shove.

"Why Switzerland?" she asked as she shook the crystal twice.

A soft glow appeared in their stones, throwing out a gentle golden illumination that resembled a microscopic sun. The murky atmosphere of the street retreated beyond the boundaries of the light and relaxed both the Austrian exorcist and the Neapolitan swordswoman.

"Much of the Vordenberg property is in Switzerland," he explained. "My great grandfather favored the Swiss preference of avoiding political battles to the Holy Roman Empire's constant squabbling. With the French Emperor battling all, I should prefer those lands to the many Karnstein ruins across Austria and Hungary."

He made a chopping gesture with his free hand. Sylvia appeared rebellious for a moment, disliking his Germanic methods of ending conversations. Then she rolled her eyes dramatically and gazed through the now open door.

A stone stairway leading into the depths led downward into a plutonian darkness. The visible walls were cut from a gray black stone and appeared perfectly smooth. There was a glassy consistency to the rock, one that added to the disquiet felt by both young people.

"This is an entry port into the tunnels beneath the city," Karnstein said, stepping inside. "From my readings, a city existed in this location before the time of the Sumerians. I do not know if this is true, but the maze beneath Paris is quite stupefying."

"Is there anything I should know?" she asked, following a few steps to his rear.

"Only that we must remain upon the central path. If we stray off, from what I gather, we shall not survive."

The door slammed shut behind Sylvia just as her feet left the first step. She did not start in surprise, but instead sniffed in annoyance at the theatrics.

"My father said the same words to me when I first walked home from church alone. I obeyed then, but strayed later," she said, placing her free hand upon her smallsword.

Karnstein did not reply and followed the staircase as it wound in a serpentine pattern into the depths of the Earth. The air felt heavy and stale, as if they were entering a newly unsealed tomb from the ancient past. This made breathing slightly harder, and he thought of a prayer to the archangel Michael as they plumbed these antediluvian nadirs:

Sancte Michael Archangele, defende nos in praelio, contra nequitias et insidias diaboli esto praesidium: Imperet illi Deus, supplices deprecamur, tuque, Princeps militiae caelestis, satanam aliosque spiritus malignos, qui ab perditionem animarum pervagantur in mundo, divina virtute in infernum detrude. Amen.

He felt some comfort in the words. Michael led the armies of the Lord against Satan and threw down the Prince of Evil. Karnstein never considered himself so exalted, but did know that, in his small way, he fought the same battle here on Earth.

Or beneath it in this case, he thought, smiling to himself.

CHAPTER XIII

"I am sorry, monsieur," the clerk said while closing a large ledger upon his desk, "Such information is not available without permission from the Prefect of Police, or by personal request from the office of the Emperor himself."

"My good sir," Lord Henry Morley replied in his best Breton accent, "I am a distant relative of the man. As I showed you, my interest is merely in the proper disposal of my relative's remains and the disposition of his life's work."

"Then you should have presented such information a year ago, monsieur," replied the clerk sniffing.

He was a small, narrow man with a thin face that somehow looked both fleshy and emaciated at the same time. Perhaps it was his hook-shaped nose, or possibly the tiny fur beneath his nostrils that resembled a caterpillar rather than a mustache? A pair of tiny spectacles was perched on the tip of his nose and looked as if they may fall over at any moment.

His name was Marcel Lozé and he was the supervisor of the Morgue Records for the City of Paris. He was a man who took his duties quite seriously and followed the rules with nearly religious fervor. An educated man, Marcel Lozé had been infamous since childhood for his lack of imagination and complete, unflagging adherence to authority.

Too weak for the military, he was an early member of the new civil service created after the Revolution. Surviving the Terror and the conflicts that followed, he found himself shunted from department to department until the day he received an appointment as head of records for the Paris Morgue.

In most governmental department, fanatical following of the rules was often viewed as foolish, even a bit strange. The highest ministers to the lowliest soldiers, all, possibly save the Emperor Napoleon himself, found means of making their lives easier. From the pocketing of minor bribes to the enjoyment of titles and high honors, few obeyed the law rigorously.

In the case of the Paris Morgue, this was not true for the records department. Proper disposal of all deceased individuals was both a legal and religious duty. Additionally, disposition of the personal effects required specific paperwork that, if done incorrectly, could slow the work of the courts and the tax collector. This was Marcel Lozé's mission in life and he spoke of these duties in the same hushed tones used by priests and nuns when explaining God to outsiders.

"If you request this information through the Prefecture, please ensure each document is stamped in triplicate and the eleven required signatures are all in place. Otherwise, the request will be returned in a blue folder to indicate incorrect paperwork," Marcel Lozé added.

Henry Morley frowned, stood, and punched the little man on the side of his bony head. The bureaucrat squeaked softly and crumpled, moaning softly at the English sailor's feet. Morley snatched up the ledger, placed it upon the table, and turned to the page the supercilious bureaucrat had examined moments earlier.

"17 January 1805, Anquetil-Duperron, Abraham Hyacinthe. Death by natural causes. Body claimed by distant relatives... interment..." Morley read.

Ripping the page from the ledger, the powerful sailor strode deeper into the chamber, checking the files randomly in comparison to the information clutched in his fist. After a few moments, he discovered the correct folder, removed it from the shelf and strode towards the exit.

"No!" Marcel Lozé said, clutching his ankle with shaking hands. "All files must remain in this vault unless specifically ordered by..."

"Shut up, you blasted swab!" Morley said, kicking his leg free.

He contemplated drawing his sword and slicing the French fool in twain, but decided against such an action. The man was down, and it would not be right, killing an unarmed landsman as he lay upon the floor. Also, one had to admire the skinny weakling's tenacity. He clung onto Morley's leg with surprising strength, if only briefly.

Tucking the file under one arm, Henry Morley strolled away from the building, appearing as relaxed as any passer-by. Within minutes, he was lost in the Paris crowds and heading for the rooms he and Ishaani used as their base.

"You succeeded?" Ishaani asked as he strode into the disgusting building.

Morley tossed the file and the crumpled page onto the table. Somehow the young woman had cleaned the furnishing and removed the layers of dust and grime, not to mention the horrific scent.

"Was there any doubt?" he asked.

He dropped into a chair. "Anything to drink?"

The young Indian woman exhaled with open annoyance and produced a wine bottle.

"You English and your need for constant spirits is quite confusing. Why should one desire intoxication or weakening of one's resolve?"

"One bottle does not deteriorate my mind, girl. It strengthens my resolve." he said, removing the cork with his hip knife.

"Before you strengthen yourself," she said, holding back the pewter cup she held in her slim fingers, "please summarize the information you received."

Morley looked rebellious for a moment, but barked out a laugh.

"You do have spirit, girl, despite being a devil worshipper. I have the location where the old grave robber is buried and who received his possessions after he died. From there, we can find out what happened to the nonsense he stole from your temple. Now, haven't you got a beggar to throttle or something?"

Ishaani stood and left, not answering his rude question. She disliked Henry Morley, found him completely repulsive.

However, he was the best chance she had at recovering the spell of Raktabīja and preventing the death of all life on Earth.

I shall ignore his sneers and fulfill our part of the bargain, she thought as she lit a rod of incense and began praying.

CHAPTER XIV

"Oh, Monsieur le Directeur! I am so glad you heard and are present!" Ludovic Gide said upon spotting Jean-Pierre Séverin striding into the Paris Morgue.

Gide was a man of average height, with a massive round face, rounded shoulders, a round paunch and an oval-shaped head. Perpetually dressed in light clothing, he resembled a massive egg walking about and smiling upon all. When Ludovic Gide walked through Paris, he invariably attracted children, all of whom found his looks delightful. Happily for them, he loved entertaining the little ones and would sing silly songs or juggle apples above his head.

As an employee of the Paris Morgue, he was a sub-director whose main responsibility was speaking to grieving families. His gentle demeanor helped many painful situations from becoming hysterical.

Seeing him in a state of high excitement was unusual, causing a raised eyebrow in surprise from the approaching Séverin. He spotted a policeman down the narrow hallways and knew something terrible occurred.

"Forgive me, Monsieur Gide," he said, "but I am unaware of any problems. I am here on another matter. However, I do wish to learn of your concerns. Please tell me now."

Ludovic Gide related the assault on Marcel Lozé.

"The poor man is badly injured, yet he refuses any pleas that he leave and receive medical attention! Such bravery in the face of danger!" Gide said, appearing close to tears.

"Does this happen often in your corpse-storing house?" Bartolomeo Dardi asked, leaning against a pillar and examining his nails.

"I should say not, monsieur! At least, not since Director Séverin confronted the body-snatchers from the Sorbonne!" Ludovic Gide replied.

The elder swordmaster shot an amused look at his friend, knowing Dardi was attempting a bit of levity in light of a terrible situation.

"As you say, Monsieur Gide. Is Monsieur Lozé at his desk in the records room?" Séverin asked.

He nodded upon hearing this was the case. Then, after issuing a few detailed orders, he and Dardi strode towards the records vault.

Once they were away from the egg-shaped morgue employee, Dardi glanced his friend's direction.

"You believe this attack is connected to the brothers whose name we should not mention in these halls?" he asked.

The swordmaster raised a hand and said, "I find coincidences of this sort often have connections to the larger problem. Attacking a records clerk, even an irritating one such as Lozé, is very odd. Somehow, this must be connected to the brothers."

Dardi grunted, though his face appeared skeptical. Stopping just outside the vault door, he leaned against the nearest wall and returned to examining his nails.

"Monsieur Lozé," Séverin said, "I came as soon as I heard of your tribulations. Please tell me all that occurred and then you must attend to your injuries."

"This office does not close until six o'clock, Monsieur le Directeur. I shall not neglect my duty…" the bureaucrat said, only stopping from a gesture from Séverin.

"You will find in the rulebook that the Directeur may order an employee to receive medical attention if he deems it necessary. I determine this to be necessary now, and will have Monsieur Gide take you to an physician of my acquaintance. You shall follow all his prescriptions. Is this understood?"

This was an easy request for the swordmaster to make. Lozé's left eye was completely shut and his nose was still bleeding. One hand clutched his side and he moved slowly and painfully.

Broken nose, possible fractured cheek or orbital bone, and broken ribs. Yet the man wishes to work despite his ap-

parent agony. We humans can be very unusual creatures, Séverin thought.

"Very well, Monsieur le Directeur," Marvel Lozé replied.

Then, at his supervisor's prompting, he related the events of the assault in an impersonal, almost bored, manner.

The swordmaster listened carefully, then asked, "What was your impression of the man? You described him physically, but what did you think of him as you conversed?"

Marcel Lozé looked confused for a moment, then answered, "You mean, besides the fact that he was English?"

Séverin frowned and studied the record-keeper for a moment.

"You said that he spoke with a Breton accent. There are many sailors from that region and they often do business with the English. Perhaps that is what you mean?"

Marcel Lozé shook his head, groaning softly from the effort.

"No, Monsieur le Directeur, I do not. When he struck me the second time, he called me a 'swab.' I learned that word when working as a member of the customs office. It is a device sailors use…"

Séverin held up a hand, stopping the flow of information.

"I am aware of the properties of a swab, Monsieur Lozé. Why is this relevant?"

"Because," the other insisted, leaning forward and wincing, "French sailors do not use that word as an invective. That is characteristic of an Englishman. I met many sailors while I worked for Customs, and only the English called me that when angered. The French usually called me 'cochon' or 'fils de pute.' That man was definitely an Englishman. But I shouldn't leave until the ledger's page is recreated and the file copy is located, and a proper copying commences..."

"Psst, Gâteloup!" Dardi said from behind the doorway, wagging a finger.

Realizing his friend wished to talk to him, Séverin excused himself and exited the chamber.

"Barto," he said, shaking his head, "you are behaving as if we were in a bedroom farce. Why did you summons me in such a theatrical manner?"

"Because the little man would not care and I always wished to act in such a way," Dardi said and guffawed. "Now all we need is a young girl screaming, her idiot lover, and a matronly woman who shall shriek back in shock."

Séverin sighed and made a hurrying up gesture with his hand. His friend was the same joyous trickster he had been when they were boys, training in his family's fencing studio.

"Allow your little man his work time. He shall be grateful you did it and we shall have no need of asking questions. Within an hour, that one will have all the information the English thief stole. Then we shall see if it connects to the brothers…"

Considering this for a moment, Séverin nodded and leaned back into the room.

"Monsieur Lozé," he said, "you may finish recreating the information stolen by the Englishman. When your task is complete, send it to my office so that I may examine the loss. Then you must attend to your health and return only when the doctor allows. Your position shall not be endangered."

"Thank you, Monsieur le Directeur," came back the soft reply.

Leaving, Séverin felt some guilt, but knew Dardi's idea was sound. By examining the stolen records, as well as the information from Ludovic Gide, he would have some chance at discovering the plans of the terrible Ténèbre Brothers.

CHAPTER XV

An hour after Franz von Karnstein and Sylvia Dardi had entered the winding stairway, the stairs ceased.

They stood in a long corridor, wide enough for five men, with a ceiling their light did not reach. It was as if a vast black curtain lay above their heads, drowning out any illumination.

"I think I believe you, *amore*," Sylvia said, removing a wooden canteen filled with water. "That walk was far longer than I expected."

Karnstein nodded in response, his lips and face taut.

"There is something about this underground labyrinth that feels unclean. I believe dreadful rites once occurred near where we stand."

Sylvia reached out and squeezed his arm. She knew her fiancé possessed knowledge different from any she or her father had encountered in their time as vampire hunters. It had not been easy, but she did trust his odd instincts.

"In that direction?" she asked after a moment.

"Yes," he said and turned towards the path. "They used a large chamber that the Maestro believes was once a dining room for a noble family of this devilish city. He and I embarrassed the cult leaders and they took their rites away. The new location is as foul a temple as any I saw since childhood."

Sylvia frowned, stepping to his side and drawing her smallsword.

"Considering we once fought a demon in a location known as the Gates of Hell, that says much of this dark temple."

"That was not a demon," Karnstein said.

He received an elbow in his side for his remark.

"I know," Sylvia said in a snarl, "I was there, *idiota*!"

"Stop calling me an idiot," he said.

"Then stop acting like one," she said. She shivered and added, "I do not like this place."

"You will like it less shortly," Karnstein.

He removed a large revolver from his belt.

His word proved prophetic as they strode slowly through the stygian depths. Odd openings appeared along the distant walls, some resembling insect or rodent tunnels, others large and precisely designed corridors. These caverns and hollows were randomly placed, some several feet above their heads, others torn from the floor or walls. Each were as murky as the distant ceiling above their heads, and none were in any way inviting.

After an interminable time, sounds drifted their direction, low skittering noises as if made from tiny talons or multitudinous legs. The jangle was barely audible, but just loud enough that neither could ignore its faint clamor. There was an almost maddening quality to that sound, one that sent involuntary shivers down their spines and cold sweat across their brows.

Then the eyes emerged from the murk, shimmering orbs from various locations, their owners just out of range of the golden crystal illumination. Some were tiny, red or silvery pinpricks visible in the distance. Others were oversized and glimmered like multifaceted jewels as the faintest traces of light glinted across their moist surfaces. The sheer inhumanity of these observers added to the inhuman horror of their underground city, truly a land of demoniac madness."

"What do we do? If they attack, we shall be overcome by their numbers," Sylvia asked.

She then realized the tunnel, formerly quite wide, had narrowed so that soon, they would not be able to walk by each other's side. The dreadful sounds, formerly low, grew in intensity as if all about them were stealthy creatures, skittering, chittering and slithering beyond their sight.

"We fight and make them realize we are not common prey," Karnstein replied. "I will admit that my last visit was less intense than this one. It is almost as if the beasts are agitated."

Sylvia's hand tightened on her sword and she glanced over her shoulder.

"I think we have no choice, *amore*, the circle is closing."

Karnstein stopped, unsurprised that she had turned her back and placed it against his without speaking. In many ways, Sylvia understood these situations better than he, having been raised in a family that prized vampire hunting and swordsmanship for centuries. After they first had met, Karnstein had soon realized her sword skills far exceeded his.

The circle, as Sylvia called it, was closer to a massive sphere, with the shimmering orbs emerging in greater numbers with each passing second. Their owners remained just short of the light, though both Sylvia and Franz had become aware of elongated legs tipped with talons and maws filled with rows of tiny, sharp teeth.

With each passing second, the hidden monstrosities crept forward. The paths forward or back were blocked, and the sounds even appeared above their heads within the inky darkness.

"*Ich liebe dich*," Sylvia said.

"*Ti amo*," Karnstein replied, as the horrific, inhuman crescendo grew...

CHAPTER XVI

Jean Ténèbre smiled as Maurice Hatry raised a glass of wine his direction. The man's wife snored next to him as their coach rolled and rattled through the streets.

"Thank you again, Baron," Hatry said for the third time, "you honor me by allowing me your company."

Jean waved a hand through the air, dismissing the thanks.

"You do yourself too much discredit, monsieur. You are far and away a greater man than the ridiculous pack of geese we left behind. They squawk and coo, and are quite ridiculous, in truth."

Maurice Hatry started, looking shocked by the nobleman's dismissive statements.

"But... I find that..." he spluttered, incapable of forming a sentence.

"Monsieur Hatry," Jean said after a sip of wine, "the days where the world is run by old families is coming to an end. Look at your Emperor. A Corsican with no bloodline, and yet the greatest leader of this age. He defeated men who trace their lineage back to the days of Ancient Rome and now rules the greatest empire of this age. Why? Talent, not blood, controls the world."

"I fail to see..." Hatry started to say before being silenced by a look from Jean.

"Listen to me, Monsieur Hatry. You built your fortune and are wealthier than any who were at the salon. Yet, you believe, because some hold titles and others are famous, that they are your better. They are not. It is men with ambition and drive that control the world. Once you realize this, such noble fools and silly creatures shall pay homage to you," Jean said, handing back the wineglass.

"I confess I never viewed the world in that manner," Hatry said after a moment.

His tiny, fussy hands returned the glass to the hidden cabinet in the coach's wall. Closing the wooden door, he depressed the hasp, which blended in with the nearby fabric.

"Consider my words," Jean said, handing over a card. "If you realize they are correct, send word to that address. You will meet like-minded men and women who are your equals."

With that, Jean Ténèbre exited the coach, having found another recruit for Strix's cult. The masked master of the satanic circle desired more members. The only demand was that they do not emerge from the noble families of old or new.

"If they have a title," Strix had said a month ago, "or a family member with so much as a chevalier, avoid them completely."

"Why?" Jean had asked.

He did not hide his confusion. From his experience, titled families with important ancestors were the easiest recruits to organizations devoted to demons and darkness.

"The world is changing, *oupire*," Strix had replied. "The old blood fails, and the new nobility shall fall as fast as the ancient families. Men of finance are the future. In the days that come, bankers and merchants shall control empires. I wish such people in my thrall."

This was before Jean Ténèbre had learned of the insane summonsing Strix planned. A cult filled with wealthy men and women made some sense in his mind. It fit the changing world as he observed it.

If they bring this demon to Earth, how shall a cult matter in any way? This still vexes me and I must find a solution, he thought as he turned several corners and entered the passage that led to his employer's lair.

"Where is your brother?" Strix asked, looking up from a long scroll of parchment.

This was his library, a tiny cubicle filled floor to ceiling with books, parchments, scrolls, and odd accoutrements. A smell of burning sandalwood floated in the air and a single candle lit the chamber, sending odd shadows across the walls and corners.

The Satanist sat in a highbacked wooden chair, one built in the shape and size of a medieval throne. Dressed in bright red robes and wearing a wooden demonic mask, complete with tiny horns, vast gnashing teeth, and a long black tongue- Strix was a theatrical figure in Jean Ténèbre's eyes.

Jean shrugged and sat down in the other chair, a rickety old seat that creaked.

"Probably seducing a newly married Countess. I saw him eying her in the same way a starving man would a cooked meal. I imagine she shall be his obsession for a time."

"A Countess?" Strix said,."I require two noble sacrifices the day after tomorrow. If he bites her, she shall be unsuitable for my purposes."

Jean chuckled and shook his head.

"That one would be unsuitable in any event. Her husband is no more a Count than I am a Baron. I know the family in which he claims membership, and he is not one of their clan."

"Are you positive about this? Perhaps he was a member of a cadet branch…?" Strix said.

"If that one was suitable for your purposes, I should have prevented Ange's interest," Jean said. "I should also add, there were no cadet branches to that noble family. They were a poor, inbred pack of fools, who believed they still ruled their city-state."

Strix made a strangling sound beneath the wooden devil mask and finally said, "I require two nobles for my next sacri- fice and…"

"I have them prepared. A pair of brothers, one of whom holds the title of Vicomte, the other his heir. They will suit you perfectly, and nobody will miss them in Paris. Oh, and I nearly forgot. Have you heard of Hatry the coachmaker?" Jean asked, crossing and uncrossing his legs with discomfort.

"Yes," Strix said. "They're the best firm in Paris, if not Europe. Why?"

"I met the man this evening and gave him my card. A prospect for your little devil cult, I should think," Jean an- swered.

Then he stood up, "This chair is more of a torture device than the rack!"

"How would you know?" Strix said.

The *oupire* favored the devil worshipper with a gimlet gaze and a show of blocky pale teeth.

"Years ago, the witch hunter, Lord Cumberland, and his apprentice, Count von Meruh, captured Ange and myself in Bavaria. The rack was the kindest of their tortures… though I should prefer that device to that chair!"

"How dare you? That chair has been in my family since I was a child!"

Jean Ténèbre laughed and said, "And syphilis has been in my family since Philippe the Fortunate. What of it? A poor article does not improve with age."

"I warn you, ghoul…" Strix snarled, stood and raised a pair of velvet-gloved hands.

The Chevalier Ténèbre yawned and shook his head.

"No, I think not, Strix. You are not the master of the Ténèbre Brothers. We help you because it serves our interests. Do not start believing you control us."

Strix reached into a voluminous sleeve and removed a small golden charm that hung on a leather thong. The round surface possessed tiny letters and designs etched with obvious care onto both sides of the coin.

"This is a charm that invokes the power of Saint Raphael, archangel and binder of demons. When used upon the undead, it purifies the body of the damned creature. Invoked against you or your rapist brother, it would reduce your disgusting forms to ashes. Now, are you sure you do not serve me, *oupire*?"

Jean Ténèbre chuckled and shook his head, his amusement evident in his bearing.

"More than ever, silly Strix. Because, if you destroy me, your ceremony shall fail. You do realize I never told you of the victims I shall provide for your Satan worshipping rites. Now, put that trinket away."

Strix's hand shook, but a moment later, the mystic sigil vanished from sight.

"Leave me! Just get me my sacrifices!"

"Very well," Jean said. "Oh, and I should tell you one final piece of information…"

"Yes?" the sorcerer asked with a warning note in his voice.

Jean waved a languid hand towards Strix's sleeve.

"That particular spell was invoked against Ange and me three times. It has limited affect. We are not so easily overcome by the works of Hermes Trismegistus as others you may have encountered."

"Leave!" Strix said, stomped a foot and pointed towards the door.

Jean Ténèbre bowed cordially and backed from the chamber. He did not hide the triumphant glint in his eyes as he vanished from view.

CHAPTER XVII

"The Antipope will meet you," a small child said as she stopped before bumping into Bartolomeo Dardi, "in the Quartier Pigalle in one hour."

She was an angelic child, a slender waif with enormous blue eyes, golden hair streaked with dirt, and a coal smudges across her face and neck. Dressed in a shapeless frock two size too large for her, this child resembled a printed etching decrying the ills of poverty and want. Her voice held the light lilt of an adolescent, but her words and gaze possessed age that far belied her years.

Jean-Pierre Séverin, knowing the rules of her guild, handed the child a pair of coins and asked, "Who should we contact?"

"You will be met," the little beggar girl sang, curtsied and vanished into the crowd.

"The Antipope? Your beggar king has a sense of humor," Dardi said. "Why does this one despise you, my friend?"

"My work resulted in a severe injury to her and, years later, the blinding of her former bodyguard. The Antipope is a very dangerous woman and has somehow retained her power despite challenges from the Emperor's police and new criminal groups."

"Perhaps she lures us into a web as recompense for your crimes?" Dardi said.

Séverin nodded slowly and said, "I think, in part, this is true. There shall be challenges meant to bring my death or disfigurement. The Antipope can do no less and remain in her position."

"Then why go at all, Gâteloup? Guilt?" the Neapolitan swordmaster asked, his bulbous eyes focusing like massive dark lamps upon his friend's face.

"No, not that. The injury was not the fault of mine, but of a vampire and his *loup-garou* slaves. As to the blinding of her former friend… that woman was insane and a professional assassin. One of her patrons was Fra Diavolo."

"Truly? Then why should she want revenge?" Dardi asked.

Séverin shrugged and waggled a finger in a circle.

"The demands of being a leader by popular acclaim. The Antipope, like a privateer captain, only maintains her power through the will of their followers. The beggars' guild follows her and rarely questions her decisions. Nevertheless, they do have rules, traditions, and demands. I believe she must place me on some kind of trial."

"I am never happy when I hear of trials in any situation. Despite that, I am with you until the end, Gâteloup!" Dardi said, throwing a powerful arm across his taller friend's shoulders.

"Of that," Séverin said, "I had no doubts."

They arrived at the Quartier Pigalle, an odd region of the city. This neighborhood of Paris possessed an odd anarchistic feeling. The small, brick buildings lining the avenues and alleys appeared elderly and crumbling, as if they had existed for centuries and would fall after the first strong wind gust. Many visiting the Quartier later said that they felt as if they had somehow fallen back in time to an era long before the Revolution, when the streets were uncontrolled and wildly transformative for all its inhabitants.

Said inhabitants were most notable to outsiders; garnering attention by their presence alone. Artists, actresses, writers, and unusual types were in evidence, crowding the lanes and walking with a supercilious air that impressed some, but disgusted others. Bearded men stood in groups, haranguing each other, selling poorly printed leaflets on obscure philosophical subjects. Tiny bookstalls lined the streets, the folios sold ranging from translated English Gothic tales to texts written in languages not easily discerned by pedestrians. The bohemian environment resembled a vast street fair with few actually enjoying the atmosphere.

"No prostitutes," Dardi said as his eyes scanned the people and locations. "Young, old, new, and those seeking some extra money or a thrill. This Antipope bars the trade?"

"She may have," Séverin said. "In this district, she need not bother. For reasons I cannot fathom, those poor wretches avoid these streets. Something drives them to other neighborhoods."

"Interesting," Dardi said a moment later, "I heard of that happening once in quarter of Cologne. The ghost of a scorned woman scared all the prostitutes away. I think she still haunts the area, preventing a return of those ladies and men."

Séverin opened his mouth in reply, when he recognized a pair of faces. The first was a tall, skeletal man with a nose that resembled the beak of a particularly large bird. His clothes were tattered rags. He walked with an indolent step, as if the act of motion was a trial upon his weakened frame.

The second individual stood just above his companion's waist. He dressed in garments that aped that of a wealthy man, though older, soiled and patched in many locations. A massive, dark blond, waxed mustache flowed across his pale, round face and joined to his thick sideburns. He walked with a confident, powerful stride, marching like a Guardsman on parade rather than a denizen of the poorest district of Paris.

"Why, Cabot!" The tiny man called out in a voice that poorly imitated the upper class drawl of the wealthier members of society. "Look who has appeared in our poor streets. None other than Maestro Séverin, the friend and confidant of our beloved Emperor!"

"Who? Is he the one who lost all his wages betting on Maison Heureuse in the Spring Stakes?" Cabot asked in the rougher tones of a Parisian street tough.

The little man shook his head vigorously, his battered, dusty, top hat shimmying back and forth across his round skull but never falling to the ground.

"No, no, my good Cabot! That was Serrurier, the bank clerk. He swore off horse racing and strong drink forever and now attends church daily."

Cabot looked dubiously at Séverin and Dardi for a moment.

"Are you sure, Geof? They resemble the pair that lost all their wages and fled for the country."

"Hello, Cabot," interrupted Séverin. "We last met at a house filled with loup-garous. Before that, we met the creatures in a basement."

"Huh," Cabot said, waggling his head back and forth, resembling a pelican more than a man for a moment. "Why, yes. You were bad luck then, and probably now too. You still want to meet…her…?"

The swordmaster nodded his head slowly.

"I do."

"Excellent!" Geof said. He stared off to his right and added, "Head that direction until you find a small bookshop with a stuffed monkey in the window. Go inside and walk down the back stairs. You shall be led to the meeting."

Séverin sighed and asked, "More theatrics? Bags upon our heads and led around in circles?"

Cabot shook his head quickly, his vast proboscis creating a small breeze between him and the swordmasters.

"No, no, why bother? Last time you knew where they dragged you even with a sack on your noggin."

"Just remember," Geof said while holding up one tiny, sausage shaped finger. "Once you walk below the streets, you live by the rules of the guild. Do not weep with the results. Life is like a horse race, my friend. There will be days when you lose every wager."

"I understand," Séverin said.

"Odd pair," Dardi said as they spotted the bookstore.

"Agreed," Séverin said. "Honorable in their own way. They seem fascinated by horses and wager upon their race contests."

Dardi did not reply, remaining silent as they entered the bookshop and headed down a well-lit set of newly-painted wooden stairs.

At the bottom of the short staircase stood the little girl they'd met earlier.

"Follow me, sirs," she said with a giggle and skipped a few steps towards a doorway while singing in a piping, tuneless voice:

"Ah ! Vous dirai-je, maman
Ce qui cause mon tourment?
Papa veut que je raisonne
Comme une grande personne
Moi je dis que les bonbons
Valent mieux que la raison."

The two swordmasters exchanged a look, shrugged and followed a moment later.

The corridor veered to the right a few steps beyond the distant doorway and the girl vanished from sight.

CHAPTER XVIII

Lord Henry Morley buttoned his trousers as he stepped out the door. He glanced at the fat woman seated in the hallway, peeling onions into a bowl in her lap. She was as broad as the English Post Captain, with vast layers of flabby skin under her multiple chins and bloated arms. Her hair was a filthy brown tangle that brought to mind an abandoned bird's nest fallen from a tree, and her brown eyes were tiny and unresponsive. She held out one swollen hand, the puffy stained fingers slowly wiggling like tiny tendrils on some horrible insect.

Disgusted, Henry Morley tossed her a pair of coins and watched as her lips quivered into a wide, gap-toothed smirk.

"Tomorrow?" the woman wheezed and released a throaty hacking cough.

"Yes," Morley said. "Just have her cleaned up first."

The woman continued coughing harshly, driving the sea captain back, away from her station.

Just as he exited, she said, "Bath costs extra."

Morley tossed another coin, fleeing the tenement without looking back. Ishaani appeared at his side, her face obscured by the hooded cape and the growing twilight.

"You waste much time, Morley sahib," she said, her stride matching his motions. "Can you not concern yourself with our business first?"

"Her mother offered her to me. Said the little one was ten, but lack of food means she is probably a shade older. Perfect age, just before they get spoiled by years," Morley said and guffawed.

Ishaani did not reply, but led him down a short alley and onto a main avenue. They walked without speaking for an hour, stopping near a small apartment building.

"Stay here," she said. "If you hear cries of alarm, come in and assist my escape."

"Why? What do you have planned here?" Morley asked, looking at the building without favor.

"This was the last home of the thief who used the name Abraham Hyacinthe Anquetil-Duperron. He stole the spells of Raktabīja while traveling through our sacred lands," Ishaani said while removing her hooded cape and tossing the article into his arms.

The Thuggee woman said no more, but simply melted into the shadows, slowly vanishing from view. Morley glanced about, but knew no trace would appear.

Savages excel at sneakiness. They are all shy and train at cowardly arts. I will work with them, but there is no trusting these soulless darkies, he thought as he paced twenty steps back and forth.

Those were the exact number of steps he had on the poop of his last vessel, the horrible 50 gun Fifth Rate *HMS Jaguar*. The ship, a crumbling, wallowing, slow, wet hulk, was one of the last of those horrible, under-gunned vessels, and he did not earn so much as a farthing in prize money after three years aboard. The only good of that period was his accidental encounter with Ishaani and her Thuggee compatriots. He had learned of them after stumbling upon three dead bodies.

"Who are they?" he had asked a Company clerk as they had gazed upon three strangled bodies.

The clerk, whose name was Keats, had lifted a small ledger book to his nose and read down a page. He had nodded twice to himself, adjusted his small spectacles and closed the folio.

"The blond man is Lindgren, from Norway. The center one is Riber, a former cook in the Royal Navy, who served the Company. The final one is an escaped American slave named Jones. Reported missing by the service for two weeks as of yesterday. Had them listed as runners. Damn those heathen thugs!"

"Who?" Morley had asked.

"Thugs," Keats had replied, shaking an ink-stained finger, "a pack of heathen devil worshippers who strangle men in the name of their goddess. The East India Company must act and destroy this blight upon their lands!"

Realizing there was no more he could learn from the clerk, Morley had wished the man a good morning and left the scene.

Returning home, he had striped, mounted his paid concubine, and then questioned her about the Thuggee. Her information had been scant, but it was a start...

Ishaani suddenly appeared at his side, interrupting his reverie of the past. Taking her cloak while falling into his pacing step, she shook her head and said, "Nothing. I found an empty document vault. We must locate the thief's library."

Morley harrumphed and said, "I will examine the file. Perhaps the name of the fool's heir will be present."

"Yes," Ishaani said. Then, she asked, "Could he have been buried with his treasures?"

"Hmm. Possibly. I do know where they lay the man to rest. You think it could be there?"

Unlike many of his compatriots, Henry Morley was not squeamish about unearthing the dead. He had done it first when he was eight years-old, when his great uncle had died and they hadn't removed the man's watch and chain from his vest. A young Henry had dug up the corpse, taken the watch, reburied the body, and tossed the filthy clothing into a fire. His family, too stricken with grief by Uncle Gordon's passing, hadn't questioned his ownership of the item.

"It is fitting," his great aunt Doris had said one evening upon hearing the repeater's gentle chime, "that the watch remained in the family. Wear it with pride, young Henry."

Henry had taken that advice to heart, secretly agreeing with the elderly woman's assessment of the situation. He had learned that simply waiting for men or God for good fortune was never enough. A brave man went out and sought his success, even if that meant breaking a rule or twelve while taking those steps.

Back in the present, Ishaani gazed in his direction and asked, "That does not upset you? Your people, like many of mine, find the touch of a corpse unholy and unclean."

Morley shook his head and snorted with amusement.

"There is little I will not do if the need arises, woman. Do you want this Anquetil-Duperron dug up?"

Ishaani did not reply for several moments, her soft breathing the only sound proving that she remained at the sea captain's side.

"Yes, I think we must. While we await tomorrow evening, please examine the file, Morley sahib. We must find the documents before someone realizes their true worth."

"Their true worth is potfuls of gems, gold, and silver. Correct?" Morley asked while sneering in her direction.

"Of course, Morley sahib. Your reward will be vast once the Raktabīja scroll is in the hands of my people," Ishaani said evenly.

Morley guffawed, having heard that same statement from her for almost one year now. He never tired of hearing of his future as one of the wealthiest men in the world.

CHAPTER XIX

"*Ich liebe dich*," Sylvia Dardi said.

"*Ti amo*," Franz von Karnstein replied as the horrific, in-human crescendo grew all around them.

"Close your eyes," he added, raising a large brass gun in one leather gloved hand.

Sylvia squeezed her eyes shut and heard a sound like air being violently expelled from a giant's lungs. Then, above their heads came a loud explosion, a single burst of noise like a thunderclap. Despite her closed eyes, she felt and viewed a light both bright and profound which filled the chamber a moment later.

The tumult about them, formerly a low rumble, grew in pitch and volume. Screeches and squeals rent the stale air and the screeching and scrabbling of multitudinous insectoid and other demoniac limbs merged with their agonized howls.

Sylvia opened her eyes as Karnstein expelled a massive metal shell from his weapon and reloaded.

"What was that?" she asked, realizing that a falling fire-ball above their heads lit the massive chamber.

"An experimental naval device," he answered. "It fires a phosphorescent flame that lingers in the air for a time. I carry it when in these tunnels."

He snapped his gun closed. "Come, we must proceed be-fore the light vanishes."

"Clever," Sylvia said, kissing his cheek as she passed his side, "The creatures of the depths may be blinded by your flame gun."

"Possibly so," he said. "However, I see some returning despite the glare. I should think we shall fight on soon enough."

They walked at a steady pace down the narrowing corri-dors, Sylvia taking the lead now. She held her sword extended before her and a long dueling pistol clutched in her other fist.

The random caverns and holes appeared as they walked, though the light above cast these sub-chambers in bright relief. The uneven floor of these rips in the walls brought to mind the vast underground tunnel networks of ants and other hive creatures.

The thought made them shudder as they shared an unspoken disgust of this infernal city beneath the Earth's surface. This sensation redoubled when, a few seconds later, the light above winked out and returned them to the inky obscurity they had formerly experienced.

From a massive, gaping cavity to their right rose a sound, a wet snuffling and a rumbling growl that echoed and increased in pitch. A pair of wide, luminescent, golden eyes appeared on the edge of the cavern, followed by a scratching sound like talons dragging across a stone surface.

The creature remained just short of the golden glow of the light crystals, but both Sylvia and Franz held the impression of a massive hirsute form lurking in the shadows.

A rippling, high-pitched cackling sound emerged from the monster as it inched forward. Vast glistening yellow fangs appeared in an extended snout and the huge head dipped slightly lower.

Karnstein began a quick said prayer, one that Sylvia had heard him perform when battling evil before. She found the sound comforting, though still wondered why he often prayed more than most priests.

"*Crux Sancti Patri Benedicti. Crux Sancta Sit Mihi Lux! Non Draco Sit Mihi Dux. Vade Retro, Satana! Non Suade Mihi Vana. Sunt Mala Qua' Libas. Ipse Venena Bibas!*"

"Amen," she answered, her eyes never leaving the demoniac being that lay in wait before them. Then she added, "Just like the vampires."

"Yes," Karnstein said, shifting slightly to her rear.

Then the high-pitched giggle emerged again from the hidden monster and the Austrian fired a musket pistol. Not at the creature crouching before Sylvia, but into the darkness at their rear.

A loud screeching sound rent the stillness and a body flopped to the stone ground with a meaty, wet thud.

Then the monster before Sylvia sprang forward, with a second from a few feet behind the first. She fired her pistol into the creature's face while extending her sword's point towards the shadowy form just visible within the cavern. She heard a second howl to her rear, followed by another shot from her lover's direction.

Before her, the first creature screeched and fell while the other leaped forward over the fallen form.

Sylvia dropped her spent gun and lunged forward, grabbing for the *main gauche* on her belt. A huge hairy form appeared momentarily in her vision before the weight of the horrific beast forced her back several steps.

An almost human sounding wail of agony pierced her ears and she soon realized that her sword had sliced the hairy breast deeply. Still, it moved with lightning swiftness, falling back before rearing back for a second strike.

Recognizing the danger, Sylvia waited until the monster pulled away before lunging forward again.

The shadowy creature leaped towards her, its massive foaming maws slashing and snapping as it attacked. Just as it left the ground, Sylvia sword impaled its breast while her heavy dagger stabbed deep into the extended neck.

A bubbling shower of viscous *vitae* sprayed across the ground and she kicked the howling horror aside.

The beast fell to the floor, twitched and moaned several times, before falling still. A hush fell across the underground city, with only the slowly drip of the wounded monsters audible.

"Franz, *amore*? Are you well?" Sylvia asked, not turning his direction.

She remained crouched in a fighting stance, her eyes scanning for another enemy. There was no movement from the cave, nor from the walkway ahead.

"Yes," he replied, his back pressing against hers a few seconds later. "Are you unhurt?"

"Yes," she echoed, glancing down at the bodies near her feet. "*Madonna!*"

Karnstein did not answer, but she felt his sinews stiffen against hers as she called out her oath. The dead creatures before her shuddered and shrunk, their thick brown and black fur retreating as their corpses quaked. It took her mind a moment to grasp the transformation as it occurred before her unbelieving eyes.

The bodies of the creatures retracted, with their paws widening into long, slender fingers, and their front legs losing layers of muscle and becoming soft, pale flesh. Their stubby muzzles pulled back into a widening head, which soon became that of men, probably in their early thirties.

The one before her had long, curling brown locks that fell across his narrow shoulders, a long, swan-like neck and a face more pretty than handsome. There was an almost rakish quality to his soft features.

"*Madonna!*" Sylvia said again, crossing herself, "What were these poor wretches?"

"Werehyena," Karnstein replied, stepping to her side while reloading his pistol. "I met one before in the Holy Land, though it was the pet of witch who worshipped a demon prince. Killing her, and these creatures, was an act of mercy."

"Was it?" Sylvia asked, looking down upon the face of the dissolute youth. "It feels less like that right now, *amore.*"

"Understandable," Karnstein replied.

He began cleaning his saber and added, "Their change after death makes them appear human. But you must remember that they are accursed. These poor unfortunates angered a sorcerer or a witch in Africa, and received the punishment of being turned into werehyena. The curse means they cannot function in society and perpetually crave living meat. After a time, according to my teacher, they lose their humanity and remain animals, until someone ends their misery. Now, reload your guns and I shall fire another flame into the air. That should allow us some respite from the creatures who are probably craving the blood and meat of these corpses."

Sylvia reloaded her musket pistol, cleaned her weapon and closed her eyes after a nod. Though raised by a vampire hunter in a family of monster slayers, there were moments when her duties were quite difficult. Oddly enough, Karnstein's phlegmatic attitude towards these dangers was something of a comfort.

Can you imagine Giovanni Maldoni or Arturo Cancio reacting so calmly to werehyenas? she thought, remembering the two suitors that had pushed the hardest for her hand in marriage.

Giovanni was the second son of a noble family, a future banker, and one of the handsomest men in Naples. His dark good looks attracted women in flocks, yet his first choice was his sword teacher's fierce daughter, Sylvia. When his second had raised the subject, Sylvia had been flattered, but had firmly rejected the courtship.

"He is weak, Papa," she had said while practicing her lunges on a dummy target in the studio. "The first sign of danger would have him screaming for guards and his carriage."

As to Arturo Cancio, he was neither as handsome nor as wealthy as Giovanni. A son of a successful baker, his main interest was the sword. His ambition was simple: to become the best swordsman in Europe. He had trained harder than anyone in the school and had received respect, even from rivals from other academies.

"Too angry," Sylvia had said when her father had raised the subject. "He is overly competitive and a poor loser. Anyone that defeats him becomes his enemy for life. He shall not live long, but should he marry, he shall leave behind a grieving young widow."

Her words had proved prophetic since three months later, Arturo had died in a foolish duel with a young aristocrat. The noble, a Count from Rome, was unskilled, but had stabbed his enemy in the neck just as Arturo's blade had entered his arm.

"Young Arturo was attempting a disarming attack as a means of showing his skill," Bartomeleo had said, having witnessed the fight without favor. "He left himself open, believing he was untouchable and unbeatable. His new young wife shall be quite sad."

Franz von Karnstein, though colder in demeanor than both of her previous suitors, and other lesser ones, possessed none of the deficiencies of the pair. Also, he willingly pitted his will against her, which made life far more interesting.

The last thing I need is a worshipper, she thought as she heard the exhalation of the flame gun and saw the brilliant light through her closed lids.

Sylvia opened her eyes a moment later and turned away from the dead werehyena pack.

"How far to the temple of your *amore*?" she asked teasingly.

"Another half hour, if we are not interrupted," he said, ignoring the joke.

"Good," she said, grinning. "You shall now describe the facial and physical features of the would-be mother of your future child."

"She stands your height, has dark hair, comes from Naples..." he replied, lifting the glowing crystal above his head.

"*Idiota!*" Sylvia said while fighting laughter as well. "I meant the satanic harlot we must entreat for assistance!"

"Oh, her!" the Austrian replied, sounding neither contrite nor ironic. "You did not specify—and stop calling me an idiot. This witch is three inches taller than you with blond hair, blue eyes, and milk-colored skin. No moles or blemishes on her skin..."

"Wait!" Sylvia said, whirling his direction. "How do you know she is free of beauty marks or other blotches? Did you see her naked?"

Karnstein looked confused and nodded once.

"I did. The first time was when the Maestro and I interrupted her cult's rites. She stood before us, completely naked, and answered our questions. But the second time, she was fully clothed. This is understandable since we were standing on the street before the fencing academy."

"And the third time?" Sylvia said, not hiding her growing fury.

"This will be the third time," Karnstein replied."Do you think I spend all my time in the company of ageless demon worshipers?"

"I was simply checking," Sylvia said.

She turned towards the path again, gripping her sword with a tight fist.

CHAPTER XX

The waif, whose name was Esmée, led them through a series of corridors, into various basements and sewer sub-tunnels. After an hour of such travels, she stopped by a large wooden door set into the wall of a dry sewer tunnel.

"Here we are!" she said.

She removed a tiny silver key from a a metal chain around her neck and handed it to Jean-Pierre Séverin. She giggled and skipped away, singing merrily as she vanished from sight.

"Gâteloup," Bartolomeo Dardi said, breaking the silence, "your beggars' guild is very odd. The king of ours, in Naples, simply rules his tiny kingdom from an abandoned church and protects his people. Yours behaves like a spider in the center of a vast web of deceit and danger."

"Very poetic, Barto," Séverin said, "as well as apt. The Antipope is no common criminal. I find her closer in focus and behavior to the leader of a spy network."

Dardi laughed and clapped his hands. "That is exactly what I said, my friend. Come, we're wasting time! *Andiamo*!"

The swordmaster did not reply, but placed the key in the lock and pushed open the door.

A pair of large burly men stood behind the threshold, alike in many ways. They were both a little taller than Séverin, and their shoulders were broader, with arms thick with ropy muscles. They both possessed heavy dark beards that hid their facial features.

The man on the left's most intriguing feature was a nose that had been broken so many times that it resembled a pitted, crushed rock. The one on the right had a stub nose; his cheek-bones appeared irregular and gave his face an odd asymmetrical look.

"Your weapons, if you please," the man on the left said in a heavy rumble. "You will get them back after the meeting."

Both swordmasters did not reply, and simply removed their swords and other weapons they wore. Handing the items to the two men, they waited and found themselves rewarded by an expected sight. Cabot and Geof stepped into view, having waited just beyond the large bullyboys.

"Good evening, Your Excellencies," Geof said, bowing low. "So good of you to join our little conference."

"If," Dardi asked in a slow drawl, "you had a faster method of arriving at this location, why did you make us travel in circles for an hour?"

Geof guffawed, a sound that appeared practiced and not a demonstration of mirth.

"Allow our noble congregation some secrets. Also, it teaches our little Esmée a modicum of responsibility. Otherwise, she might find herself an unprepared victim of the harsh world outside."

"Also," Cabot said while waving them forward with a loose, filthy, flapping paw, "we enjoy sending nobles crawling about the dirty cellars of our neighborhood."

"I am no noble, monsieur. I am a Republican," Séverin said as they strode down a rickety wooden stairs.

"Yet, you serve Bonaparte? You seem at odds with yourself," Geof said.

They stopped by a small door. "We now enter one of the cathedrals of our guild," he continued. "You shall find we are a raucous bunch, but none shall assault you here as you take your place on the stools before the throne. Then the trial shall begin."

"Is my friend allowed legal representation?" Dardi asked.

Cabot snorted, an explosive sound from the massive nostrils that took both swordmasters aback.

"What do you think we are?" he asked. "We will be in the row just behind you and shall help where possible. You shall find Geof and my good self thoroughly on your sides. We requested the right to advocate for your collective cause."

"Collective cause?" Séverin asked. "My friend here has no part of your trial. He was not even present in France when we battled the *loup-garous*!"

"He is with you now. That means he shares in your crimes," Geof said. "There can be no mitigation in such circumstances."

Séverin opened his mouth to protest, but found himself cut off by a shrug and a laugh from Dardi.

"Leave it alone, my friend. We've shared in all areas since boyhood. I will stand at your side, no matter what the danger!"

Cabot and Geof watched the discussion without comment and exchanged a look. An unspoken exchange occurred between the two men and they nodded simultaneously.

"Let us proceed!" Geof said, and he threw open the door.

The chamber within was a wide circular room with rows of seats rising in ever-widening spirals upward. At first glance, it resembled a vast amphitheater, one similar to the older stages once used by ancient kings.

Upon closer examination, the theatrical likeness fell away, replaced by a sinister cousin to the ancient theaters. This room was an underground arena, one designed in the same style as that used by insane rulers such as Caligula, Nero, Commodus, and Caracalla.

Filling the seats were men, women, and children of all ages, sizes, and infirmities. There were elderly men with long beards, skeletal faces and the dull gaze of cattle in an abattoir. There were old women with haggard, lined, downcast faces and children with eyes far older than their bodies belied. There were men with missing limbs or lacking eyes, women dressed in rags, resembling famine victims, and healthy people with the feverish look of fanatics.

This arena was a theater of the castoffs of Paris, the people born in an unspoken untouchable class that existed in every part of the world. Wealthy and poor strode past these sad sufferers whose only crime was to belong to the wrong section of town. They were a bedraggled army and they gazed down upon Séverin with hate-filled eyes and snarling, bloodless lips.

A low series of hisses and snarls broke the silence as Cabot and Geof plopped down onto benches situated behind a pair of elderly three-legged wooden stools. The seats, ones found in nearly every home in Paris, were not remarkable in any manner. However, the chair that rested five feet away was a remarkable sight, even for experienced world-travelers like Séverin and Dardi.

Eight feet high and made from a pale wood that sparkled in the flickering brazier light, the seat could comfortably fit Dardi and Séverin, with room left for the slender Cabot. Its creator had carved its arms in the shape of roaring lions and an enormous faded crest filled the back of this rutilant throne.

"Do you recognize that crest?" Dardi asked, tilting his head as he examined the engraving.

"I believe that is the lost throne of Louis the Fat, sixth king of the Capet line. Legend had it that the English took it as a prize after they defeated the French at the Battle of Brémule."

"You are correct, Maestro," a woman said from somewhere beyond the massive throne. "The foolish French king abandoned this seat of power while fleeing from his English cousin, Henry of England, who took the throne, and later gave it to his daughter, Empress Matilda. It has remained in a cellar in Anjou until a Parisian noble stole it. Later, we, the beggars, appropriated it as a symbol of our power."

A hush fell over the arena, thick with tension from all quarters. The crowd held its collective breath, and many leaned forward as a tiny tapping sound echoed with increasing volume.

A long wooden cane peaked out from beyond the ancient seat of power, followed by a pale, slim arm.

The woman that emerged from hiding was tiny, dark-haired, shapely, and moving with a slow, cautious gait. A thick woolen bandage covered her lovely face and she tapped the ground constantly with each faltering step. With each step the loose ringlets that haloed her head bounced and vibrated, proving almost hypnotic to any viewer.

"The beggars' guild is an ancient brotherhood that accepts all but criminals who violate our laws," the woman said, her strong, light voice echoing though out the massive chamber.

"I know," Séverin said. "I believe you were expelled from it for becoming a professional assassin, Lisebette."

"Oh, so you remember me, Maestro? I thought your kind forgot those whom you destroyed!" she said.

"You challenged me to a duel, during which you admitted you were a killer for hire. I later learned that you were Fra Diavolo's favorite assassin, though he proved disinterested in revenge when we met. Yes, I remember you, and take no pleasure in my actions. Nor do I regret removing a sadistic killer from the streets of France," The swordmaster paused and asked, "Is this the trial to which we must submit?"

Lisebette, whose face had grown redder with each of Séverin's comments, shook her head. A slow smile spread across her attractive features.

"No," she said, "that complaint was denied when I rejoined the guild. Happily, I have a new crime for which you are guilty. I shall act as your prosecutor and, I hope, your executioner."

"I think I am grateful you blinded this one, Gâteloup," Dardi said. "She is mad like a dog with a foaming mouth."

Séverin nodded once, but did not speak. His eyes shifted across the room, to a patch of darkness in which a tiny light emerged. The light was a candle, held without a holder in the slim fingers of a woman, her face hidden by a black hood. Hot wax dripped and drizzled across her fingers, though she appeared unmoved by the burns. Her step was slower than Lisebette's, performed with a ceremonial deliberation.

The beggars rose—at least those capable of standing— and chanted a single word in a hiss.

"Antipope, Antipope, Antipope..." they chorused as the newcomer ceased her motions just before the massive throne.

"The light of this candle is the illumination of eternity, the guiding force that brings life to high and low," said the new woman.

Her voice was strong, husky, and held the attention of all present with ease. "From the dust we rise in the light; into the dust we fall in time. In the name of the Beggars' Guild, we the Queen of the fallen and broken, who is called the Antipope, do open this trial. Sit and serve as witness, my sisters and brothers."

With the same slow deliberation, she removed a tin candle holder, fitted the wax into the center and sat in the titanic seat. She threw one leg over a carved armrest and lounged with open mockery of the antique seat of royalty.

The beggars ceased speaking and sat, and another heavy silence fell over the arena.

The Antipope pointed one wax-covered finger towards Séverin and cleared her voice.

"Jean-Pierre Séverin," she said, "you are charged with bringing death to our people. We, the beggars of Paris, do demand justice!"

The dozens of men, women and children of the guild screamed and howled, stamped their feet, clapped their hands said. The inhuman sound shook the arena and dust fell from the ceiling in a slow shower upon all present.

"How do you plead?" the Antipope asked.

"Please plead innocent," Lisebette said. "Your trial and death is all I seek in this life..."

CHAPTER XXI

A gaping opening lay before Franz von Karnstein and Sylvia Dardi, one which glowed with a distant flickering illumination. She glanced in his direction and he nodded, reaching under his cloak and removing a tiny pistol half the size of his hand. The weapon had a wide barrel made from a heavy piece of iron. It resembled a ship's cannon in miniature, and it looked quite odd, even to Sylvia's trained eye.

"What is that?" she asked, as they entered the tear in the stone wall.

"A gun," was the phlegmatic reply that earned Karnstein a black look.

The opening proved to be a jagged rip, one that looked remarkably like dozens they had passed in their journey. The only difference was that the walls and floor appeared rougher and older. There was a clear path in the stone, though it did not appear to have been carved as much as created by the stride of thousands of feet over ages. No etchings or carvings appeared in their field of vision, giving the impression of an ancient forgotten edifice only recently unearthed by mankind.

Karnstein held up an arm and stopped Sylvia's progress several feet from the flickering firelight. With a nod forward, he edged several feet and stopped near another rip in the rocks. Kneeling, he glanced within the glowing chamber. Looking over his shoulder, he nodded and remained in his low crouch, his pale eyes returning to the room.

There, a circle of black hooded figures knelt around a brazier, their hands pointed downward, their heads nearly touching the floor. None made a sound, but one suddenly stepped from the praying people and stood before the flaming embers.

"Hear me, O infernal names, Satan, Belial, Asmodeus, and Leviathan! I raise this chalice of unhallowed infant's blood in your name. I call forth the Princes of Hell, Satan from the north, Asmodeus from the West, Belial from the south, and Leviathan from the east. Come to me, your servant, and give me the gifts promised. In the name of darkness, I do plea for power."

The person speaking was a woman, a matronly lady with the vestiges of beauty still visible in her lined countenance. She had a patrician nose, a high clear brow, and a Cupid's bow's mouth, though her skin was a map of age spots, and a smattering of unpleasant pustules. Her gray hair fell in a loose, limp tangle from under her hood and seemed more like a cobweb atop her sculpted skull.

"Shall I?" Sylvia asked.

"Allow me," Karnstein said.

He rose and raised a long dueling pistol in his gloved right hand.

Seemingly without aiming, he fired, causing a booming, echoing sound through the underground lair. The chalice, made from a gold-plated baby's skull, exploded, sending a shower of crimson *vitae* and bone shards in every direction.

The elderly lady shrieked, a sound echoed by many figures in the circle. Some stood, others crouched lower, a few pulled wicked curved knives from under their ebony tunics.

"Who dares…?" bellowed a powerful, bass voice from the right side of the gathering.

Karnstein dropped the expended weapon and stepped into view. He held his small firearm in one hand and gripped the hilt of his saber with the others.

"As always, deluded, damned fools, I dare," he said in a tone so chilly that a few cultists flinched.

"Baron Franz von Karnstein," another woman's voice said in a dulcet tone. "Have you chosen to accept my loving embrace? Our children shall be great and beautiful…"

A second woman rose from the rear of the circle, throwing back her hood as she strode forward through the cultists. Her golden hair spilled like a shower of sunlight across her shoulders, framing her high cheekbones and tiny pointed chin. Her brilliant smile revealed a row of perfect, pearly teeth framed by pale, pink lips. She was lovely, though as cold as a Greek statue of some pagan goddess. There was an inhumanity to her beauty, an untouchable quality that empowered her and rendered her both engaging and frightening at the same time.

"*Madonna!*" Sylvia said, stepping around the corner and pointing her pistol at the priestess's chest. "This is *putana* you mentioned? I am not impressed!"

"Who are you, peasant slut?" the priestess asked, stopping in the center of the circle.

Sylvia, whose hand did not waver, chuckled and replied, "Careful what you say, *cagna*. For now, I am amused by your pathetic attempts at seducing my *fidanzato*. That will not last."

"You dare insult the Brotherhood of the Ram?" a male voice screamed.

A man rose up. He was tall, a few inches higher than Karnstein, with a barrel chest and massive hands. He threw back his head, revealing a massive, craggy face, a heavy black beard and dark, hypnotic eyes. He gripped a sword in his right hand, a heavy bladed weapon capable of slicing a horse in half with one mighty swing.

"I have been insulting your ridiculous pack of sadists since I was a child," Karnstein added. "You are Petrov, right? Igor Petrov, brother of Count Mathias Petrov?"

The man appeared nonplussed.

"How do you know me?" he inquired.

"I slayed your mentor, Edward Kelly, three years ago in the Roman catacombs. He died, begging for mercy. It was a pathetic sight for one so old," Karnstein replied, grinning.

Igor Petrov leaped forward, his massive sword glinting in the firelight.

Karnstein fired his odd pistol, which, like a dragon, sent a massive tongue of flame towards the sorcerer. His chest exploded as if a cannonball had struck his body, sending him sailing backwards onto the empty stone floor, beyond the brazier.

"Igor!" another man shrieked, rushing towards the fallen figure.

He returned seconds later, his step a hard march. He reached beneath his robe, drawing forth a gilt encrusted small-sword. His face was like that of Petrov, though thinner and possessing a nobility that the brutish Russian had lacked.

"My name is Vladimir Petrov," he said in heavily accented French. "Igor was my cousin and closest friend. I challenge you to a duel of honor!"

Karnstein threw back his head and laughed while tossing aside his pistol. Its massive barrel appeared twisted and shrunken, and its wooden frame shattered when it struck the stone floor.

"Honor? From a worshipper of the Dark Prince? That may be the most ridiculous statement ever spoken by one of the Fallen!"

"Sir!" Petrov said, his back stiffening, "I am a swordmaster, formerly employed in the Tsar's court. I may choose the left-handed path for my soul, but I retain my dignity as a student of the sword!"

"*Amore*," Sylvia said, putting away her pistol, "I know of his name. He is known for his correct behavior in his duels while employed by the Russian Emperor."

Vladimir Petrov saluted her with his sword and nodded slowly.

"My thanks, madam. Your name, if you please?"

Sylvia handed her gun to Franz and saluted the Russian swordmaster back with equal precision.

"I am Sylvia Dardi, daughter of Bartomeleo Dardi, and I shall be your opponent this day."

Petrov shook his head and said, "I do not fight women and call you out, Baron Karnstein, a coward."

"You shall not have the chance," the Austrian said, still smiling. "You made her angry and she will not rest until you lie dead at her feet."

Petrov looked confused, his head swiveling back and forth between Karnstein and Sylvia.

"You are serious? You allow a woman to fight your duels of honor? This is… undignified…"

Karnstein shook his head and replied, "When I must fight, I do so—and kill my enemy. But I see no honor in swinging swords. On the other hand, my fiancée, Signorina Dardi, trains day and night in the art of the blade, and she shall be one of the few acknowledged female swordmasters in history."

Sylvia stopped at the center of the floor and waited several seconds before spitting on the floor near the Russian's foot. Her face twisted into a derisive sneer and she sliced her blade through the air with a loud swish.

"Either step forward and raise your sword, or lay it down and admit you are a coward."

"No man or woman calls me a coward and lives!" Petrov said, stomping forward.

"Before you begin," Karnstein said, revealing that he held two more pistols, "if any Satanist dares intervene, I shall shoot them dead before they can take a single step."

"How do we know you shall not shoot Igor?" a woman asked, her voice coming from the far edge of the cluster.

"He shall not," the priestess said with an angry look in Sylvia's direction. "The Austrian is a believer in the false God and he shall not violate their foolish laws."

Vladimir Petrov stopped six feet from Sylvia and threw off his robes. Underneath his clothing was the dark jacket and skintight pants favored by some duelists. He held his blade with a calm assurance and his arm was raised with smooth precision.

"So be it," he said. "I doubt there is honor in dueling a woman, but every man has the right to his champion. After I slaughter your slut, I shall defame your name throughout Europe and destroy your reputation in society."

Karnstein contemplated Petrov for a moment, then shook his head. He was clearly silently laughing, and his amusement spread to Sylvia and, surprisingly, the satanic priestess. She spoke up first as a few titters emerged from the crouching cultists.

"Vladimir," she said, giggling. "His name is Franz von Karnstein. Do you know anything of his family's history? No? Then I shall summarize: They are among the oldest families in Europe, but possess the blackest reputation. His ancestors includes Princess Asa Vajda and many of the most feared vampire witches. You cannot embarrass a man raised in a family that has demons among its ancestors."

"Yet, somehow," the Austrian added, "I became a member of the order of Exorcists and of the Holy Inquisition. Princess Asa Vajda was only part Karnstein. But this talk is unnecessary. I have no concerns for my fiancée's safety."

Vladimir Petrov looked confused for a moment, then his resolve returned, and he raised his sword in salute.

Sylvia answered in kind, and they crossed blades. A moment later, the battle commenced.

Petrov leaped forward, his attack furious, his sword licking out like a slim sliver of silver light. His arm and body moved with uncanny celerity, his actions appearing almost blurred to the onlookers.

Yet, for every attack, Sylvia's sword either parried the Russian's blade, or simply was out-of-range. Her motions appeared languid, almost relaxed, as she only occasionally attacked the tall Russian swordmaster.

"You are fast, but cowardly, *suka*," Petrov said as he lunged towards her heart again.

Sylvia parried and rolled her eyes.

"And you attack with all the finesse of a mountain ape, *mudak*."

Petrov clenched his teeth and attack with greater fury, his face turning red and sweat dribbling across his brows and cheeks.

"Engage, damn you! Fight me!" he said.

"Why bother?" Sylvia asked. "You are defeating yourself with greater skill than I."

Petrov's flashing assaults continued, the smallsword stabbing and slicing towards the Neapolitan woman, who appeared almost disinterested.

"This grows boring. Shall I end this, *amore*?" she asked.

"Yes," Karnstein answered, sighing. "Send him into the arms of his dark master. I shall pray for his soul."

"You are too good," Sylvia said.

She parried and lunged forward with her blade. The sword pierced Vladimir Petrov's throat and he fell back, crimson blood pouring across his chest in fountaining spurts. The gilt-covered sword fell from his now-nerveless fingers, and a moment later, he dropped to the stone floor, twitching and slowly dying.

None of his fellow cultists moved to his side and he died in that terrible place seconds later.

The evil priestess shook her lovely head with obvious annoyance.

"Men! They never change. Perpetually acting with foolish finality. Ah, well, we must replace two more in this coven before we attempt any further rites. What do you want, Karnstein? If it is not for my embrace, but that of your aging peasant slut, do explain quickly."

Karnstein touched Sylvia's shoulder and they shared a smile. Handing her a cloth, his face turned stony as his eyes gazed upon the dark coven.

"Before we discuss my reason for interrupting your black mass, a question: who among you killed an infant for its blood?"

Nobody spoke up, but all eyes fell upon the aging patrician woman who held the chalice earlier.

"I… I… No…" she stammered.

Karnstein shot her in the head with his revolver, sending her tumbling backwards in a welter of blood and bone. The cultists near her shrieked in fear, then quieted down as the Austrian exorcist drew another gun from his cloak.

"Do you know who you just killed, Austrian?" the high priestess asked. "That woman was Madame…."

Her words stopped as Sylvia leveled her own pistol.

"Oh, do continue, *putana*," she said.

"Before you begin issuing threats our direction," Karnstein said, "spare us the exercise. Satanists are rarely original, and neither of us are frightened. Simply answer our questions and we shall each walk away this day."

"How do you know I shall be truthful?" the priestess inquired, dropping her hands to her sides.

"Because it is in your best interest. We shall eliminate another of your competitors," Sylvia said. "You gained power the last time *mi amore* and the Maestro fought an enemy. Just tell us who employs the Ténèbre Brothers."

"The Ténèbre Brothers are in Paris?" another woman said, stepping next to the beautiful priestess.

She threw back her hood, revealing a plain face, round with chubby features, tiny brown eyes and mousy-colored hair. She reached out with a pale hand and gripped the sorceress's dark robe with white knuckled intensity.

"Mistress! Please, is it true? Are the Ténèbre's in our city? Please tell me! They are greatest servants of the Prince of Air and I would serve them in any way they allowed!"

The high priestess reached out with one slim hand, her long fingers encircling the throat hidden by the cloak. Seemingly without effort, she lifted the clutching woman off her feet and held her above the ground.

The woman who had expressed a desire for servitude gagged and kicked the air, incapable of freeing herself from the iron grasp of the seemingly delicate cult mistress.

"Understand me, fools," she snarled, her mouth suddenly filled with massive, oversized incisors. "It matters not whether the Ténèbre Brothers are in Paris or not. Your service is to the Lord Lucifer, and I stand in his stead. If you move away, you shall violate the covenant you made with the Lightbearer and he shall claim your soul immediately. You... belong... to... ME!"

She tossed the dangling woman aside, watching as the cultist gagged, vomited and rubbed her neck with weak hands.

"That was your warning," the priestess said. "If I ever hear such rot again, I shall murder the speaker and torture another of you randomly for the crime. Is this understood?"

"Yes, mistress," the remaining cultists choroused, kneeling and pressing their heads to the stony surface.

The priestess nodded and turned her angry eyes upon Franz von Karnstein and Sylvia Dardi.

"Go now! I shall send word to you when you are on the surface."

"By tomorrow night," Sylvia said. "Or we shall return."

"We shall not use this site again for our rites," the priestess said with a smirk.

Karnstein shrugged and shook his head.

"That matters not. I shall find you in any hole you and your accursed brethren use for your unholy ceremonies. There is no place you can hide from me, creature…"

"Yes, yes," the other said, waving them away like a housewife shooing a pesky fly from her freshly baked pie, "you will seek me hither and yon without stopping. I met an Englishman with your disposition once. He was a Puritan and famed for chasing enemies across entire continents. Like all humans, he died eventually. Your life spans are so very short. Go… I shall speak to you and provide what you wish… I must now chastise my flock…"

Sylvia and Karnstein backed from the dark chamber, hearing the shrieks of pain and wails of terror echo in their ears for a long time as they headed back towards the surface.

The monsters of the depths were still in evidence, yet they remained distant this time.

"That was very successful," Karnstein said as he reloaded one of the pistols he had tossed aside earlier.

"How do you know?" Sylvia asked, narrowing her eyes.

"We are alive and unhurt. This is a blessing. For the rest, we shall see…"

CHAPTER XXII

Ange Ténèbre tightened the bonds that held the Count in his chair and patted the man's face with a soft hand. The false nobleman's eyes stared at him, with low moans issuing from his gagged mouth.

"Your wife," Ange said, "is quite lovely. Too bad she does not know the truth... She believes she married a Count who is a scion of an ancient line. Shall I tell the ravishing creature the facts?"

"What facts?" Maria Favrini asked.

She lay upon her bed, her hands tied to the frame, her Psyche knot in complete disarray. Salty wet tears streaked her tiny face and her lower lip quivered as she looked at the blond vampire.

"That the family in which he claims lineage died ninety-four years ago. The few remaining members died, their corpses only being discovered when the stench from their home became unbearable to everyone in the district," Ange answered, caressing her face gently.

Maria Favrini tried biting him then said, "How would you know, monster?"

Slithering close, the vampire flashed his fangs and said, "Because my brother and I killed them in an orgy of torture that lasted four days... Ah, I can still taste the blood of the youngest children... so pure and innocent..."

"What? What? No, you lie! You are a creature of Satan, trying to deceive me. Hail Mary, full of grace..." she prayed, closing her eyes as the words tumbled from her wide mouth.

Ange turned his back on her and straddled the false Count with a giggle.

"She does not believe me, Your Grace. I think I shall make you a bargain. Tell your slut wife your identity and, as a gift, I shall spare your life. Is that not kind of me?"

The Count was a handsome man of middle height, with soft, olive-colored skin, light brown hair and deep brown eyes covered with lacey lashes. He was wasp-waisted and spoke in a languid style reminiscent of pre-revolutionary French aristocracy.

He nodded vigorously, his gagged mouth making appreciative little sounds, his eyes wild and hopeful.

Pulling a tiny knife from his shoe, Ange Ténèbre sliced the cloth gag that silenced the false nobleman.

"Speak, my good count… or should I call you, Monsieur Balsamo?" the vampire said.

The Count coughed several times before turning his startled countenance upon the tiny undead man in his lap.

"How did you know? I am not… he was not…"

Ange giggled again and clapped his hands.

"How did I know? Because I knew your relative when he haunted this very city. Yes, I recognize that you are not the son of Joseph Balsamo. You must be a son of a cousin, but the corruption of the line is recognizable from a distance. Now, please fulfill your part of our compact."

The false Count glanced at his prone wife and back to the cackling undead being.

"You promise… If I tell her my identity, you shall kill her, not me?"

"What?" Maria said, staring at her husband with wide eyes. "I am your wife! You pledged to love me until the day we die!"

"I prefer that my death be a long time away. Also, we were never truly married. My cousin Jacomo performed the ceremony. His greatest disguise is that of a priest…"

"You impotent bastard!" she screamed. "How could you do that to me?"

The Count chuckled weakly and shrugged.

"I required a wife for my disguise as an Italian aristocrat visiting Paris. Once the Corsican on the throne defeats the Prussians, I planned to leave you behind and find a dispossessed baron's daughter or someone equally useful. Now you know. My true name is Ernesto Balsamo, cousin of the legendary Joseph Balsamo, who rose to power under the title of Count Cagliostro. I do not possess his ambitions, but hope I shall find a banker's daughter or a wealthy widow, and live my days in luxury. I shall miss you for a time... but your death shall give me an excellent story for melting the hearts of young ladies... Now, vampire, free me as you promised!"

Ange Ténèbre patted the Count's face and hopped from the man's lap. He shook his head slowly and moved to Maria's side.

"Now you see your beloved husband in all his unpleasant glory. Are you not enraged? Do you hate him?"

Maria's sobs drowned out her words; yet, she kept staring with the utmost abhorrence at the man she believed had loved her. She struggled against her bonds while shrieking, her lips peeling back in a rictus of fury and insanity.

Ange sliced her bonds and pressed his tiny blade into her hand. She reared up, ignoring the handsome vampire by her side, and charged her false husband. Her shrieks and squeals echoed through the bed chamber, and the gibberish emerging from her mouth was barely comprehensible.

The first slice was across the false Count's handsome face; he moaned as the thin, sharp blade drew a crimson gash across his cheeks and nose. Maria Favrin screamed and sliced her false husband's face, the weapon transforming him from a handsome man into a ruined, tattered, ripped bag of bloody flesh. There was nothing human about the false aristocrat within a few moments, and he was dead long before his wife fell to the floor in a swoon.

Licking some of the blood from the horror that was once a man, the vampire received his fill before throwing open a window and screaming long and loud into the dark night. Screaming again, Ange turned and walked out the rear door of the home, leaving behind the devastation and death he created.

Jean was waiting a block away, munching on a smelly dead rat. Like all *oupires*, he did not find rotting flesh repulsive, but point-of-fact preferred it to new meat.

"You look as if you had some fun," he said. "What did you do, rape the woman before the husband's eyes?"

"Nothing so dull," the vampire said.

He told his tale in brief, then asked, "Why are you here?"

"I sought one of our victims, but he was nowhere in Paris. We must find Baron von Karnstein. I grow tired of Strix's complaints and I kidnapped the other noble and placed her in our patron's hands."

Ange frowned and shrugged without interest.

"We will find him. That is the one you spotted going to church every day."

"Yes," Jean said. "Finding unattached nobles is less easy than you may believe. This one is unmarried and lives by himself in a room over a bakery. He spends his days practicing shooting, fencing, praying, and arguing with a Neapolitan female."

"Oh?" Ange asked and smirked. "Tell me of this woman…"

"She's taller than you, has a large bust, black hair. She's of peasant stock and has a tongue like a fishwife," Jean said, chuckling at his brother's crestfallen expression. "Cheer up, Ange. Soon Strix's experiments shall be complete and we shall enter Selene. Then, revenge shall be sweet…"

"I still do not trust Strix. Any occultist who desires to raise a demon that could consume all life is too insane to be trusted…" Ange said. "We do not even know his identity!"

Jean's eyes narrowed as he studied his vampire brother.

"You do not know Strix's true name?"

Ange winced and looked away, his narrow shoulders hunching.

"No," he said after they walked another mile.

Jean refrained from chuckling or insulting his less curious, but quite dangerous, smaller brother.

"No matter, my brother, I shall explain. Have you ever heard of a woman named Catherine Monvoisin?"

"No," came back the short reply.

"We were in Greece at the time, but I learned all about her from a warlock who had escaped custody. This woman, who was known as *La Voisin,* was the leader of a black magic cult of poisoners responsible for two thousand deaths over one hundred years ago..."

"This matters why?" the vampire asked.

"I shall tell you of Catherine Monvoisin and her clan, and all shall be clear. Back in the days of the French King Louis XIV, men and women sought power from that monarch. One of those seekers was his mistress, Madame de Montespan..."

CHAPTER XXIII

"How do you plead?" the Antipope asked.

"Please, plead innocent," Lisebette said. "Your trial and death is all I seek in this life…"

"How can I enter a plea," Séverin asked, "if I do not even know what crimes you speak of? If I violated your ways, I must know how before I answer."

"There, you see it!" Lisebette said, pointing her cane towards the swordmaster. "The noble monster speaks down to those he views as being beneath his boots. I simply wonder why he did not die by the hands of Jacobins as an aristocrat who opposed the glorious Revolution!"

"Because," Dardi said in a deliberately insulting drawl, "Jean-Pierre Séverin is, and was, a republican who opposed the monarchy before the Revolution. He was even imprisoned for his beliefs."

A low titter filled the arena as several beggars understood the implications of Bartolomeo Dardi's reply.

"Yet, now he serves the Emperor! He abandoned his lofty ideals!" Lisebette said, spitting on the ground between Séverin's feet.

"No," Séverin said. "I am still a republican and said so to Napoleon when he was still an officer without a rank in the army. I said that again when he requested my assistance. No matter, we are wasting time. What crimes do you lay upon my shoulders?"

"Five members of our guild died by strangulation, and seven more had their blood drained from their bodies," the Antipope said. "Of those drained, all lacked limbs. Then we find you are back on our streets, seeking information. We lay these wrongdoings at your feet, Jean-Pierre Séverin."

"When was the first body drained and partially consumed?" Dardi asked.

"This summer, in June," Lisebette answered.

"Then, of those murders, I am innocent," Séverin stated. "I was in Naples battling demons and other fiends for King Joseph. I returned only months later. The name of the ship, for both arriving and departing, was the *Loire*. Feel free and check her manifest. You shall find myself and my pupil Franz von Karnstein listed among her passengers."

Séverin sat upon the stool and concluded, "I shall wait."

The Antipope shook her hooded head.

"No, I think we shall not bother. You know something of these crimes, yet you were not the reason they occurred. Had you been hunting some monsters upon our streets and allowing these deaths, we would hold you responsible. Those charges are expelled. We now charge you with the strangulations. All five occurred in the last three days. You and your student were in Paris. How do you answer?"

"Innocent," the elder swordmaster said. "I seek two brothers. They are ancient, evil, and undead, but neither uses strangulation. However, I do seek full understanding. What was the instrument of death?"

"Strangulation! The way strangulation works is the innocent victim has their air blocked by constricting the neck and life leaves their body. If necessary, we can have this demonstrated on your body," Lisebette said, adding for the assembly with mocking laughter, "Wealthy fool!"

"Strangulation has many methods, madam," Dardi said. "It is rarely so simple. For example, the Camorra in Naples use a thick rope with a knot tied in its center…"

"In Bonn, there was a man who used a circular metal bar and shattered the throat in one pull," Séverin added.

"The tongueless servants of the Ottoman sultan use a wire," Dardi said. "Then they drop their victims into the river in a heavy sack. It is said they sit at the bottom like a forest of corpses."

"Do you remember the giant Spaniard who simply used his hands?" Séverin asked his friend. "He nearly throttled us both at the same time, one in each fist."

The Neapolitan swordmaster rolled his eyes dramatically, "I still have pains in my neck and my back when it rains thanks to that maniac."

Dardi then turned his attention back to Lisebette and the Antipope.

"As you now understand, we have some knowledge of the subject. Please explain the marks across the neck and body."

"Body? They were killed by choking, not a beating!" Lisebette said.

"Persons attacked in this manner," Séverin said, "do not simply stand still and die. They fight back in some manner. Killers often place a knee in their victim's back. This knocks the victim off-balance and adds to the difficulty of escape. We must know more before we can provide an answer."

The Antipope nodded and said, "Bring Ivo the Pale here. We discovered his body hours ago and he has not received a farewell from his brothers and sisters."

"Antipope, I do not think…" Lisebette said, her voice dropping and sounding lighter in tone.

"You charged these men with responsibility for the deaths of our people, Lisebette. We follow all the rules and allow them their rights. If you disagree, you may leave our guild again. We took you back in because you promised you would obey our ways. Are you choosing to leave again?"

"No, Antipope! Please do not cast me out again!" the blind woman said, her head drooping.

"Then we shall follow our rules, ones that even I may not disobey. Bring the body here and we shall first examine the method of his death. Then we shall pay tribute to our fallen friend once these outsiders leave our august body," the Antipope said, waving a finger towards the dark corner from which she had emerged.

Four men came out a moment later carrying an unpainted door with a body across the surface. A thin gauzy shroud covered the corpse, but could not hide the emaciated state of the dead man. He was a small, narrow man, with an emaciated frame that appeared skeletal despite the cloth covering.

The men lay the door in the center of the arena, with one tossing back several feet of the shroud. Ivo the Pale possessed a gaunt, waxen face that probably appeared nearly as sallow as fresh flour in bright sunlight. His sunken cheekbones and long stick like neck exuded a mummified quality, as if he never possessed a fluid of trace of fat across his bony body.

Jean-Pierre Séverin and Bartomeleo Dardi slid closer to the corpse, observing a livid black mark across the unyielding flesh. Kneeling closer, the ligature marks proved narrow, a solid line of death that had ended the sad life of the poor beggar.

Dardi crossed his himself and said a quick prayer.

"Gâteloup, you recognize this method?"

Séverin frowned and exhaled slowly.

"Yes, though I hoped we would never see such a sight again in our lives."

"Them? Here in Paris? One of them would stand out as clearly as an Ottoman hiding among Swedes!" Dardi said.

Straightening, the swordmaster said, "Paris is a large city and they are experts in hiding…"

"What are you saying?" the Antipope asked. "You recognize this method of murder?"

"Oh, yes," Séverin said. "When my friend and I served on a privateer in the Indian waters, we encountered an ancient cult who strangled people for their dark goddess. They believed that every death by strangulation satiates their mistress, at least for a time. Then she does not bring death and chaos to the world."

"They are a small group," Dardi said, "mistrusted by the millions of people in those lands. Some are simply bandits and die the death of a robber when captured. The followers we discuss are true believers. They have rules they must obey for fear of angering their goddess."

"Who…" the Antipope began, though a yell from above drowned out her voice.

"This is all lies! Lies! I demand the challenge! Only through the challenge will we know the truth!" a man's voice said.

The beggars, who had fallen silent once the Antipope had produced the body of Ivo the Pale, erupted in cheers, screams, and stomping feet. Their near animalistic shouts and caws shook the arena and they only fell silent when the Antipope raised one hand.

"He who issues the challenge, come forth," she said, returning to her throne.

She adopted the same indolent, insolent pose on her seat of power and waved her hand in a circle. Her actions were an open mockery of royal behavior of past days, though they seemed more of an act than insult.

The large, muscular male with the shattered nose stepped forward, his face twisted in with disdain and disgust. He spat at the feet of both swordmasters and touched his forehead to the Antipope.

"Antipope, brothers and sisters," he said, his voice a booming basso, "the false republican lies to us. He speaks of foreign lands and tales from the penny press, stories stolen from sailors, no doubt. Yet, when he returns to our city, who dies? Do the friends of the false Emperor fall, or do our people perish? He lies, my friends! Did we confront such evil before Jean-Pierre Séverin appeared? No! He lies, he lies, he lies and we die, we die, we die!"

The beggars screamed, voices chorusing the last words with astonishing speed.

"He lies, we die! He lies, we die!"

The muscular male raised his hands again for silence, which took a wait of several moments. Finally, the last echo of the chant died away, the arena drifting into an anticipatory hush.

"I demand, as a member of the guild, the right of challenge. Let this liar prove he is more than honeyed words spread across our ears! Challenge! Challenge!"

"Challenge!" the beggars screamed back, repeating the words with ever-growing intensity.

The Antipope regarded the room for a moment, her hooded head circling the chamber without comment. Eventually, she stood and stepped between Séverin and the huge man.

"Thierry issues the challenge to you, Jean-Pierre Séverin. Under our ancient laws, this means trial by combat. Refusal means you plead guilty and the guild decides your punishment. What do you say?" the Beggar Queen asked.

Séverin shrugged and said, "We're wasting time again, but I accept. What happens if I win?"

Lisebette pushed forward and grinned up at the taller swordmaster.

"Nobody ever beats Thierry when he issues the challenge, fool! You shall die, screaming for mercy... which shall never arrive... Pray while you have time, dead man..." She added with a girlish giggle, "Finally, I shall have my revenge!"

CHAPTER XXIV

Ishaani sighed as Henry Morley left again, his need for raping children controlling his actions. He had been that bad back home, where the poor *Dalit* families sold him their children for pennies. He was repugnant then, worse now.

"I like your little ones," Morley once said in her hearing. "Once clean, they are useful creatures. Good for a poke or two until you tire of them. Then they go back their gutter, grateful for a few coins."

Disgusting, Ishaani thought then, and again now.

She still remembered the day they had discovered that the stupid, blond, rutting boar was an impressive warrior. It had happened during one of his treks to a district that people of the city, both wise and foolish, avoided for fear of their safety.

It was a short two years ago when four men had attacked the tall English sea captain. They had known that he carried money and liked children. If he died, the Company's masters would only look briefly for his killer.

"Who are you, you filthy swines?" Morley had asked while flexing his broad shoulders.

"Give us your money," a squat, toothless man of twenty-six named Dhruv had replied.

Dhruv was a criminal from birth, one whose life had moved on a downward trajectory since he was twelve and who had become a robber instead of a nightsoil collector like his father and older brother. Never a particularly successful criminal, he and three of his fellows, none of whom Ishaani or her grandmother knew, robbed English visitors who wandered into the worst streets by accident. They were like a pack of wild dogs, dangerous as a group because they operated as a team, but individually small and weak.

Dhruv had pulled out a long, rusting knife he had stolen from a French sailor and licked his flabby lips with a long scabrous tongue.

"Give us your money and your clothes and your boots and we will let you live…" Dhruv had lisped as he waggled the knife left and right with an amused glint in his eyes.

Henry Morley had reached down, looking as if he would pay. Ishaani knew that this pack of savages were never content with anything they stole. The Englishman would be lucky if all he received was theft, rape, and a beating this day.

The long heavy knife that had appeared in Morley's hand nearly decapitated Dhruv a moment later. The sea captain's other hand removed a rounded wooden rod, which he used to smash the jaw of the second man.

The final two had fled, shrieking in fear, Henry Morley a step behind their frightened forms. Within seconds, both lay dead at his feet and the Englishman merely paused long enough to clean his knife on their bodies.

"We watch that one," Ishaani's grandmother, also named Ishaani, had said, "He may be the tool we require."

Ishaani had sighed unhappily, disliking this duty. Yet the guru of their sect, her great grandfather, an elderly wisp of a man named Rudra, had started this search months earlier.

"The French advisors who escaped when our poor Tipu Sultan died have granted me knowledge," Rudra had said in his surprisingly strong voice for a man who looked like a bundle of stick with a white beard. "I know the name of the creature who stole the scrolls of *Raktabija*. He, too, is French and considered a great scholar among their people…".

"Then ask the French for the holy parchments and promise them jewels and other precious objects in return," Mohan, Ishaani's grandfather, had said in reply.

Mohan looked like a slightly heavier version of his father, a shrunken man with a heavy gray beard and rounded shoulders. He spoke in a reedy voice and there were times outsiders from other temples believed Rudra was his brother instead of his father.

"No!" Rudra had said, "If we do that, the French will wonder what the holy texts contains. We require a greedy man, one who is a white, but not interested in anything save his wealth. He must be dangerous and clever, but hold no curiosity of the greater aspects of life."

The temples had scoured the settlements, discovering many who might fulfill these conditions, but ultimately each proved unsuitable for one reason or another. A wealthy trader was too greedy, a Company army captain spoke French poorly, and so on...

Morley had proved the best of a poor lot. He was greedy, a trained killer who rivaled any European they encountered. Even the English army sergeant who had killed their beloved Tipu Sultan would have found this navy captain a difficult foe. He held no interest in the reason they sought the scrolls of Raktabija, only that he would receive more gold and gems for his services.

"Just for my kit and... ahem, entertainments... ahem, and I shall help your man," Henry Morley had declared after receiving a small gem and the offer.

"Woman," Ishaani said and sat at his side.

Morley had stared at her and laughed, howling like an ape at the sight of the kneeling woman. He had reached out to pat her on the cheek.

"Dear little girl, do not..."

His next words had been a shriek of pain as Ishaani swept him to the ground and placed a blade at his neck.

"Do not underestimate any from this temple, Morley sahib," Rudra had said. "We train in the killing arts and are, even by your English standards, formidable. Ishaani is the youngest of our people, yet the best able to complete the quest."

Morley had thought for a moment, then continued laughing. Though this time it was not with derision, but genuine delight.

"Very well, darkie, very well," he had said between laughs. "Send the gal and we shall find these old papers you need. But if you try and trick me, I will bring your temple down around your ears and sell your people into slavery!"

The bargain was made. Henry Morley and Ishaani, the priestess of an underground sect worshipping Kali, goddess of destruction, traveled secretly from southern India to the heart of the French Empire.

"I swore to you, Black Mother Kali, I shall succeed in this task. Even if it costs my life and that of every living being between here and your holy temple!" Ishaani prayed.

CHAPTER XXV

"I shall tell you of Catherine Monvoisin and her clan and all shall be clear," Jean Ténèbre said, clapping his brother on the shoulder. "Back in the days of the French King Louis XIV, men and women sought power from that monarch. One of those seekers was his mistress, Madame de Montespan…"

"I remember Louis," Ange said. "He was the beardless king who listened to any astrologer for advice on all subjects. He loved spies and we nearly ended up dead when he kidnapped that count's wife and daughter."

Jean shook his head and said, "No, that was his ancestor, Louis XI, the Spider."

Ange frowned and asked, "Was he the Louis who allowed Richelieu rulership over France?"

"No, that was Louis XIV's father," the *oupire* said, suppressing a sigh.

One of the difficulties of a long life was that remembering humans was rarely easy. They died so easily and lived short lives filled with nonsense.

"Louis XIV was called the Sun King, and he was an impressive man, intelligent, well-read, and politically clever. However, he was very vain and had many mistresses. One was Françoise-Athénaïs de Rochechouart, Marquise de Montespan. She was the mother of seven of the king's children and, for a time, was queen in all but name. A true beauty, but she fell victim to that which plagues all the living…"

"Age," Ange said with heavy finality.

"Correct, my brother," Jean said. "She grew older and other lovely ladies arrived in court, hoping to become the new King's Mistress. Many would weep or marry a wealthy duke, yet Madame de Montespan chose a different direction… One that you shall find quite amusing… She took the left-handed path."

Ange giggled and threw back his head of thick blond curls.

"She became a witch? Killing black cats, sacrificing babies and drinking blood from the skulls of the dead?"

Jean nodded gravely and said, "That, and more. She met with a woman named Catherine Monvoisin, better known as La Voisin. That evil woman created an organization devoted to evil witchcraft and, most importantly, poison. La Voisin and her competitor, a woman called Marie Bosse, were responsible for over one thousand deaths, as well as the spread of black magic throughout all levels of Parisian society. They even considered killing the Sun King and installing one of his bastard children by Montespan, creating the first truly satanic kingdom."

"They were late to that game, brother. Cesare Borgia and his father, Pope Alexander VI, chose that path three hundred years before," Ange said.

Shaking his head, Jean said, "No, Ange, you are wrong. The Borgias were truly evil, but they were not satanic or demon worshippers. They had other interests; ones that I will not speak aloud... Remind me to show you Cesare's folio when we return home. I think you shall find the pages quite... instructive..."

"I shall," Ange said and glanced up at his brother. "Why are you telling me this admittedly interesting history of murder and silliness in France? You never discuss such matters without a reason."

"If you recall, the original discussion was of our employer, the demon worshiper named Strix. What do you know of Strix?" Jean asked while quirking an eyebrow. "I ask this because my information regarding *L'affaire des poisons* shall play an important part in the tale of the one we call Strix."

"Sexless, based on smell," Ange said. "I cannot sense male or female upon that creature for some strange reason. Smells of brimstone, blood, and sulphur... always dressed in magician's robes with a mask that covers the entire head. Has no personality and spends every waking hour studying occult books and scrolls. Did I miss anything?"

Jean shook his head.

"Nothing except the name. Strix has two meanings. The first is another word for an owl. The second, for a type of witch. A witch known as a *strix* is a poisonous creature, a being that lives to spread of horror and chaos in the world. Additionally, Strix mutters of the past, remembering an extended life. I listened and recognized the truth…"

"Where did you learn of witches called strix?" Ange asked, eyes narrowing.

"In Selene," Jean replied, effectively ending all discussion.

They both fell silent as their minds drifted back through the centuries to a city of darkness and horror. The spectral land of ancient vampires, known to the world simply as Selene…

CHAPTER XXVI

"In time, all fall," said Bartolomeo Dardi. "Diodorus Siculus, the ancient Greek historian, once wrote of a fallen Egyptian statue inscribed with the words, '*King of Kings Ozymandias am I. If any want to know how great I am and where I lie, let him outdo me in my work.*' Even a mighty ruler fell in time. Your Thierry is a fool if he believes none shall defeat him."

"Once I kill your friend, little man," Thierry said, "I shall snap your back and watch you die slowly…"

Dardi yawned, opening his mouth wide, a ridiculous display that, none-the-less, earned many titters from observers.

"I have been threatened by demons, vampires, strigia, and my late beloved wife—God rest her soul. Your words are unimaginative in the light of such dangers," Dardi replied with an eyeroll.

Thierry surged forward, but fell to the ground. He struck the stone floor with bone-crunching force, the air knocked from his lungs. He gasped and groaned, his face reddening from the exertion and embarrassment.

"Who… did… that…?" he gasped.

"I stuck out my foot. You did not attend and tripped," Séverin replied with a Gallic shrug while turning towards the Antipope. "May I know which method is used in this challenge?"

"Combat, of course," she answered. "You and Thierry shall fight in this arena. We shall place weapons along the walls, or you may use your hands. The battle does not end unless one party yields, and the surrender is accepted by the other fighter. Or if either or both combatants dies, of course."

"Of course," Séverin replied.

He unbuttoned his jacket and said, "Shall we commence? We are wasting time and demons still prowl our streets…"

"The challenge is accepted," the Antipope said.

The assembled beggars shouted with delight, many screaming without actual words. This response was an explosion of pure exultation, a celebration of the coming contest of blood and honor. Transport these people back in time to the days of the Emperor Commodus or Diocletian and the screams and celebratory shouts would have been identical to those of the ancient Romans.

This was humanity's inner monster—the being that resided in the hearts of even the best of our species, the hidden creature that was a demoniac whisper in the back of our minds. It desired nothing more than blood, pain, and animalistic sexual congress as a means of satisfaction.

To some, this voice was naught but an easily ignored whisper—their darkness they denied or despised. To others, this aspect of the psyche emerged without warning, often leading to unexpected death and pain. However, to a rare few, that dark voice within their mind and body was the only driving force in life. The sadist who enjoys torturing weaker victims for pleasure and power, the robber who murders and rapes without cause or control, the ruler who treats their people as toys to be broken at will—these were the obvious members of humans who embraced their inner darkness.

The shrieking, stamping, and clapping members of the beggars' guild did not fall within this category. Though many were angry at all life for reducing them to the lowest caste of society, they did not seek the death of all life. Their anger emerged now, as they watched their protector, Thierry, prepare for battle against a handsome, older, cleanly dressed man.

The target of their rage, swordmaster Jean-Pierre Séverin, did not dress like an aristocrat, nor did he behave like one who looks down upon those present. But this did not matter. He possessed clean clothing, access to fresh food, and a bed of his own. He would serve as a representation of the world that had tossed them aside and reduced members of their guild to their sad state.

Later, Séverin had no doubt that many would feel shame for their behavior this evening. But for now, they would call for blood and pain and demand a brutal death.

Five men carted away the Antipope's throne and she took a seat in the first row of the arena. The candle she carried in earlier lay by her side on the bench, flickering, as the assemblage howled for the commencement of the duel.

"This one," Dardi said, "has the look of a sadist. He will go for the painful wound first."

"Yes," Séverin agreed. "I believe incapacitating me is his first priority. Then he would wear me down with slow, painful attacks."

"Teach him a lesson, Gâteloup," Dardi said, clapping his taller friend on the shoulder, "and beware of treachery."

Nodding gravely, Séverin watched as his friend found a seat among the masses. The Antipope stood and raised one gloved hand, calling for silence from the throng.

"Lisebette, a member of our covenant, issued the challenge rather than a ruling on the guilt of Jean-Pierre Séverin. Though an outsider, the latter has accepted the duel. Thierry, our chief guardian of the weak, acts as her champion. Bring forth the arms of battle!"

From four directions of the arena came a line of men and woman, each bearing items they held above their heads. They carried long knives, tiny throwing darts, huge clubs with spikes across their surfaces, a massive, rusting basket-hilted sword, a heavy flanged mace that made the holder wheeze and sweat with each step, a woodman's axe, and a wooden staff about six feet long.

After a signal from the Beggar Queen, the men and women walked to the walls of the arena and placed the weapons on the stone floor. They then broke apart and ran into the crowd, taking seats among their fellows and joining the merriment.

"Are you prepared?" the Antipope asked as she gazed down on both men.

"I am!" Thierry said and raised a fist above his head.

The elder swordmaster bowed and said, "*Ave, Imperator, morituri te salutant.*"

"What does that mean?" Lisebette said, dropping into a bench near the Antipope.

"It is," Dardi replied with a chuckle, "an old Roman salute performed by gladiators in the arena. They turned to the Caesar of the day, raised their hands, and called out those words. The statement means, '*Hail, Emperor, those who are about to die salute you*'."

In the arena, Thierry dropped his arm and looked to the Antipope.

"Let the challenge begin," she said in a hollow voice.

The massive Thierry expelled a loud scream and turned, running directly for the small pile of darts. Séverin turned to his left and reached for a different weapon. The multitude fell silent, holding their collective breath as the fight commenced...

CHAPTER XXVII

Sylvia Dardi and Franz Karnstein released each other reluctantly, with the Austrian Exorcist taking a step away from Madame Annette's doorway.

Sylvia had a room in this small home, one owned by the widow of an Admiral killed fighting the English. Madame Annette was a large woman with a massive bust, a booming voice, and the face of an aged Sergeant Major. She accepted young women in her home with the understanding that they obeyed her strict rules.

"No visitors, man or woman, church every Sunday, no eating in your rooms, all male escorts must meet the lady of the house and be approved by her..." and a host of other regulations.

Jean-Pierre Séverin knew the powerful matron from years past, having taught her husband, middle son, and nephew, fencing when they were back from the wars. She approved of him, especially since he had shown no inclination for re-marriage after the passing of his dear wife.

"Too many young people," she said one day when they met in passing, "view marriage as a temporary estate. I thoroughly do not!"

Sylvia found the formidable woman familiar, just like her aunts back in Naples. She agreed to take these rooms without argument, knowing this would add some comfort to her father and Séverin.

She introduced Franz to Madame Annette.

"This is my *fidanzato*, Franz , Madame," she said.

Franz clicked his heels and said, "Please to meet you, Madame. I am Franz von Vordenburg-Karnstein."

"You are a Prussian?" Madame Annette asked, a warning note in her tone.

Franz shook his head and smiled briefly.

"No, Madame, I am Austrian," he replied.

"Franz's family is among the oldest in Europe," Sylvia added.

Madame Annette stared at them for a moment and then nodded once.

"You may visit, young man, but you shall not enter this house. You shall meet Mademoiselle Dardi at the door and await her when you meet socially. Violation of my rules shall mean casting the young lady in the street like a common harlot!"

Bowing in acceptance, Karnstein obeyed the rules without question. He knew Sylvia liked the daunting matriarch and that was enough for him. Their partings were never easy, their mutual desire for each other did not slow in time.

Bowing towards the curtain behind which Madame Annette spied upon them, he turned on his heels and headed towards his home. The distance was only a few streets, but he gripped a small wooden club in one hand and a pocket pistol in the other. The streets of Paris were still a dangerous place at night, despite the State's declarations to the contrary.

Suddenly, a figure stepped out of a doorway a few feet ahead, standing directly in his path. Karnstein raised his revolver and pointed it towards the hidden individual without pause.

"Calm yourself, Franz Karnstein," the satanic priestess said with a bubbling laugh. "It is only I."

She stepped into view, standing in a circle of silvery moonlight. She wore her blond hair swept up and in curls, and her cotton dress did not hide her impressive décolletage and narrow waist. The spare light made her appear almost ghostly in the gloom.

"I know," the Exorcist replied, without lowering his weapon. "What do you want?"

"You, young Karnstein," she said with a girlish giggle, stepping closer. "I told you that the first time we met. A Karnstein for a mate would grant me a child who would rule the world."

"And the devil said unto him, 'All this power will I give thee, and the glory of them: for that is delivered unto me; and to whomsoever I will I give it. If thou therefore wilt worship me, all shall be thine.'" Karnstein replied. *"And Jesus answered and said unto him, 'Get thee behind me, Satan: for it is written, Thou shalt worship the Lord thy God, and him only shalt thou serve,'"* adding, "Luke 4:5-8."

The priestess laughed and shook her head. Her laugh was the same as used by malicious children as they watch a weaker creature suffer. The Austrian found the sound repugnant and reminiscent of earlier horrors in his life.

"You always quote from the false God's bible when something unnerves you, Franz Karnstein. Your will is strong, but I am ancient and knowledgeable. It is time I broke your spirit and taught you your true path. Take him!"

Dark figures spilled out of the shadows, five cultists dressed in black, armed with makeshift clubs.

Karnstein turned his weapon upon one without looking back and shot a woman with dark hair and a pretty face marred by a nasty grimace. The bullet entered her eye and sent her sprawling backwards. She was dead before her body flopped upon the pavement.

Tossing the unloaded weapon into the face of a second attacker, the Austrian cracked the knee of a third. Both men yelped in agony, while the remaining one strode around his fellow cultists, finally swinging for Karnstein's skull.

The Exorcist ducked the attack and grabbed his attacker's arm. A moment later, the cultist flew through the air, landing on his back several feet away.

"Bastard!" the priestess snarled, stepping forward.

Suddenly, a thin blade appeared by the side of her neck, the sharp point just short of piercing the skin and sending showers of crimson blood across the cobblestones.

"You should leave my *fidanzato* alone, you blond cow," Sylvia snarled. "Can't you see that he has no interest in your pale, flat-chested body?"

"Bitch," the priestess said, her eyes burning with uncontained fury.

"Say that again, *putana*, and I will slice your pale face into a pile of blood and meat. *Capice?*" Sylvia replied, her voice cold and taut with fury.

"I would do as she says," Karnstein advised as he retrieved and reloaded his pistol. "The last woman who cast eyes in my direction only survived out of necessity. We only require your information."

The priestess stared at the Austrian, her gaze shifting back and forth between him and Sylvia.

"Lords of Earth and Air... You lust for this peasant... over... me?" she asked.

"Yes," the Exorcist replied. "I informed you thusly earlier today. You are pleasant to the eye, damned creature, but I see your true face. You are inwardly as hideous as the demons you worship."

"No man," the priestess said, "denies me. Great heroes, evil mystics, men of purity and faith. In the end, all yield to my desires. Two children I had in ancient days; both died. My third shall herald the new age... The day where the Dark Angel rules Above and Below. You shall give me your seed and your allegiance, Franz Karnstein. Lust after peasant girls and pray day and night. Your true nature, the ancient black blood of your clan, shall call you to my side."

There was a moment of silence as the words hung in the air. Nobody moved and it felt as if the very world awaited a response from someone present.

The answer came several seconds later as Karnstein tittered. His face, normally cold, stern, and unyielding slowly spread into a smile and his pale cheeks glowed with a scarlet blush.

Then he began laughing, howling with uncontrolled mirth as he stood on the dark Parisian boulevard. Tears streaked his face and his entire body shook as he said and screamed with uncontrolled, hysterical, merriment.

129

Sylvia looked confused, but joined the laughter seconds later. She did not know what made her fiancé laugh so hard, but found his reaction infectious. This was the most she had ever heard him laugh in their entire time together.

"What," the priestess asked through clenched teeth, "do you find so amusing?"

"You!" he shrieked, pointing her direction. "The ancient black blood of my clan... shall call me... oh, I cannot finish..."

The priestess stood and haughtily watched as the Austrian hooted for several more minutes. He leaned against a nearby wall for support and appeared exhausted as he slowly straightened.

Finally, Karnstein shook his head and breathed slowly, clearly fighting to regain control of his emotions.

"I shall try and explain, but I cannot promise complete control. When I was eight years old, a relative came to my home... An exquisitely beautiful woman named Mircalla Karnstein and her two servants, Otto and Jana..."

CHAPTER XVIII

Karnstein Castle, Styria, 1784

Franz Karnstein did not speak; he stepped deeper into the room and pulled the brass cross his grandfather had given him as a present a while back. It was an old item, a relic a Vordenburg had earned during a war, hundreds of years in the past.

Both women recoiled at the sight of the holy object. Their eyes grew wide and their faces fearful. Lena looked away, shielding herself with her gown. Mircalla raised her hand in defense, her sharp teeth revealed.

"Otto! Jana!" shouted Lena, as she shrank back even further.

Franz heard the drumming, thrumming, pound of feet approaching and reached into his bag.

Otto appeared in the doorway, his face twisted with fury. He stepped towards Franz, not noticing the dueling pistol in the young man's hand. The boy squeezed the trigger and a loud explosion echoed in the room. Otto crashed to the floor, half his head missing. His blood began pooling upon Lena's beloved carpet.

Mircalla and Lena were still frozen by the cross and stared in shock at Franz plucked a second pistol from his bag. He pointed the weapon at the doorway and fired when Jana appeared. The seductive servant fell to the ground beside Otto, her face destroyed by the heavy pistol ball.

Franz then dropped the pistols back into the bag and pulled out a small pouch. This he opened with one hand and tossed it at the feet of his mother. The contents spilled across the floor and Lena stared down, unable to tear her eyes away.

"Lena, no! I command you!" said Mircalla with a ragged voice.

Lena Karnstein ignored her dark mistress and dropped to the ground. Her soft voice floated through the air.

"One, two, three..."

The contents of the pouch were tiny seeds.

One lesson Franz had learned from his grandfather was that new vampires were unable to resist counting fallen items. The way to stop such creatures was to drop seeds or rice at their feet. Their hunt would cease as they dropped to their knees and counted each item. It was a mighty weakness.

Mircalla turned her haughty expression upon Franz.

"Guns will not kill me, little boy. And soon you will tire. Then I will bite you and tear your heart from your chest. And your last memory will be watching myself and your mother feasting upon your blood and meat."

Franz did not answer. He merely stooped down and pulled an object out from beneath a large couch. This was the article he had hid in the room before daybreak. Another gift from his dead father. A cavalry saber. The blade gleamed in the sunlight as he stepped close to Mircalla.

"No! No!" she screamed as she tried to back away.

She struck the wooden wall and shrank downward, pulling herself into a ball.

"Yes. This is for my Vordenburg family. And even for my father," said Franz.

He swung the heavy blade downward. The steel sheared through Mircalla's neck. Her head fell away from her body and a fountain of dark blood spread across the stone floor.

Stepping around the corpse of his vampiric cousin, Franz stepped next to his kneeling mother. She was still counting, her soft voice rhythmic as she separated the seeds.

"...fifty-three, fifty-four..."

Lena never looked up as Franz raised the sword in two hands.

"I am sorry, mother."

Franz's voice shook as he swung the blade down hard and fast.

A spray of blood spattered across his face and his mother's head rolled next to that of Mircalla.

Back in the modern day...

Sylvia knew the story, having heard it shortly after they had met. She still felt a stab of agony, imagining herself in Franz's place, being eight years-old, killing two humans and two vampires. Worst of all, one of those undead leeches was his own mother! The thought was horrific, and she wished she could hold him right now.

The priestess remained still, her lovely form statuesque and coldly inhuman as she contemplated the young Austrian.

"As you probably realize now," Karnstein continued, "resisting evil is not difficult for me. Poets declared Mircalla Karnstein was the Helen of Troy of her time. Possibly, you are as well, but it matters not to me. You are as evil as she was, and I should sooner take holy vows rather than pollute my body and soul with your presence."

"Then why do you trust I shall give you correct information?" she asked, her eyes narrowing.

"Because it serves your interests, of course," he replied. "The vampire and the ghoul that haunt these streets, and their damned employer, endanger your position. We shall do battle again, creature, but not today. For now, we share the same goal."

The priestess's eyes shot daggers in his direction, but she did not move or even appear to breathe. After what felt like hours, her face twisted into a moue of distaste and she sighed.

"Very well. The one you seek calls herself Strix. She is older than human years and is a witch of great power and madness. Seek her and her followers near the Place Beauvau. That is all I know. Strix and her ilk find the desperate and the stupid. Why else would she employ the Ténèbre Brothers?"

Karnstein frowned and nodded once.

"That makes some sense. However, is not the Place Beauvau a location used by the government?"

"I do not care. That is where they exist, though more I cannot discover. When confronting witches who seek chaos, the wise enemy moves with care. They are often insane and vastly powerful... now, you know all. I shall leave!"

Sylvia looked in his direction and Karnstein moved a finger. So she removed her blade and stepped aside, her weapon still at the ready.

"Leave now, *putana*," she said.

The priestess turned on her heels and marched away, stopping when she was just barely visible.

"I curse you both, in the name of Belial and Lucifer! Your ends shall be painful, and you shall die slowly by my hand!"

She then melted away into the night.

"They always call out such threats. I should have died in terrible ways since age eleven when I helped my aunt defeat a strigia and her vampire daughter," Sylvia said.

Then she kissed him quickly. The Austrian looked confused, tilting his head slightly in response.

"What was that for? I do not object; I simply ask for information."

Sylvia took his arm while rolling her eyes.

"You are truly an innocent at time, *amore*. If you think, you shall realize why this confrontation makes me happy."

"Oh my," Jean Ténèbre said as he crossed the street. "Young lovers, so sweet and delightful. Are you not moved my brother?"

Ange appeared at his side and shook his head. His blond hair bounced freely with the movement and appeared almost white in the pale illumination.

"No," he said. "An Austrian Baron and a Neapolitan peasant? Very uninspiring."

Jean tsked several times and shrugged.

"My brother has specific views of behavior and physical appearance in females. I am not so sanguine with such prejudiced views. In any event, my lord Baron, it is a pleasure to meet you. My name is Jean Ténèbre, and this is my brother Ange. We require you for our mistress."

"Do come quietly and we shall allow your strumpet a chance of escape," Ange added, flashing a long, sharp incisor.

"Reject our kind offer," Jean concluded, while fluttering his elongated fingers, "and we shall break your arms, legs and jaw, and you shall still do as we bid…"

CHAPTER XXIX

Thierry snatched up the pile of darts and yelled in triumph. Spinning, he raised one hand and flung the weapon towards Jean-Pierre Séverin's leg.

What the beggar's guild knew was that, though Thierry was a giant, his massive, mighty strength was only his second best weapon. His favorite method of attack was throwing weapons such as daggers, sticks and, most importantly, darts. Though these devices were rarely fatal, they severely weakened an enemy and rendered them helpless in a battle that lasted longer than ten minutes. This was one of the reasons he had never lost a challenge; he fought strategically to the end.

The dart flew true, though a second later it dropped from the air in midflight. Thierry looked confused and tossed a second missile, this time towards Séverin's face.

Again, the dart fell useless to the stone floor, the metallic sound echoing through the now-silent arena. A confused hush ruled this amphitheater devoted to judgment and death.

Stepping forward, Thierry realized the swordmaster held a long wooden staff in one hand. Seeing the giant's slow approach, he spun the weapon in one hand, the action a blur of wood and flesh.

Thierry faked a throw towards Séverin's head and tossed the dart towards his unmoving right arm. But the staff slashed out in an almost invisible arc that batted the dart aside. The swordmaster then spun it again, switching several times before bringing the wooden weapon to a sudden halt.

"*Connard*," Thierry spat, dropping the remaining darts on the stone surface.

Taking three fast steps to his right, the giant grabbed a pair of daggers—each weapon a little more than a foot long. He clashed the weapons together over his head, sending sparks flying into the air. The crowd loved the display and cheered, their words mixing and mingling into an incomprehensible buzz.

Séverin shrugged and tossed the staff aside, walking to his right, picking up the rusting sword. Testing the blade and balance, he stepped to the center of the arena. Assuming a stance where the sword covered most his body, Séverin waited for his opponent.

Thierry dropped into a low crouch, moving his daggers back and forth. He danced to the left on light, soft feet.

"Come at me! Fight!" the giant hurled.

Séverin gave no indication that he had heard his words. The elder swordmaster, held the large blade with a steady, unwavering hand.

Thierry reared back, preparing for a long bound. Then, he threw both weapons, nearly at the same time. This was a tactic he had used only twice in combat against highly capable foes.

The swordmaster's massive blade sliced the first dagger in half. However, the blade was too slow and unwieldy for a second parry in defense. The second attack had been aiming for his left shoulder. Even a glancing blow could incapacitate a strong man, and Thierry, knowing this, had smiled as he had released the blades.

But Séverin's left hand lashed out, the motion appearing almost unhurried. He snatched the missile from mid-air, raising the dagger to eye-level. He examined it with a practiced eye, turning the blade left and right.

"Approximately fifty years-old," he said, then tossing it aside. "Acceptable workmanship, but uninspired."

Thierry screamed with rage as he ran to his left and snatched up a huge, spiked club. The weapon was five feet long and covered with metal nails that protruded in multiple places. Raising it above his head, he howled like a beast, his humanity lost in his growing rage. He was now a barbarian, a savage Gaul like those who had fought Rome with fury centuries ago. Spittle flew from his foaming mouth, and his wild eyes were terrifying to behold.

Séverin stood his ground, the basket-hilted sword held before his body, blocking his torso. He appeared relaxed, despite the crazed giant charging in his direction.

Suddenly, he exploded forward, his sword slashing out with a silver and red lightning bold.

Thierry's club fell to the stone floor, bouncing and skittering across the surface. The giant lowered his hands and stared at the handle of his weapon. The wood stopped a mere inch from his hand, sliced cleanly by the swordmaster's attack.

The crowd inhaled in shock, many realizing the expertise required for such an attack. Séverin had intentionally disarmed his enemy without injuring him. Some cheers rose from the arena, though they were muted. After all, Thierry was still one of their own and the elder swordmaster was an outsider.

Thierry was past comprehending such details. His crazed, berserk mind ignored the implications and he threw the remaining piece of the club towards Séverin. His aim was true, but the swordmaster merely caught the wooden piece and tossed it aside.

Grabbing the huge, oversized flanged mace, the giant beggar bayed like a starving wolf and charged again. A collective intake of breath filled the arena, for all knew that the slightest strike from such a weapon would destroy anything it struck. It was designed for the destruction of metal armor as well as the human body beneath the heavy, steel plates. An unarmed human head would burst into a horrific mass of blood and bone when hit by such a mace.

Séverin stepped forward, reversing his grip on his sword. He then threw the weapon at Thierry's legs. It tangled in the giant's feet, cutting him and sending him toppling to the ground. The mace fell from his nerveless grip and rolled several feet away.

Thierry rose slowly, his eyes wild, staring in Séverin's direction. With a loud howl, he opened his hands and ran towards the unarmed swordmaster. He dwarfed the tall Séverin, appearing colossal, a modern representation of the minotaur to the latter's Theseus.

Reaching out with hands that appeared mere blurs to the observers, Séverin grabbed both Thierry's arms, shifted his stance, and sent the giant sailing through the air.

The huge beggar landed with a sickening thud and several teeth flew from his now-bloody mouth. Séverin leaped onto the man's back and twisted both arms, holding them in painful locks.

Thierry struggled and screamed in pain. His convulsions popped both of his shoulders from their sockets, rendering his arms useless. He flopped on the stone floor like a fish out of water, his screams dropping into soft, mewling, whimpers.

Séverin rose and stepped aside, sighing loudly and shaking his head.

"It is done. Take this man to a proper bone fitter. With some rest, he should be well in a short time."

"No!" Lisebette said, rising and pointing her cane in his direction. "He has not surrendered and is alive. The duel is not finished!"

"No. I will not murder a man for being stubborn or foolish just to satisfy your bloodlust. Thierry fought bravely and now could not defend himself against a child with a rock until he receives proper treatment. The battle is over."

Lisebette opened her mouth, but the Antipope rose and clapped her hands three times.

"An outsider demonstrates more mercy than one of our own guild members. Yes, the challenge is over, and Jean-Pierre Séverin proved his innocence. Do you agree, my people?"

A discordant cry in the affirmative pierced the air and several men carried the quivering Thierry away on a large door. The Antipope raised the nub of a candle to her hooded head and flew out the flame, handing the holder to a young girl who appeared at her elbow.

The beggars turned away and filed out, heading towards unseen exits, resuming their invisible life in the city of Paris.

Within fifteen minutes, only the Antipope, Lisebette, Dardi and Séverin stood in the arena.

The Antipope turned towards the blind woman and asked, "You have a final message for these men?"

"I do," she said, drawing a sword from her cane. "DIE!"

The blind woman stabbed out, her blade aiming straight for the Antipope's chest!

CHAPTER XXX

Franz Karnstein drew his pistol and fired, striking Jean Ténèbre in the face, sending the tall *oupire* tumbling backwards with a shocked cry.

Sylvia Dardi lunged forward, her blade piercing Ange Ténèbre's heart and sending a showering of scarlet *vitae* across his chest.

"We reject your offer," she said, taking a step back as her fiancé drew his heavy saber.

Jean popped onto his feet, his face ripped and crumpled. He looked as if his entire head was imploding, with a vast, cavernous indentation pulling his nose and mouth inward.

Yet no blood leaked from his terrible wounds, the skin appearing waxen and oddly pliant to their unbelieving eyes. His face slowly expanded and shifted, transforming back to his normally serene countenance within a few seconds.

The blood on Ange's chest ceased pumping at approximately the same moment. The puckered hole caused by the sword blade vanished a second later, leaving behind smooth, unblemished skin.

"Bastards!" Ange said through a massive maw of frightening fangs.

"That was unnecessary," Jean said, his face having resumed its normal shape. "We only need you alive. But if we break every bone in your German body, our employer would not mind. Shall we, Ange?"

"Yes," the vampire growled, "but first, I will feed upon this blood bag's lifeforce. Jean, take the sacrifice. I need food…"

"*Madonna!* Did he just call me a bag of blood?" Sylvia asked as she pulled a dagger from her boot.

"Yes," Karnstein replied.

"I think I want this creature dead for that alone!" Sylvia said, circling to her left.

The Austrian did not reply. Jean had already leaped forward, slapping aside the heavy sword. With a powerful openhanded blow, he sent Karnstein sailing through the air and landing several feet away.

The Exorcist rolled to his feet in one smooth motion and swung his sword for the *oupire*'s neck.

Jean ducked the attack and slapped Karnstein aside again, sending him rolling down the street and rising more slowly. The Austrian reached under his cloak, removing a musket, which he raised and fired in one motion. The weapon discharged, striking Jean Ténèbre in the chest, forcing him back several feet.

Nearby, Sylvia sliced Ange's hands every time he reached in her direction. The vampire snarled, his pretty face slowly turning ashen and inhuman as they danced left and right. Suddenly, he leaped forward, piercing his chest with her smallsword, giggling as he slowly slid closer to the young Neapolitan woman.

"Got you now, blood bag," he said. "I love peasant food. It is so rich and unsullied."

Sylvia gripped her blade tight and, with her left hand, stabbed Ange in the neck with her dagger. She then kicked him in chest, sending the undead monster back several feet. Backing away, she knew she was almost completely disarmed, but had trust in her partner.

"That hurt, human slut," Ange croaked in a rough voice as he tugged at the dagger protruding from his throat. "I will kill you and rape your corpse!"

Sylvia backed away further, pulling out her final weapon. It was a tiny dagger that she held in a tight fist, the point extending several inches beyond her knuckles. A variant of an Indian weapon, her grandfather had designed the punch dagger in case of an emergency.

Against a vampire, it is useless, she thought, *but I will not give up. Franz,* amore, *please keep safe!*

"Sylvia!" Karnstein shouted, tossing his saber in her direction.

142

She caught the weapon, blew her beloved a kiss, and spun the heavy sword through the air with ease. She handled the weapon better than he, her skill apparent as she brought the blade to bear.

"Do try, leech!" she said with a happy laugh. "This sword killed Mircalla Karnstein and many more vampires. Shall Ange Ténèbre be its latest victim?"

The vampire surged forward, his movements inhumanly fast. The dagger still extended from his neck as did the small-sword from his chest. The sounds emerging from his demonic face were more the snarls of an animal than that of a man.

"Disarming yourself, human?" Jean asked, straightening his coat. "While I applaud your noble behavior, I also find it rather stupid."

"It is not chivalry, *oupire*," Karnstein replied, pulling out his last musket and firing the weapon into the creature's face. "I am not particularly effective with a sword."

The musket ball missed the fast-moving ghoul, who stood several feet away from his prey.

"You are not particularly good at that either, Baron. Bullets from guns and slicing swords cannot kill the Ténèbre Brothers. We are not weaklings like those of your family who embraced the world of darkness."

"I know," Karnstein said. "But it does not matter. You shall die one way or another by my hand."

Swinging a hard hand again towards the young Exorcist, Jean's wide mouth opened in shock as the blow missed. He reached out, intent on grabbing his enemy and slicing him open with his jagged talons. But again, the attack missed, and Karnstein raised an eyebrow in open mockery.

The *oupire* sprung forward, landing mere inches away from the Austrian, chuckling as he reached for the exposed neck. Oddly enough, Karnstein did not recoil, but pressed closer. His arm encircled Jean's waist and, with a shift of his hips, he sent the undead monster flying through the air.

"I am, as you can see," Karnstein said, "very good at wrestling, French *savate*, English boxing, and other methods of killing your kind."

"You think you can defeat me and my brother with your hands alone?" Jean asked incredulously.

Karnstein shook his head and pulled out a metal flask. He slowly unscrewed the top and smiled, an evil glint in his pale, lupine, eyes.

"Of course not," he replied. "This is water from the Sea of Galilee, blessed by three Popes and held in a sealed holy vessel for a hundred years in the Holy See. A potent weapon that kills the undead with one drop upon their skin's surface. I think I shall make you drink that drop…"

Before Jean could answer, a loud shriek, like that of an animal in agony, ripped through the night. Ange Ténèbre stumbled backwards, black blood shooting from the stump of his right arm. His hand lay upon the street, shriveling like an insect under the gaze of the scorching sun.

Jean exploded into action, scooping up his brother and vanishing from sight in a blur of motion.

A heartbeat later, they had vanished from sight, leaving Karnstein and Sylvia alone on the boulevard.

"*Gott in Himmel!*" the Austrian exclaimed, sagging against a nearby wall.

"Thank you for the sword, *amore*," Sylvia said, extending the weapon his direction.

Karnstein shook his head slowly.

"No, I think not. You keep it. You use it better and take it from me most times we are in a battle."

"That *cazzo* stole my favorite smallsword and a good knife!" Sylvia raged, staring at the flask he held in his hand. "What is that?"

"Water," he answered. "Blessed water I keep in case we encounter Hell's servants."

Sylvia's eyes widened and she asked, "Blessed by *il Papa* himself?"

Karnstein shook his head and took her arm.

"No, just from the church I pray at every morning," he said, as they headed back towards her home.

"Thank you again for the sword," Sylvia said, kissing his cheek as he handed her the sheathe and belt. "I know it was a gift from your father. You will need one in replacement."

"It was not so much a gift as a spoil from his gambling winnings. My father treated me like a pet puppy he hoped would one day grow up to something useful, and I shall discuss a replacement for it with the Maestro tomorrow at our training session."

"I think speaking is all you will do tomorrow. You shall be bruised badly in the morning. I shall come and help you with your recovery," she said in a teasing manner.

"An encouraging event at last," Karnstein said, wincing as she elbowed his side.

CHAPTER XXXI

Henry Morley sliced the sextant's throat with a long dagger and tossed the man's body into the heavy brush. Picking up his shovel, he walked with a swaying step into the graveyard, opening his lantern periodically and getting his bearings.

"Here," he said, reading the name on the tiny tombstone, "Abraham Hyacinthe Anquetil-Duperron, may he rest in Hell. Are you sure this is the best chance of recovering the stolen documents?"

"Yes," Ishaani said, appearing before the headstone like a spectral presence. "He will know what happened to the Raktabīja spell."

Morley's face creased in a frown and his shook his head.

"Why this unholy parchment exists still confuses me. None-the-less, I shall do as you ask since we have a pact. And a Morley always honors an agreement!"

"That is well enough for my people, Morley sahib. Do as we ask and your reward shall be as great as you imagine."

Ishaani sympathized with the Englishman's view, but that did not matter. The spell of Raktabīja existed and that was her only concern. The story flowed back to her as she watched the sea captain dig into the hard earth.

She had heard her aged great grandfather telling the tale when she had been two years-old, days before the elderly warrior had died in his sleep…

"Raktabīja was a demon king who battled the Gods and sought the death of all life," the old man said, weaving the tale with his soft voice and frail, shriveled hands.

The entire clan sat before him, their guru for more lifetimes than any imagined. None stirred or made a sound as he told the tale that was central to their beliefs.

"He had one gift from birth, a terrible power that made Raktabīja feared by all who knew his might. The clue was in his name... which meant, 'He for whom each drop of blood is a seed'. If an enemy cut or stabbed Raktabīja, a duplicate of the mighty demon sprung to life. One battle with the creature could flood the universe with evil."

The elderly man closed his eyes and shook his head sadly.

"The goddesses wounded the demon, but when he started bleeding, dread Kali intervened. She licked up each drop of blood as the demon bled. We, her true followers, celebrate her bravery by killing in her name through bloodless strangulation. Every soul we send her prevents her from bringing the Kali Yuga, the last age of life in the universe. When Kali brings the time of chaos, none shall survive..."

In the present, Ishaani knew she was a faithful Thuggee, a protector of humanity. The cost of a few lives was worth the effort. She, like her fellows, preferred the death of the beggars and other parasites of society to that of Mankind. None missed such untouchables, and their loss benefited all in the end.

"I reached the casket, woman," Morley said, popping his head over the gravestone. "Shall I break it open?"

"Yes, I must see the body from head to foot. If there is a shroud, toss it aside."

Morley swore and vanished from sight. The sound of wood splintering rose and a gauzy shroud appeared over the stone.

"Done," Morley said, stepping away from the hole. "I shall walk to the trees south of this position. Call me when you wish the body returned to the ground."

Whistling tunelessly, the Englishman strode from sight, leaving the lantern behind. Ishaani waited until he had vanished into the night, then circled around the marker, staring into the hole. Opening the lantern, she smiled quickly and reached for the pouch hidden on her back.

The body of Abraham Hyacinthe Anquetil-Duperron was a leathery bundle of sticks, colorless hair and yellow, shrunken skin. He formerly pudgy hands and fingers appeared like jaundiced claws across his chest and the fingernails protruded several inches beyond the fingertips.

"Perhaps in death you may still indemnify my people for your theft, Abraham Hyacinthe Anquetil-Duperron," Ishaani said as she studied the corpse. "You were a monster in life, but death did not rob you of being useful to those you wronged."

Hopping into the hole beside the body, the Thuggee priestess retrieved a small limp rat from a pouch. She had drugged the vermin earlier, knowing she required a life for this ceremony. A rat would do for obtaining information from the dead. Should she require an unliving servant, a greater, more vital life was required.

Slicing the rat's throat, she dribbled the creature's blood across the colorless lips, cheeks, forehead, and chin. With a reed brush, Ishaani drew a series of symbols and images across the dead flesh, each marking possessing details only an expert could discern.

Focusing her mind with a simple mantra and meditative technique, Ishaani placed her hands over Abraham Hyacinthe Anquetil-Duperron's unbeating heart and dead mind.

"*Aham aSTavAdane pratyAgacchAmi samudrakukSi pAtAla malina bhUta Abraham Hyacinthe Anquetil-Duperron,*" she said, whispering the words three times.

A heat grew in her palms, rising with each passing moment and sending a light, sickly yellow illumination about the graveyard.

The closed eyes of the dead man slowly climbed open and his mouth moved up and down without making a sound. Ishaani dropped the remaining, drying drops of rat vitae into the slowly working mouth and tossed the dead animal aside.

"Abraham Hyacinthe Anquetil-Duperron," she said in Hindustani, "you are awake."

"I am dead," came back the hoarse, almost inaudible reply.

"Yes, you are," the Thuggee priestess said, "and you will return to the peace of death after you answer my questions. Where are the scrolls of Raktabīja?"

"I do not know. *She* stole them as I died. The scrolls are gone," Anquetil-Duperron answered, his unblinking, dry eyes gazing her direction.

"Who is this woman who stole the parchments?" Ishaani asked.

"She calls herself Strix... I never learned her real name... worshipped devils or something... lovely body and face... taught her Sanskrit and other ancient languages... then she... then she... then she..." the dead man stammered and his body shook lightly.

This was something Ishaani never knew was even possible: a raised dead who exhibited traces of fear! Until this day, dead men and women never demonstrated the slightest trace of emotion. Something about the transition from the world of the living to that of the dead robbed them of any feelings they had, positive or negative. This trace of terror was fascinating, if slightly unnerving.

"Where does she reside?" she asked, knowing the mission was more important than what caused Anquetil-Duperron's fears after his death.

"She took me to her temple on the Place Beauvau... I never learned where.... wore a hood... thought it was all in fun... then she... then she... then she..." the dead man stammered.

"Then she, what?" Ishaani pressed. "What did she do?"

"Then she... then she... stole... the soul..." Anquetil-Duperron's shaky voice cracked upon the last word, sounding like a mouse's squeak rather than human speech.

"Stole a soul, how?" the Thuggee priestess said, pressing closer.

"..."

The mouth of the dead man opened and closed, but no words emerged. Nor did he form any sounds. His motions were that of a damaged creature, a man whose mind had shattered upon viewing something beyond comprehension. Ishaani knew that Anquetil-Duperron, explorer, thief and sensualist, no longer possessed even the trace of a mind that she had granted him through her ancient spell. He was little more than a corpse whose body held a spark of life.

Even if I sacrificed twenty strong men, she thought, *he would not speak again. Whatever he viewed was so horrific that reliving it again shattered him completely.*

Though she despised this man as a thief, Ishaani was not cruel. Smudging several symbols, she dropped a clump of dirt upon his face and removed the spell. The quivering face fell slack again, resuming the peaceful repose of death.

Hopping out of the hole, she opened her lantern and summoned Morley.

The sailor strode into view a moment later, the smell of brandy overwhelming the scents of soil and rotting flesh.

"Return the dirt to the grave," she said. "Then we must find a temple located on the Place Beauvau. There we shall find the scrolls of Raktabīja. That is your path to fortune and glory, Morley sahib."

"The Place Beauvau? You do not need my help in finding that location. It is a well-known location," Morley said, casting dirt back into the unearthed grave.

Ishaani accepted that explanation and said, "I am sure you are correct. However, I doubt we shall find the dwelling place of a witch of terrible power so easily. We must search carefully…"

"I would search the petticoats of the French Empress if they held your damned fool's papers. Just tell me where I should look," Morley said. Then he asked, "Tomorrow?"

Ishaani nodded, "Tomorrow."

CHAPTER XXXII

"It hurts!" Ange Ténèbre said while gripping his wounded arm as he writhed upon the ground.

"I do not doubt it," his brother Jean said as he pulled the musket ball from his body. "We must feed and repair ourselves, brother. Feed and heal."

"Jean! That bitch cut off my hand!" Ange said, his pale face appearing almost spectral as he looked up at his *oupire* brother. "How can you be so calm?"

Jean stared down at his brother, revealing his tattered face to the fallen vampire. A huge gash lay across his creek, revealing red muscles, dead black veins, and clean white bone. He looked frightful, a monster out of ancient legends. Yet he stood there, phlegmatic as ever and speaking in the same level tone he used when discussing the weather.

"I had a musket ball fired in my face, Ange. I healed, but the lead remained. I pulled it free, but I, too, must feed and regain my strength. We both must indulge ourselves if we are to get this crazed witch to Selene."

Ange, who had ceased screaming upon sight of his injured brother, rose and swayed upon his feet.

"What do you suggest?"

Jean pointed at a small house across the weed-covered field where they stood. No lights emerged from the dwelling, with only the vaguest outline of a building visible.

"That is the home of Chevalier Oscar Augustin. Fat Louis, the headless king, knighted him shortly before the family fled from the Revolution. He's returned to France, and they live in their ancestral home with no servants. The knight is almost eighty, his wife just as old, and his son, daughter-in-law and a child reside there as well. We shall capture the old man for Strix and you shall consume the lives of the others. I shall eat my fill of their dead bodies and we shall have completed our mission."

"If you knew of this man," Ange asked slowly, "why did you not choose him instead of Karnstein and his slut?"

"First, because Augustin rarely leaves his house. That meant we should have to kill all in the home if he became our quarry. Second, he is aged, and I am uncomfortable around old people. They remind me of that which we lost in Selene. Third, because he is aged, he may die if we take him, and that would destroy all our hard work. Finally, I dislike all Karnsteins. They are dangerous when left alive. Do you remember Wandessa? She nearly brought about your end!"

"Wandessa? She was not a Karnstein, but a Nadasdy!" Ange said, flashing his teeth.

Jean shook his head and tut-tutted.

"By marriage. She was a member of the Spanish branch of that family. I am also sure you remember Lady Viy and Carmilla as well. Viy may be the founder of their black bloodline, and I know of at least five vampire witches who used the name Carmilla. All Karnsteins, my brother! Their presence in this world places us in danger. I sought to eliminate a future threat."

"Unsuccessfully—at least for now. Damnation and hellfire! My arm burns!" Ange gasped.

Jean clasped his brother by the shoulder and said, "Come, we must not be subtle. They have no neighbors and we must complete our tasks quickly."

Vampire and *oupire* fell in step, moving quickly, but not using their undead celerity. They knew the encounter with Franz Karnstein and the woman he called Sylvia had weakened them sorely. They would use what strength they had left for the orgy of blood and death coming in the next few hours.

Opening the lock with a skeleton key he kept inside his belt, Jean stepped inside, softly closing the door after Ange had entered.

The house was a small two-story dwelling with a tiny kitchen, a dining room, a drawing room, and a tiny cell intended as a servant's quarters on the ground floor. Upstairs were two chambers, originally intended as a single bedroom and a sitting room. With the loss of fortune from the Revolution, Chevalier Augustin had turned the rooms into two bed-chambers. He and his elderly wife slept in the front room, with his son and daughter-in-law in the rear room.

"How do you know this?" Ange said after his brother had explained the layout of the house.

"I visited the family, pretending that my father was an old comrade of the family. They believed me... especially after I brought them wine and a large duck dinner..."

"Clever," Ange said, sniffing the air. "I smell tender flesh. A young boy?"

"Ten years-old," Jean said, pointing down the hall. "Do be quick though. I must feed on the body and then we shall consume the others. Just leave the old man unhurt."

Ange giggled and walked down the hall, his agony momentarily forgotten. He slowly opened the door and gazed down upon the face of a young boy with light brown hair and a red complexion partially covered in bright freckles. His breathing was low and sound, and he did not stir as the vampire crept to his side.

Ange's vampiric fangs slowly emerged from his expanding maw, their ivory surface practically glowing in the gloom. Without a sound, the vampire lunged forward, the incisors slicing deep into the tender flesh. The young boy died without pain, his death instantaneous at the hands of his undead attacker.

Low slurping sounds drifted in Jean's direction as Ange lay atop the tiny body. His shoulders shook as he greedily sucked the dead child's blood, treating each drop as if it were a rapturous feast.

After fifteen minutes, Ange Ténèbre stood upright and turned around, his mouth and face hidden beneath a layer of crimson *vitae*. He smiled, his stained teeth once again appearing tiny and human, and sighed happily.

"Oh, Jean," he said, "the little ones are a feast. So much life bursting from every precious drop of their tiny bodies. I want more..."

"Go upstairs and kill the old lady, the son, and the daughter-in-law. Bind and gag the old man. He must live long enough for Strix's latest experiment."

Ange clapped his tiny, stained hands and pressed forward, brushing past his taller sibling. Pausing in the doorway, he had a thought and glanced back.

"What of you?"

The ghoul licked his lips slowly, sensually, and turned his eyes upon the tiny lifeless form hidden in the shadows.

"You left me my meal, brother Ange. I shall feast upon this one and regain my power. Then we shall deliver Strix her latest victim and rest for the day."

The Ténèbre Brothers shared a meaningful look and simultaneously nodded. They had no need for conversation after centuries spent together.

Ange's blond hair shimmered in the gloom as he silently stole upstairs. Jean closed the door and approached the dead child, his wide mouth practically salivating as he lifted one chubby arm towards his mouth…

The blazing fire in the Augustin home provided the Ténèbre Brothers illumination as they strode towards their employer's dwelling. The rolled carpet across their shoulders proved a small burden, not by weight, but by sheer bulk. Chevalier Augustin periodically twitched, but he made no sounds after Ange delivered a few stinging blows to the man's stomach.

"Do you think anyone shall miss one body?" Jean asked, glancing back as flames burst from the roof.

Ange shook his head and giggled, a childish sound completely at odds with his behavior.

"No, Jean, no. I covered the floors and walls with every drop of lamp oil in the house. All that the brave rescuers shall find is a pile of ashes. The Turks perfected this method and that crazed Wallachian was even better at their brutal arts. No, none shall miss Chevalier Augustin… oh… my arm hurts…!"

"Yes, I expected as much. Your hand shall not grow back overnight, but within days, you shall have something at least. We shall fill you with blood several more times, and then you shall regrow that which our enemies stole."

"You never did finish the tale of our employer. It is a long way back to her home…"

Jean chuckled and replied, "Very well, Ange. As I was saying, before we spotted the strolling Baron Karnstein, over one hundred years ago, there was an infamous event known as *L'affaire des poisons*… The leader of a cult of Satanists and poisoners was a woman named Catherine Monvoisin, better known as La Voisin. It is with that black-hearted villainess that the tale of our employer begins… "

CHAPTER XXXIII

Lisebette's blade was inches away from the Beggar Queen's chest when a hard blow sent her sprawling aside.

The sword whistled through the air, only lightly scratching the Antipope's arm.

"Bastard," Lisebette snarled at Bartolomeo Dardi as he stood between her and the Beggar Queen.

Dardi threw back his head and laughed, his huge eyes nearly vanishing as the mirth overcame him.

"No, no, Signorina *Cagna Cieca*," he said, "this is not so. My mama and papa were married and lived together forty-three years—God rest their souls. You on the other hand..."

The blind woman screamed wordlessly and lunged forward, her sword aiming for the little Neapolitan man's heart. But he danced aside, remaining just out of the reach of her lunges, once, twice, then three times.

"Barto!" Séverin said, tossing the fallen wooden sheathe which had hid Lisebette's sword to his old friend.

"Thank you, my brother!" Dardi replied, catching the device and parrying the blind woman's attacks. "Now, let us test your skill, ha, ha!"

Sword and sheathe met as wood and weapon slashed through the air. Lisebette appeared unhampered by her blindness, attacking with slashes that were both fast and impressively accurate.

Bartomeleo Dardi was quite the contrast. He moved as if he was dancing as he capered about the arena floor, laughing as if this was a wonderful lark. He appeared as joyful as a child at a fair and as ridiculous as a street comedian... until one examined the motions of his arm.

Every attack, ever parry, every still moment possessed a precision that was almost astonishing. Dardi never wasted a moment or a motion and, after several minutes of back-and-forth battling, no sweat had yet appeared upon his brow or bearded face.

Lisebette, for all her impressive talent, gasped for breath; her free hand pushed aside tendrils of tangled, damp strands of hair. Her attacks became wilder, less accurate, and all artifice of skill and precision vanished as the duel continued.

"You are good, Signorina *Cagna Cieca*, but you rely on the foolishness of your enemy. I underestimate no being, living, dead, sighted, or blind. Now, it is time I take you seriously," Dardi said as he evaded her latest attack.

The Neapolitan swordmaster's attacks suddenly increased in speed, force, and danger. Lisebette, for all her skills, backed down four times as the sheathe met her sword. Soon, they stood were the fight had begun, with Séverin and the Antipope stepping aside as the blind ex-assassin stumbled their direction.

"Have you said your prayers, Signorina?" Dardi asked.

"What? I... Stop talking!" Lisebette replied.

"A pity," Dardi said, "that was your last chance."

He then lunged, his arm and weapon fully extended. The wooden sheathe struck the blind killer in the throat, the force shattering both her weapon and her neck.

Lisebette silently gasped and dropped backwards. Her body collapsed and her face turned first red, then a dull shade of blue, and finally black.

"A bad end to a bad woman, may God rest her soul," Dardi said, making the sign of the cross.

"Her insanity was worse than I had imagined," the Antipope said, sitting down on a bench. "My thanks for saving my life, as well as ending Lisebette's. I had hopes, earlier, of reforming her, but I failed."

"You could not succeed," Séverin said, dropping into a seat by her side. "Some men and women are born with compassion missing from their heart. Others lose that piece of their soul through living a difficult life. I know not which applied to your former bodyguard, Lisebette, but I always knew she was one of that kind."

"Yes, yes," the Antipope said. "I knew that much since I took her by my side. I still view the current proceedings as my failure. No matter, back to business. You seek the location of an undead pair. We have no knowledge of them, but we shall provide you with the locations of the main satanic circle in Paris and one near our city. The first meets in tunnels where my people never go. The few that descended into those depths never returned."

"We know of that black pack," Séverin said.

"I am not surprised. The second exist in the hamlet of Courcelles. A group meets there regularly, with the men dressed as nuns and the ladies dressed as priests. They sacrifice goats, dance, drink pig's blood and then rut like cattle in a field."

"Not them," Dardi said. "Fools of that sort exist in every city. Most are sons and daughters of wealthy families who are bored with their life of ease. Most end up going mad from the pox before they turn thirty."

The Beggar Queen released a sound that could be a laugh or a choke. She remained silent for several moments, her eyes sliding back and forth between the two men.

"We only have the barest knowledge of a third group," she said, shaking her head. "They meet somewhere near the Place Beauvau and kill outsiders who stumble upon their black masses. Perhaps they can provide you with information? The beggars of Paris know nothing else."

"The last group is unknown to me. When were they formed?" Séverin asked, rising.

This time, the Antipope laughed, her reaction lacking in mirth but filled with mocking irony.

"Jean-Pierre Séverin, better known as Gâteloup, Spoiler of Wolves, friend of the Emperor, and Republican," she said acidly, "and yet, also a blind fool!"

"Your meaning?" he asked.

The Antipope reached up and patted him on the face, with a mocking gesture.

"You have eyes, yet do not see. That black brotherhood has always existed in Paris, and will continue long after we are dust. The earliest record my people have of them was from the days when John the Good sat on the throne. We were less organized then, but the beggars knew that the devil worshippers of that section of Paris were dangerous and evil."

"Then they may know of the brothers we seek. How can we find them?" Dardi intervened.

The Antipope shook her head. "I neither know, nor care, unless they kill my people. As you now know, someone else is strangling my fellows. If you discover who it is, send word to me. I would make them pay for their crimes."

"I shall," was all Séverin said as the Beggar Queen led them away from the arena.

"One question," the Antipope asked Dardi. "What did you call Lisebette in your language?"

"Signorina *Cagna Cieca*," Dardi said with a snorting laugh. "It means, *Blind Bitch* in your tongue."

The Antipope guffawed. "I shall remember that insult."

"A question for you," Dardi said. "Why do you wear a hood?"

"You do not need to know," the Antipope replied, while she led them away.

CHAPTER XXXIV

"Where is your sword?" Jean-Pierre Séverin asked as Franz Karnstein returned from his morning prayers.

Tossing his cloak and hat upon a bench, the Austrian did not answer for a moment. He placed a heavy wooden cane in a bucket near the door.

"I gave it to Sylvia last night," he finally said. "Did she tell you of our battle with the vampire and the *oupire*, and our conference with the satanic priestess?"

"Yes," the Maestro replied. "In great length as she had her morning lesson. She is now with her father, relating the same tale to him."

"Then you should know the location of my sword," Karnstein concluded as he stepped onto the training floor. "Why did you ask?"

"I imagined you would purchase another such blade after your prayers. The lack of weapon intrigued me. You are not attached to the heavy cavalry saber?" Séverin asked, watching his pupil with narrowed eyes.

Karnstein, who was reaching for a practice saber, stopped and turned slowly. His pale eyes rose and met those of the Maestro and confusion appeared in the luminous orbs.

"No more so than any other weapon. Why?"

Séverin nodded approvingly and clapped the young man on the shoulder.

"You carried that weapon in the same way a monk wears a hair shirt. It never suited your style of fighting, but you kept it upon you almost as a tribute to your past sins. Yet, now you cast the sword aside without ceremony. This is very interesting—and gratifying. I would ask for your reason for such a decision."

The Exorcist frowned for a moment, his eyes losing focus as he contemplated the question.

"The decision was not made with much thought. This was the second time Sylvia and I found ourselves in danger from the undead. On the previous occasion, she'd taken my sword without asking, and slew her enemy."

The corner of Séverin's face twitched as he remembered the lovely Neapolitan woman's reason the next day. She had not shown the slightest contrition and even her father, a master of the blade himself, could not help but yield to her assertion of greater skill.

"I remember," he said. "You were only slightly miffed on that occasion."

"Simply because she hadn't told me of her plans in advance. When facing the vampire and his *oupire* brother, she required that saber more than I. She shows superior skill with the weapon, and her smallsword and dagger proved useless against the damned creature," he said, lifting a practice saber from the rack.

But Séverin led him further down the racks towards more exotic weapons.

"Sylvia told me you threw the ghoul with a wrestling hip toss," said the Maestro. "I am impressed you managed such a feat. *Oupires* are dangerous creatures. Their strength is equal, often surpassing, that of a vampire. Killing them is nearly impossible, even for a team of well-trained hunters. Now, please return that saber to the rack. You shall only train in that weapon to maintain your current skills."

"My current expertise is minimal," Karnstein replied as he returned the sword to its proper location.

"You are probably equal to that of an average cavalry officer in the French or English forces. You will never rise to the abilities of many of the German soldiers. Many of those gentlemen, especially that of the English regiment known as the King's German Legion, train exclusively in their few chosen weapons."

Karnstein's eyes narrowed as he concentrated on these trivial facts.

"What happens if they find themselves unarmed?"

161

Séverin shrugged and replied, "They either adapt or die. Such has been the way of life for warriors since the dawn of time. Now, I shall continue—you did learn one skill from me, which I find mildly interesting. Do you remember the battle against the vampire two days ago? Yes? Good! How did you attack the largest vampire as he charged your position? Your first attack only."

Karnstein thought and responded slowly, "I drew my saber and cut the damned beast's neck. Why?"

Séverin sighed, then chuckled. "*Mon Dieu!* Franz Karnstein, there are times I despair at your inability to realize virtue and success. A vampire moves with uncanny speed. This is why they are so dangerous. When a very fast creature attacked you, you drew your sword and nearly removed its head. Had you held a superior weapon, the beast's undead life would have been ended in that one swing."

"What of it? You, Maestro Dardi, and Sylvia could each do just as well," the Exorcist replied.

"Possibly so, possibly no. Barto and I trained in such arts, but it is not our emphasis. Our dear Sylvia has no interest in such training, though she has some skill in the area. However, skill is unimportant. We turn to philosophy. If you only had a sword with which you could kill a foe, how long should the battle last?" the elder swordmaster asked.

"How long? The shortest possible time, of course," Karnstein replied.

Séverin silently applauded again, with only the faintest trace of amusement on his face.

"Precisely, my friend. You care nothing for the history of duels, the beauty of the blade, of the code of the duelists, and the many techniques used with each sword. This, I comprehend. The difficulty lay in your inability at releasing your past torments. The difference was, you allowed yourself the gift of love after you met Sylvia Dardi. Now we can truly begin your training. Regard the sword to your right."

Karnstein turned his head and examined the weapon that hung upon the wall. It was curved like a half moon, about three feet long, and hidden beneath a dark wooden sheath. Silken cords wrapped around the handle and an inlayed circular guard rested before the hidden blade.

"That is a *katana*, a Japanese sword of excellent design," Séverin continued. "The warriors of that distant land believe drawing their weapon and killing their enemy in one stroke is perfection. That is a particularly fine example of their swordsmithing art. My teacher, a former soldier named Kronos, received it many years ago. I own five, as well as the matching small swords which are called *wakizashi*. Kronos and a teacher I had while in the Orient taught me the use of the *katana* and the *wakizashi*. I shall now pass on this skill, called *iaido*, to you."

"That is intriguing," Karnstein said, still studying the sword.

"I think the fast draw of *iaido* shall suit you well. I considered a Chinese sword call the *Jian* as well. It is a noble weapon with a useful, dangerous form of combat. However, the philosophy behind it would clash with your way of thinking…"

The swordmaster removed two wooden swords from a chest. They were carved in the shape of a *katana*, though lacking the round guard. Karnstein later learned that that protective piece was called *tsuba* and its creation was also an art form in Japan.

The lesson that followed was long, slow, and humiliating. For two hours, Karnstein learned the stances of the Japanese warriors, which the elder swordmaster called *samurai*. The method of drawing the weapon possessed similarities to his prior training, and he did slightly better in that area.

It was in actual sparring where he truly felt mortified. The unfamiliar weapon moved clumsily in his hands and he never came close to striking Séverin even once.

"You are overextending yourself, Franz. Maintain spinal integrity when you move or swing your blade. Try again."

Karnstein lunged forward, swinging his wooden sword towards the Maestro's neck. Séverin parried and shifted position, sending the Austrian sprawling on his face upon the training floor.

"That did not look particularly elegant, *amore*," Sylvia said from the doorway. "You looked like a duck falling from the sky."

Karnstein sat up slowly and rubbed his chest.

"I think you are being kind, *liebling*," he said. "The Maestro taught me how little I comprehend the Japanese sword. Question, what shall I use when next we go into battle?"

"What would you choose?" Dardi asked, appearing by his side and helping his future son-in-law back to his feet.

"It does not matter," Karnstein replied. "Sylvia will take it from my belt the moment she requires it."

This brought about a slight twitch of a smile from Séverin, a loud guffaw from Dardi, and a mock slap on the arm from Sylvia.

"Consider your equipment as you cleanse your body and break your fast," the elder swordmaster said. "We shall meet here in two hours and plan our search. Before you ask, I shall search with Sylvia, and you shall do so with Barto. We shall be conspicuous, but moving individually shall make us vulnerable to the Ténèbre Brothers. Sunlight does not hinder their actions and they are already quite angry with you both."

Karnstein frowned briefly, but the straightening of his back indicated acceptance without argument. Sylvia looked rebellious momentarily, but then waved a hand quickly, signifying her metaphorical acceptance of these conditions.

"Sylvia, Barto, I have a cold spread awaiting us. Franz shall join us later," Séverin said as his pupil exited the academy.

"Is he as hopeless as he looks, Uncle Jean-Pierre?" Sylvia asked as they walked upstairs to his living quarters.

Both swordmasters turned her direction, seeing the concerned look across her lovely face. They exchanged a look of amusement, recognizing her fears for the man she loved so passionately.

"My dear," Séverin replied slowly, "he held that sword approximately two hours and had minimal instruction. No man or woman, no matter how talented, could have looked effective in so short a time."

Bartomeleo Dardi hugged his daughter tight and kissed her on both cheeks.

"Your *fidanzato* has some natural skill, though he lacks the mind and spirit of a swordmaster. He possesses a determination for survival, even when confronting the demons of Hell, that may surpass Gâteloup and I. He shall master this one sword style because it fits his...what is the right word...?"

"Discipline," Séverin answered. "The *katana* is an excellent weapon for killing with the fewest possible motions. My teacher, Kronos, once killed three assassins in two swings of that very blade, and returned the weapon to its sheath before they realized they were dead. Impressive, no?"

"Worry not about your young man, child," Barto said, dropping into a chair before the small spread of cold meats, cheeses, bread, and wine. "Concern yourself with your own training. What is this I hear of you being disarmed twice this morning?"

Sylvia flushed and took her seat.

"Uncle Jean-Pierre punched me in the arm!"

"A popular street fighting technique," Séverin said, filling his plate with food. "Your father and I nearly died fighting a pair of brothers who used that as a weapon against their enemies."

"Ah!" Dardi laughed and popped a piece of cheese in his mouth. "The Rosero Brothers of Madrid! This is a wonderful story! We were in Madrid, searching for a nobleman vampire named Don Sebastian de Villanueva, when Gâteloup caught the eye of a lovely lady..."

CHAPTER XXXV

Henry Morley was bored, very bored, and growing angry. The area called Place Beauvau was a busy location, filled with government offices, soldiers, and merchants seeking commerce. There were dozens of Frenchmen everywhere, most well-dressed, many resembling the irritating pen-pushers he had encountered in the Admiralty. That thought added to his irritation because he remembered well his last encounter with that most terrible breed of creatures known as a bureaucrat.

Walking into a small alley between buildings, he leaned against the wall and waited. Ishaani's sandalwood scent tickled his nose and Morley affected nonchalance.

"I see nothing," he said softly in English. "This is a place of pen pushers and fat merchants. There are no cults hidden here."

"Do you remember Pankot Palace in the north?" Ishaani asked.

Morley frowned and then replied, "Yes, I visited it once with the Company. They sought a mining agreement."

"A particularly virulent group of my people rule that place. Did you know that, Morley sahib?" she asked, amusement bubbling up in her voice.

"No," the English sea captain replied, not hiding his astonishment. "That can't be!"

"None-the-less, Morley Sahib, it is so. Religions whose members are misunderstood often hide in plain sight. This allows greater protection than secrecy. You must look with an eye that seeks that which is hidden," the Thuggee priestess said.

Morley then spotted a face he recognized and flushed with barely contained rage. Stepping back into the shadows, he bumped into Ishaani, but did not ask her pardon.

"I think that will not be necessary. I believe I just spotted the one who shall lead us to that which we seek," he said through clenched teeth.

"Who?" Ishaani asked, pressing forward and crouching at his side.

Morley nodded towards a tall man who was crossing the market square with a tall, dark-haired woman in tow. His face showed some age, but he moved with the light step of a dancer and his sad eyes examined the street and buildings with slow deliberation.

"Jean-Pierre Séverin," Morley said. "The man who killed my closest friends years ago... I swore I would hunt him down one day..."

"What has that to do with our search for the scroll of Raktabīja?" the Thuggee priestess asked, as the man and his female companion stopped before a small doorway.

"That French bastard murders those who study ancient magic and other nonsense. If he is here, he is looking for the same ones we want. We shall let him be our goat..." Morley said, his eyes narrowing.

Ishaani studied the Englishman for a moment and recognized the truth as well. Morley, like many idiots from this decadent, cold, portion of the world, valued hunting animals as a pastime. Their favorite game was shooting tigers, but few Englishmen dared stalk the great beast into its dens. Instead, they tethered a goat under a tree and waited until a tiger heard the poor, helpless creature. Then, after the tiger had killed the goat, men like Morley shot the massive cat and took their hide as a prize.

That is how Morley shall use this Jean-Pierre Séverin. He shall follow him, hide, and pounce after the holders of the scroll of Raktabīja attack. It is a good plan and we shall see if it works, she though.

She slipped away, keeping the English sea captain in her sight.

CHAPTER XXXVI

"My daughter tells me you will live in Switzerland one day," Bartolomeo Dardi said as he and Franz Karnstein strolled along a lane near the Place Beauvau.

The Neapolitan wore a bright red suit with silver buttons, green hose, and silver buckled shoes that shone in the bright sunlight. The Austrian wore his customary black suit and white shirt, a small metal crucifix being his only adornment. Formerly, he had worn a signet ring with his family crest, but he had placed that on Sylvia's fingers after their engagement.

"That is true," he replied, stopping before a plain building with no plate outside the door.

They spoke in Italian, not hiding their origins to the world. A pair of foreign visitors were slightly unusual, but only in a small way. Few would suspect their search for evidence of black magicians, vampires, and ghouls in a wealthy district of Paris like the Place Beauvau.

"Why is this so? I know you have much land in Austria and other places. Why Switzerland over, say, lower Styria, or Lake Balaton?" the Neapolitan asked.

"Politics and history," Karnstein replied in his normal clipped tone. "My family has a poor history in those regions. Few members of our clan still reside in our ancestral lands, most having been driven out because of their evil activities."

"This I can understand, no offense meant, boy," Barto said with a broad shrug.

Karnstein raised a hand in agreement, continuing as if his future father-in-law hadn't spoken.

"Our lands in Switzerland are from my Vordenburg relatives. If we use that as our home, we shall have some peace and neighbors who were not raised with tales of Count This, or Baroness That, slaughtering their families and friends before being slain by a crusading priest or a warrior of good."

168

Dardi nodded and chuckled, waving Franz away from the unmarked building.

"Not that place, Baron. I spied the office earlier and it is merely the counting house of a parsimonious man named Harpagon. The family is very wealthy, unpleasant, and old. As to your Swiss thoughts, I agree with your reasoning. My family has always avoided politics and we've survived many horrific regimes. Do you have a house there?"

"Yes. A small castle near the city of Zurich," the Austrian answered. "Are we to just wander about until we spy a vampire?"

Dardi continued laughing softly, his ugly, bearded face almost glowing in his mirth. "You have fought cultists in the past, yes? What do they all do the same?"

"Sell their souls to the devil, murder innocents...." Karnstein started saying, but was cut off by a hard look from Dardi.

"No, no no. You see the surface evil of these men and women and stare down at them like an inquisitor facing an old herb woman..."

"I am a member of the Inquisition..." Karnstein began, but stopped again at the same dangerous expression.

"Cease chattering and listen, *genero*!" Dardi said. "You hate followers of the devil and sneer at their very mention. This means you underestimate them because you believe their motives to be simple and base. This is a weakness, and it could get you killed someday. I do not wish you dead and my daughter mourning you forever!"

Karnstein thought for a moment and remembered that the word *genero* meant "son-in-law" in Italian. Instead of replying, he simply nodded and listened.

"In the battle of dark and light, despising the followers of evil is natural. The trick is you must never view them as simple and stupid. Many are highly intelligent, especially the leaders. They act with far greater cunning than you realize, and theirs is not the cleverness of a beast. Some sit by the side of those in the seats of power and they are not fools," Dardi continued in a low voice.

"I heard this was so," Karnstein said.

Dardi held up a finger and waggled the digit slowly.

"Good, good, now you learn. So stop seeking crazed pleasure seekers and damned souls. Think of the behavior of men and women of true power and how they act. What shall they do to hide their activities in a place of power such as this one?"

Karnstein thought for a moment and shook his head.

"I confess, I do not know. My apologies."

Dardi clapped him on the back and laughed again.

"*Genero*, you learn slowly, but never give up. Do not look for slavering beasts and black-robed fools," the tiny Neapolitan said. "Those shall come to their temple dressed as any ordinary person. We seek something that appears slightly incorrect, but would be ignored by any normal citizen. Once your teacher and I found an entire nest of noble vampires because one of their members wore dark glasses on a foggy day. This, you shall now learn... Look out across the avenue... Who does not look correct..."

Karnstein's eyes slowly moved across the lane, his face resuming the calm, unemotional expression that was his normal countenance.

"That lady in blue," he said, spotting a pretty woman with long, red hair and a tight, blue cotton dress. She was pretty in an obvious manner, her lips painted bright red and her long, thick lashes fluttering at each appreciative look she received from passing men.

"A good choice," Dardi said, kissing the air. "I spotted her earlier, though I doubt she is dangerous to us."

"How do you know this from her looks alone?" Karnstein asked as he watched the lovely lady stroll with slow, sensual movements.

Dardi snorted and rolled his large eyes.

"That is a lady who seeks attention from men. She prowls about a location known for wealthy, powerful men.

Her walk and coquettish behavior are an act intended to seek a patron. You miss this because you are young and in love with my daughter."

"And if I paid attention to such ladies, she would first seek their death and then mine," Karnstein replied, permitting himself a brief smile.

Dardi clapped him on the back again and said, "This is why all men shall respect you, Franz Karnstein. Not for your service to *il Papa* or your title, but for your survival in marriage to my Sylvia. Her aunt, grandmother, and mama all shared the same disposition."

Karnstein did not answer, but they resumed their walk. He came to a sudden halt and said, "I believe I see something outlandish... Please look to my left, near the foundation of the building we stand before."

Dardi stared for a moment at a beautiful woman and then turned his head quickly, as if ashamed of his attentions.

"I see nothing, *genero*..."

"There is a chalk drawing approximately four inches wide etched on the stone," Karnstein said.

He turned his attention to a man dressed in a bright blue uniform with a conical hat.

"Yes, yes," Dardi said impatiently, "a childish scrawl of *il diavolo*. What of it?"

"Correct me if I am wrong, but do not most drawings of the enemy of our Lord portray him with his trident pointed upright or above his head?" the Exorcist asked.

"Yes, what of it?" Dardi said.

"This scrawl has him pointing his weapon to the right. Is that not somewhat odd?" Karnstein asked.

Dardi repeated his action of staring at the young woman and then looking away.

"I do not know, but it is an interesting observation. Shall we walk that direction and search for a second drawing?"

"It is better than walking in circles, looking for strange women," Karnstein said with a resigned expression.

CHAPTER XXXVII

"I see a Satanist, uncle Jean-Pierre," Sylvia Dardi said, smiling brightly. "Look at the gentleman on your left."

Jean-Pierre Séverin slowly glanced in that direction and his eyes tracked an elderly priest walking slowly with two canes, his head low and watching the ground.

"Amusing, Sylvia," he said, realizing the joke.

The young Neapolitan beauty giggled and proceeded forward, the picture of gay loveliness.

"Sorry, uncle, but you looked far too serious and morose I felt the need for a little relaxation which can help sharpen the mind."

"How well does that work on Franz?" Séverin asked dry-ly.

Sylvia snorted and rolled her eyes.

"It does not penetrate his Austrian exterior. He does not so much as twitch or smile under such jests. I love Franz, but he lacks any sense of humor."

"Possibly," Séverin replied, "though he may simply not find your jokes amusing."

Sylvia's eyes narrowed and then she realized the elder swordmaster was teasing her back. She laughed, sighed and danced forward.

"A clean strike," she said. "I should know better than fencing with you. Have you spied anything of interest since we arrived?"

"Nothing," the Maestro replied, "which either proves that this is a ruse, or that this cult has survived thanks to some very impressive planning…"

"I should think it was the latter if they are as old as re-ported," she said, ignoring the appreciative looks and noises from a group of well-dressed young men.

"Agreed," Séverin said.

He stopped as he examined a small plate outside a new brick building.

"*Madonna!*" Sylvia said, turning her back quickly and staring with unseeing eyes at the brass plate.

"What did you see?" Séverin asked.

"There is a man, as tall as you, dressed in a blue suit with a red waistcoat…" she answered in a taut tone.

"The one lacking earlobes?" Séverin said, tracking the man with his peripheral vision.

"Yes," Sylvia said. "That is the *oupire*, Jean Ténèbre. My dear Franz shot him in the face, yet he strolls though Paris as if nothing had occurred!"

"Sylvia," the swordmaster said, "he is undead and hundreds of years old. A pistol shot in the face is an inconvenience, but not a true danger. In truth, I know of few methods capable of destroying those monsters. You do affirm that he is one of the Ténèbre Brothers?"

"Yes! His brother is slighter, with a pretty face and golden hair. I cut off his hand," Sylvia answered, touching the saber under her heavy cloak.

"Then we shall follow him," Séverin said, turning slowly.

"So that he may lead us into a trap?" the Neapolitan beauty asked.

Slowly striding after the *oupire*, the swordmaster replied, "Of course. It is the best means of locating his brother and everyone associated with those monsters. I trust your father and fiancé shall either meet us there, or arrive soon enough."

Sylvia looked rebellious for a moment, but then shrugged quickly.

"Very well, I have no better plan. Part of me hopes I shall meet the little *stronzo* again. I wish I'd removed his head rather than his hand!"

"That would be a mistake, Sylvia. The Ténèbre Brothers have died in the past—at least seven times according to my information. But they always return. They are not common members of the undead, like these poor creatures to which we gave a merciful release two days ago. The Grand Turk had them impaled, but a year later, they took his favorite concubines from his harem," Séverin said as they followed Jean Ténèbre down a lane and into a smaller side street.

"Then I shall try other methods," Sylvia said. "I shall find a means of ending their miserable existence."

"I wish you luck, child," the elder swordmaster said, "but they have survived beheading, impalement, burning, and hanging."

Sylvia sniffed and replied, "Common, unimaginative methods. The Camorra of Naples could teach you northerners better methods when it comes to destroying your enemies."

Séverin did not reply but observed the *oupire* walk to a door and remove a key from above the sill. He unlocked a heavy brown door with a name plate for a lawyer listed out front. He replaced the key and vanished from sight a moment later.

Holding a hand out to prevent Sylvia's advance, the swordmaster said, "We wait fifteen minutes and ensure this is not simply a mere visitation."

"This is the worst trap I have ever viewed, uncle Jean-Pierre. That creature obviously knows we followed him to this location."

"Agreed," Séverin replied. "None-the-less, it is our best method trapping them. We wait."

They moved to separate locations, within sight of each other and the doorway. For fifteen minutes, they spied five men and three women as they entered the location as well as many pedestrians on this busy lane. The visitors to the office all arrived via coach, ducking inside, unseen by the populace, while their transports left immediately after they had alighted. Otherwise, there was no sign of the Ténèbre Brothers.

Sylvia appeared at the swordmaster's side.

"Now?"

He nodded. "We enter. You have a revolver?" he asked.

"Two," she answered, pulling one out and keeping the weapon hidden by her body.

"Keep one in hand and draw your sword once we are inside the building," Séverin said, drawing a pistol of his own while reaching for the key. "Are you prepared? Excellent. May the Lord guide us in this endeavor."

With that prayer, Séverin unlocked the brown door, replaced the key, and drew the small cutlass on his belt. He stepped inside and immediately knew that danger lay ahead...

CHAPTER XXXVIII

The tiny devil drawings led Dardi and Karnstein on a ramble throughout the district. They looked the same, each appearing childish in style, yet precisely similar in every detail. The trident in the demonic hands always pointed towards the next position, leading the Neapolitan and his future son-in-law on a tour of the neighborhood.

"Ah, here we are," Bartolomeo Dardi said. "Our entryway into the adventure. Are you prepared?"

"Why does it always occur in sewers?" Franz Karnstein said, looking down and sniffing.

The tiny devil drawing pointed towards an opened doorway that was a stairway leading downward into the famous Parisian sewer tunnel system. A pungent odor of feces and ammonia drifted their direction and there was a tiny devil drawing on the second stair.

"It shall not occur in the sewers, *genero*, but this shall lead us to their side," Dardi declared, striding inside and walking down three steps. "Close your eyes tight when you are near the gloom and count to sixty. That shall adjust your eyes to the dark better."

The Exorcist obeyed and found that this proved quite effective as they slowly walked down two flights to the tunnel beneath the street.

"*Il Diavolo* is to the left. You shall adjust to the smell soon enough. Your teacher and I once tracked a terrible vampire through the sewers beneath the Ottoman sultan's palace. That was a horrible place, with several smaller tunnels choked with dead bodies of the ruler's enemies. We had the vampire before us and the Sultan's silent eunuch assassins at our rear. What would you do under those circumstances?"

Dardi splashed through a small stream of black and gray foaming water.

"I do not know," the Exorcist replied.

"That is wisdom," the Neapolitan laughed. "A willingness to admit ignorance demonstrates a mind open to learning. Ah ha! Our little devil friend leads us away from the stench!"

Dardi's words proved true. The chalk devil etching lay before a stone walkway with a heavy black metal door at the barely visible summit. A circular, rusted lock clasped the door shut and there was no handle attached to the surface.

"I see one difficulty with our entry..." Karnstein said as they approached the door.

"Only because you choose to view this as an obstacle," Dardi replied.

He studied the lock and shook his head.

"Attend to what I do."

Reaching into a pouch, he pulled out a circle of jangling keys. Selecting one, his powerful hand gently slipped the key into the lock and moved the metal back and forth. A moment later, the lock opened with a light snap.

"Understand the art of lock picking and you shall never find yourself denied entry throughout the world. My daughter shall teach you."

"You mean she can call me an *idiota* even more as I learn the skill," the Exorcist said phlegmatically.

Dardi elbowed him affectionately and replied, "Now, *genero*, prepare yourself. We shall face the horrors momentarily."

Karnstein did not reply, but helped pull the door open. It was a heavy portal though it swung inward after they gave it a hard shove.

A short man with flaming red hair, a long-pointed nose, and a nasty sneer on his face stared their direction. He checked a large gold repeater in his hand and sniffed superciliously.

"It is about time you were here! You were almost late! Which of you is Count von Meruh?" he asked in a fluty voice.

"That would be I," Karnstein said in accented French while clicking his heels.

"I thought you would be older," the red-haired man said.

He then looked to Dardi and said, "You would be Chevalier Dutourd? Fine, fine, we have no time in which to waste. Your robes are in the next chamber. Dress quickly and join the others. The mistress will complete the unholy sacrament within the hour."

He rushed out through a heavy purple curtain that covered the one doorway, never looking back. They stood in a plain room with white painted walls, a single flickering lamp and a scent of incense intermingled with a sweet, cloying odor.

Karnstein made to follow the red-haired man but found himself halted with a hard hand and head shake from Dardi.

"We wait here, *genero*," he said.

A moment later, the sounds of voices drifted their direction and the door swung open. Two men, the first tall, heavyset, blond and in his mid-thirties, filled the doorway. He entered with a slow, arrogant stride and looked down upon Dardi.

A step behind him was an emaciated man with graying brown hair, a thin beard and mustache and expensive clothing at least twenty years out-of-date.

"You are late!" Dardi said, his voice an imitation of the reedy voice of the red-haired man. "I assume you are Chevalier Dutourd and Count von Meruh?"

"I am he, Count von Meruh, and this is my companion, Ritter Dutourd. Who do you happen to be, little man?" the heavyset man said.

Dardi glanced in Karnstein's direction and nodded. They sprang forward, with the Austrian grabbing the knight and Dardi attacking the German noble. Both men were shocked by the assault and froze—a fatal mistake.

Dardi plunged a misericorde into von Meruh's throat while Karnstein seized the Frenchman's neck. Within a few seconds, both Satanists were dead in the arms of their attackers.

"Push them down the stairs. Do you feel guilt by these actions?" Dardi asked.

Karnstein shook his head and said, "No, but I shall pray for their souls when I next attend church. Their participation in this den of evil damns them to Hell until the good Lord forgives their trespasses."

Dardi grunted but did not reply as they heaved both dead men out the door and into the sewer. They closed the door and Karnstein pushed a thick bolt home, locking the portal closed.

The next room was a small closet with two bright red hooded robes hanging from a pair of pegs. At the other end of the room was a matching purple curtain with a bright, flickering yellow glow from behind its edges.

Dressing quickly and pulling the hoods low over their head, they quickly moved some weapons about on their body and walked through the curtains. Keeping their heads down, their eyes became dazzled by a large room filled with thousands of candles and a massive circular brazier.

The chamber was a black painted rectangle, about thirty feet long and half that wide. Low unbacked, unpainted wooden benches lay in five rows leading towards a coffin shaped altar at the front. An inverted crucifix hung above it, with the image of Christ painted with bright red lips, rouged cheeks, and green eyelids. The look was grotesque, an intentional merger of the Christian savior and a painted street harlot.

Similarly robed men and women sat in the rows, with the rearmost seats available for Dardi and Karnstein. There was a low murmur of conversation from a few knots of hooded people, but no words were audible from their location.

From an alcove near the altar, a black robed entity stepped into view, a horned wooden demon mask hiding the facial features. Slim, white fingers clutched a heavy yellowing scroll in one hand, waving a long knife in the air with the other.

With great ceremony, the robed figure lay both items across the altar and folded her hands in a position of prayer, then turning them downward in an inversion of the traditional pose supplication to God.

"In the name of the Prince of the Air, Master of the Earth, Satan Almighty, I bid you welcome. Let us hail our master as we say these words... Satan, Belial and Leviathan, master of Hell, kings of the Earth, we hail to thee..."

The congregants said the words along with the masked priestess, moving their hands in a mockery of the sign of the cross. Their performed their actions with their left hands and moved upward, then left and right.

"Bring forth the sacrifice!" the priestess in the demon mask said.

The red-headed man appeared, a baby held in his arms.

"No!" Karnstein said.

He rose from his bench. A dagger appeared in his hand and he thrust the blade into the red-haired man's back.

The robed Satanist gasped and collapsed. The Exorcist grabbed the child from his arms before it could fall down to the wooden floor.

"Who dares to interrupt this unholy rite?" the devil-masked priestess shrieked, pointing her dagger in his direction.

Karnstein threw back his hood, his face a cold sneer as he gazed back at the Satanic cult leader.

"Who are you to ask, damned thing?"

The priestess reared back, as if struck by lightning, and replied in a voice taut with rage.

"I am Strix, favored priestess of Satan, Lord of the Earth and the Air. I was old before your mother's mother was born. Now, who are you, you stupid child?"

"My name," Karnstein spat back in a soft voice, "is Franz von Vordenburg-Karnstein, Baron Karnstein, Baron Vordenburg, heir to Count Karnstein of Styria, advisor to Pope Pius VII, knight of the holy order of Malta, member of the holy order of Exorcists, and sworn inquisitor of the Supreme Sacred Congregation of the Roman and Universal Inquisition. I declare that this unholy horror ends now!"

"A Karnstein inquisitor, how very ridiculous..." Strix said, barking out an odd sound.

The cultists, all of whom now sat ramrod straight in their seats, did not move or make a sound. They rose at the exact same moment, as if yanked upright by invisible strings held by a giant puppeteer. As a body, they spun in place, facing Karnstein and the whimpering baby he held in his arms.

They stared at the Exorcist, their faces impassive, their eyes black and unwinking. Five men, four women, their ages diverse, but their expressions exactly the same.

"*Madonna,*" Dardi muttered, throwing off the scarlet robe, "they are possessed..."

He drew a cutlass in one hand and a long knife in the other.

"Correct, little man," Strix said. "The rite shall continue whether I have an unbaptized infant child or not. I merely need a life for completion of the ritual. The child was simply to enthrall these slaves further. I shall not waste anymore breath up on you... Robert, come here... The rest of you, kill them!"

One man from the ranks detached himself and ran to Strix while the rest reached into the robes. They pulled out a collection of swords, knives and other vicious weapons. With a bestial howl, they surged forward, reaching for Dardi and Karnstein.

"*Madonna!*" Dardi yelped again.

He smiled and leaped into the fray.

181

CHAPTER XXXIX

The Ténèbre Brothers stood at the end of a narrow stairway, each clutching a revolver. Jean smiled up at them while Ange spat upon the ground, his angry eyes never leaving Sylvia.

"Now, no foolishness, Monsieur," Jean said, raising the weapon slightly higher. "Close the door, lock it and walk slowly down the stairs. We are both expert shots and will happily kill you both now if we must…"

"I want to feed on that bloodbag bitch," Ange said as his pointed fangs rose in his oversized maw. "Give her to me!"

"Calm yourself, Ange," Jean said in a soft voice. "She shall be yours soon."

"Not soon, now! Look what she did to me!" Ange shrieked and raised his other arm.

The extremity at the end of the arm was a hand only in the barest sense of the word. It was a bright red mass of bone, gristle, dripping with black ichor. Elongated talons protruded from the four fingers as well as a nub where the thumb should be.

"It shall be normal again after you feed upon her and several others, brother. Simply wait and it shall be so," Jean said, moving closer to his sibling and placing a hand upon his shoulder.

Ange Ténèbre did not reply, but his eyes narrowed and his breathing grew faster and heavier.

"Monsieur, you shall come down first," Jean continued, nodding towards Séverin. "Walk slowly and keep your hands visible. I am an excellent shot and a man your age shall never match my reactions."

The swordmaster did not reply, stepping slowly down the stars, his hands visible. He was halfway down the short distance when Jean raised his revolver and narrowed his eyes.

"No tricks, old man," he snarled.

Before Séverin could answer, the door above burst open. Henry Morley charged inside, screaming and roaring, knocking Sylvia aside and stopping at the first step.

"Jean-Pierre Séverin! I am here for your life!" he shouted in English.

"Do I know you?" Séverin asked, looking over his shoulder.

"Bastard! Murderer!" the English sea captain said, leaping forward.

Séverin, surprised by the insane act, moved aside from the blade, but fell backwards as Morley's heavy body struck him and sent them both falling down the remaining steps. They rolled together, crashing on the landing and sending Jean sprawling.

The *oupire*'s musket pistol discharged harmlessly into the ceiling, sending a cloud of plaster and wood harmlessly showering down over their heads. He climbed back his feet, his eyes slowly blinking as he tried comprehending the current situation.

Ange shrieked and leaped over the two fallen men and charged up the steps. In two leaps he was at the top, staring into the barrel of a weapon remarkably like his brother's.

"Bloodbag?" Sylvia asked, shooting the vampire in the face.

Ange fell backwards, rolling end over end down the steps and tripping up his brother. Vampire and *oupire* found themselves tangled in a mass with Séverin and Morley.

Sylvia reached for her saber, when a silken cord encircled her throat and a hard knee pressed into her back.

Immediately, she found herself incapable of breathing and a soft voice said a series of words she did not understand.

"*Om khargang chakra-gadeshu-chapa-parighan shulang bhushundlng shirah shankhang,*" the soft voice said as the knot about her neck grew tighter and more painful.

On the floor below, Morley's hands finally reached the swordmaster's throat, his grip tight, his eyes filled with madness.

"You killed my cousin! You murdered my friends!" he gasped out.

"She shot me in the face," Ange shrieked, "the bloodbag shot me in the face! The bitch shot me in the face!"

"What is going on here?" Jean said, pulling himself free, stepping away from the human mass roiling on the floor.

Sylvia stumbled backwards, feeling weak as the knee in her back dug deeper. Her vision was swimming and she felt the cold edges of unconsciousness rising in her mind.

"*Sanda-dhatIng karistri-nayanAng sarbanga-bhusha britam. nIlashma-dyutimasya pada-dashakang,*" the woman behind her said.

The elder swordmaster broke Morley's grip and took a deep gasp of air.

"I do not even know who you are, idiot!" Séverin shouted, pushing the man away from his body.

"*Sebe maha kalikang yamastou-chhaite harou kamalajye hantung madhung kaitavam,*" the woman behind Sylvia said, her voice rising with each passing moment.

Sylvia grabbed a small blade from her belt with fumbling fingers. She knew she had to act immediately, or her death was imminent. She also realized that pulling forward would result in greater pain.

"Think creatively when danger arises," her father had preached since she'd been a child. "Never act in a way your enemy can anticipate. A predictable action is one that leads to death…"

Thrusting backwards, the pain in her back exploded as her attacker's knee grinded deeply into Sylvia's back. The strangling cord loosened fractionally, which was the opening she needed.

Slicing upwards with the tiny knife, she cut the cord as well as scratching her own flesh painfully. The attacker, caught mid-chant, fell backwards, and Sylvia kicked out, catching the falling woman in the stomach.

184

The Neapolitan girl stumbled forward, coughing and gasping for air as she pulled the silken scarf from her aching throat.

Retrieving her fallen saber, she turned and faced her attacker. The slightly built woman had lithe muscular limbs, a face hidden beneath a scarlet scarf, and a medium length curved sword that had just appeared in her small hand.

"*Marana tyaag Kali ke naam par!*" she said, slashing out with her sword.

Morley, rolling a few feet from Séverin, came up to his feet, a dagger in hand.

"You don't know? How dare you? You murdered my cousin Jedediah Morley, and my friends Stephen De la Poer, Richard Karnstein…"

"And three others," Séverin said as he rose, throwing his cutlass to the left of the Englishman.

Morley, who was a foot or more from the flying weapon, dove sideways and knocked over the writhing vampire.

"Ha! Missed me, you French bastard!" he said.

"I was not aiming at you, idiot," Séverin said and pointed.

Pinned to the wall by the sword through his neck was the *oupire*, Jean Ténèbre. His mouth opened and closed, yet no sound emerged from his massive, gaping maw. Black ichor mixed with yellow fluids bubbled from his colorless lips. The undead creature struggled for release, incapable of gaining hold of the sword's hilt.

Meanwhile, Sylvia parried Ishaani's attack and replied in kind. The Thuggee priestess thwarted the Neapolitan swordswoman's slashes with impressive dexterity. Their swords danced and clashed—the narrow Indian blade swifter than the heavier Austrian weapon. Yet, Ishaani never scored even the slightest scratch, no matter how vigorously she sliced or thrust…

"Die!" Morley growled

He moved forward, knife held in a fighting grip, his other hand in front of his body defensively.

The elder French swordmaster drew his own blade, an Italian dagger with a razor sharp edge and circular metal ball at the end of the hilt. He circled away from Morley, his eyes scanning for a weakness.

This English lunatic is a skilled knife fighter, Séverin thought as his enemy left no openings as they danced to the left and right, *experienced from many battles.*

Each performed swift probing attacks, with neither scoring a hit for a full minute. Then Morley stepped to the side and switched the hands holding his weapon. He stabbed out and caught Séverin across his shoulder, narrowly avoiding a neck strike.

"Ha!" Morley said. "You are done for, old man!"

Séverin did not reply, but circled away, his face briefly registering pain.

Above, Sylvia parried Ishaani's sword and pressed forward. They appeared evenly matched for strength, locking close and freezing in place. They stood mere inches apart, their breathing slow and measured as they sought an advantage over the other.

That was when the Thuggee priestess lashed out with her lead leg, striking Sylvia's inner thigh. The Neapolitan swordswoman stumbled and then found herself swept from her feet by a whirling step from Ishaani.

She fell forward, immediately rolling to her right, and narrowly avoided a downward stab from her enemy. She turned onto her back and raised her sword, blocking a downward slice that would have split her head in half.

Ishaani flicked her wrist and sent the heavy saber sailing out of Sylvia's grasp. She heard the weapon crash into the wall behind her, just out of reach.

"Marana tyaag Kali ke naam par!" Ishaani repeated, raising her sword high from a downward thrust.

Below, Séverin reversed his hold on the dagger and flung the weapon into the English sailor's face. Morley laughed and batted the weapon aside. He opened his sneering mouth just as the French swordmaster's rear leg lashed out and hammered him in the midsection.

Séverin's Hessian boot struck Morley with the force of a bucking stallion, rocking the huge man back and knocking the wind from his lungs. The English sea captain did not fall, but the air in his body flew from his mouth like a massive bellows, turning his face bright crimson.

Snatching up his fallen dagger, Séverin swung the heavy ball end into Morley's knife hand. The delicate bones shattered under the impact, with the dagger dropping from the Englishman's now-useless fingers.

Morley gasped and wheezed as the agony of the broken bones filled his body. Forgetting his enemy, he grabbed his injured hand and dropped to his knees. His lungs and chest burned and he fought for air as lancets of pain pierced him with every heartbeat.

Though he loathed killing a wounded enemy, Séverin knew that this man was a permanent danger.

Morley, De La Poer, and Karnstein were a coven who snatched children and sacrificed them to the ghost of a witch. I still do not know who was behind their cult... They were simply followers who performed the act as an act of sadistic satisfaction, Séverin thought as he stepped nearer to the fallen man. *Also, he is the same man who stole the files from the Morgue...*

With a quick swing of his arm, the French swordmaster sliced the jugular vein of Henry Morley, ending his dreams of wealth and power forever.

Above, Sylvia threw her small knife at Ishaani's hand, piercing the skin between thumb and forefinger. The Thuggee priestess yelped in pain, her swing arrested in mid-air. Sylvia then kicked out with both feet, striking her enemy in the face.

Ishaani fell backwards, momentarily senseless. Sylvia rolled backwards, snatched up her sword and lunged.

"Hold!" Séverin said, appearing at her side. "Not yet, we must have answers first!"

187

Sylvia stopped her attack, the edge of her blade less than an inch from Ishaani's throat.

"She spoke no language I understood," Sylvia said, "and what of the Ténèbre Brothers?"

"They fled together, badly wounded from you and I," the Maestro replied, "and I recognize her language. She spoke Hindi, a prayer to her goddess, Kali."

Ishaani looked up at Séverin, her dark, luminous eyes blinking slowly.

"You know Kali?" she asked in accented English.

Séverin nodded slowly and said, "I do. You are one of the society of stranglers called the Thuggee?"

"I am," Ishaani said. "Kill me now if you must, for I will not stop until I hold in my hand the scroll of Raktabīja!"

"Who is Raktabīja?" Sylvia asked, her English heavily accented and less understandable than Ishaani's.

"A being who would destroy all life on this world," Séverin said. "Lower your sword, Sylvia. We may have common cause with this young lady."

With ill grace, Sylvia obeyed, but did not sheathe her blade.

"A *fanabla*!" she said, retrieving her pistol.

CHAPTER XL

Taking two steps back, Franz Karnstein kept the baby cradled in one arm while closing his eyes for a moment.

When he opened them, the sockets where his eyes lay now pulsed with a luminous pale energy.

This was his true power—one that made him a real threat to evil beings throughout the world. Only a few on Earth knew the secret that lay within the Austrian baron, and those people held the tale as sacrosanct.

Karnstein suddenly spoke, his voice ethereal and odd, sounding closer to an echo of a distant powerful being than that of a man. The words that emerged were gibberish to most ears, but they did possess an odd, rhythmic pattern.

"*Anshargal Ati Me Peta Babka Nisme Annu Isten! Usmi Annu Isten Ina Akhkharu Ma Ina Maskim Xul, Ina Kashshaptu, Ina Lilit, Su'ati Mursu In Matum!*"

A silver sigil appeared before his body, vanishing a heartbeat later. The world transformed, becoming a universe of energy and spectral creatures floating in an endless void. Karnstein viewed the world in its purest form now, where humanity represented a mere spark in a cosmos that stretched endlessly through time and space.

With long-trained concentration, he forced his mind back to this world, focusing upon those present in this single room. He saw Bartolomeo Dardi, a golden flame of positive power, as well as the corrupt, decaying horror that filled Strix's damaged soul. There was another power present, somewhere within the altar... but the nature of the being appeared... blocked...

That never happened before, Karnstein thought, incapable of penetrating the altar.

That was when he spotted the black chains of force. They emerged from within the altar and spread out to every cult member present. The energy emanating from the altar to the cultists rose and fell with each expenditure. The Satanists themselves were simply shells, each possessing only a tiny drop of humanity left.

Karnstein realized that these people were truly dead, mere simulacrums of life, because the being inside the altar allowed it. Should the unseen creature wish it, the cultists would simply fall over and decompose.

God save their lost souls, the Exorcist thought.

The silver images appeared before his body, a star suspended in a circle surrounded by odd, disquieting symbols.

"*DALKHU TARU SERU ESERU ETUTU INA ETUTI ASBU DARISAM!*" he shouted in the same odd tone.

The light before his body rose and lashed out at the cultists. They screamed, shook, and wailed, their bodies quivering and smoking beneath their red robes.

Standing near the altar, Strix moaned in pain, slumping forward onto the wooden surface.

"Mistress, are you well?" Robert her servant asked, touching her arm.

Strix spun and stabbed upward, piercing her follower's chest. He whimpered like a kicked puppy, blood welling from his mouth, his eyes staring glassily forward.

Raising the bloody knife, she slashed the air several times and barked out several sounds that were like that of buzzing insects rather than speech.

A heavy black smoke filled the air where her blade had sliced, slowly forming into an oval shape.

"At last! At last!" Strix said, her voice rising.

The Satanists fell over, their bodies collapsing. A noxious smoke arose from their corpses, driving Dardi and Karnstein back several steps.

As the smoke slowly coalesced into a solid object, about three feet-long, Ange and Jean Ténèbre appeared near the altar. Ange clutched his face and stumbled, whining with each movement. At his side was Jean, his neck and chest covered with a viscous black yellow ooze.

"Help us…" Ange said.

Strix ignored them as she reached out and folded her arms about a massive black skull. The shape was vaguely human, though the dimensions and proportions were oversized. The teeth were ivory colored and elongated, resembling that of a massive cat, and its eyeholes were bulging and reptilian in design.

"Take the altar, we leave now! Vampire, kick over the brazier!" Strix ordered.

"*Genero*, your gun!" Dardi yelled.

Karnstein handed him his long revolver, which Dardi raised and fired.

The ball struck Strix's demonic mask squarely in the forehead, shattering the heavy wood and sending splinters flying every direction. Oddly, none hit the satanic priestess, though her mask fell away in pieces.

The woman beneath the mask possessed a lovely oval face, high cheekbones, full ruby red lips, and large violet eyes. She also lacked any traces of hair on her head, eyebrows or eyelashes. Her bald pale skull was the last thing Dardi and Karnstein viewed as Ange kicked over the nearby brazier. Flames leaped out, spreading across the floor as if oil had permeated the wood, and set it ablaze.

Coughing and gagging, both men were forced to retreat through the curtained doorway. Heading back into the sewers, they returned to the streets moments later, the infant still blessedly asleep.

"Franz! Papa!" Sylvia said, throwing her arms around both men's neck., "Why are you holding a baby?"

"The Satanists planned using the child as a sacrifice to their devil," Dardi said.

He stared at Ishaani as she and Séverin approached, "You have a tale to tell as well, I believe."

"We do, though you will have to exercise your limited English. This is Ishaani of the Thuggee. She came here with a mad Englishman on an important mission…" Séverin said, leading them away.

CHAPTER XLI

"Why," Franz Karnstein asked an hour later, after events had been relayed, "does this terrible, demonic scroll exist? The very existence of such an item endangers the entire world!"

Ishaani, who unwounded the scarf across her face, looked back at him with open disgust.

"You think we did not try and destroy the Raktabīja parchment? Do you think we, a religion founded thousands of years ago, would not try every means of destroying the scroll? By the time your Christ walked the Earth, we, the Thuggee, had made thousands of attempts. It does not burn, tear, or remain buried. One of my ancestors placed the page in a heavy steel chest and dropped the weighted trunk into the ocean. Before he returned to land, the trunk and scroll were back in the secret temple. We know not who carried them back, or how, and yet there they were..."

They sat around a table in the lodgings located above the fencing school. Ishaani sat at one end, Jean-Pierre Séverin at the other. Between them, Franz and Sylvia sat on the right side, Bartomeleo Dardi on the left. Wine, bread, cheese and tea lay untouched on the table.

The baby was well and, surprisingly, in the arms of her mother. The woman lived only two streets away from the satanic temple,; she was mad with grief and had described the red-haired man as her attacker.

"What happened to him? I want him dead!" she had said, quieted quickly as the baby started fussing.

"He is dead and paying for his crimes in hell, Madame," Karnstein had replied, handing her a small purse of coins. "God be with you."

The woman had tearfully accepted the gift, kissed the Austrian on both cheeks and fled into the night. The others had remained silent for the rest of the walk back to the fencing school, where they had related the day's events.

Sylvia was particularly angry about Ishaani's murder attempt, rubbing her throat and whispering, "*Vaffanculo*," under her breath.

"Yet somehow," Dardi continued, "the document that you claim cannot be destroyed, has vanished. How do you explain this?"

"The scroll of the demon can be moved. It vanished twelve times before—this is the thirteenth. We do not understand how or why, but a French thief named Abraham Hyacinthe Anquetil-Duperron took possession of the scroll of Raktabīja and hid it away. Before he died, a woman named Strix stole it and wishes for the demon king to be brought back to Earth. This is a calamity!"

Ishaani concluded by slapping her open hand on the table.

"Before the fire," Dardi said, "this Strix received a massive black skull from somewhere unholy. This is the head of this demon?"

The Thuggee priestess nodded.

"It is, and now they must find a place in the open air where there is only darkness. Then she can enact the final rituals and Raktabīja shall return to Earth. They only have until the next full moon, or they must begin again."

"What is this creature?" Karnstein asked, "Raka…"

"Raktabīja," Ishaani corrected with an indulgent smile. "In ancient days, creatures you call demons ruled the Earth. One of the worst was Raktabīja. A king among his kind, his blood held a terrible power. If a drop of blood from his body strikes the ground, an exact duplicate of the demon appears. That is what Raktabīja means, 'He for whom each drop of blood is a seed.' That is why his return is death to all life… This monster would consume all life in the universe if left unchecked."

"How was it killed?" Sylvia grudgingly asked.

"Kali, the black goddess, swallowed the duplicates and drank every drop of *Raktabīja*'s blood that struck the ground," Ishaani said.

Séverin, who remained silent after learning of the events in the temple, sighed.

"We now have all answers necessary. The unmasked Strix confirms my concerns. That creature, whatever she calls herself, is a vampire."

"No, she is not," Karnstein said, "she is a black witch."

"She is both," Séverin said, "or a very odd variant of one whose existence I learned from my teacher, Grost. You know of the vampire city, Selene?"

Dardi, Sylvia, and Karnstein nodded in the affirmative. Ishaani looked confused, but did not reply or move.

"The creatures that emerge from that city are not vampires in the sense we understand. They are not even like the hopping undead of China, known as *jiangshi*. They steal the souls of their victims by piercing the neck with a forked tongue and lapping up the blood. Once the soul is within the vampire, the creature can revive their victims as servants. The master can also control the form they take. I once encountered a servant of these vampires who was in the form of a talking parrot," the swordmaster said.

"That explains something I viewed," Karnstein said, but he shook his head and added, "my apologies; please, continue."

Séverin acknowledged his student with a brief nod.

"One characteristic that renders these vampires easily detectable is that their female victims return to the world completely hairless. I cannot explain why this is so, but this is clearly the case with Strix."

"I am not so sure," Karnstein said. "The power that controlled the cultists emerged from the altar, not the priestess. I viewed clear lines of dark, corrupting power from it to the men and women assembled. Only the bright-haired one she sacrificed was a human among that circle of the damned."

The swordmaster contemplated the wall above his student's head for a moment and frowned.

"That is odd, but I believe we shall find out more in the future. I do have a theory based on Grost's work. I shall study his writings as we travel."

"We? You are taking this *porca vacca* to travel with us?" Sylvia said.

"Yes," Séverin replied, "she knows more of this scroll than any of us. Additionally, she is a dangerous warrior and we shall need every strong arm we can recruit."

"Where are we going?" Ishaani asked, haughtily ignoring Sylvia's enraged expression.

"To the most dangerous place in the world. To the dark city, in the land where the sun never shines, Selene, the Sepulchre, the Vampire City itself," Séverin replied.

"*Ach du lieber Himmel*," Karnstein said, crossing himself.

CHAPTER XLII

The woman called Strix adjusted the dark wig that lay upon her head. She stared at herself in the mirror and frowned. The hair was human and stiff curls framed the outlines of her face.

"No, this one makes my face look fat. Bring me the next," she said, pulling the wig from her head and thrusting it into the shopkeeper's hands.

He was a man in his late forties or early fifties with a moon-shaped face, three chins, a wig of tight curly hair, and a waxed beard and mustache. He wore heavy, flowery perfume and behaved like a fussy matron rather than one of the premiere wigmakers in Paris. His name was Anton and he never told anyone his last name.

"Oh, how very sad, tsk, tsk, tsk," he said, fluttering away behind the counter.

He returned seconds later with another wig, this one as dark as the previous one, but with shoulder-length hair that held a mild wavy quality. Gently placing the item on Strix's head, he adjusted the fit and teased out the ends with a silver-topped brush.

"This one is a true masterpiece," Anton said, "I placed each strand in place personally, not stopping even for food for sixteen hours."

Strix gazed upon herself and barely hid her expression of surprise. This was precisely what she looked like over one-hundred years ago...

1676, Paris

The loveliest woman in France, if not all Europe, sat primly on a plain wooden chair. She held herself upright with a proud carriage that suggested the seat beneath her pert bottom was that of a royal throne.

A voluptuous woman, she had high, firm breasts, a narrow waist and, supposedly, beneath the layers of silk and petticoats, a perfect derriere. Long, thick, curling, golden hair flowed across her shoulders and back, and her large blue eyes appeared intelligent and guileless.

Her name was Françoise-Athénaïs de Rochechouart, Marquise de Montespan, better known to all as Madame de Montespan, the favored *maîtresse-en-titre* of King Louis XIV of France. Though Louis's wife was Maria Theresa of Spain, the true Queen of France was known everywhere to be Madame de Montespan.

Mother of seven of Louis's children, her highly intelligent and often piercingly witty mind allowed her the position of unofficial advisor to the Sun King. Though other mistresses had captured Louis's momentary fancy, Madame de Montespan had remained throughout the years.

"You say the king has another lady? My friends in court tell me this happens often, but never lasts," the witch said as she sat down in a matching chair.

"Yes," Madame de Montespan said. "However, I believe this is no short infatuation. Louis is dressing himself in ribbons, dancing, singing gaily, and purchasing diamonds and feathers."

The witch frowned and asked, "Is this a problem?"

"Yes!" Montespan insisted. "Little Marie Angélique de Scorailles is young, beautiful, and enchants him daily with her naïve gentility. Louis is so enamored with her... he does not realize the little sausage is as stupid as a basket of nails!"

"Ah," the witch said, showing her rows of yellowing teeth, "so you come to me for help! What do you wish? The death of your rival? The love of your king again? I can promise both—but there is a price."

"Name your price, La Voisin, I shall pay what you demand for both!" Madame de Montespan said, her head low.

Catherine Monvoisin, better known as the poisoning witch La Voisin, smiled upon the royal mistress with delight.

Soon her plans, all in the name of her master Belial, First of the Fallen, would come to fruition.

"Very good, child," La Voisin said, standing up. "You shall first pledge your body and soul to the powers of darkness. Then my daughter, Marguerite, shall assist your every need."

"Your daughter?" the royal mistress asked. "Why her?"

Catherine Monvoisin giggled and called out, "Marguerite, come here, girl!"

The queen of French poisoners heard movement from above and turned back to Madame de Montespan.

"My daughter is better suited towards satisfying your demands. She is young, learned in the dark arts, and can pass for a lady's maid at any time. Would you wish one who looks as me wandering about your king's court?"

Madame de Montespan visibly shuddered at the thought. One could as easily be the source of gossip for an unsuitable servant. In addition, the squat, earthy, clearly peasant stock, La Voisin resembled precisely what the court believed a witch and poison dealer to resemble.

"You are correct," the royal mistress said as Marguerite Monvoisin entered the room.

Slightly shorter than de Montespan, her long, unfettered dark hair, thick dark lashes, and wide brown eyes, were simply lovely in a peasant manner. Her skin was tanned and a bit coarse, and her hands were rough from labor, but Marguerite Monvoisin appeared pretty enough for the royal court in a servant's role.

Marguerite curtsied slightly awkwardly and said, "How may I assist you, Madame?"

The royal mistress tapped her own chin softly with one finger, planning her strategies. She never acted swiftly when major decisions loomed, having learned at the feet of her beloved Louis the workings of conspiracies.

She is pretty, but I cannot suddenly have a new servant trailing my tracks. However, she could serve in a secondary role to dear, pretty, little Claude, she thought.

"You must learn to curtsey better, girl," de Montespan said, "for you will appear on occasions at the Royal Court. You must keep your eyes downward at all times there and never show any sauce. Do you understand me?"

"Yes, Madame," Marguerite said, casting her eyes downward.

"Very good," de Montespan said. "I shall assign you to the service of my mistress of the bedchamber, Mademoiselle Claude des Œillets. She shall conduct all business in my name from this day forth."

"If that is your wish, Madame, it shall be so," Marguerite said.

The she looked up and added, "First we must complete the rites of binding. Please follow me."

Madame de Montespan rose, her face creasing with annoyance.

"I am not some servant you may order about, girl!"

"Here," La Voisin said, her face breaking into an amused smirk, "you are very much the servant. You have no knowledge of the dark arts, or the ways of the prince of darkness, Belial. In the art of sorcery, even I, mistress of this coven, obey Marguerite."

The royal mistress's frown deepened, yet she followed the young girl down a hall and into another building. They stopped before a rack filled with woolen black robes. Marguerite grabbed one without looking and placed the garment over her head.

"Place one about your body, Madame. It is necessary for the ceremony, and the cloth shall protect your clothing," she said, pulling her hood over her head.

"Protect my clothing from what?" de Montespan asked as she reached for a clean robe.

"Bloodstains, of course," Marguerite said, laughing as she pulled aside a curtain.

The room within was a tiny chapel, probably built within the last century. The walls were simple brick and several large unadorned rugs covered the dark wooden floor. A simple wooden altar lay several feet from where they stood, near an upside down cross that appeared nailed into the wall.

A cooing baby lay in the center of the altar, chubby arms and legs gently waggling, tiny fingers opening and closing. Near the baby's head was a long straight knife and a gold inlayed chalice that resembled a screaming skull.

"Take up the knife, Madame. When I complete the prayer to the Devil, Belial, and Leviathan, kill the child. I recommend a thrust to the heart. It ends the life faster," Marguerite instructed, taking up the heavy, gold cup.

Picking up the dagger, Françoise-Athénaïs de Rochechouart, Marquise de Montespan, better known as Madame de Montespan, *maîtresse-en-titre* of King Louis XIV of France, averted her eyes and simulated deafness.

I do this for my Louis, she thought. *I cannot lose that which is mine…*

"*Nema! livee, morf su revilled tub nushyaitpmet ootni ton suh deel su tsnaiga sapsert…*" Marguerite chanted, speaking the famed Lord's Prayer in reverse.

"Strike," she said to de Montespan as her words ended.

Madame de Montespan thrust downward, the blade sinking deep and through the tiny body. A nearly inaudible wail rang out, ending seconds later. The tiny arms and legs went slack and there was a moment of heavy silence about the demonic chapel.

Marguerite was unsurprised that this titled, royal whore sold herself to their lord Belial without a murmur or regret.

There is steel in this one. If she chose a path in the dark arts, this slut could surpass me. Fortunately, she does not realize this and I shall never teach her the left-handed path, the satanic priestess thought.

Dipping the middle finger of her left hand into the dead child's blood, Marguerite looked to her newest recruit in their ancient circle.

"Do you agree to give your body and soul up to Belial, angel of enmity, master of the sons of darkness, first of the fallen?"

"Yes," de Montespan replied in a clear voice.

"Then your wishes shall be granted by your new master," Marguerite said, drawing a reverse cross across Madame de Montespan's lovely pale forehead. "Your name within our circle is now Lamia. None but one of our numbers shall know it…"

Paris, modern day

That was the beginning of the end, Marguerite thought, smiling at her image in the mirror.

"I shall take it," she said.

Anton bowed deeply, practically scraping the floor in his obedience to her.

"Thank you, thank you, dear madame! Now, will you please tell your friends they may release my wife and children?"

"Jean! Ange!" she called out in the same deep tone she used as Strix, "to me, if you please!"

There was movement from above and the light step of someone heading down the backstairs. Ange Ténèbre appeared seconds later, her face practically unrecognizable under a mask of gore.

"What… what… what did you do?" Anton said, staggering backwards.

"Your wife tasted bad," Ange replied, licking his lips. "She had many diseases and was dying. Your children, they were a little better, but not by much. Jean is eating the remains."

Marguerite, pointed at the quivering, shattered wigmaker.

"Toss that one into the altar and lock it tight. That should serve as a meal for at least a week. We can find someone on the road that shall serve until we reach Selene."

Ange pounced upon Anton, his tiny hand encircling the fat man's throat. The wigmaker kicked and flailed his arms about, but the vampire appeared unmoved and disinterested.

He dragged the struggling Anton from the room and towards the back door.

"What are you doing? Help me! Please stop! I will give you anything, no please…" the wails suddenly cut off as the back door banged closed.

Fifteen minutes later, Ange returned while Jean walked down from the upstairs apartment. The *oupire* held a thigh bone in hand and gently gnawed on the dripping meat like a child savoring a treat.

"Travel," Jean said after gulping down the contents in his mouth, "will not be easy. The borders will be guarded, and the trek is long. We must abandon the coach before we reach the smuggler's roads that Ange and I used when escaping this country."

"I have money; we shall buy what we need," Marguerite replied. "Our pursuers do not have my resources."

"True," Jean said as he waved Ange ahead. "But they have a Karnstein. Though feared in those lands, they still have power and influence. We must stay away from main highways and travel the hidden routes known to criminals and, of course, my brother and I."

"That one is no Karnstein!" Marguerite said, climbing in the rear of the carriage with Jean. "He serves the Roman Pope and used an ancient form of exorcism that I thought was only a myth! No Karnstein would carry such power!"

"Nonsense," Jean said as the coach lurched forward. "Kriavi Vajda was a Karnstein and the Grand Inquisitor of Moldavia and Hungary. He executed his own sister for witchcraft and impaled Ange and me for our crimes. The Karnsteins are creatures of extremes, light or dark, and fully committed to either."

"What happened to that Karnstein?" Marguerite asked while studying the *oupire*.

"He died in his bed of old age, cursed by his witch of a sister. We never did pay him back for his treatment of us, but we did desecrate his remains forty years ago…" Jean replied, before returning to his snack.

CHAPTER XLIII

Sneaking across the border proved easier than Jean-Pierre Séverin and his party had believed possible. The frontiers were no longer harshly guarded since the Austrian defeat at the Battle of Austerlitz and the subsequent Treaty of Pressburg. Napoleon's attention now lay upon Prussia, as well as the lesser countries of that region.

Their party traveled in a wagon, one Séverin owned but rarely used. Purchasing a set of draft horses from a dealer, they had set off a day after the encounter at the black mass. Franz Karnstein drove the cart with Sylvia at his side.

"We can travel openly now?" Bartolomeo Dardi asked in halting English as they arrived upon a wide road.

"We can," Karnstein replied as he shook the horse's reins, "but we should not use my name too often. There are many villages who remember my ancestors. When we are in Styria, it shall not matter."

"Why?" Sylvia asked.

Karnstein snorted with open amusement and looked at his fiancée with a sardonic grin.

"Do you believe," he asked, "that I would not be recognized the moment I arrived in the lands that my family has held since the days of Rome? We must be on our guard. Some may treat us with... disrespect..."

That effectively ended the conversation, though an hour later, Dardi broke into song, his strong voice ringing across the busy highway:

"Ah, ah, ah, questa è buona, or lasciala cercar; che bella notte! È più chiara del giorno, sembra fatta per gir a zonzo a caccia di ragazze. È tardi? Oh, ancor non sono due della notte; avrei voglia un po' di saper com'è finito l'affar tra Leporello e Donn'Elvira, s'egli ha avuto giudizio!"

"What is he doing?" Ishaani asked, her voice floating from the back near the trunks of food and weapons.

"I was about to ask the same question," the Exorcist said.

"That is called singing, you barbarians! It is the words and music of your countryman, the great Mozart. The opera called *Don Giovanni* is perfection, and even tells the tale of man and the Devil! Do you not know anything of your heritage, *genero*?" Dardi asked, laughing and punching the Austrian on the shoulder.

Karnstein winced slightly at the impact; his future father-in-law's hands felt like mallets.

"Music? No, only church hymns. Sylvia took me to the opera last week. It was very long, and nobody stopped singing. I still do not understand why this was entertaining," he said.

Dardi and Sylvia exploded with laughter and the corner of Séverin's mouth twitched slightly.

The Maestro turned to Ishaani and bowed slightly her direction. "We must talk of matters that do not involve you," he said. "Please forgive us, but we shall speak briefly in another language."

The Thuggee priestess did not reply but closed her eyes and breathed slowly in her nose and out her mouth.

"I think I shall ask a question I never ventured," the elder swordmaster said in his native tongue. "Franz, how do you exorcise demons with such ease? You said that the language you speak during those times is Sumerian, and I believe the truth of your words. However, I know of no other exorcist who dispelled a demon in less than an eight-hour ceremony. But you do so in seconds…"

"I should wish this knowledge too, *genero*. Secrets do not serve among family…" Dardi began, but stopped after spotting an amused expression from Sylvia.

"Franz told me the day after we were engaged. I never asked, he volunteered that information and several other secrets," she said, kissing the Austrian's cheek.

"What other secrets?" Séverin and Dardi asked at the same time.

"That is not important," Karnstein said, frowning. "However, I shall inform you of the tale of my apprenticeship and the source of my power…"

CHAPTER XLIV

Karnstein Castle, Styria, 1784

"What happened here, boy?" Father Sandor asked as the Bishop's people examined the bones and said the word "vampire" under their breath.

"Cousin Mircalla was a vampire. She made mother into a vampire. I… sent them away… they're gone… were already gone," Franz Karnstein mumbled.

Then, he seemed to pull his shattered spirit together. He looked at Father Sandor and the Bishop's representative and spoke in a more even tone:

"I killed my mama. She was a vampire too."

And then, he burst into tears.

The priest, a gruff but saintly man, placed an arm across the young baron's shoulders. The child silently wept, never snuffling, wailing, or any histrionics. Franz Vordenburg-Karnstein, though merely eight years-old, talked in the same manner than one expected from an adult.

"Your grandfather, Count Karnstein, shall take charge of you. Perhaps you shall live with him in his home in Vienna," Father Sandor said after the boy had wiped his tears and stared unseeingly into the distance.

"No," Franz said. "He does not like children. When I went to Vienna or his castle, I was kept away and silent."

"Then perhaps he shall send a…" Father Sandor's words stopped as a large, well-appointed coach bearing the arms of the Bishop Prince of Seckau arrived.

Ten cavalry guard road before and after the carriage, and they leaped off their massive chargers upon stopping near Karnstein Castle.

The man alighting from the coach was not the bishop, but an elderly man with a skeletal face, a few wisps of gray white hair, and hard blue eyes that pierced everyone he gazed upon like a knife. He walked with the help of a heavy black cane with a shiny silver top and was dressed entirely in plain black clothing.

Father Sandor pulled Franz to his feet and bowed low before the man, signaling that the boy should follow suit. He obeyed, keeping his eyes low and his lips tightly clamped shut.

"My Lord, you honor us with your presence. Lord Inquisitor von Spielsdorf, may I present Baron Franz Vordenburg-Karnstein," Father Sandor said, bowing again.

Franz found this obsequious behavior on the part of the priest quite odd and in opposition to the man's nature. Father Sandor was gruff, tough, harsh, demanding and disinterested in the rights of nobles or their traditions. Even Franz's late, unlamented mother held a great deal of respect for the priest, sensing he was fair and learned.

"Look at me, boy," the elderly inquisitor said, "I would see your eyes."

Franz looked up at the man, feeling tiny under the harsh, unflinching gaze. Part of him felt like fleeing or hiding behind Father Sandor, but he did not. He never knew why, but he stared back and withered under the terrible eyes of this ancient skeleton.

"Your mother and the vampire Karnstein," von Spielsdorf continued, "shall be buried in unhallowed graves after their remains are burned. Unless you demand otherwise."

"No," Franz said, adding, "I shot Otto and Jana. Do the same to them, please."

The elderly inquisitor leaned downward, his thin pointed nose mere inches from the boy's face.

"Then we celebrate their death?"

Franz thought for a moment and shook his head.

"Then we pray for their soul's deliverance."

A rictus grin slid across Lord Inquisitor von Spielsdorf's face and he straightened.

"This boy shall be under my charge from this day forward."

Father Sandor took a step back, his face registering shock and fear.

"A Karnstein, my lord? Truly?"

The elderly inquisitor nodded once and said, "Yes, a Karnstein. I am as surprised as you, considering I destroyed three of his ancestors. Now, show me the bodies and pack the child's clothing and books. His learning begins today..."

Father Sandor obeyed and that night Franz Karnstein's lessons in the ancient languages of Sumerian, Akkadian, Sanskrit, Aramaic, and other other obscure tongues began. That was the first step preparing the boy for a vastly different life than he imagined possible.

CHAPTER XLV

"These routes are very slow," Marguerite Monvoisin said, as they slowly went up and down a trail that just fit the small wagon that the Ténèbre Brothers had stolen from the outskirts of Paris.

"We have no choice," Ange said, lazing in the back and staring at the sky as they bumped along. "The French and Austrians were still at war only last year…"

"Once we are miles from here," Jean added from the driver's seat, "we shall return to the main roads. We shall steal another carriage and return to our best disguises. I as a noble knight, Ange as a priest, and you… well, we must think of a disguise for you…"

Marguerite ceased listening as the Ténèbre Brothers discussed different possibilities. She was not their age, but, like the vampire and *oupire*, knew more about life than most humans….

1679, Paris

Madame de Montespan lay nude upon the altar as Marguerite Monvoisin and the dark priest, Abbé Étienne Guibourg, painted her body with ancient sigils in honor of Satan, Belial, and Leviathan. Her desire for power grew daily and even her return to the favored position in the Sun King's bed did not satisfy her desires.

"*Nema! livee, morf su revilled tub nushyaitpmet ootni ton suh deel su tsnaiga sapsert…*" Guibourg said, his voice heavy and disapproving.

A short man with a square head fringed with white hair, Étienne Guibourg looked the very model of a congenial local priest. He had a wide, happy smile, a gentle manner of speech and conduct, and soft brown eyes that resembled that of a cow.

This only showed how looks could be very deceiving. Étienne Guibourg was a man devoted to personal pleasures in every form. He had two mistresses, a woman of twenty-five and her sister, a child of thirteen, an appetite for strong drink, and a desire for occult and temporal power. There was no vice he would ignore, and he had indulged in most since choosing the path of the dark priest.

Dressed in a silver stitched robe covered with occult symbols, he nodded his head and a robed acolyte lit six black candles that exuded a noxious scent. Lifting a silver chalice that still held an infant's blood, he placed the vessel upon the soft stomach of the famed Madame de Montespan and pointed at the tiny broken figure beside the altar.

"Dispose of that refuse," he said with a hand flick. "We shall begin the rites now."

La Voisin scuttled over to the side of the altar and picked up the dead child. She walked across the chamber and winced as she approached the oven that heated this entire building. The flames dancing in the brick and stone kiln were white hot and exuded a powerful heat that burned the very air.

Tossing the dead baby into the fire, she turned away and wiped the traces of blood across her black robes. Resuming her place around the altar, she pulled her hood low and watched the proceedings as a faceless member of the coven.

Since the entry of the powerful and famed Madame de Montespan into the La Voisin organization, their power and clientele had grown with impressive speed. Their patrons now included Henri de Montmorency, Duke of Luxembourg and Marshal of France, the former mistress of the king, Olympia Mancini, Countess of Soissons, Marie Louise Charlotte, Princess of Tingry, and Marie de Broglio, Marquise of Canilhac. Poison and evil were a powerful aphrodisiac to the wealthy and bored.

There had been another transformation of the coven since Madame de Montespan had joined their circle. Though La Voisin acted as leader, her only role was that of fortune telling and mixing poison for her patrons. A student of black magic, she possessed neither the knowledge nor the power of her lovely daughter, Marguerite. Even La Voisin's lovers, learned students of the occult since before Marguerite's birth, now deferred to the young woman.

Étienne Guibourg and Adam Lesage, another sorcerer, obeyed Marguerite with an almost religious fervor. Both were La Voisin's lovers, but she knew they would sacrifice her if her dark daughter ordered such an act.

Fortunately for Catherine Monvoisin, Marguerite had no such desire. She appeared content in her role as student of magic and leader of their temple. All that the young woman had told her mother was this:

"When I tell you that someone should not be inducted in our coven, you shall not mention its existence to them. The Duke of Luxembourg and the Princess of Tingry are to only receive poison or fortune-telling. If they hint at anything involving black masses, you are to recoil in horror. Is this understood, mother?"

"Yes," Catherine had replied with a downcast expression painted across her face.

By the time of this ceremony, the one inducting Madame de Montespan from acolyte to member of the coven, over one thousand men, women, and children had died from La Voisin's poisons. Over one thousand more infants, stolen or purchased from poor families, had died in their dark ceremonies. Their coven had eschewed from the murder of cats and dogs since Marguerite had taken command of the ceremonies.

"True evil," she had told her mother, Guibourg, and Lesage, "despises weakness. Cats and dogs are animals, and as such, of little interest to our demonic masters. The death of innocents destroys the light. Infants. We shall steal or buy babies, the younger the better, and use their blood and bones in our rites."

They had all obeyed, using their growing number of followers; the children of the poor were easily obtained. After a hundred or so, even the squeamish members of their circle no longer winced at the pitiful wails and whimpers of the babies as the knife sliced into their tender bodies.

In the present, Étienne Guibourg completed the backwards Lord's Prayer that all present knew by heart. Raising his hands upwards, he pointed his palms downward and said out the final portion of the invocation.

"...O Princes of Hell, Satan, Asmodeus, Belial, and Leviathan. Honor our sister with the love of all the princes and princesses of the Court, that the King deny her nothing she requests!"

Marguerite lifted the chalice from Madame de Montespan's breasts and walked to each member of the coven. They sipped the wine mixed with baby's blood and spat the viscous liquid upon the floor. Guibourg placed a piece of bread in each of their mouths and they also spat this out and ground the soggy remains beneath their feet. It was a final act of disrespect to the Church, desecrating the solemn rituals.

After the black mass, when all had returned to their homes, Marguerite Monvoisin found her mother admiring herself before a mirror. Her fleshy body lay hidden beneath a soft red robe with gold and silver eagles stitched across the cloth. The garment was gaudy and ridiculous, an item chosen by a woman lacking in any sense of style and decorum. A beauty like de Montespan could possibly wear such an item as a joke—a costumed jape, like when the wealthy dressed like peasants and played at performing farm work. But on La Voisin the robe was simply ridiculous.

"Where did you get that?" Marguerite asked, "and how much did it cost?"

"I ordered it especially for meeting with clients. It only costs one thousand three hundred in gold. That does not even cover a tenth of what my latest patron gave me. His name is Eustache Dauger de Cavoye, and he is one of the young blades who..."

Marguerite did not protest but left unhappy at the purchase. Yes, they had that much money and more to spare. But the trouble was that they were becoming too well-known among the nobles as suppliers of poisons. With the recent arrest of a fortune-teller and minor poisoner named Magdelaine de La Grange, their organization required more discretion and fewer new members.

That was, Marguerite soon discovered, the beginning of the end of their brief period of power in Belial's name. It was that imbecile, Eustache Dauger de Cavoye, who brought down their circle and transformed Marguerite's life irrevocably...

CHAPTER XLVI

"Lord Inquisitor von Spielsdorf?" Bartolomeo Dardi asked. "He was a time-waster. He never performed any arrests and even freed several accused witches in Hess and Styria. Not that I disapprove—most inquisitors are simply woman haters who use their power as an excuse for rape and sadistic murders... present company excepted..."

Franz Karnstein snorted again and said, "Thank you for that. What you believe and what is true are not the same. Though a foul-tempered man who loved the cane a little too much, von Spielsdorf was a true holy crusader who spent his life defeating demons and followers of darkness. I learned much at his feet, and together we put to rest another of my ancestors."

"Let me guess," Sylvia said, smiling his direction. "Her name was Countess Mircalla, or Baroness Carmilla, or some strange version of that odd name."

"*His* name," the Austrian answered, matching her smile, "was Emil, and he was the fourth son of a third son of a Karnstein baron. He ran a circus of vampires and evil creatures. We destroyed him and his followers before their evil show contaminated another village."

"*Idiota!* You are telling this story in the slowest way possible. We will be out of Austria before you finish your tale!" Sylvia said.

"I am telling the events as they unfolded—and stop calling me an idiot," Karnstein replied.

"Then stop acting like one. You trained under the witch hunter—a German named von Spielsdorf. Tell them what you told me before I see white in my hair," she said, elbowing him in the side.

Bartomeleo Dardi and Jean-Pierre Séverin exchanged an amused look as the young couple squabbled. The once agreed that as long as Sylvia and Franz argued, they were happy.

Should they ever start behaving politely and quiet, they would have cause for concern.

"I think," Séverin said, "that I should prefer jumping to the end this one time, Franz. What did Lord Inquisitor von Spielsdorf teach you besides languages and rituals?"

The Exorcist thought for a moment and exchanged an unreadable look with Sylvia. Their gaze lingered for a heartbeat and she nodded once and squeezed his hand.

Behind them, Dardi and Séverin glanced in each other's direction. The Neapolitan swordmaster shrugged broadly, indicating his complete ignorance at the young lover's silent communication. Séverin smiled briefly, rolling his eyes and waited.

"What do you know of the religion of the followers of Muhammad?" Karnstein asked.

"Much," Dardi replied. "My father and grandmother had us read their Koran and learn of their ways. We later fought against and by the side of the Barbary Pirates."

"We assisted in a battle against a cult who worshipped the elder gods in Egypt as well. The followers of the Black Pharaoh were a terrible cult who sacrificed entire villages to their god," Séverin added.

"Good," Karnstein said. "Then you know the tale of the ring of Solomon?"

Dardi and Séverin sighed at the same time, with the latter shaking his head sadly.

"Franz," he said slowly, "that is a myth. The wise king never wore a ring that granted him the power to control demons."

Dardi chuckled, still shaking his oddly shaped head.

"I wish I could tell you how many times Gâteloup and I received word that someone had found the ring or some peddler held it for the right buyer. It is a tale told by silly occultists."

"Of course, it is, Papa," Sylvia said, grinning. "Do you think my *fidanzato* is credible enough for such stories?"

Karnstein briefly smiled at her and then his face returned to his normal, stern expression.

"Who was the first exorcist?" he asked.

Séverin shook his head and said, "There is no answer to such a question. There are tales of ancient kings of Egypt casting out demons."

"The first exorcist in the known world," Karnstein said, "was Ninurta, son of Enlil. In ancient days, he destroyed the followers of Mušḫuššu, cast out the terrible demon Asag, and revealed that the wife of a minor king was a demoness named Alal."

"How do you know all this? It exists in no known texts that I or my teachers ever studied," the elder swordmaster asked.

"There is a tradition," Karnstein said, speaking as if he hadn't heard the question, "of one man, or woman, holding the power of exorcism, first granted or found by Ninurta. The holder of this power somehow knows his successor and seeks him out. In the age of Solomon, the woman who held this power was a wise Egyptian woman whom the king referred to often as a 'jewel of wisdom.' Somehow, scholars misunderstood his words and she became his 'ring.' My master, Lord von Spielsdorf, held that power and he trained me for all his remaining years. When he died in the Holy Land, I inherited his power—though not his position."

Silence fell over the wagon, with only the soft breathing of Ishaani in the rear and the crunch of the wagon wheels rising to their ears. Finally, Dardi broke the hush by exploding with laughter. He howled and shrieked for several minutes, ignoring the puzzled expression from Karnstein, the angry flush of his daughter, and the amused glint in Séverin's eyes.

Sylvia broke through his hilarity by asking through clenched teeth, "What is so funny, Papa?"

Dardi, still giggling madly, clutched his chest in paroxysms of pain. "For centuries," he said, "alchemists and worshippers of demons have sought high and low for the famed Ring of Solomon... the great device that controlled the creatures from the darkest pits of Hell. Little did they realize that the legendary controller of demons lay in… Madonna, this is killing me!... a church-attending, Karnstein!"

"There is something unusual about that detail," Séverin said, his dour face reflecting some traces of humor. "I assume that means you cannot order demons about and have them build temples and palaces for you?"

"I should think not," Karnstein replied. "I can exorcise the creatures of Perdition and view the world in its purest form. More than that is unknown, since word of mouth is the only method used in passing the lore of Solomon. I do know that the holder knows, which is where his heir is. More than that remains a mystery."

"Interesting, we shall speak more upon this subject another day," said Séverin. "But I hear a large troupe of horses approaching from our rear and others in our lead. Franz, pull the wagon to the side of the road."

Séverin placed a pair of loaded pistols near his hands. Karnstein obeyed and checked the weapons he wore hidden beneath his cloak. Sylvia placed a hand on her heavy saber by her side, and her father moved to the furthest portion of the wagon. Only Ishaani appeared unmoved, her eyes closed and her breathing slow and inaudible.

Two minutes later, five horses halted several feet from the rear of the wagon. Three more were in front. The riders were all tall mustachioed men with gleaming red uniforms and rounded conical helmets. Each wore heavy cavalry sabers on their saddles and they rode their powerful charges with apparent assurance.

A handsome man in his mid-thirties trotted closer to the wagon and asked, "Lord Karnstein?"

The Exorcist nodded and tilted his head slightly back while examining the soldier. "I am Karnstein."

The soldier flicked his eyes over the others with little interest. "I am Colonel Kurt Schwaiger of the Imperial Dragoons. Your presence is required for a brief conference. Please follow us and you shall be escorted a short distance."

"Very well," Karnstein replied, picking up the reins.

Within a moment, they rumbled along, the soldiers from the rear never approaching closely, and the men in the lead cantering ahead. One horseman in the front group bolted ahead several minutes later.

"Who knew we were in Austria?" Sylvia asked as she studied the soldiers.

"I would guess," Dardi replied, "that your *fidanzato* is easily recognized by his countrymen. The Karnstein legacy is long and powerful."

"Correct," the Exorcist said, "though I cannot guess the identity of who wishes my presence. There are any numbers of powerful men capable of ordering a Colonel of Dragoons."

The horsemen turned off-road and onto a small, flat track that was barely a road, but still quite passable. Ancient trees lined it and small groups of men periodically appeared and vanished as their wagon rumbled past.

"Those were infantry," the elder swordmaster observed. "Someone of great importance lays ahead."

"That does not shorten the list," Karnstein replied.

They fell silent for several minutes.

The horsemen came to a halt fifty yards ahead, with the Colonel returning to the wagon.

"Lord Karnstein and the woman shall come forward. Please leave behind all your weapons. The rest must wait here and remain in your conveyance. Leaving shall result in arrest. I shall have my men provide you with some food and wine as you wait. This shall not take long."

Franz and Sylvia exchanged another unreadable look and then alighted from the wagon. Reaching from under his cloak, the Exorcist removed two pistols, a nasty looking Sicilian dagger and a light cavalry saber. Sylvia removed a single pistol and a small stiletto she pulled seemingly from nowhere.

"You carry more weapons than I do," the Colonel said with a chuckle. "Are you heading to war?"

"Mankind has always been at war, Colonel," Karnstein replied. "John 3:12, *not as Cain, who was of the evil one and slew his brother And for what reason did he slay him? Because his deeds were evil, and his brother's were righteous."*

The Colonel stared at the Exorcist for several seconds, his eyebrows rising and vanishing beneath his heavy helmet.

"A Karnstein quoting the bible... What other wonders shall this world provide?"

He dismounted and led them towards a path lined with armed infantrymen. The soldiers stood at attention and none so much as glanced in their direction. Their uniforms were a light blue, perfectly pressed, and held shining silver buttons down the front of their tunics.

A small manor house lay at the end of the path and several guards and liveried servants strode in different directions around the small structure. The Colonel stopped a passing servant, said a few brief words, and the latter scurried away quickly.

They stood waiting for another half hour, with Colonel Schwaiger standing ramrod straight the entire time. The door then opened and a tall man dressed in a green coat nodded in the Colonel's direction. The cavalry officer barked a harsh command and the soldiers froze in place. The servants melted away, moving behind the house and out-of-sight.

"Kneel," the Colonel said towards Franz and Sylvia as a man appeared in the doorway.

They obeyed, keeping their heads bowed as a strong voice said out in clear, unaccented German.

"Remain kneeling in the presence of Francis the First, by the Grace of God Emperor of Austria; King of Jerusalem, Hungary, Bohemia, Dalmatia, Croatia, Slavonia, Galicia and Lodomeria; Archduke of Austria; Duke of Lorraine, Salzburg, Würzburg, Franconia, Styria, Carinthia and Carniola; Grand Duke of Cracow; Grand Prince of Transylvania; Margrave of Moravia; Duke of Sandomir, Masovia, Lublin, Upper and Lower Silesia, Auschwitz and Zator, Teschen and Friule; Prince of Berchtesgaden and Mergentheim; Princely Count of Habsburg, Gorizia and Gradisca and of the Tirol; and Margrave of Upper and Lower Lusatia and Istria."

There was a brief pause and the Emperor of Austria stopped several feet before the kneeling Franz Karnstein and Sylvia Dardi.

"Baron Vordenburg-Karnstein and Signorina Sylvia Dardi," Francis said, "we grant you leave to rise and speak. We would discuss matters of some importance."

CHAPTER XLVII

Marguerite Monvoisin chewed slowly the salted meat they kept in a cask for her benefit. Ange and Jean Ténèbre did not require regular food and only partook of such delicacies if strongly flavored.

"Food," Jean had said to her a few weeks earlier, "is tasteless for Ange and me. The exceptions are ones with very strong flavors. Wines and spirits, highly salted meats or ones with eastern spices. Those are a treat, though ultimately they provide no sustenance. I do not believe you would wish an explanation of what we do with the lingering items we consume that do not assist our continuation... or do you?"

"No," Marguerite, then as the masked Strix, had replied, visibly shuddering at the image.

Jean had smiled briefly, and bit into a rotting rat he had found in the basement. The *oupire*'s feeding habits were truly revolting, even more so than his vampiric brother.

The undead are disgusting, she had thought that day and glanced at the coffin she used as her altar, *truly revolting creatures*.

Despite her position as the true mistress of a satanic circle, Marguerite Monvoisin had never met a member of the undead until after their fall from power.

"Eustache Dauger de Cavoye," she whispered aloud, thinking bitterly, *the greatest fool in history. It was all yours and mother's foolishness that brought me to this low state.*

1679, Paris

Marguerite knew he was trouble from the first time her mother La Voisin had presented him as a potential new initiate for their circle.

Eustache Dauger de Cavoye, the eldest son of a father who had served as a Captain in the Cardinal's Guards, ap-

221

peared at his induction ceremony drunk on cheap wine, carrying a flask filled with pig's blood.

"He is perfect," her mother had said. "He's friends with many young and wealthy young men. He is also deeply in debt and we can use him as a means of selling poison."

Marguerite frowned and disliked what she viewed. This de Cavoye had the weak look of one raised in luxury and never having risen above the stature of a demanding child. He had watery brown eyes, a weak chin, and a mean expression that reminded her of children who kick beggars and stray dogs.

"You wish to sell your soul to Belial?" she finally asked.

Eustache Dauger de Cavoye hiccupped and asked, "Who? You're saying the devil, girl? He can have what I got if I get some money. I'm already damned... I might as well get some cash for it."

Marguerite soon learned this young idiot had once killed a pageboy while in a drunken brawl, danced naked with a pair of serving girls while sodomizing a third with a crucifix, and joined in an orgy and black mass as an amusement.

Still, Catherine Monvoisin wanted him as a member of the coven in order to spread her poisonous wares. As the face of the organization, she had some power, though very little in reality. Her growing alcoholism and spendthrift ways rendered her less useful to the cult.

"He already knows our ways," La Voisin said, "so we must let him in."

Despite her misgivings, Marguerite had agreed and inducted the idiot that night. The only part of the ceremonies that interested de Cavoye were the drinking of blood and the orgies performed as part of the desecration of the Roman rites. He never learned any Latin and simply mumbled along with the group, waiting for the parts he found exciting.

Three months later, the doors and windows of the Monvoisin home burst inward and armed men swarmed inside. Everyone within found themselves shackled and gagged as a short, broad-shouldered man with a scraggly brown mustache and no beard surveyed the place. His heavy dark wig denoted him as a man of some status, and he carried himself with an assurance that silenced everyone.

"What have you found?" he asked one of the men holding Marguerite flat on the floor.

"General," the man began, clearing his throat, "excuse me, we have discovered poisons, and a church devoted to… to…"

The soldier stammered, shivered, and crossed himself. This gesture was replicated among several others, with every man, save the one they called "General," sweating profusely and looking alternatively between frightened and furious.

"Doctor," the General said, his head moving with slow deliberation toward a wizened figure dressed in a long frock coat and leaning on a black walking stick, "provide me with your preliminary discoveries."

The elderly man adjusted a gold-flecked gilt-encrusted pair of scissor spectacles and cleared his throat with painstaking slowness.

"The filthy excuse for a pharmacy room in this hovel held at least twelve forms of poison I recognized at first glance. There were several containers holding mixed toxins suited for the poisoning of an adult male of average or excessive proportions."

"Well done, Doctor," the General said, nodding and turning towards a man hovering by his left elbow.

The doctor tapped his cane on the ground and cleared his throat a second time. "I have not finished my statements, General!" he said.

"My apologies. Do continue."

The doctor took a full minute in his throat-clearing action before speaking again.

"Ahem… Within a cold furnace, your men discovered burnt bones—both whole and in fragments. I glanced briefly, but I can certify that they are human in origin. The ones I studied were of three different children, none older than three…"

Two men present ran from the room, retching violently as they fled. A large man with a round face and a fringe of blond beard kicked La Voisin in the side, while a shorter man with long, oily black hair and a huge gap in his teeth spat in her face.

"Enough," the General said. "Take them away. Keep the witch La Voisin separate from the others. Lock them all at a good distance from each other. We shall question them later. Their offenses against our beloved King as well as our Lord in Heaven shall be punished..."

Only later had Marguerite discovered that the General in question was none other than Gabriel Nicolas de la Reynie, the powerful and terrifying Lieutenant General of Police of Paris. Rumor held that de la Reynie would commit any act, no matter how heinous, to protect the King and the laws of France. His involvement in this situation was bad for them.

Dragged away and dropped in a lonely cell with no human contact, Marguerite only later learned the entire story from a female guard. The woman, a large, powerfully strong, religious woman named Clara, provided her with food and a short explanation.

"Your fellow poisoner, Eustache Dauger, killed the wrong person. After being arrested, he told the police all your names," Clara said, after spitting in Marguerite's soup. "Your witch of a mama had her trial yesterday. Tomorrow, they'll burn her at the stake."

There would be no trial for the lesser members of the cult, like Marguerite. A few wealthy patrons were sent into exile—most simply lost the right to appear at the Court.

"The rest of you will live the rest of your damned lives in a cell. Whether you live or die is of no importance to anyone," a young assistant to the Lieutenant General of Police said as he stepped out of her prison cell.

The implications were obvious. Her service to Madame de Montespan as an occasional "maid" could embarrass the King. The enormity of de Montespan's possible crimes would have condemned her, but for one factor. She was the mother of many of King Louis XIV's legitimized children. If anyone knew her part in the satanic conspiracy, the results could destroy the monarchy.

Hiding me and others away forever would be the best solution... for them... Marguerite thought as the cell door slammed shut behind the young man.

For three years, that was her life. Clara appeared twice daily with food and water and little or no conversation. Any questions from Marguerite received an honest, if short, answer, followed by her jailer spitting into her food.

Realizing she had to keep busy, Marguerite exercised twice daily and spent the remainder of her time practicing her dark arts. She knew that lacking the trappings and codices of the left-handed path would slow her progress, but what else did she have in her life?

Her powers grew slowly, with her inner strength providing a barrier against the daily boredom of her solitary life. Her meditations ate away the hours and she knew that, one day, this growing inner power of hers would provide a means of escape.

If only I could get control of Clara, she thought many times, *I could receive some comfort.*

She needed a lock of the jailer's hair or blood, which appeared impossible. The occasional spittle in her food proved useless for reasons unknown to the young, powerful witch. She was on the verge of despair, but still not giving up.

That was the day the raven appeared on her windowsill...

CHAPTER XLVIII

"Why would an Emperor waste time with an unimportant baron?" Bartolomeo Dardi asked after Karnstein and his daughter had vanished from sight.

"I would guess he learned of Franz's presence in the vicinity and wished a meeting," Jean-Pierre Séverin replied. "Consider the confusion our young pupil causes to their political structure. A baron with much land, who serves the church, is an advisor to the pope, the heir to a powerful title with more land, and yet rejects involvement in any form of politics. The Austrian Emperor would naturally demand an explanation—if one is available."

It had not been hard for the two swordmasters to guess the identity of the man behind the summons. The sheer volume of troops, all well-dressed and moving with clockwork precision, meant that the Emperor of Austria was nearby. Neither man had ever met Francis I, though they knew his country had received recently a humiliating loss in the war against France.

Dardi snorted out another laugh.

"He will find a cold reception. Our Franz is a good man, but as icy as an Alpine peak—except when with my dearest Sylvia. She makes him more…"

"Human, yes. I despaired he would become a witch hunter and ride about murdering innocent herb women in the name of God," Séverin said.

That had been both their fear, his and Dardi's, though Sylvia's skill at angering the young Exorcist had provided them a ray of hope.

"Keep them together," Dardi had said in Naples that summer. "They quarrel like an old married couple and are obviously struck by the thunderbolt. They will either duel or fall in love. Either way, we will have a solution."

Séverin, despite himself, had laughed and agreed immediately. The results were obvious and they had later found a better path for Karnstein.

"Why are we sitting here in the woods?" Ishaani asked, breaking into their reverie.

"One of our numbers received a message from his ruler, requesting an audience," Dardi said, waving a hand towards the front of the wagon.

"We must not tarry here, wasting our time on unimportant matters. The fate of all life in the universe demands we leave your man and his woman behind!"

Dardi looked in her direction, his face unemotional, his bulbous eyes hardening.

"That is my daughter and son-in-law you are speaking of, Thuggee."

"Among my people," Ishaani said, "family ties are unimportant when danger arises. Our guru would sacrifice the life of any of his followers if it protected the world from the return of Raktabīja. He for whom each drop of blood is a seed shall return, hungering for life."

"That does not matter," Séverin said. "You are among our kind and we do not abandon our own for reasons of convenience. Additionally, a small army of soldiers, mounted and infantry, surround our wagon. We cannot leave without permission."

Ishaani opened her mouth in protest, but fell silent from a raised palm by Dardi.

"If you leave, even if you could get away, what shall follow? You are in a strange country, hundreds of miles from our destination… a location even Gâteloup and I cannot discover easily."

Séverin added, "We have the same goal. Do not fear our commitment. Simply wait and hope the Emperor keeps their conference brief."

The Thuggee priestess frowned, but nodded slowly.

"Very well," she simply said and returned to her meditations.

Séverin and Dardi exchanged a look, knowing each other's thoughts based on their many years as friends, brothers-in-arms, and unofficially adopted brothers. Neither trusted the Thuggee priestess, but they required her help for the moment.

CHAPTER XLIX

Francis I, first Emperor of the Austrian Empire, was a man of medium size. He had narrow shoulders, a solid frame, and was dressed in a simple, even slightly shabby, brown coat without designation of rank. He had a stern face with high cheekbones, a pointed chin, and kind brown eyes that gazed upon them with interest.

"We learned of your travel through this district and requested you appear before us. You interest us, Baron Vordenburg-Karnstein."

The Emperor spoke German with a smooth Viennese accent, the cadence sounding slightly odd, but quite understandable.

Franz Karnstein clicked his heels softly and bowed slowly. "I cannot imagine why, Majesty. I am simply another citizen of your vast empire."

"Now, now, Baron, no false modesty. You are quite religious according to reports. Perhaps you simply view the world from that view. This is possible, but it does not matter. Our servant in France, the good von Metternich, reported that you rendered some service to the French Emperor. Is this true?"

"Yes, Your Majesty. I was in Paris for the coronation as part of His Holiness's staff. I became embroiled in an affair that involved unholy beings seeking to murder those present. Then, at my request, I took tutelage under Jean-Pierre Séverin, a swordmaster with an expertise in battling the servants of Satan," Karnstein said, bowing again as he completed his explanation.

"Yes, we heard of this Séverin," the Emperor said while sitting on a chair brought over by a silent servant. "A believer in Republican causes. We find that troubling, Baron. Such men brought about the death of our aunt, Marie Antoinette..."

"He does not fight for the cause or involve himself in politics in any manner, Your Highness. Maestro Séverin's

229

only concerns are the teaching of the art of the sword and battling the monsters that plague mankind."

The Emperor studied the young Austrian for a beat and smiled gently.

"We heard that of you, Baron. You reject any involvement in politics, reserving your strength only for holy work. Will this remain so, should we give you permission to marry?"

Karnstein bowed deeply, sensing that a nod would be greeted with disfavor by this ruler. He had learned that during his first audiences with His Holiness and several important Cardinals. The only time he had met the ruler of Austria previously, his grandfather's only instruction had been very simple.

"Stand still, bow when I do, and hold your foolish tongue," the elderly Count Karnstein had growled before his single meeting with Emperor Francis, then ruler of the Holy Roman Empire.

Now, rising slowly, Karnstein kept his head deferentially lowered slightly and said, "I shall never involve myself in politics, Your Highness. It does not suit members of my family. Nor shall I take up regular residence in any of our family's homes. The fear caused by my ancestor's behavior often causes unrest among the people."

The Emperor studied Franz for another minute, then asked, "If we were to send word to you, requesting your aid in duties similar to those you performed in Paris and Naples, would that be politics?"

"No, Your Highness, that is not politics but the saving of souls. I would come as quickly as I could," Karnstein replied.

The Emperor beamed for a moment and then looked to the man in the green jacket.

"Give Baron Karnstein the envelope as our consent in passing through our realm," he said, and added to Franz, "You have our permission to withdraw, Baron. We look forward to a longer meeting in future days."

He waited as the young Exorcist bowed deeply, while Sylvia dropped into a deep curtsey, before striding back into the house. As the door closed behind him, the man in green appeared by their side and handed Karnstein a pair of small envelopes.

"Escort the Baron back to his conveyance and send them on their way, Colonel," he ordered in a nasal voice before sliding away quickly.

Colonel Schwaiger, once again acting as guide, led them through the trees towards their wagon.

"My men will lead you back to the main road. There we must leave you, for our duties lay here," he said before swinging into his saddle a moment later.

Once they reached the main road, Karnstein pulled the envelopes from his tunic and read the first.

"Our consent in the Emperor's name to pass all tolls free of charge and any borders without prejudice. That is kind."

He handed the pass over to Séverin.

"What of the other?" Sylvia asked. "And why did you not introduce me to your king?"

"One does not introduce anyone to a ruler without their consent," Dardi called out over his shoulder as he drove the horses forward. "Once Gâteloup and I stood before the Empress of Russia for three hours as my father spoke to her and her ministers. None looked in our direction."

Karnstein read the second note for a moment and handed it to Sylvia. She scanned the lines several times before exploding with a single loud word.

"*Madonna!*" she said, crossing herself and hugging her fiancée.

"The only letter that could cause such a strong reaction would be a decision by the Emperor regarding your proposed nuptials. So he consented to your marriage?" Séverin asked.

Franz and Sylvia were not listening, by this time, but locked in a tight embrace. They separated reluctantly a minute later, while still holding each other.

Karnstein answered while sounding slightly breathless.

"Yes. I believe he decided in our favor based on two questions."

From the front, Dardi snorted out another laugh and smiled over his shoulder at his daughter and soon-to-be son-in-law.

"I would assume the first was your remaining uninvolved in politics."

"That is correct, Papa. I think that Emperor was relieved we would not take residence in the Karnstein estates," Sylvia said, while grinning back at her father.

The French swordmaster nodded gravely.

"A wise decision. Some families are simply ill-suited for such lives. That sailor I battled, Morley? His family would return their country to feudalism, complete with *jus primae noctis* and serfdom. Keeping such families from power is a gift the English still perform for the world."

"He also asked if we would assist in battling monsters if he so requested. I assented, though did not stress that we would do so for any ruler in need," the Exorcist said. "I think he did not realize the depths of my disinterest in politics."

"We must plan the wedding now," Sylvia said while looking thoughtful. "In Naples, of course."

"Why Naples?" Karnstein asked.

"*Idiota!* That is where I was born!" Sylvia said, pulling away from his arm.

"I know that is where you were born! I asked why that city instead of Styria or Rome? And stop calling me an idiot," he said.

"Then stop acting like one! In a wedding..." and they were off, arguing again and ignoring the triumphant expressions that crossed the faces of Jean-Pierre Séverin and Bartomeleo Dardi.

CHAPTER L

The smugglers' roads proved slow travel for the Ténèbre Brothers and Marguerite Monvoisin. They bypassed main thoroughfares, preferring slower routes, only occasionally approaching small towns. Few people crossed their path throughout the days that followed. The occasional farmer or hunter were but furtive figures who slipped away from sight behind elderly trees and thick brush.

The forest they were passing through appeared almost new, with tall spritely trees, thick bushes and chirping birds above their heads. There was a gentle calm to this region that ignored the witch and her undead minions. The feeling, they later realized, was that their presence was unimportant compared to the majesty of nature.

The Ténèbre Brothers guided their coach silently and changed drivers every few hours. They ignored Marguerite and simply scanned the surroundings with the wary eye of fugitives from justice.

That was well for the satanic priestess, who was still lost in her reveries of days past...

1682, Belle-Île-en-Mer Prison, off the Brittany coast

For Marguerite Monvoisin, life changed as suddenly as her imprisonment had begun the day the raven appeared on her windowsill. The bird, a massive black animal, fluttered a pair of massive wings and settled upon the edge of her small window.

Marguerite, who was asleep, opened her eyes at the movement, and stared dumbly at the bird. The creature stared back, its reptilian gaze somehow feeling almost intelligent. Its eyes moved with careful deliberation over the imprisoned witch in a manner that made her shiver slightly. The reaction was an innate, antediluvian loathing that all humans feel for the cold inhumanity of certain members of the animal kingdom.

"Nevermore," the raven croaked, "have I viewed a creature as pathetic as you, Marguerite Monvoisin. Devotee of demons, knowledgeable witch, poisoner and actress. Yet here you languish, trapped forever in silence until you die of old age, or someone slips poison in your soup."

"You are not a raven," Marguerite said, standing and approaching the bird.

The raven cawed several times, its long beak clacking with each cry.

"I am a raven—and yet, I am not. My real name is Radka and I serve Veselina Dushev. My mistress has an interest in you and may wish your presence in her service. I must discover if your time alone has driven you insane. Are you mad?" the raven asked, fluttering its large wings and landing near the straw pile Marguerite used as her bed.

"No," Marguerite answered, sitting cross-legged upon the stone floor.

"Huh," the raven somehow said, "but you would say that, wouldn't you? At least they gave you a big room. Your friend Marguerite Delaporte's in four paces long and only three wide. That old biddy whines and moans all day long. Another of your sisters, Catherine Leroy, has the same size cell as Delaporte and stares at one wall all day long."

Marguerite shook her head and laughed softly.

"They were weak. Delaporte wanted money, fearful of abandonment. Leroy was a slattern who attracted young wealthy idiots into her bed and suggested they solve their problems with poison."

"And you are a strix," Radka the raven said.

"A strix? Don't you mean a *strigoi*? A witch who serves the dark powers?" she asked.

"Yes," Radka croaked, flying back to the windowsill. "Can you turn into an owl?"

Marguerite waved a finger around the room.

"If I could, would I still be here?"

"My mistress may grant you that power, if she finds you suitable. Expect a visit tomorrow," Radka said, squeezing through the bars.

With a harsh, croaking cry, the raven flew away, vanishing even before Marguerite could pull herself up to the bars. She dropped to the floor and fell onto her pallet, staring at the ceiling.

Have I gone insane? Shall I become one of those poor creatures who speaks to people who are not present? she thought all day and deep into the night.

It was after midnight when her cell creaked open and a figure wrapped in a heavy brown garment stepped inside. A slim, pale hand threw back the heavy hood, revealing a plain square face with sallow skin and a spray of freckles across a long, pointed nose.

The woman standing before Marguerite was about her height with head of thick, curly auburn hair, wide green eyes and thin lips. Her smile was wide, bright, and infectious, transforming her from plain to striking in appearance.

"I am Veselina Dushev and you would be the poisoning witch, Marguerite Monvoisin," she said in heavily accented French. "I watched your mother burn at the stake; it was an ugly, painful death that was boring once the screaming had stopped."

"If you say so," Marguerite said, waiting.

"You met my servant, Radka. She liked you, even though you smell worse than a cesspit. I can free you from this imprisonment, but it will hurt at first. Then you must enter my service forever. Do you agree? I could use a poisoner and you are the prettiest and smartest of your dead mother's organization."

Marguerite thought for a moment and realized she could not lose by accepting. Her soul belonged to Belial and her body languished in durance vile. If she died, her master would have her eternal service sooner rather than later.

"Yes," she said.

Veselina giggled and opened her mouth wide. As swift as a striking serpent, a red streak emerged from her gaping maw. Marguerite felt a sharp pain in her neck and gaped in amazement as the object pierced her flesh.

That was her tongue! she thought as she felt the warm *vitae* spill across her filthy flesh.

The long, crimson tongue retracted back into Veselina's mouth, a single scarlet spot of blood appearing near the corner of her mouth.

"Oooh, you do taste delightful," Veselina said, grabbing the captive witch with a powerful grip.

Marguerite felt herself swooning as the auburn-haired woman leaned forward, lapping the dribbling blood like a cat a saucer of cream. With each drop slurped by the waggling tongue, the young witch felt her body dying and her soul drifting away from her body…

A vampire… Marguerite thought as a gentle blackness drifted over her eyes and her body started to feel heavy.

Her soul slowly fell away from her fleshy prison, falling into Veselina's cavernous form. There were others within the Bulgarian vampire's shell, three women and an elderly man, and they served their mistress without question. The construct known as Veselina Dushev controlled them with threads of dark magic that Marguerite viewed just as her soul joined the terrible being whose power grew with each life she stole.

The vampire appeared larger than everyone and far more beautiful than her actual features showed. Within this construct that held the souls of her victims, Veselina towered above them, resembling an ancient goddess whose power and beauty dominated all present. Her face was no longer a featureless square, but a strong, triangular structure with an aquiline nose and vast, liquid green eyes the color of newly grown grass. Her figure was a perfect hourglass and the toga draped across her perfect body clung to her unblemished flesh like a second layer of silken skin.

"Marguerite Monvoisin, welcome to our gathering! I think you shall emerge from me soon, though you may be shocked by your appearance. This shall ease, in time."

Laughter bubbled to her lips.

"Yes!" a tiny woman with large breasts and the face of a twelve-year-old girl said. "Usually after ten or twelve years!"

The gathered souls howled with laughter for a long time, mockery evident in their mirth.

Marguerite bore their taunts while studying the magic that surrounded the vampire and her followers. That was of great interest to her…

CHAPTER LI

The Austrian countryside was lovely and alternated between the feeling of being in a modern country, and that of an ancient land filled with eldritch oddities. The people ignored the small party and the inns they used as stopping points were congenial enough, if lacking in interest. The food in most was plain, the wines and beers tasty but standard, the people completely disinterested in a passing nobleman and his servants.

"We must only let Franz speak to the people," Jean-Pierre Séverin said as darkness neared the first night. "His accent and behavior will stop any questions. Silence shall serve us best, preventing any unnecessary questions."

The swordmaster's statements proved correct. For days, their occasional encounters with local people and even officials of the military or local governments moved smoothly.

"I will take three rooms for the night with food," Karnstein said every time they stopped in a traveler's inn. "I am Baron Vordenburg and I shall pay now."

The use of his other title was his choice, one he had not discuss with the others beforehand.

"My other name is legendary in these lands," he finally explained. "I should not inconvenience us with anger and fear. We shall encounter enough of that later when we pass through my estates."

Styria was the traditional seat of the Karnstein clan, dating back to either the Roman Emperors Diocletian or Constantine the Great. Related by blood to the Celts and other tribes that inhabited that region, the family possessed an ancient reputation for fierce warriors and black rites that may predate known civilization.

A hilly, ancient land filled with thick forests and pre-Roman ruins, traveling through Styria felt like traveling back to the ancient days when savages still ruled Europe. Though there were towns and cities, as well as many modern conveniences, these additions almost felt intrusive upon this primeval region.

"We are near your lands?" Ishaani asked in English.

"We entered them yesterday," Karnstein replied, nodding towards a distant castle barely visible in the distance. "We shall stay there for the night."

"Is that where you...?" Sylvia asked, touching his hand, hesitant at resurrecting the terrible memories of her fiancé's past.

"Put my mother and ancestress to rest? Yes," he replied in a surprisingly even voice. "The difficulty is not the castle, which is mostly empty now. It will be the villages surrounding it. We must pass through several and head toward the monastery, a short distance from the lands."

Bartolomeo Dardi, sitting in the rear near Ishaani, chuckled. "Allow me to make a prediction... The local inhabitants shall greet us in a manner lacking enthusiasm."

"Correct," the Exorcist replied, adding, "Please stop the wagon so that I may drive."

Séverin did so and the Karnstein took the reins, with the swordmaster at his side.

"I think we shall drive to the nearest tavern, which is owned by the Mueller family," the Austrian said. "They do not like my clan, but are less hostile than the owners of the inn in the town closer to the church. The owner of that business lost his wife and eldest daughter when I was a child."

The tavern in question was a three-story rectangular stone structure with a sign that read *White Stag Tavern* in large Gothic letters. A pretty barmaid opened the large wooden door, her long blond hair and prominent bosom bouncing as she greeted them with a wide, bright smile. The happy look dropped from her face when she saw Karnstein at the reins of the carriage. With a low cry, she fled inside, her high-pitched shrieks audible but incomprehensible from their location.

The door flew open a moment later and a squat man with a round balding head, massive forehead, bushy salt and pepper eyebrows and a long gray mustache waddled outside. He

239

glanced in Karnstein's direction and twisted his meaty hands into tight, white-knuckled fists.

"We have no rooms for the night, Herr Baron!" he said.

Karnstein alighted from the wagon and bowed slightly.

"I did not ask for rooms, Herr Mueller. We only wish food and drink, and for a message to be sent to Father Sandor at the monastery. Once he sends a response, we shall leave."

"We have no..." Mueller said but stopped at a raised hand from the Exorcist.

"Herr Mueller, please spare me your protests at having no food or drink. If you claim that, I will merely pay the messenger and sit in your tavern until Father Sandor either comes to us, or we to him. The only loss to you shall be the price of our meals. Now, lead the way and do as I asked."

Mueller harrumphed and stormed inside, leaving the door open. Karnstein and the others followed, entering a large room with thick, dark wooden beams, metal lanterns, a roaring fire in a nearby fireplace, and a room full of men and women who stared at them in a heavy silence.

They sat at a table near the far wall. The barmaid deposited two bottles of dark wine while staring with wonderment at Franz Karnstein and Ishaani. She fled without a sound, though joined the others staring in their direction.

"Karnstein," a gray-haired man said, "now the deaths will begin again."

"A Karnstein killed my mother," a sharp-faced woman with coiled brown hair and a tight brown dress called out.

"And mine," added her companion, a strong-looking youth with blond hair and a stern, angry expression.

"Is that true?" Sylvia asked the Exorcist.

He nodded and answered, "Possibly. The Karnsteins in this region occasionally return and indulge in their appetites."

"He admits to his evil!" the youth said while slamming his fist into the table. "We should save our families and kill him now!"

Karnstein sighed and placed a musket pistol on the table next to his plate.

"Shall you be the first, Mein Herr?" he said, pointedly. "I have no desire for violence, but if you incite a mob, I shall kill you first."

"He threatened me! You heard it! The Karnstein threatened my life!" the young man yelled while standing and backing away.

"He did! He did threaten Hans's life!" the brown-haired woman screamed.

"Damned Karnsteins!" the gray-haired man said. "You killed my grandmother!"

"That would be Count Stefan Karnstein, yes?" the Exorcist replied. "Very possibly true. I executed him when I was fifteen, while in the service of Lord Inquisitor von Spielsdorf."

That hushed the room, with even the angry young man and his companion blanching at the name Karnstein had just invoked.

Mueller broke the terrified hush.

"You were von Spielsdorf's acolyte? I was there... that could not be you..."

"I wore a hooded white cloak with a red cross on the front. My only adornment was this ring," Karnstein said, lifting Sylvia's hand and showing the crested family ring she always wore, "and a metal cross. My mask was red and I executed the vampire with a cavalry saber. You carried the faggots we piled across his corpse, and Polgármester Steiner lit the flames."

Mueller nodded, his shoulders slumping in obvious relief.

"My apologies, Baron, I did not mean... I... we... have rooms... if..."

Karnstein held up a hand and stopped the flow again.

"Please send word to Father Sandor at the monastery that my party is passing through the region. We require one night in either the castle or the church, and then we shall leave."

Mueller bowed quickly and trotted away, calling out for the pot boy and barking out orders.

"So you are just passing through and leaving the monster behind? Typical Karnstein!" the youth scoffed.

"What monster?" Dardi asked, frowning at the taste of the wine.

"Two girls are missing and then you show up! You brought another vampire and shall leave that monster behind as punishment for hating your damned family!" the youth's female companion said.

Karnstein and the others, save Ishaani. rose, with Séverin meeting Hans's eyes.

"Take us to the scene of the abduction, young man. We hunt and exterminate vampires wherever they hide. If one exists, we shall slay it."

"Fine!" Hans said, turning towards the door. "The site of the tragedy is in Karnstein Woods, a place of true evil!"

CHAPTER LII

Hans and his female companion filed out with the vampire hunters, leading the party to a path near the edge of town. The woods within were high, thick, dark, and choking in their closeness. Only the squawk of large birds broke the silence, and a low buzzing of unseen insects was heard as they passed through the heavy brush.

They walked for twenty minutes until they reached a clearing, turning as they approached its center. Hans smiled, showing his sharp teeth and his companion flashed a similar toothy grin.

"Well, that was entirely unexpected," Séverin sighed in affectation, before glancing about. "Bring out your fellows," he added.

Hans giggled and waved his hand. Three men and four women stepped out from the brush. Each were young, smiling, and flashing their fang-filled mouths, giggling madly.

"The Ténèbre Brothers send their regards," Hans said, rubbing his hands together. "We shall kill you all, hide your bodies, and blame our future slaughters on your family."

Karnstein shot Hans in the face and drew a second pistol.

"You talk too much," the Exorcist said.

But Hans bounded to his feet and made a sound that the other vampires echoed. That serpentine noise drowned out the other murmurs of the forest. The undead creatures slithered forward. They were all young, with plump, well-fed bodies, and clothing that looked expensive but lacking in taste.

"Bullets cannot kill me, Karnstein!" Hans screamed.

His nose was now a gaping crater, caved inward by the musket ball. The flesh reknitted itself slowly, though his formerly handsome face now seemed monstrous.

"No," Karnstein agreed, "but they do hurt a great deal."

He then shot the vampire's female friend in the eye. She screamed and toppled to the sward, climbing to her feet a moment later. Her left eye was now a puckered, gaping hole that leaked viscous ichor as the flesh around it slowly re-formed.

Screaming, the female vampire with one eye charged forward, her black talons poised like claws before her body. She shrieked incomprehensibly through her oversized jaws.

Sylvia stepped forward, drawing the saber strapped to her hip. In one swift motion, she beheaded the attacking vampire and stepped aside as the now-silent skull bounced past her.

The other vampires shrieked like wounded creatures and closed the gap between them and the four hunters. Their inhuman amber eyes narrowed as they panted and snarled with each step.

Séverin lunged forward, his rapier piercing a male vampire's heart. The creature wailed in agony, froze, and fell away, his undead form crumbling a moment later.

"How did you do that?" Hans said. "Nothing can kill the royalty of the night!"

"Royalty of the night? Did he actually call this pack of leeches by a noble title?" Dardi asked, stabbing another male vampire through the heart.

As the vampire expired in the same manner, Sylvia sliced the head from a third.

"He did," Séverin replied. He looked to Hans and said, "Our weapons were blessed by a cardinal and two bishops and bathed in holy water. They are like salt to a slug, instant death to your kind."

Near his side, Karnstein drew a short wooden dagger from under his cloak. He ducked the swing of a female vampire and thrust the sharp wood into her breast. She moaned and fell the ground, the dagger piercing her heart.

Sylvia spotted Hans dashing in their direction and knew he was about to leap upon her fiancé before she could respond. She was correct and the vampire threw the Exorcist to the ground. Snarling like a rabid dog, Hans reared his head back and launched himself towards Karnstein's exposed neck.

A silver object flashed through the air and Hans froze in place. He looked puzzled for a moment as a welter of black blood bubbled from his mouth. Turning his body in confusion, the vampire's head fell from his shoulders and his body fell heavily onto the Exorcist's.

"You are welcome," Ishaani said while retrieving a circular metal object from a nearby tree.

CHAPTER LIII

Jean Ténèbre closed the spyglass and frowned. He climbed down from the top of their latest carriage, a large wooden vessel that creaked and moaned as it rattled along the roads. They bought the object from a salesman in the municipality of Scheifling.

"Drive on, Ange, our attempt has failed," he said, waving his brother forward. "Our enemies slaughtered those idiots with ease."

"You do not appear moved by the death of your fellow undead," Marguerite Monvoisin said.

Jean shrugged and leaned back in his uncomfortable, bouncing wooden seat.

"Why should I care? They were idiot children."

Marguerite did not reply, reminded again that all vampires and undead creatures were beings who were easily despised. She had learned that shortly after Veselina Dushev had consumed her soul with the idea of making her another slave.

Marseilles, 1684

The first time Marguerite Monvoisin returned to the world was a Wednesday, some years after her "death" in prison. Veselina Dushev held her in the dark shell that was her being, leading the taunting of the young witch along with Radka and the others.

"My darling, Marguerite," the vampire said, "it is time that you return to a form of life. Would you like that, my little one?"

"Yes, my lady," Marguerite said.

That was what the other slaves called Veselina, even though she held no nobility within her bloodline. In truth, the vampire was a crass, unlearned fool who enjoyed the trappings of wealth without comprehension of how to live as a member

246

of that class. She spent money on silly objects and expensive clothing, losing interest in each item days or even hours after the purchase.

Marguerite felt a force pulling her from the dark hole that was her home and up into a world of bright light and sound. Overwhelmed, the young witch closed her eyes and placed her hands hard over her ears. The silence helped, as did the slowly leaking light on the edge of her vision.

That was when she realized another sensation, an odd one that she did not understand for several long minutes. It was her hands, or all least what she did not feel beneath the flesh extremities.

Where is my hair? she thought, moving her fingers experimentally across her scalp.

She only encountered soft, warm flesh and no trace of follicles across the expanse. She heard guffaws about her, and she slowly opened her eyes, gazing into the inhuman black eyes of a large, black raven.

"Missing your hair, little girl?" Radka's voice squawked from the bird's beak. "Get used to it!"

"Yes," Veselina said. "You shall never have hair across your skull; that is one of the prices you pay for service. I shall decide your other forms in time. I think you shall be a pretty little parrot some days, or a copy of me… or maybe a cow… I always wanted a pet cow…"

Radka screeched with laughter, but Marguerite held her tongue. She had much to learn from this vampire and her slaves. She spotted the lines of force and realized one touched her, but held no power over her mind.

This Veselina Dushev thinks she controls me, but all she can do is remove me from her empty soul, the satanic priestess thought, while holding her head low and behaving like a whipped dog before a cruel master.

She traveled with the vampire for another month, emerging regularly and behaving as if everything was wonderful.

"Oh, mistress," she said, hugging Veselina's legs, "you honor me so with your gifts. May I serve you in some way?"

The services the vampire sought were usually assistance in discovering her next victim, or cooing over the latest, foolish purchase. Sexually, Veselina only received pleasure when her tongue pierced her victims' necks and she lapped up their scarlet *vitae*. Men, women, children, animals... they were all merely toys she played with like the dresses and hats she purchased with stolen money.

The other slaves inside the vampire were a pathetic lot, chosen almost randomly at first, and later, in the case of Radka and Marguerite, because others of her kind had similar servants. Radka was a seductress, a courtesan who had counted a member of the Russian royal family, a German Prince, two counts, and several politicians and bankers among her lovers. Veselina had stolen the girl when two of Radka's lovers had shot each other in a duel for her favors, both dying from wounds that day.

"Their families," Radka confided in her one day, "were baying for my blood. Our mistress offered me an escape!"

The others were unimportant and easily forgotten; only Radka possessed a clever mind capable of spoiling Marguerite's plans. The young woman might realize the satanic priestess's actions and attack her when most concentration would be required.

That day came after a week's wait within the vampire, with the others celebrating the finding of some toy or book Veselina desired. The vampire summonsed Marguerite and pointed towards a large, wood and brassbound book.

"Read to me, little Marguerite, read to me," Veselina said, reclining upon a long couch covered with red fabric.

She wore a long gown, one suitable for a taller, bustier woman, but ill-fitting on her figure. The folds hung loosely about her torso and she resembled a child trying on her mother's clothing. A rope of brilliant white pearls encircled her neck, falling almost to her waist, adding to the ridiculous image.

"Yes, mistress," Marguerite said.

She read the cover, "*El Cantar de mio Cid… The Poem of the Cid…* Do you speak Spanish, mistress?"

"No, idiot! Why else would I call you forth as my reader!" the vampire said, grabbing an ostrich feather fan and waving the article before her face.

"Give me several minutes, mistress, and I shall translate," Marguerite said.

She began the spell she had careful prepared.

"*Bellum exaudi orationem meam…*" she said, beginning her prayer to her master and seizing control of the black magic within Veselina Dushev.

An hour later, she pushed the lifeless vampire into a trunk and changed into one of the nicer gowns. Veselina Dushev had made a big mistake, stealing the life of Marguerite Monvoisin.

Her power flowed out of her like an uncontrolled river. I became her dam. Now, her power is mine and I shall live without aging forever! Marguerite thought.

She giggled, "I am immortal! How wonderful!"

She found, within a few years, that this belief was not true. Immortality was, in fact, a curse…

CHAPTER LIV

They traveled fast and lighter from that day forth, having realized that the Ténèbre Brothers were ahead of them, or following closely behind. They could not allow those monsters and the crazed witch access to the vampire city of Selene.

"Why does this place exist?" Ishaani asked, echoing the thoughts of several others in the party.

The Thuggee priestess occupied an odd status among their group. She behaved respectfully towards all, but also remained apart. She was often silent, occasionally observing and often whispering prayers in a language none could identify.

"I hear traces of Sanskrit in her words, but the intonation and phrases do not translate into meaning for me," Karnstein once reported.

Her rare questioning always led to silence, followed by a discussion in English. This moment was no different, though the information was of interest to both Sylvia and Franz.

"According to legend," Bartolomeo Dardi answered, "Selene is the location where Lucifer crashed onto Earth after his expulsion from Heaven. From there, he shattered the ground and fell until he reached the fiery pits of Hell."

"The Greeks believed that Selene was the location where Orpheus's descent into the depths of the underworld began," Jean-Pierre Séverin added. "The Romans never bothered explaining the location. They simply ignored the region. There are many theories and no explanations. My teachers, Kronos and Grost, once visited there with an odd doctor whose name I never learned. Grost described the city as dark as night with spiraling towers and minarets overlooking a massive graveyard."

Sylvia frowned and said, "I read there is only one large structure, a vast spiraling temple. Also, that only the vampires of Selene may enter its gates."

"There are ways inside," Séverin said, "but the methods are simply quite difficult. It is the land surrounding the Sepulchre. The area about that region is queer and dangerous, filled with terrible, inhuman animals who hunt those violating their territory."

Those words effectively ended the conversation and the party fell silent. For several days thereafter, discussion of Selene appeared suspended, even after they entered the land of the Bulgars.

The border crossing was swift, though the Ottoman guards they observed stared at them silently with suspicious expressions across their bearded faces.

The land, formerly a hilly terrain filled with small farms and friendly villages, grew wilder and exuded an ancient, antediluvian air. It looked as if they had traveled back into an earlier age, one where savages still ruled the wilderness and civilization was a distant dream.

The hills, though low, were rocky, and odd ruins appeared in the distance. The occasional farmer or inhabitant were squat, powerful-looking people with furtive eyes and dark expressions. The wooded patches looked thick and unpassable, and the few animals they observed stared at them with hostility apparent in their gaze and posture.

"If we meet someone," Dardi said in a hushed voice, "speak either French, German, or Italian. They probably will not understand your words, but the Bulgars only minimally despise the people of those lands. If they say anything to you in Arabic, pretend you do not understand. It is a trick they use for catching Ottoman spies."

"Timely advice," Karnstein said, nodding ahead, "Three horses approach."

"Stop the wagon, Franz," Séverin said, climbing next to him on the driver's bench.

Karnstein obeyed and, a moment later, men swarmed out from the surrounding bushes. They held ancient, heavily inlayed, matchlock rifles and curved swords strapped to their hips. Like the others in this territory, they were short men with powerful bodies, dark hair, and heavy beards. Their clothing varied from modern outfits to the heavily stitched robes of the wealthy Ottomans.

Two of the riders stopped before the wagon's horses, with the third trotting closer. That third rider was a taller man with a straight black, broad shoulders and a blue-black beard streaked with white whiskers. His hooked nose and a scar across his cheek gave him a piratical air.

A burst of laughter boomed out from his great chest. "What have we here?" he said in heavily accented Arabic.

Everyone in the wagon, Ishaani included, understood his words, but everyone feigned ignorance. Dardi tilted his head like a confused dog and glanced around, as if looking for an interpreter.

The other man chuckled and asked in even worse German, "What have we here?"

"We," Karnstein replied in a thicker accent than he normally used, "are traveling through your lands."

"Are you now? My, that is so very kind of you! However, you must pay us a toll, as is the custom," the other said, guffawing again.

"That seems fair. What do we owe you?" Karnstein replied in a mild tone.

The rider considered for a moment and then pointed at Sylvia. "I will take her as payment for passing through my lands."

Sylvia opened her mouth to spit back a threat, but the Exorcist raised a hand slowly. She subsided, though her lovely face appeared murderous.

"No," Karnstein stated, "you shall not touch her for she is my wife. Nor may you harm anyone in our group."

"Oh?" the rider said, moving his horse closer, "You think you can stop me if I take her?"

"Yes," Karnstein replied, raising the musket pistol in his hand and pointing the barrel between the rider's eyes, "I know I can."

The men surrounding the wagon surged forward from all sides, raising their rifles and swords while shouting in their harsh tongue.

The rider raised his hand and glanced about, his eyes flashing. "Sprise! Sprise!' he shouted, bringing them to a halt.

Turning back towards Karnstein, who had not wavered or even glanced in the direction of the other brigands, he studied the young Austrian for several seconds.

"If you pull the trigger, everyone dies," he said.

"You first," Karnstein replied, "then, the two men behind you."

He nodded his head backwards and Sylvia sat upright. A pair of similar pistols now rested in her hands, pointed at the men near their horses.

The rider stared into the cold, icy gaze of Franz Karnstein and then studied the dark-eyed fury that was Sylvia Dardi. A wider smile spread out across his face and he threw back his head and howled with laughter. His men soon joined in, their mirth both genuine and hardy.

"He who pulls out a knife, by knife shall die," he said, waving to his men again. "Any man who touches her or any woman that touches you would die a painful death. A wolf mates once and the pair is forever."

"This is true," Barto Dardi said, "She is my daughter and I think he would fight me for her, even though he would lose!"

This brought another bark of laughter from the rider, who nodded his head sagely.

"I see that, little man. I find you interesting. Come with us for the night and you shall receive the bread and salt of hospitality. I am Krum Karposh, the *maĭstor* of these people. Tell us your story and sleep safe for the night."

"We accept," Séverin said, "We shall honor the obligations of guest to host."

Karposh nodded, laughed again, and took Séverin's extended hand.

"Follow my sons and I."

Moments later, they left the main road for a small track, just wide enough for the wagon. Karposh and the others cantered ahead, but remained in sight as the rumbled down the bumpy road.

"Are we safe?" Karnstein asked.

"Very," Dardi said, "He offered the traditions of hospitality, salt and bread. If he violates those rules, his own people will view him as treacherous."

Séverin nodded while adding, "For our part, we shall not demand anything more than food, shelter, and protection of their home. If someone attacks their camp, we must assist in the defense of their people. When we leave, we shall give Karposh a gift and a symbolic token of our appreciation."

"How do you know this, Papa? Uncle Jean-Pierre?" Sylvia asked.

Dardi smiled and exchanged an amused look with his friends.

"This story begins before Gâteloup and I met. He was in the service of your aunt Sylvia and she brought him to the land of the Bulgars. I was an active youth and my grandfather..."

CHAPTER LV

The horses were dead, the Ténèbre Brothers having driven the animals too hard throughout the day. After a bad stumble, the massive beasts slowed, stopped in place and slowly collapsed. Within ten minutes, both horses gasped, wheezed, and died in the middle of the road.

They were deep in the Bulgar Mountains, once again traveling ancient roads that the vampire and *oupire* knew from their past journeys. This trail was a wide one with the remnants of a stone road beneath a light layer of dirt, dust, and weeds. The trees were sparse and they did not spot any humans, only small animals who had fled upon sight of their carriage.

Marguerite Monvoisin adjusted her wig and held back her impulse at kicking the dead horses or the Ténèbre Brothers.

"What do we do now?"

"I shall run to a village not far from this location. I shall buy or steal one or two animals and we shall continue. I shall return tomorrow night," Jean said as he dropped from the carriage.

He turned towards the north and glanced over his shoulder.

"Ange, search the area for people. Feed on them if you like. Madame Strix, please remain in the carriage."

With that said, Jean vanished from sight. Ange turned his head left and right and sniffed the air experimentally.

"Goodbye," was all he said before striding purposefully back down the road.

Paris, 1744

Marguerite stared at her hand and wept, realizing the finger was growing back again. The heavily engraved knife clattered to the floor as she pressed her palms over her eyes and sobbed at her lot.

Immortality, the most terrible curse imaginable, she thought as she fell to the floor and wept.

At first, upon seizing control of her vampiric mistress, she had rejoiced in her new life. She lived, breathed and could walk the Earth a free woman. With the help of various wigs, she could move freely in society and live a contented life.

Until the power emanating from Veselina Dushev weakened... The young witch's firm body had slowly withered inch by inch. Her hands had grown clawlike and each day, deep runnels and lines had spread across her face and body. Within two weeks, Marguerite had turned into an aged, bent crone. capable of movement only with a pair of sturdy canes.

In desperation, the dying witch sought new remedies, brewing noxious potions, praying to mighty Belial and even attempting a grand summonsing.

Seated on the floor, using the last of her special black candles, she uttered a dark spell, seeking an ancient and terrible demon. A pot filled with blood from a dozen dead doves lay in the center of the circle at the center of the empty chamber.

"Marbas, mighty one, Great President of Hell, thirty-six legions of demons, heal me or give me answers to my plight," she prayed.

Within the pentagram appeared a puff of smoke, followed by a flame that grew wider, yet exuded no heat. As the fire vanished, a vast lion sat within the circle. The beast, even seated, was over eight feet tall and covered in black, tawny fur that rippled with massive thews.

"Thou summons me, witch, and unliving being. I cannot heal thee, for you have no life within your shell," Marbas said in a voice that sounded terrifyingly human. "Thou did ask for answers, and that you shall receive. Your undead sire dies faster than thee, witch. You leave her unfed and her power waxes. She will not die, but shall remain a living corpse. You shall wither further and fall into dust, yet never die."

"How may I heal the vampire?" Marguerite asked, "and how may I be free of her?"

"To the first, two methods. You may return to her home in the Sepulchre, a place called Selene by the mortals. There, in that great city of endless night, the dark priests of the temple can place a key in her heart and repair her body. The second, you can feed her blood. She shall grow stronger, but never rise unless you remove thy wards and spells."

The barked out a laugh that was a terrible combination of a human giggle and a feline purr.

"As to freedom, unliving witch, there is none for thee. No death for thee. Vampires of the Sepulchre steal souls and hold them within their being. A living death is thy fate until the stars grow dark and silence sits upon the universe."

Marbas then vanished from sight.

Marguerite obeyed, pushing a drunken porter into the coffin and watching as the vampire fed upon his soul. By the end, nothing remained of the man, not even his clothing, and the witch found her body young, strong, and lovely again.

She then spent years testing the truth of the demon's words. She stopped eating or drinking; yet nothing happened to her body. Soon she forgot even the act of feeding herself. Marguerite lived two months in that manner, later discovering food and drink were mere ashes in her mouth. Flavors vanished and soon she gave up that piece of humanity.

Then she tested her body, attempting every manner of death. She walked into the Seine and sat on the bottom for two hours, returning to the surface unhurt. She leaped from the top of a four-story building in the middle of the night, shattering her bones and falling unconscious, but by morning, her body was normal, unharmed by the horrific pain.

I tried burning, hanging, cutting open my wrist and neck... nothing worked... she thought in despair.

The final act was attempting the slow removal of body parts and hoping the body would not heal small injuries. It was her last hope, but once again, she failed.

That was when, after ceasing her sobs, she thought back to the final words Marbas had said to her that fateful day.

"...The living death is thy fate until the stars grow dark and silence sits upon the universe..."

That was when the satanic priestess known as Marguerite Monvoisin made her decision, one that led her to the ancient, moribund satanic circle and Abraham Hyacinthe Anquetil-Duperron.

"I must exist until the end of time," she vowed as she watched her finger reform, "then I shall destroy all life. There must be a way..."

CHAPTER LVI

Krum Karposh's camp was only half an hour away and was located in the ruins of an ancient hill fort built by either the Greeks, the Macedonians, the Romans or the Goths. The Bulgar leader did not know, though Jean-Pierre Séverin and Bartolomeo Dardi spotted traces of all four empires as they approached.

The people, about forty families, lived in long one-story cottages with stonewalls and newly thatched roofs. Narrowly placed homes lined a central square, revealing passages between the residences which only one man could pass.

"These people live in war," Ishaani said. "Towns to the north arrange their homes this way, forcing invaders into tight passages."

"People used to raiders either accept their fate or learn methods of fighting efficiently," Dardi replied as they stopped and alighted from their vehicle.

Karposh barked out several phrases in his language, receiving a roar or laughter from the people, who immediately went back to their work. Those passing smiled upon the group, but did not linger.

Karposh clapped Séverin and Dardi on the back and said, "You have freedom of the camp; you are my guests. Do not venture past the castle, or you shall fall outside my protection. Now, come with me and I shall give you bread, salt and much, much more!"

The bandit chieftain proved an excellent host, sitting them in places of honor and feeding them bread, salt, fresh game meat, and thick, strong, dark ale. He proved a congenial host, full of amusing tales and jokes.

"…and I told him, 'You may be an Ottoman, but your wife thinks you're one of the eunuchs'!" he said, causing laughter from everyone, save Ishaani who did not understand German.

Dardi recounted an amusing tale of a fisherman, a priest, an escaped convict and a blind man that added to the laughter. It was a pleasurable evening and, by the end, most were a little dizzy from the heavy drinking.

"Now, my friends," Karposh said in a softer voice, "we have laughed and drank and feasted together. I ask you only one question: where do you head? South or east?"

"South-east," Séverin answered.

"Hmm," the powerful Bulgar said, "then you must not take the main roads. That shall lead you far west and then back towards your destination. We shall show you faster road, a secret highway known by few. You shall ride on it for two days before you come to a fork in the road. Take the gentle path and you shall join the main highway in half a day. It shall save you four days travel. Do not take the dark road! You shall know of what I speak when you view that path. All who head down that track vanish forever!"

"We thank you, *maĭstor* Krum Karposh," Séverin replied. "You are the best of hosts and you honor us with your kindness and wisdom."

Karposh bowed, clapped the dour swordmaster on the back again, and left the room. Soon four young men appeared each carrying piles of straw that they arranged into pallets. Night was falling and room, unlit save by a brazier, grew dimmer with each passing moment.

"They only made four beds," Franz Karnstein said in French.

"*Idiota!*" Sylvia replied, taking his hand and pulling him to the largest straw pile. "We are married. They honor us by giving us one bed!"

"Hmm," the young Austrian said, realizing his mistake. "It appears calling me an *idiota* is correct this time."

"It is correct every time!" Sylvia said. "*Idiota!*"

"It is not, and stop calling me an idiot!"

"*Vai a letto ora, idiotas,*" Dardi said as he collapsed into his pallet and closed his eyes.

"What does that mean?" Ishaani asked.

"Go to bed idiots," Sylvia replied, pulling Franz down onto their pallet.

The next morning, they rose with the sun, meeting Karposh and his men as they stepped from their chamber. The massive bandit scratched his heavy beard unconsciously as he stretched and yawned.

"You do not rise like soft city folk at least," he said. "Do you know there are city men who do not wake until the sun is overhead?"

The parting that followed was short, with a quick flowery speech by Karposh thanking them for accepting his hospitality. Dardi stepped forward with an equally elaborate, but quick reply, and bowed deeply towards the bandit chieftain as he backed away.

Karnstein stepped forward, a flat wooden box in hand, and bowed to Krum Karposh as he handed the powerful man the item.

"As a thank you for your kindness and protection, we would give this to you as a sign of respect."

Karposh's craggy face split into a wide smile and he nodded in the slow, calm manner of a nobleman receiving a tribute from a serf. Tossing open the box, his eyes widened at the artistically crafted matched dueling pistols nestled within the case.

"I accept with gratitude. If you come through this territory again, you must spend more than a day with my people. We will show you sights you cannot imagine! For now, safe travels and remember what I said of the path!"

With a wave and a cry of farewell from Krum Karposh and his people, the vampire hunters left the Bulgar village behind. They rumbled along, Dardi at the reins with Ishaani at his side.

"Those guns," Sylvia said. "Those were the ones you used as a child?"

Karnstein nodded. "Yes, those are the weapons I used that day when I slew Mircalla and Lena."

Séverin clapped his student on the back. "Giving up past pain is never easy, Franz. Happily, you progress forward."

"Unlike when I met you and you behaved like an angry priest with saltwater in your veins," Sylvia said. "Now, we must discuss your choice of clothing. You still dress like an *imprenditore di pompe funebri!*"

"I do not dress like an undertaker…" Karnstein retorted and they began arguing again.

CHAPTER LVII

Ishaani sighed inwardly as the lovers began bickering again. She found them wearisome, always debating and then ending their debate with passionate embraces. The two older men either ignored the cycle or found the behavior amusing, neither finding the actions dull.

These whites are different from the English, she thought, having observed them for days now. *More polite towards me and others openly. The difference is larger, since they are an odd group.*

Glancing at Bartolomeo Dardi, who tunelessly sang an odd song as he steered the cart, Ishaani reflected on the four Europeans.

The little one, Dardi, behaves as if life is one large jest. Yet he fights as a warrior born, singing and laughing constantly... The tall one, Séverin, is like my grandfather, a supremely skilled combatant with much knowledge. Yet he appears sad and hides a secret pain... The loud woman, Sylvia, nearly beat me in battle... I did not expect such skill in a white woman. She reminds me of Belawadi Mallamma, who fought with the Marathas, leading an army of her fellow women. I do not like her, but I respect this Sylvia... As to her cold-eyed Franz, I like him least. He has a darkness within him, like a holy man who takes the path of the Aghori, using the power of evil and death in hopes of protecting the world from worse.

This much was her opinion, though she did recognize a few truths. First, they did not trust her because Séverin and Dardi possessed some knowledge of the religion and practice of the Thuggee. This did not mean they despised her, as had the disgusting Morley. They simply did not trust her motives.

Second," she thought, *they have no interest in betrayal. They seek the preventing of the return of Raktabīja and shall fight for the destruction of our mutual enemy. And finally, they*

263

do not know they must die when this battle is complete and I hold the scroll of Raktabīja.

This was a truth Morley had not realized either. Oh, the temple would supply him with the wealth promised in India. They would bestow jewels upon him, gold, and baubles to his heart's content. Then, shortly after he returned to his cold, wet land, Ishaani or one of the other Thuggee would strangle him and prevent knowledge of the parchment spreading beyond the temple.

Ishaani held no guilt for this position, knowing the path of her religion was a lonely one.

We protect the world from demons and the return of Great Kali to the Earth. The world does not love us, but we are a necessary force.

Having reflected enough, Ishaani said a brief prayer to the goddess, grateful the pair behind her were no longer yelling.

Om Maha Kalyai, Ca Vidmahe Smasana Vasinyai, Ca Dhimahi Tanno Kali Prachodayat... she thought as the wagon rumbled along the road.

CHAPTER LVIII

"Dead horses on the side of the road," Bartolomeo Dardi announced, pointing ahead.

"How recent?" Jean-Pierre Séverin asked, sliding forward and peeking his head out from the back.

The Neapolitan did not reply, but pulled their beasts to a halt and hopped out, his smallsword in hand. He sniffed the horses, gently touching the creature's legs with his sword tip, and returned after cleaning the blade with a cloth.

"The smell and stiffness tell me half a day at most," he said, sending the horses racing forward.

"Papa, you fear the Ténèbre Brothers left the poor animal dead by the road?" Sylvia asked while holding tight to the side of the bouncing wagon.

"Yes!" he replied. "The undead forget that the living require rest and food. Killing horses through neglect is their way!"

"Let us not kill our own animals in our haste," Séverin said as the fast ride continued for several minutes.

Dardi eased the blowing horses back to a slow trot, nodding to his friend.

"Too right, Gâteloup!"

He then asked the Thuggee in English, "Is the ceremony for summonsing this demon a long one?"

Ishaani shook her head and said, "No, a few hours under the correct conditions. The location must be a place of ancient death and pure darkness, and then the proper sigils are inscribed with blood and ashes. After correctly completing the drawings, the witch must read the spell three times. Then Raktabīja shall return and we will all die."

"Pure darkness and death? That means Selene," said Séverin. "The city is invisible unless one catches a glimpse of it by chance. Then it appears different to all. Entry is barred by ancient magic, but we shall find a way."

"How can you be sure?" Karnstein asked. "What little I learned from you and Sylvia, that city is unpassable, save for vampires."

The swordmaster shook his head slowly.

"You forget, two of my teachers entered the city. There are methods of entry—the trek is simply quite difficult. The Lord shall provide a method, Franz."

Karnstein closed his eyes and prayed silently for several moments. He then performed the sign of the cross before kissing the plain metal cross he always wore around his neck.

The day passed and they traveled until the horses required food and rest. There were no signs of other humans along their trail, nor hint of another wagon along the trail. Sleeping in shifts, the vampire hunters and the Thuggee priestess passed the night with scant conversation. An indefinable tension had entered their group, with even Sylvia and her fiancé refraining from their normally loud arguing.

Dardi attempted a song in hopes of lightening the mood, but stopped before he even reached the chorus. Sleep came fitfully for all that night, without need of waking those assigned to guard duty.

A second day also passed much in the same way, with an equally strained group sitting silently and only speaking when the need arose. Even the dour Séverin appeared tense as he took his turn driving the horses down the deserted path.

"No signs of life," he eventually said. "Our quarry may be moving at the same horse-killing pace."

Nobody speculated on this statement, even after he stopped the wagon for the night. While Dardi and Karnstein fed and rubbed down the horses, and Sylvia built a fire, Ishaani sat down and brooded.

"I feel," she said, "a heaviness in the air. As if we were in the monsoon season back home, and I fear a terrible storm is coming..."

Sylvia glanced over her shoulder and studied the Indian woman. Detecting no humor or sarcasm, she tossed a few sticks on the fire and turned in Ishaani's direction.

"I feel it too. Though not as a storm, but as if we were in a funeral procession for a loved one. A weight bears me down and makes even thinking difficult."

Dardi dropped next to his daughter and nodded, no laughter in his face or bulging eyes.

"I feel the same, though not as you two do. It is as if I were sinking in sand and my limbs are struggling without hope of pulling me higher. Thinking is difficult… Even breathing is difficult…"

"What of you, *genero*?" he asked as Karnstein joined them. "Do you feel the weight of darkness and doom upon your soul?"

The Exorcist, who took Sylvia's hand, replied, "Every second of every minute, of every hour, of every day…"

Séverin clapped his hands together, a sound closer to that of a tree limb snapping than applause.

"*Pardieu!* We chase a witch, a vampire, and a ghoul, and now feel darkness and impending doom. How can the two not be related?"

Karnstein nodded slowly and said, "Possibly true. A subtle curse that slows one's down and weakens one's resolve. I shall see if I can lift it…"

He closed his eyes, prayed for several moments and uttered a series of sounds that grated upon the ears. When his eyes opened, his normally blue orbs now pulsed with silver energy.

"*Arre Yaar!*" Ishaani said, leaping backwards with a knife in hand. "What is happening?"

"My *fidanzato* is talented," Sylvia said. "Now, *stai zitta!* He is working."

"*Ach du lieber Himmel!*" Karnstein said. "The void… We travel into the void!"

267

CHAPTER LIX

As Franz Karnstein opened his eyes, the world transformed before him. Now he viewed all life as patterns in a vast skein, a webway that existed throughout the world and connected all beings to the vast, infinite universe.

People and animals appeared as flickering flames of energy, their aura transformed by their choices in life, and the emotions that ran through their mind, body, and soul. Sylvia always appeared to him as a being of brilliant, intense light, chased with blue and red stripes of emotions. Bartomeleo Dardi's energies were also blue, but possessing a lighthearted glow that was not merely an act for the world. Jean-Pierre Séverin's was grayer, as dour as his public persona, but with an inner illumination hidden beneath the cloudy outer shell.

The Thuggee priestess Ishaani's was the oddest of all. There was light and darkness filling her being, an inner war that she did not realize existed within her mind and spirit.

She sees her motives as good, though her actions are evil... much like me, but darker... he thought.

Then Karnstein lifted his vision higher, allowing more of the greater world into his mind. A thin dark cloud floated above them like a noxious, infectious mist. A dark power existed within, filled with a corrupting power that sapped the light from everything it touched.

Forcing his spirit through the dark cloud, he observed a miniscule tendril of power that flowed into the vast webway of life. Following this strand, he spotted the source in the distance, a single being using a sleeping demoniac creature as a source of horrific black magic.

"I see you," the bald witch said, though her words were mere echoes with little connection to Karnstein.

He did not reply but opened his mind to the even greater scope of all life. This was dangerous, a risk that could consume his mind and soul instantly. Vast ancient powers of darkness and light drifted through the cosmos and, once at-tracted to a tiny human energy spark, often sought the mortal soul as a minor extension of their greater being.

Once in Naples, the only reason he had survived an en-counter with such an ancient horror, his mind remaining intact, was because Sylvia's intervention had rescued him from being consumed by that fiend.

Opening his mind to his full surroundings horrified Karnstein in a manner that he had not imagined. Beyond the witch and her dark energy was something that filled him with a terror that shook his very soul.

This was because what lay in the distance was pure noth-ingness, a vast void without any traces of life or light. Within this eternal murk were beings, some as tiny as ants, others as vast as cities, moving about and staring inward towards their home. Occasionally a terrible eye emerged, an immense orb of negative magic seeking the light that existed outside the terri-ble, infinite nothingness.

"*Ach du lieber Himmel!*" Franz exploded.

Sylvia's voice, drifting from somewhere, pierced the veil and rose to his unlistening ears.

"…Franz… pull… away… come… me…" her words said with increasing volume.

Looking away from the terrible void, Karnstein turned himself away and pulled himself back into his own body. Just before he returned to the meaty shell that was his body, he stopped and examined the thin corrupting cloud above their heads.

This I can defeat, he thought, feeling stronger for the moment.

Reaching into himself, he uttered the ancient Sumerian spell that empowered him against demons and black magic.

"*DALKHU TARU SERU ESERU ETUTU INA ETUTI ASBU DARISAM!*"

He felt the powerful eldritch energies flow through his body.

The silver light struck the dark mist and expelled it, destroying the corruption and shattering the strand from which it had emerged. A pitiful wail sounded in the distance, a thin cry like a dying animal which vanished in an instant.

Karnstein returned to his body and collapsed, feeling the horrific sensation of a soul confined by a prison of flesh and bone. As always, he felt horrified by this experience, then reasserted his control over himself and recalled the necessity of breathing.

The needle pinprick of a blade point touched the side of his neck.

"Prove to me that you are my Franz," Sylvia said.

Karnstein slowly opened his eyes, the glare of the fire and the stars hurting his eyes.

"The first time we met, I beat you in a duel with swords," he muttered.

The dagger's point vanished, and Sylvia dropped to her knees and hugged him tight for a moment. Then she slapped him behind the head with a hard, calloused palm.

"*Idiota!* You only won that duel because you shocked me with what you said."

"I still won—and stop calling me an idiot," he replied.

"Then stop acting like one!" she said, and they embraced, holding each other with an intensity whose fierceness was inexplicable to all save each other.

CHAPTER LX

Marguerite Monvoisin shrieked and collapsed, her body completely devoid of even the slightest trace of strength. Ange and Jean Ténèbre, who were standing a distance away with the horses, exchanged a look and tied the animals to a nearby tree. Then they ran to the side of their employer, spotting her crumpled form laying near her coffin altar.

"The silver light," she muttered, "the silver light…"

Ange turned her over and recoiled at the sight that greeted his unbelieving eyes. Marguerite's black wig slipped from her head, revealing a wrinkled, wizened, shrunken skull whose skin resembled a rotting apple transforming into dust. Her hands and neck were mere withered sticks that looked as if a sharp wind would shatter them into tiny shards, and her eyes were sunken and turning a urine-colored yellow with each passing second.

"The light… burned… help…me…" she rasped, her voice dry and barely audible.

Jean sniffed the air and frowned, shaking his head slowly.

"I smell no humans nearby. Only creatures whom I cannot understand. These lands are no longer as I remember, Ange."

Ange sniffed too, and glanced about, viewing their dark wooded surroundings. He shuddered briefly and looked away from the near corpse in his arms.

"We left the main road five hours ago. If one of us goes back, perhaps we shall find traces of a human, or at least an animal. I smelled the blood of the living before we chose this path."

Jean nodded and opened his mouth in response, only to stop from a fierce look from his vampire brother.

"I shall go, Jean, and bring back living beings. I cannot promise humans, but they shall be alive when I return."

Jean shook his head and crossed his arms across his chest.

"I should retrieve the living, Ange. They hold no appeal to me. Your needs are only fulfilled by warm blood. We cannot risk the death of Strix because you are overcome by hunger…"

Ange lowered the shriveled form of Marguerite and rose, baring his sharp teeth. He held a small sharp knife in his hand and reared back, his shoulders hunching and hooding his skull like a vast, pale, serpent.

"No! I must go! I cannot spend one more moment in the company of this failing corpse!"

Jean, who was crouching himself, revealed his jagged, ragged talons, then froze, considering the words from his brother.

He fears the living death Strix is undergoing. If he does not feed on blood, will he wither and fall into dust? Would I, too, if I do not feast upon the dead? he thought.

"Very well, Ange. But please be quick and bring back whatever you sensed," Jean said, withdrawing his claws.

Ange straightened and his beautiful face resumed its normally falsely angelic persona. He returned the knife to his sleeve and raised a hand in farewell.

He ran away, running faster than any man, but not at his maximum speed.

He is not running as fast as he could. He doesn't place himself at risk of growing hungry. I underestimated him again, Jean thought, retrieving a blanket for the apparently dying Strix.

Jean Ténèbre the *oupire* did not perform this simple act of kindness out of any respect or friendship for the witch who employed him and his brother. He honestly did not care if she lived or died, though the money she gave them was impressive and secured some loyalty. If this shrunken creature died, his only feeling would be anger that she did not gain them entry into Selene.

The Sepulchre, the dark city where Ange and I received our curse. The city to which we owe a debt of blood and death. Strix must live so that the Vampire City of black jasper falls, he thought, while slowly building a fire for his employer.

CHAPTER LXI

"If I may interrupt?" Bartolomeo Dardi asked, rolling his eyes and grinning for the first time in two days, "what did you see?"

Ishaani, who still crouched at a distance with a knife in hand asked, "What did you do? Your eyes glowed like an *asura*'s!"

"He is not a demon, Thuggee," Séverin said, waving the knife away. "He is an exorcist... one who fights demons."

Ishaani's eyes narrowed and she slowly nodded.

"Then you could use such power against Raktabīja should he return to our world again?"

Karnstein snorted and rolled his eyes.

"Most assuredly not. A being, such as the one you told us is far beyond my talents. A creature like that one is, I imagine, as dangerous as a fallen angel or a demon prince, and would find my attempt only mildly irritating."

"But you said..." Ishaani said, returning her knife to her belt.

"...That I am an exorcist? Yes, that I am. But I am also a human. I cannot contend with beings whose magnitude of power is incomprehensible to the mind of any living being," Karnstein said, his voice weary. "When a demon inhabits a human body, even a dead one, they are weakened and less powerful than they are outside of a body. An exorcist can expel them back to their world, destroying the connection between Hell and Earth. They cannot exist on this world without possession, I do not know why. This is simply a fact. But if somehow a demon, a fallen angel, or even one of the Lord's own angels, were to manifest in our world, they would hold power capable of destroying cities,"

"Sodom and Gomorra..." Sylvia said.

Karnstein nodded once.

"Yes, exactly. The angels destroyed these two cities in one night and turned Lot's wife into a pillar of salt for gazing upon their mission. This *Raktabīja*—did I pronounce that word correctly? Thank you, I am glad—is as terrible as those I mentioned. If you need a fuller comprehension, here is the analogy my master taught me when I was a child. You are sitting on the ground and a singular ant crawls upon your hand. The tiny pincers in the creature's head clamp onto your skin. It is a mild irritant and you brush it away... perhaps gently and grant the ant life... perhaps roughly out of anger... or perhaps slowly and torture the tiny life for pleasure... I am that small ant, tinier than a grain of sand. Your demon is a man, perhaps one the size of Paris, or some other large city."

Ishaani sighed and closed her eyes.

"I shall pray to Samhara Kali, she who is destruction to all who contend with her power. For if an expeller of demons cannot defeat the *Raktabīja*, we must prevent the return of *He for whom each drop of blood is a seed.*"

She walked away behind the wagon and vanished from view. No sound emerged from her location and none followed in her path.

"That was the longest speech I ever heard you make, *genero*," Dardi said and laughed. "Now, what did you see?"

Karnstein looked up from his seated position, his eyes bleak but controlled.

"First, I found a spell that sat over us. Maestro Séverin's belief was correct; the witch had cursed us with her power. I found her, but in doing so, I spotted... I viewed... nothing... but emptiness..."

"Explain, if you can, Franz," Séverin interjected.

Sylvia placed an arm around the young Exorcist, who was shivering slightly from the memory.

"I viewed... it was darkness, an infinite pit of nothingness... but there were beings who lived in that horrible place... some gazed out, most did not... I cannot explain, but it was as bleak a place as any I viewed since I took on this... It was not as deadly as when I looked upon that fiend in Naples, but I fear we approach that... that... emptiness..."

He closed his eyes, shivering slightly again.

Dardi and Séverin exchanged a look and both swordmasters nodded after a moment. They sat down by the fire and Séverin pulled out a leather flask. Taking a quick drink, he handed the container to Karnstein.

"Take a drink," he said, "that is very good brandy and it will brace you a little. Once we each take some in, Barto and I shall explain what you viewed."

Karnstein took a small gulp and winced at the taste before passing the flask to Sylvia. She swallowed a larger amount and appeared neither disgusted nor interested in the alcohol. Dardi emptied the remainder in a quick pull and licked his lips.

"Ah, refreshing! French wines are acceptable, though Neapolitan vineyards are superior. However, no other country produces brandy so perfectly as your people, Gâteloup!"

"Agreed on the brandy, we shall discuss the wine another day. You were wrong when we were children; that has not changed since you grew an inch or two," Séverin said.

The two old friends exchanged an amused look and then resumed their neutral expressions.

"What you viewed, Franz," the swordmaster continued, "was the city of Selene. It can be nothing less than the ancient city of vampires. Selene is said to be a vast city clouded in darkness. Grost said the streets and buildings are black jasper and the very air feels heavy and unnaturally still..."

"Imagine walking in an endless graveyard," Grost had said all those years ago, "where each step brings you to another funerary procession filled with mourners and painful gloom. Now picture a city filled with spiraling towers, some that resemble Ottoman minarets... others the magnificent onion shaped towers of Muscovy... that is what I saw... What about you, Kronos?"

Kronos, the aging swordmaster, tapped his pipe empty for a moment and then slowly refilled the bowl with his large, dexterous fingers.

"I saw nothing save an endless graveyard. There was one building only. It stood in the center. A white stone roof with white marble columns leading to an arena or amphitheater," he said as he relit his pipe.

"That was a long speech for Captain Kronos," Séverin said. "He could go days without saying more than ten words."

"My great grandfather told my grandfather, who told told my father who told me of Selene," added Dardi. "He went there seeking a vampire who had stolen the soul of his half-brother. I do not know how he entered it, but Padrone described Selene as a city of darkness and emptiness. No other life stirred, save the vampire woman whom he had chased into that terrible place. Only small buildings, each the size of a large coffin standing upright."

"I find this confusing. Is it a city of mosques and minarets? Russian shaped towers or emptiness, save a Greek theater?" Karnstein asked.

"We do not know," Séverin admitted. "Perhaps all, perhaps none. The only consistency I ever discovered in my research of Selene is that there is a white columned building in most accounts. That may be the location of greatest importance in the city."

"A city we cannot see and cannot enter," Sylvia said dryly. "If we told this tale to anyone, save in silly penny tract fiction, they would confine us in a home for the insane."

"True," Séverin said. "However, they would probably do that for any of our many adventures."

Dardi laughed and said, "Such as the time we battled a warlock who stole living bodies of beautiful, wealthy people in hopes of taking over their life of luxury and sex. This was in Bremen, when Gâteloup and I were fifteen and assisting my Papa in a mission…"

CHAPTER LXII

Ange Ténèbre returned the next morning with an unconscious elderly man under one arm and a small pig under the other. Jean smiled at his brother, nodding as the vampire approached.

"Well done, brother. Perhaps that shall be enough for Strix's continued existence," he said, dusting the seat of his pants.

Ange preened slightly as he walked over to the coffin Marguerite Monvoisin used as her altar. Kicking open the lid, he gazed down at the skeletal creature that lay within. Though a vampire of considerable age, he felt an acidic tang rising in his throat at the sight before his undead eyes.

The body was in the form and shape of a woman, but that was where the similarity ended. The monstrosity's skin was gray, gnarled, and covered in vast puckered sores that wept viscous yellow and green puss. The hands were misshapen and fused into three bloated, wart-covered digits. The claws on each finger appeared reptilian rather than mammalian in origin, and shimmered like glass in the light.

But it was its face that truly revolted Ange and made him wince when it came into sight. The head was round and there were no features left. Instead, there was a round puckered hole that gaped and quivered, while a long forked black tongue slithered across the unyielding flesh, spattering milky white fluid with each movement.

He dropped the pig within the coffin; the animal bleated once as the terrible tongue wrapped itself around its torso. Its pointed ends thrust through the animal's head, killing it instantly.

Ange closed the lid as the bloody carcass fell across the body and pieces of it vanished within the cavernous hole in the skull. He glanced towards Strix's prone form and his eyes narrowed.

"Does she look... fuller than before?" he asked.

"I believe so," his brother the *oupire* replied.

Marguerite did indeed look less like the dying body of a ninety-year-old spinster than she had moments earlier. Her face appeared slightly fleshy and her neck did not resemble a dried stick covered by a layer of wrinkled, withered, flesh.

The Ténèbre Brothers waited another hour and then simultaneously glanced at the coffin.

"Your turn," Ange said. "I fed it last time."

There was firmness in his tone and a glint in his eyes that exuded a willingness for violence should this become a point of contention. Jean breathed heavily through his nose but rose and picked up the unconscious peasant in one hand while approaching the casket.

Opening the lid with his hand, he groaned at the horrific sight that lay within. As always, the skeletal form bore no trace of the previous feast, nor did the creature had regained any semblance of humanity. As always, Jean's keen eyes sought out the round hole—a mark of all the vampires of the Sepulchre.

That is where the dark priest inserts a key and turns, saving the vampire from death. I do not understand these creatures, he thought.

Turning his head away, Jean Ténèbre tossed the unconscious farmer into the casket and swiftly slammed the lid shut. He still heard the tearing of the meat and the bubbling of the fluids, as well as a noise that resembled a leechlike slurping.

Backing away, the *oupire* dropped next to his brother and observed Marguerite. Before their eyes, her body reformed, growing firmer, stronger and younger. By the end of the next hour, she resembled a girl of about twenty, though she remained completely bald.

"The silver light," she said, sitting upright, then touching her face and chest. "Oh!"

"Ange saved you," Jean said as the witch gazed upon their seated forms. "He fed the vampire and returned you to your human form. Now, what silver light? We viewed no light save the stars above our heads when you screamed."

Marguerite groaned and covered her face with her narrow, long hands.

"I placed a curse on our enemies... a minor one that fills them with sadness and weakness. It would have slowed their progress. But the Karnstein spoke ancient words and destroyed my spell with a silver light... it burned..."

"Hmm," Jean said, rubbing his chin. "That is a story unlike any I have ever heard. Whoever heard of silver light as a weapon? Ange?"

The vampire shook his head and said, "Never. Flames of red, blue, green, or yellow, yes. Golden light like the sun, too. But silver? Never."

The Satanic witch located her wig and carefully fitted the article in place.

"I will not place myself in danger from that one a second time. Now, we must proceed. Our enemies are following us to Selene."

"We must walk from here, Strix," Jean said. "The horses shall not walk one step further. When we tried, they rolled their eyes in terror and foamed at the mouth."

Marguerite stared at the placid animals who stood facing away from the road, slowly chewing on some grass. Neither appeared crazed, however both never once looked towards the direction of Selene.

"We must bring the coffin and the skull of *Raktabīja*. How shall we transport it?"

"On our shoulders, of course," Jean said.

CHAPTER LXIII

It was midday when they reached the abandoned carriage and their horses came to a full stop. The beasts whinnied reared, bucked, and backed away from the road ahead. From a visual point-of-view, none could blame the poor animals.

The road ahead was, as Krum Karposh hinted, darker, and held a sinister quality that caused a shudder among the vampire hunters. The thick trees that lined it were tall, yet none held leaves of pines needles. Furtive creaking and chittering sounds drifted in their direction, and the bones of small animals lined the brush near their position.

"No birds or squirrels or any other forest creature," Bartolomeo Dardi said in a whisper.

Somehow his soft speech felt correct. Although they were on the edge of this wild zone, there was a forbidding atmosphere that made them feel like intruders. Yet none suggested they should turn back.

Without discussion, the group undertook the necessary steps. Dardi and Karnstein led the horses back several yards away, near a grassy sward and a small brook. Séverin filled packs with food and flasks of water while Sylvia and Ishaani removed the weapons from a heavy chest.

Within half an hour, they took the first steps into the forbidding forest, their shoulders hunched slightly from the weight of supplies and weapons as well as the dark road.

"How far is the walk to Selene?" Karnstein asked after silent hour.

"Half a day by horse, I believe. Perhaps one by foot," Séverin replied.

His answer did not cheer anyone, though none raised objections. The tall, dour swordmaster walked in the lead, with Karnstein behind him and Sylvia next in line. Ishaani walked behind the Neapolitan woman, her stride so silent the former occasionally glanced back wondering if the Thuggee priestess

281

had vanished into the woods. Dardi came last, a smallsword in hand, his large eyes scanning every location as if expecting an attack.

The gloom of the trail increased as the day wore on, with only furtive sounds greeting them as they passed under the massive, bare boughs of the ancient trees. Massive spider webs covered whole branches, with small lumps hidden within the white strands feebly and futilely struggling for freedom.

Close to twilight, they came upon a wide clearing, one filled with weeds and large rocks yet bathed in a soft illumination. The vampire hunters gratefully stepped into the open space, each removing a weapon in case the location was a trap set by local predators. Strewn among the weeds were pale white stones that crackled and shattered beneath their feet.

"Walk carefully," Dardi said, "we are stepping on the bones of the dead."

Sylvia, Karnstein, and Ishaani recoiled at the statement, staring down at the random collection of human and animal dead, contemplating the creatures that performed such heinous acts.

"This is not a graveyard or a burial site," Séverin said, "but a warning against approaching Selene."

"How do you know this?" Ishaani said.

"Why else would the bones be only partially buried? If a predator had merely been careless, we would have found more, in larger piles. If the remains were ancient, they would not appear in such great numbers and so carefully placed. This is a message from the denizens of the vampire city."

He carefully stepped over a flat, white plate. They followed him, walking through the clearing with careful steps.

Karnstein muttered a prayer in a soft voice:

"Pater noster, qui es in caelis, sanctificetur Nomen tuum. Adveniat regnum tuum. Fiat voluntas tua, sicut in caelo et in terra. Panem nostrum quotidianum da nobis hodie, et dimitte nobis debita nostra sicut et nos dimittimus debitoribus nostris. Et ne nos inducas in tentationem, sed libera nos a malo."

Séverin, Dardi, and Sylvia each performed the sign of the cross and said, "Amen."

Coming to the edge of the clearing, the path appeared wider, with skeletal trees occasionally peaking above low brambles, each holding wicked, sharp thorns. Large gray blocks transformed the rough road into a paved avenue, like the still functional Roman highways that crossed Europe.

"We now approach the outer edge of Selene," Séverin said, striding forward onto the gloomy path "Be on your guard. Nothing you shall see will be like that of the rest of the Earth."

The road wound around a corner, which was as forbidding as before. A loud slithering sound broke shattered the silence of their passage and the bushes near Karnstein and Sylvia shook for a moment before falling still and silent.

"I do not like this place," the Austrian said.

"That demonstrates sanity, *amore*," Sylvia replied in a soft voice.

They continued for another hour, with occasional crashing sounds in the distance emerging from the untamed, bizarre forest. Nothing approached their party, nor did they see signs of humans, animals, or heard even the light buzz of insects.

"This is a dead land," Dardi said as they turned another twisting corner.

"Not completely, my friend," Séverin replied, pointing ahead.

As they turned the corner, they gasped at the sight before their eyes.

"*Ach du lieber Himmel*," Karnstein whispered, crossing himself.

"*Madonna!*" Sylvia and her father exploded, also making the sign of the cross.

Even Ishaani staggered and mumbled, "*Om Klim Kalika-Yei Namaha.*"

"Quite so," Séverin said, shaking his head.

CHAPTER LXIV

"Why have we not reached the gates yet, Jean?" Ange Ténèbre asked as they turned down yet another path and more forbidding roads lay ahead.

"I have heard," the *oupire* said, "that the city often moves its gates."

Ange spat on the road and shook his head.

"That makes no sense! How can a city move anything? A gate is a passageway. You can build it with walls around it, but it cannot move, except opening and closing!"

Marguerite Monvoisin chuckled and shook her head, a motion unseen by the brothers. The coffin across their shoulders prevented them from seeing anything beyond the road ahead and their own feet.

"Vampire, you forget where we are heading," she said. "This is Selene, the Vampire City, the Sepulchre and the Scholomance! Sanity has no place in such a location! Every visitor that steps into that dread land tells a different story of that gloomy, spectral land of eternal mourning and darkness! A gate moving is no stranger than one man speaking of high towers and another telling of only a single, massive columned amphitheatre!"

"You think we do not know this, witch?" Ange said. "We know more of Selene than you... for we visited that terrible land in our youth!"

"You lie!" she said, almost stumbling in her shock.

Jean Ténèbre guffawed behind her, a rasping sound that his brother echoed a moment later.

"How do you think we were transformed into the eternal beings who exist to this day, woman?" Jean asked. "The brothers Ténèbre gained their powers four hundred years ago, in that dwelling of specters and black magic..."

The spoils following the Battle of Hermannstadt were poor at best, with the greater share going to Hunyadi and the Church.

Though a knight and a warrior highly prized by the General, Jean Ténèbre received little compensation for killing so many Ottomans. His brother, Ange, received even less, since his master, Bishop György Lépes, had perished in the battle.

"There is a way, Jean," Ange said in their tent as they shared their mutual woes.

"That map you stole from the Ottoman's chest? It is a fool's errand, Ange," Jean replied, burping loudly from the cheap wine he finished moments ago.

"Yes, the map! Brother, the Ottomans planned a raiding party for this city, Selene. According to their notes, there is an ancient temple filled with jewels and gold dating back to the time of Alexander! If this is so, we can steal as much as we can carry and possibly return with an army of mercenaries. Would you not prefer meeting Hunyadi as an equal, rather than a follower?"

Ange pulled a small brass scroll case from his pack. Jean burped again and stared at his scarred hands. It still rankled his noble spirit that he was nothing more than a lesser nobleman among the Hungarian forces. His lineage was as old as that of their general, and his skill at arms was nearly as impressive. Why should he languish like a stray dog, feeding on scraps dropped from Lord Hunyadi's table?

"Hunyadi will now travel to speak with King Vladislaus," Ange said, leaning closer to his brother. "We could leave and say we are going home but will rejoin his service later. With Lépes dead, the Church shall not miss my presence. By the time they decide upon a new bishop, we could be as wealthy as the Ottoman sultan,"

The choice was a simple one for Jean Ténèbre; he desired riches, power and the pleasures that only the great nobles

enjoy. If he and Ange held the wealth that the Ottomans believed Selene hid, their days of penury would end.

*A wealthy man leading a team of mercenaries would re-
ceive favors from Hunyadi and perhaps replace Bogdan the
One-Eyed as master of Moldavia. Vladislaus would prefer one
who does not submit to the Turks with such willingness,* Jean
thought as Ange droned on about the possibilities.

When his brother paused, Jean said simply, "Yes, I
agree."

Within a week, they left the side of the young Hungarian
general and rode toward the city of darkness—a location that
would forever transform the Ténèbre Brothers forever...

CHAPTER LXV

The vampire hunters' explosive reaction was understandable, for the sight before their eyes was a vision that would have made even the greatest of men question their very sanity.

They stood before another clearing, one in which the stone road cut through and wound into the distance. Ruined buildings lay to the left of the clearing and hung into the path. The wreckage of a spiraling arch rose three or more stories high, the shattered remains ceasing before the structure rose above the path.

"I see no seams," Ishaani said. "That looks as if it were carved from a solid, massive stone...."

She was not wrong and, as they studied this structure, details emerged from the outer surface. Faces, some tiny, others as large as a man, appeared along the edges and gaped their direction with unseeing, blank, bleached eyes. The heads were a chimerical mix of human, serpent and insectoid life and each held expressions that were astonishingly human in appearance.

Tentacular protrusions extruded near every face, some nearly human in dimensions, others resembling the extremities of the odder organisms from beneath the ocean depths. The affect was disquieting, but no more so than the surroundings.

On the right, rising above them was a large, stony hill with jagged angles distending randomly like vast gray waves across the surface of the rise. A second hill lay beyond the first, rising to a vast narrow point that resembled a steeple on some ancient cathedral. The hills were still, empty, and appeared so forbidding that the effect was as unsettling as the ruins themselves.

"Is that Selene in the distance?" Karnstein asked, pointing towards the high-peaked hillock.

"It is not!" a tiny, high-pitched voice said from the far end of the clearing.

"That is the former palace of the Samojudas. They made war upon the dark city and their palace turned to stone," an equally childish, if slightly lower-pitched, voice said.

Hopping up on a stone in the center of the path was a young boy, a youth of eight or nine based on his height. He had light brown hair, tan skin with a spattering of freckles across his nose, and a round, nearly chinless face. His clothing was the simple dress of a child raised on a farm, brown homespun wool, a white cloth shirt and elderly boots that appeared patched in several places. He clutched a long staff in one small hand and smiled their direction. His tiny dark eyes nearly vanished into his face and he giggled as he extended his other hand behind his back.

Holding his hand was a smaller girl, probably a year or two younger than him. Her hair was the same color, but longer, and flowed across her shoulders and curled at the ends. Her face appeared softer, though also lacking a chin, and her almost pretty features held no freckles or blemishes. She wore a light green dress with a white collar, a darker round hat that fell past her ears. She too giggled, but covered her mouth with one tiny hand.

"My name is Mladen and this is my sister Mariana," the boy said, giggling again. "Look at your faces! You big people are scared!"

"Don't be mean," the little girl said, elbowing her brother. "They seem nice!"

The boy, Mladen, examined them for a moment and nodded his head gravely.

"Yes, they are. Not like the mean people that passed here two hours ago. Should we help them, Mariana?"

The girl tapped a tiny finger on her teeth and said, "Maybe. Let's play a game with them and see if they *are* nice."

"We do not have..." Karnstein began, quickly silenced by a look from Jean-Pierre Séverin.

The swordmaster bowed towards the children and said, "We should be happy for a short game with you, Mladen and Mariana."

Both children jumped up and down with glee and then primly sat down on the edge of the stone. The others realized that an odd, misshapen face leered out from the base of the rock, somehow approximating the stump of a massive tree.

"We will play the question game, it is short," Mladen said. "I will ask you a question, then it will be your turn. After three rounds, if we think you are nice people, we shall help you. If not, we will leave."

"That is a good game," Dardi said, making a slicing gesture towards Franz, Sylvia, and Ishaani.

There was no violence in his action, but rather a simple request for silence on their part. All three appeared puzzled, but they indicated their acceptance.

"Why do you head toward the dark city?" Mladen asked while swinging his legs back and forth on the stone.

"A witch, a vampire, and a ghoul are headed to the city and plan a terrible thing," Séverin answered. Then, he asked, "Where do you live?"

"Near here," Mladen said, but closed his mouth when Mariana elbowed him again, "Ouch!"

"My turn!" she said. "Will you hurt anyone in the city?"

Dardi shook his head and answered, "We will do our duty and leave. We shall not take anything, and will only fight the vampires of the city if attacked. Will you show us the way into Selene?"

Both children smiled again and nodded, their heads moving at the same time.

"Yes, if you answer the next question correctly," Mariana said, looking at her brother.

The boy pointed to the left and asked, "Will you attack Pluzhek when he passes you?"

The vampire hunters and the Thuggee priestess turned their head as a segmented triangular head with two vast, oval, pearl-colored eyes emerged from beyond the ruins.

A green scaled body slithered forward and a squishing, slurping noise accompanied each rippling motion. The creature resembled a slug, with characteristics of both a reptile and a sea creature. A trail of yellow slime followed the slinking motions and the bizarre creature moved between them and the children without stopping.

"Not," Séverin answered, "unless it attacks us. Who were the mean people you mentioned?"

"Pluzhek only likes dead food," Mladen replied. "The mean people were the ones you are looking for. They must go the longer way because they are not nice. We will show you a faster way and take you inside the city."

"Follow us, but do not step in Pluzek's tracks. The juice will burn your shoes," Mariana added.

The children slid off their rock and turned to take the trail behind the arch, pushing aside a pair of bushes. A thin path lay behind them, winding away down a small hill.

Mladen waved them forward, saying, "Down the hill and take the first turn on the left. You will see the gate to the Scholomance."

"Stop the mean people and do not steal anything," Mariana added, waving them forward with her tiny hand. "The vampires and the priests get mad when people steal."

Séverin bowed towards the children as did Dardi. They gestured to the others, looking at them meaningfully.

After a moment, all three followed suit and the children smiled and nodded.

"Nice people," Mariana said, vanishing from view as they released the bushes.

"What just happened?" Sylvia asked as they walked down a steep slope for several minutes.

Turning into an equally tiny trail on the left, Dardi called back from the rear.

"We shall explain later. Just know that manners serve well in strange situations."

The path wound left and right for half an hour before opening into a tiny square meadow about ten feet wide.

In the center of the field lay a black stone arch that rose eight feet high and ten feet wide. Beyond the gate lay a dusky darkness, one that appeared penetrable with the eyes, and yet still eluded their vision.

"The gate to Selene," Séverin said. "Let us hope we are not too late."

Staying in the lead, he plunged forward, stepping gingerly over the edge.

The others followed him, their step hesitant, their eyes immediately blind as they plunged into the infamous, ancient Vampire City.

CHAPTER LXVI

Marguerite Monvoisin gaped like a child first visiting a big city, staring about her with open-mouthed awe. The sights that greeted her as they strode through this city of darkness and despair almost made all the years she had suffered as slave of a vampire worth the toil.

They strode through an immense cemetery, the black stoned streets of which were lined with tombs and mausoleums of various sizes and opulence. Some were simple stone boxes capable of fitting one person, others massive palace-styled structures covered with dark, unsettling designs and massive gargoyles. Yet they were minor sights compared to the distant buildings that rose above their heads and appeared tiny from their vantage viewpoint.

Circular towers, some so lofty that their peaks were indistinguishable to the naked eye, loomed in the distance. Some resembled Ottoman minarets, others were carved in the shape of massive fingers jutting towards the starless black sky. Some were topped with the onion-shaped domes of Muscovy palaces, and a few were simply columns that seemingly supported the very sky. Black jasper or mirror-like obsidian were the building blocks of these titanic buildings, though somehow, they were distinguishable despite the perpetual dusk.

"Ignore that nonsense," Jean said. "I am not sure those towers even exist. This city will trick your mind. We seek the temple."

Marguerite wished she could turn her head and look at the *oupire* with venom in her eyes, but she could not. The coffin and skull that lay upon his brother's shoulder blocked her view.

I need the bitch in this casket one last time for my great spell. Then I shall close my eyes forever! she thought and glanced left and right.

"It is to the right," Ange said, one of his tiny, pale, finger pointing in that direction.

If the massive towers had amazed Marguerite, the temple of the vampires overwhelmed her very senses. It was a spiraling structure built in the shape of a Greek shrine, lined with twenty-four doric columns, each made from alabaster, decorated with green and blue stones. A massive porphyry blue statue of a lion tearing into the body of a buxom woman lay before twenty-four steps, each made from jade, amber, coral and many other unknown stones, which led to an amphitheater that looked as vast as the famed Roman Coliseum.

They turned in that direction, their stride increasing in speed. Each had their own reason for heading towards the temple. Marguerite dreamed of the end of all existence and the silence of the grave. The Ténèbre Brothers had their own reasons, which they had never told to anyone else.

"I think you have walked far enough," Bartolomeo Dardi suddenly said, stepping out from around a smaller mausoleum. "I think we end this now."

Lowering the coffin to the ground, Ange stepped forward, pulling out his tiny, sharp, knife, while his brother sniffed the air.

"Four others... the two who hurt us plus two we do not know," the *oupire* said. "Come out, humans," he added, "you cannot hide among the dead. The scent of the living is like food in this city."

Jean-Pierre Séverin appeared beside his oldest friend, his rapier in hand. Franz Karnstein and Sylvia Dardi emerged a short distance away, the later holding a light smallsword, the former a musket pistol.

"Your fifth is afraid and will not emerge?" Jean said. "No matter, we shall kill and eat her later."

The *oupire* looked to Marguerite and added, "Go! Take the skull and head into the temple. We shall follow after we destroy these humans."

Marguerite grabbed the package tied to the top of the casket and ran towards the temple.

Suddenly, Ishaani emerged from hiding and ran in her direction, leaping on the witch's back. Her strangling cord encircled the exposed neck and she pulled deep.

Grabbing the cord, Marguerite, ripped the object from the Thuggee priestess's hand and turned. She grabbed Ishaani by the wrist and threw her against a nearby wall.

The Thuggee priestess struck it with a sickening thud and lay unmoving on the cold, black stone ground.

Not looking back, the satanic priestess dashed towards the temple, her movements swift though unsure.

The Ténèbre Brothers moved with blinding swiftness, appearing between the vampire hunters and the fleeing, undead woman.

"That one is mine!" Ange said, pointing his knife towards Sylvia.

"And that one is mine," Jean snarled, pointing a ragged claw towards Karnstein.

The Austrian shot the *oupire* in the face, smiling slightly as his target stumbled backwards.

"You talk too much, eater of the dead," he stated.

Sylvia fired her own gun at Ange, but he moved aside in a blurring motion. Bowling over the French and Neapolitan swordmasters, he sliced at her arm with his knife, which she barely parried with her sword.

She drove the vampire back with her own swift slice and he was forced back to his brother's side. The *oupire* rose, his eye hole a gaping black wound that oozed viscous black ichor.

Dropping her gun, Sylvia drew a slim dagger and called out, "*Amore*, follow the witch. Leave this one and his disgusting brother to us."

Karnstein did not reply, but glanced in her direction for a heartbeat, then ran after Marguerite. Dardi and Séverin's blades were now pointed towards the dreaded Ténèbre Brothers.

"Once we finish these fools off, we must capture the Austrian. He must suffer for all these indignities!" Jean said.

"*Mi amore* was right," Sylvia said. "You and your brother talk too much. *En Garde!*"

And then, the battle before the temple of Selene commenced…

CHAPTER LXVII

The temple itself was a titanic, unadorned, chamber with a single black stone located in the center of the round amphitheater. Its walls were bone white and unmarked by even the smallest blemish. There were no torches or brazier, yet the single oversized room, this darkest of locations in Selene, was easily viewed, even more so than the rest of the city.

Marguerite Monvoisin crouched in its center, her hands slowly painting sigils in a twelve-foot circle. She did not look up as Franz Karnstein halted eight feet from her position and fired his gun into her back. She fell over, but somehow kept her brush and pot from dropping.

Rising and turning, she looked in his direction and moved her hand behind her back.

"No weapon can hurt me, imbecile. I am immortal!"

"Let us test that theory," the Austrian replied, drawing a long dagger from his belt.

Marguerite knelt and carefully placed the pot and brush behind her. She then traced a sigil in the air with one long finger, creating a green eldritch image between the Exorcist and herself. The symbol vanished in less than an eye blink, but a crackling energy lingered in the air

Karnstein cried out and fell backwards, dropping his blade as a long, jagged cut appeared across his right cheek. The pain thrummed across his face and he gritted his teeth and fought back yelling again.

"I owed you that, human," Marguerite spat, raising both her hands. "I would tear your body apart limb from limb, but I have no time. I think I shall simply kill you now and bring the destroyer of all life back to Earth."

Karnstein reached under his cloak, pulled a second pistol and shot the satanic priest in her chest. He then said a quick prayer, closed his eyes, and uttered a few words in ancient Sumerian.

By the time Marguerite rose again, his eyes were pulsing with silver light.

"I think you shall find that it will not be so simple, witch," he replied, focusing upon the darkness that existed within his foe. "Oh, and your wig is askew."

"Bastard," she muttered, summoning more power from the unmoving body of Veselina Dushev.

Her eyes also transformed, turning into pure black orbs that reflected the void within the vampire's dark shell. Marguerite viewed the being before her, a vessel for an ancient power that she could not comprehend. She found herself repulsed by this man, this human who glowed silver before her and appeared unafraid of her power.

I must kill him, she thought, *and then I shall end all life on this horrid little world.*

"Die, human!" she shouted, tracing another symbol in the air.

"You first, damned soul!" he replied, performing the sign of the cross between his body and that of his enemy.

The heavy, macabre temple shook as unearthly energy flew between the combatants.

In the distance, three hooded figures emerged from hidden entrances and stood with the stillness of corpses as the two foes battled for supremacy.

CHAPTER LXVIII

Ange Ténèbre snarled and exploded forward, his blood red eyes pulsing in the gloom. He sliced across Sylvia Dardi's stomach, drawing a thin line of blood from her torso. She winced in pain and slashed his direction, missing him by inches.

Jean Ténèbre dropped onto his hands and feet and charged forward, moving with the swiftness of a galloping horse. He slapped aside Bartolomeo Dardi and landed atop Jean-Pierre Séverin, his powerful hands grasping the swordmaster's arms and digging his jagged talons into the flesh beneath his jacket and shirt.

Leaping through the air, the vampire landed behind Sylvia and slashed across her back. This time, the blade only lightly scoured across her skin, a stinging attack but more an irritant than a danger. Sylvia thrust backwards with her smallsword, driving the vampire back and preventing a second strike.

Jean slowly dug his claws into the elder swordmaster's arms and leaned close to his ear. "Scream for me, human.," he hissed. "I want to hear your wails of pain before I slowly peel the flesh from your skin. Scream for me!"

The pain grew with each passing second in Séverin's body. Sweat poured down his face, his breath emerged in low rasping gasps, and his eyes grew wild as the agony increased. Yet he stared up at his foul, inhuman, demoniac, corpse-eater foe and would not utter a sound.

"I shall slice you apart slowly, you bloodbag bitch," Ange said, licking the blood from his blade. "You shall die by inches and just before you expire, I shall feast on your blood as I rape your dying corpse and feel your heart stop beating. Then my brother shall feast upon your remains. Won't that be wonderful?"

The vampire feinted low and moved closer, slashing Sylvia's arm. Her smallsword fell from her bleeding hand and she fell back, feeling the weakness rising though her injured body. Ange slowly licked the blood from his knife again, smacking his lips and sighing audibly.

"You are a refreshing meal, bloodbag. I shall remember you fondly…"

CHAPTER LXIX

Franz Karnstein and Marguerite Monvoisin, the witch known as Strix, stood within the vast skein of energy that was the real world.

Surrounding them was the terrible, infinite void that was Selene, the Vampire City. In the distance there existed the flame of life that empowered all beings, from the simplest blade of grass to the greatest leaders of humanity. But there were also other beings within this vast web, dead, undead, unquiet spirits, and even avatars of light and darkness from other universes.

This was apparent to both witch and exorcist, yet they ignored all save each other. They circled, seeking any weakness they could exploit, each performing probing attacks, light and darkness energy lances extending, yet vanishing before they reached their target.

Marguerite acted first, raising her hands high and invoking a name in a guttural tongue that shook the very air. A swirl of dark energy emerged between her position and Karnstein's, coalescing into the shape of a demon lord.

He stood eight feet-tall, radiating black magic from the tip of his goat-horned head to his sharp taloned toes. He smiled and fangs the size of a man's hand appeared in his massive, oversized maw.

"What is thy bidding, my mistress?" the demon lord asked.

His voice was sweet and horrifying upon the ears. It was a sadistic purr, the sound of poison and cruelty condensed in six simple words.

"Kill this one. You may have his soul as payment," Marguerite ordered.

The demon lord turned toward Karnstein and stepped forward. Then he stopped and a low whimper emerged from his mottled mouth.

"The hammer of demons!" he whined.

Karnstein glowed from within, the silvery light over-whelming the witch for an instant.

"*DALKHU TARU SERU ESERU ETUTU INA ETUTI ASBU DARISAM!*" he shouted.

The energy struck the demon lord, and the creature shrieked and melted away, his immense body vanishing beneath the silver force. Within ten seconds, nothing existed where he had stood.

The silver energy fell away from the Exorcist's body, weakening his power.

That was when Strix struck. A black shaft of power encircled Karnstein with crushing force. He screamed and dropped to his knees, feeling the corrupting magic rip into his body. He felt as if thousands of tiny shafts of ice had pierced his skin and were slowly digging deeper with each passing second.

"You may frighten even a demon lord, Baron Franz von Vordenburg-Karnstein," Marguerite said, circling his kneeling form, "but I am so much more. I am the destroyer of all life. I am Marguerite Monvoisin, daughter of Catherine Monvoisin. I am Strix, the high priestess of Belial, the archangel of enmity, and a witch of the left-handed path. I could kill you now with a word… but I shall not…"

She walked over to her circle and picked up her pot and brush. Slowly she inscribed more sigils and symbols across the floor and spoke without looking back towards the agonized, shivering Karnstein.

"You shall live long enough and view my greatest triumph. I shall bring about the return of the dark king, *Raktabīja*. You shall be his first feast before he destroys all life in the universe…"

CHAPTER LXX

A gun roared and Ange Ténèbre fell backwards, crashing into a small mausoleum.

Bartolomeo Dardi appeared near his daughter, a small pistol in hand.

"Karnstein was right. You two speak too much. Now, leech, you face my daughter and me. Let us see if you are as brave as you act."

Meanwhile, Jean Ténèbre was digging a little deeper with his claws into Jean-Pierre Séverin. Then, an odd look crossed his face. He reared back, his talons pulling free from the swordmaster's body with a sickening, tearing sound. He fell sideways and silently writhed in obvious agony. As the *oupire* turned, he spotted a steel circlet protruding from his back, imbedded deeply within his spine.

"You are welcome," Ishaani said as she appeared at his side.

Blood flowed down her face and she had her right arm tucked into her waistband. Her left hand held a small short sword and she walked with a slow, halting step.

Ange swiftly appeared at his brother's side and tore the *chakram* from the *oupire*'s back, throwing the sharp disk into the distant graveyard. The low whistling sound of the weapon's flight faded away in seconds and the Ténèbre Brothers slowly rose and faced their four opponents.

"That attack," Jean said, tiredly lowering his hands to the ground, "was the last. We shall not torture you slowly, we shall simply kill…"

His speech was cut off as Séverin fired his single musket pistol into the *oupire*'s chest.

Picking up his rapier, the swordmaster said, "Let us end this pair, if only in hopes they shall cease their prattling."

Dardi threw back his head and laughed—a sound that echoed throughout this grim, terrible city. The mirth lingered longer than anyone expected for reasons they didn't understand.

"Yes, Gâteloup! Let us destroy the Ténèbre Brothers and have minstrels sing of the deeds for years to come. *En Garde!*"

The fight began in earnest, with Séverin and Ishaani battling the powerful *oupire*, Jean. Nearby, Dardi and Sylvia attacked the fierce vampire, Ange. Despite injuries from by the initial assault of the undead brothers, the human hunters fought without hesitation. Their undead enemies were slower, thanks to repeatedly receiving musket balls in the face and torso.

The fighting styles of the brothers were as vastly different as their outward appearances. Jean, larger and stronger, attacked with crushing sweeps of his terrible talons. He moved with unnatural celerity on two feet, or with hands on the ground, simulating an animal's motion. He absorbed small injuries and slashes, and avoided attacks that could damage him deeply. Fighting Jean Ténèbre was like engaging in a test of strength against a giant bear or a massive bull.

Ange, in contrast, fought with a swiftness that outpaced his inhuman brother. He darted in and out, slashing and slicing exposed limbs while avoiding any contact with the Dardis' blades. He snarled, and even giggled, as he ran in any direction, licking his blade clean of any collected blood. Battling him was like fighting a pack of hyenas, each attacking in the hope of wearing its opponent down through injuries.

Séverin and Ishaani were not unmarked by Jean's attacks, though their responses did not stop the ghoul's assaults. Every cut from their sword closed within seconds, and the *oupire*'s vicious talons came closer with each passing moment.

While this battle occurred, Sylvia and Ishaani exchanged a glance. Each subtly nodded at the other and they acted simultaneously and with a swiftness that nearly matched that of their undead enemies.

Sylvia raised her knife high above her head and flung the weapon, just as Ishaani did the same with her small sword. The two weapons whistled through the air and thudded deeply into the legs of the Ténèbre Brothers. Vampire and *oupire* yelped in pain and shock, surprised by an attack which had come from behind.

The reason the brothers found themselves caught off-guard was because Ishaani and Sylvia had attacked each other's opponent. Sylvia's dagger had sunk deep into Jean's flank, while Ishaani's small sword had nearly removed Ange's spindly left leg.

Dardi and Séverin did not hesitate to capitalize on this unusual occurrence. Springing forward, they sunk their weapons deep into the undead pair's backs, pinning them down to the black stone ground.

"The Karnstein sword, Sylvia!" Séverin shouted. "Quickly!"

Sylvia drew the heavy saber her *fiancé* had given her and tossed it to the Maestro. Catching the weapon easily, Séverin raised the blade high and swung downward in an arc towards Jean Ténèbre's neck. The *oupire* shrieked loudly, a horrific, atavistic sound that was cut off abruptly.

Without waiting, Séverin tossed the weapon to his Neapolitan comrade, who kept a foot firmly pressed into the back of the struggling vampire.

"No! No! NO!" Ange Ténèbre screamed, struggling vainly.

"Yes! Yes! YES!" Bartomeleo Dardi said, slicing the monster's head from his shoulders.

The headless Ténèbre Brothers lay still, their skulls several feet from their bodies. These extruded the same viscous black discharge that had appeared whenever they had received a cut. The fluid ceased pumping a few seconds later and the bodies lay still.

"We must get to Franz! He is alone with that monster!" Sylvia said, turning towards the temple.

"One moment, Sylvia," Séverin said, frowning. "I believe there is a method to end this quickly. Look over there…"

Dardi spotted the object and smiled, laughing again, "Brilliant, Gâteloup!"

Sylvia and Ishaani exchanged a confused look but followed the pair several feet from the battle towards an object on the avenue.

"A coffin?" Sylvia asked. "But there must be thousands of them in this city of the dead."

"Possibly so," Séverin replied.

He kicked open the lid, and added, "However this one is special."

He pointed downward and smiled briefly.

"Come, we must end this now!"

CHAPTER LXXI

The pain grew slowly across his body, yet Franz Karnstein did not cry out a second time. He mumbled brief prayers, but could not summons the concentration needed for an exorcism.

Also, he thought as his body tensed as the chill increased, *it might not work…*

Strix, for that was how he thought of her, studied her work carefully and performed several minor adjustments. She then sighed loudly and removed a small yellow parchment from a pouch in her dress.

"This is perfect. It shall not be long now, Franz Karnstein. Do you know I once met one of your ancestors? A lovely lady named…"

"Mircalla or Carmilla or Millarca? She was probably lovely, blond, and spent most of her time seducing the maids, young pretty noblewomen, and the occasional male. No doubt she died screaming with a wooden stake in her heart while one of her lovers sobbed in agony at her passing," Karnstein said.

It was a trial, sounding casual as the pain throughout his body grew with each passing second. Yet, somehow, thanks to his training from Séverin and the Lord Inquisitor von Spielsdorf, he maintained a casual pose.

Marguerite Monvoisin studied him for a moment and slowly nodded her head.

"Her name was Countess Mircalla Karnstein and she was tall with a lovely face and figure and blond hair that I envied. How did you know that? Are you her son?"

Karnstein snorted derisively and looked up at the vampire witch with the same cold expression von Spielsdorf had used when someone behaved stupidly.

"The name was easy… it is a family tradition… a particularly stupid one in my opinion. As to the rest, I know of at least ten female ancestors in my extended line who fit that description. Like you, vampires are predictable, stupid, and selfish creatures."

Marguerite's face transformed from curiosity to rage instantly and she reached for the dagger by her feet. She stopped herself, closed her eyes for a moment, and opened them slowly. Now, she looked placid, almost disinterested, in his direction.

"I am not a vampire, Baron Karnstein. I am a priestess of Belial and a witch."

"You," he replied through gritted teeth as the invisible strands of ice contracted slowly about his body, "are more vampire than any of the damned creatures in my line. You may not drink blood, or steal youth, or souls, but you are one of their kind. Your actions prove my point. To maintain your youth, you murder people. When you discovered immortality is as much a curse as a gift, what did you do? Use the years and improve yourself and all humanity? Explore the world and discover hidden secrets? No. You decided you should destroy all life in the universe in the hope of ending your torturous existence. You, Marguerite Monvoisin, are the queen of all vampires, and you are the most damned soul I have ever encountered."

Marguerite listened to Karnstein's recitation without flinching or replying. After a moment, she raised her left hand and balled her hand into a tight fist.

The Exorcist moaned as the invisible strands constricted even more tightly. The tiny icy needles thrust deeper into his body and he could barely breathe, or even see. Collapsing on his side, his eyes lifted slowly to Marguerite's, and watched as she removed the wig that lay askew on her head.

"Perhaps you are right, Karnstein. In the end, it does not matter. I hold in my hand the scroll of *Raktabīja*, the demon king. With his return, I shall finally know true peace," she said.

Just as she raised the yellow parchment to her eyes, a pair of heavy boots thundered across the white marble floor.

They stopped next to Franz Karnstein and assumed a fighting stance.

"I do not think so, *porca puttana*! Now, let my *fidanzato* free of your *stregoneria*!" Sylvia said, slashing the air with her heavy saber.

CHAPTER LXXII

"Another fool," Marguerite Monvoisin said with a sniff. "Very well, you shall join your lover in agony as the demon king rises and consumes the world."

She opened her closed fist and said a few words. She then looked confused and said the words again, performing an odd gesture in the air.

But nothing happened.

Marguerite said the words louder and gesticulated wildly.

"Is that it?" Sylvia asked, rolling her eyes. "The old women in my neighborhood spoke better curses at their ungrateful children than you, vampire."

"*Et in die dolore!*" Marguerite said, pointing her finger at Sylvia.

"*Vaffanculo!*" Sylvia said. She looked down at Franz and asked, "How are you, *amore*?"

As this exchange occurred, Karnstein felt the constricting spell weakening and slowly vanish from his body. The pain remained, though diminished as the needles slowly vanished.

"Better," he replied, sitting upright.

"What happened? What did you do?" Marguerite asked, taking a step backwards.

"I think I can answer that question, little witch," a feminine voice said from the other end of the chamber.

A woman strode out of the shadows, her step slow and hesitant. She was entirely nude with a head of soiled auburn hair and skin streaked with dirt and dust. The smell that wafted from her body was noxious and pungent, a terrible mixture of rotting flesh and filth.

"You! No!" Marguerite said, staggering backwards.

Veselina Dushev nodded slowly and said, "Yes, my slave, me. I have returned and I find you are a very naughty girl. The others and I shall teach you proper manners now."

She suddenly exploded forward, appearing at Marguerite's side. Her mouth opened and a long serpentine tongue flew from her mouth and wrapped around the witch's thin, pale arm. The tongue slowly retracted, pulling Marguerite closer.

"No, no, please! Have mercy! Help me!" Marguerite screamed, looking towards Sylvia and her *fiancé*.

"No," Karnstein said as Sylvia helped him rise, "but I shall pray for your soul's deliverance one day."

Just as the shrieking witch slid next to Veselina, human hands morphed from the vampire's body. They were of various shapes and sizes, each gripping Marguerite's body with crushing force. They pulled her against Veselina's stained figure and, a moment later, the French witch had vanished from view.

"My thanks," Veselina said, turning her head and looking at the approaching trio from behind.

Jean-Pierre Séverin, Bartolomeo Dardi, and Ishaani strode out of the gloom, their movements as slow as the vampire. All three held swords in their hands and they studied the naked, soiled, Veselina.

"Fear not," she said, raising her hands. "I shall never attack any of you for as long as you live. You did me a great service this day, and I do not forget those who help me and my servants."

"Stay out of France," Séverin said, lowering his rapier.

"And Naples," Dardi added.

"And Austria," Karnstein said.

Veselina Dushev nodded once, turned and bowed towards the three hooded figures. Without another word, she walked from the temple, heading towards the graveyard beyond the walls.

Ishaani moved forward and picked up the scroll. She studied the page for a moment, sighed with obvious relief, and slipped the roll into her shirt.

"Will you try and murder us now?" Dardi asked, studying her closely.

Ishaani stared at him for a moment, frowned and shook her head. She turned away and stomped down hard on the massive skull that lay in the center of the mystic circle. The bone splintered and she kept kicking the remains until only a fine powder lay upon the floor.

"You are not believers, but your deaths would not serve our cause. The worshippers of Kali are not monsters and murderers. We sacrifice lives and prevent Kali from rising and, in her black madness, bringing about the *Kali Yuga*... the age of chaos and discord. You fight against such an event in your own unbelieving way."

"Very well," Séverin said, lifting his blade slightly. "However, if you do return to France, the beggars' guild will kill you, no matter your skills or weapons."

Ishaani bowed once and turned away.

"I shall make my own way home. You shall not see me again. I do not recommend any of you visiting my country. If you do, I shall not protect you from my people."

She walked out of the temple, her steps soft and vanishing a moment later.

"I do not like her, but I respect her skills," Sylvia said, groaning as her injured arm bumped into Karnstein's side.

"How did you know she planned our deaths?" he asked.

Dardi chuckled and gently clapped the Exorcist on his back.

"Her people have been secretly guarding that scroll since ancient days. I do not doubt she would have killed her English partner after first paying him whatever he had demanded. The Thuggee have little concern with the lives of non-believers."

Sheathing their weapons, all four limped or stepped slowly towards the temple exit. Sylvia and Karnstein joined hands and they stared up a moment later at the spiraling towers.

"Lovely, but very strange," Dardi said. "I shall not miss this gloomy graveyard of a city."

"Nor I," Karnstein said. "What did you do that led to the witch's defeat?"

Sylvia giggled and rolled her eyes.

"Did you forget the secret of the vampires of Selene?"

Karnstein looked puzzled for a moment and then frowned.

"A keyhole in their heart...?"

She kissed his cheek and said fondly, "Thankfully Uncle Jean-Pierre remembered that fact..."

CHAPTER LXXIII

Moments earlier

All four lifted the coffin, which was surprisingly light and moved with careful steps up the stairs.

As they reached the entrance, Jean-Pierre Séverin waved them to a halt and studied the scene before their eyes.

Marguerite Monvoisin was kneeling upon the floor, slowly painting and ignoring everything else. Franz Karnstein knelt a few feet from her, his body shivering slightly, his head bowed. The witch examined her work and moved on to another area, sketching slowly with her brush.

"She may begin the ceremony soon," Ishaani said. "I must stop her."

"You cannot," Dardi said. "If the only one of us capable of dispelling her power has failed, you shall die before you take two steps her direction."

"But I must!" Ishaani said.

"I have a solution," Séverin said, "Sylvia shall delay her before she begins. She will make a show of protecting her *fiancé*. Barto, Ishaani and I shall carry this coffin quietly to the left side of the temple and over to the three men in hoods."

From the temple, Karnstein's voice suddenly echoed with a strain evident in his sneering tone.

"...or Millarca. She was probably lovely, blond, and spent most of her time..."

"*Mi amore* provided your distraction. I will join when she is no longer interested in him," Sylvia said.

"*Si, andiamo!*" her father said.

He lifted the back half of the coffin alone.

Ishaani looked rebellious for an instant, but glanced in Sylvia's direction. The Neapolitan swordsman gave her the same subtle nod she had during the battle with the Ténèbre

Brothers. She frowned, returned the gesture, and lifted her side of the coffin.

They moved with deliberate slowness, each stepping slowly and carefully along the unadorned, shadowy wall of the massive temple. The voices of Karnstein and Marguerite echoed in their direction, fading as they moved towards the hooded men. The distance seemed inconceivably long and more than once, they wondered if they could reach their destination before the witch's spell commenced.

As they stepped, a motion near the wall a few feet ahead arrested their stealthy stride. A hooded figure emerged from the gloom and stopped in their path. An elongated gray-skinned hand with emaciated fingers emerged from the folds. With slow deliberation, a single nailless digit pointed down towards the alabaster floor and did not move.

"*Madonna!*" Dardi said.

He lowered the coffin, followed by the others. All drew their swords as they stepped away. They took defensive positions, but kept their weapons low as the sinister newcomer did not appear threatening.

The hooded figure never looked up, but the other claw like hand emerged into view. Within the fingers lay a long, thin, ornately carved, bronze key. Bending over the coffin, the mysterious character inserted it and slowly turned the metal object with cautious movements. A moment later, he straightened, bowed towards the three staring humans, and backed into the gloomy darkness.

A naked woman with tangled auburn hair sat up, softly groaning, her head swiveling wildly.

"Where am I?" she asked in French.

"Selene," Séverin answered, raising his sword. "Are you the vampire who enslaved Marguerite Monvoisin?"

Veselina Dushev stood up slowly, apparently unconcerned by her nudity and a century's worth of dirt and filth across her entire body.

"Yes, damn her tricky ways. She placed me under a spell that made *me* her slave!"

Just then, the witch's voice drifted in their direction, her words firm and controlled.

"…end, it does not matter. I hold in my hand the scroll of *Raktabīja,* the demon king. With his return…"

"That is her," Séverin said, nodding towards Marguerite. "She has a spell capable of destroying all life on this world."

"Yes," the vampire said, "that would be her mad choice. No matter, I shall put a stop to her foolishness now."

Veselina turned and smiled, an ugly sight for all three on-lookers, and strode into the gloom.

They followed at a safe distance, still unsure of her motives…

CHAPTER XLLIV

"*Madonna!*" Sylvia Dardi exclaimed as they exited the temple, "The bodies! They are gone!"

She was correct. Neither of the Ténèbre Brothers' corpses lay where they had left them moments ago. There was still a light film of dark, viscous fluid where each had suffered beheading, yet they could find no evidence of the two undead creatures.

"I am unsurprised," Séverin said. "According to tales, the brothers Ténèbre never remain dead for long."

Turning away from that portion of the enormous graveyard, they turned a corner and found the massive gates of Selene only a short walk away. The stone edifice appeared larger, more imposing, yet a glimmer of light sparkled around the edges.

Without speaking, all four walked as quickly as their battered forms allowed and left the city of eternal darkness without a glance to their rear.

Several minutes later, they stepped into bright, nearly blinding sunshine, and a mutual sigh of relief escaped their lips.

"You did as you promised," Mariana said, her tiny form visible under a large, looming, black stone ruin. "You are nice people."

"Excuse me?" Sylvia asked. "How do you mean?"

Mladen appeared at her side and tapped his pole on the ground.

"You stopped the heretics and their mistress, prevented the bad magic, and did not steal the wealth of the temple."

"Not that it mattered, but we did not see any wealth in that empty place," Karnstein said.

The children exchanged a look and broke into giggles.

"That is because you did not look for it. Had that been your interest, you would have seen more riches than the dreams of all the kings living and dead," Mladen said.

"Who are you?" Séverin asked, stepping a little closer. "You are not simple peasant children. Are you vampires of Selene?"

"Perhaps," Mariana said in her same singsong, childish voice, "or perhaps we just speak for those within the city?"

"Telling you would simply confuse your limited imaginations," Mladen added, "just as Selene does to all who are not vessels for her power."

"I think I understand," Séverin said. "That which we call Selene is both a city and not a city. The vampires within are tiny tendrils believing they are more…"

The children grinned up at the tall, dour, elder swordmaster.

"All we can say is perhaps, Jean-Pierre Séverin. A goddess does not grant true answers to mortals," Mladen said and bowed.

"Though if you wish a place in Selene, you need only walk this way again. You and Bartomeleo Dardi would find large tombs awaiting your eternal undead existence," Mariana added.

"We thank you," Dardi said, bowing to the children.

The children, who were not children, bowed in return and pointed their tiny fingers towards a path to the right.

"Walk that way for one hour and you shall find yourself by your horses," Mariana piped up.

"If you head three miles on the road, you will find yourself near Sofia. There is a doctor near the city named Petkova. He will help you with your cuts and pains," Mladen added.

He stepped behind the ruin.

"Goodbye," Mariana said, following her brother.

By the time all four had reached their location, the children had vanished. Sylvia and Franz exchanged a confused look, which brought about a loud laugh from Dardi and a small smile from Séverin.

"You are confused by Selene?" Dardi asked as they walked towards the path. "Good! A city of the undead should not be one we can understand easily."

"Yet, you, Maestro, appear to understand what those children said," Karnstein said.

Séverin performed a Gallic shrug and replied, "I may, but also I may not. What they said was the city may be the living or undead body of a fallen angel or a goddess by the name of Selene. The creatures we call vampires are just tiny vessels for the power of this city, which might not be a city after all. This could explain why we only viewed an empty graveyard and a massive temple."

"Though this all could be nonsense and the city is a dark hole and the inhabitants truly are vampires," Dardi said, grinning.

Karnstein and Sylvia exchanged a look and then stared back at the older swordmasters with the same skeptical expression on their faces.

"That does not make any sense, Papa," Sylvia said.

Dardi nodded, kissed his daughter's cheek and said, "Correct. We are confronting ancient supernatural powers. Simple answers are rarely the correct ones. Do you know there are some fools who believe all vampires are simply men and women who have a disease of the blood? A doctor in London once experimented to find a cure for the undead."

"What happened to him?" Karnstein asked, interested despite himself.

Dardi clapped his future son-in-law on the back and said, "The vampires made him one of their kind and watched him slowly grow insane as his experiments failed. I believe he lives in a sewer drain feeding on rats. No easy answers, *genero*."

"If we are truly near Sofia," Séverin said, "we shall find it easier to reach the coast and take a ship home."

"And stop in Naples first, of course," Sylvia said with a wide smile.

Karnstein looked confused and asked, "Why Naples?"

"*Idiota!*" she said, pulling her hand from his in obvious anger. "We have permission from your Emperor and now may marry! Or have you suddenly changed your mind?"

"I have not changed my mind and stop calling me an idiot!" Karnstein said, looking annoyed.

"Then stop acting like one! We shall get married in Naples because..." Sylvia yelled.

Bartomeleo Dardi and Jean-Pierre Séverin exchanged an amused, if long-suffering look. Sylvia and Franz were behaving normally at least, and that was some comfort. No doubt their arguments and passionate apologies would keep them entertained throughout the easy travels ahead.

"Were you tempted by the offer of eternal life among the undead, Gâteloup?" Dardi asked as the fight between the young lovers grew louder.

"Not even for a moment, my friend," the swordmaster said. "I will greet death, when it comes, as a friend, and see my beloved wife and son awaiting me behind St. Peter. You?"

"Possibly for a moment," Dardi said, shaking his head, "But life eternal is a curse to those unprepared for the pain of loss. Seeing my Sylvia die of old age while I continue living would tear the heart from my chest. No, I shall join my wife and then you and I shall meet in Heaven and battle each day and see who the better swordsman is."

Séverin nodded and extended his hand to his oldest friend.

"I accept the challenge and shall defeat you in the end."

Dardi clasped the extended hand and chuckled.

"No you will not. Now, I think it is time for a song,"

He cleared his throat and sang, "*Non so piu cosa son, cosa faccio, Or di foco, ora sono di ghiaccio, Ogni donna cangiar di colore, Ogni donna mi fa palpitar...*"

The song echoed through the empty Bulgarian hills, while Sylvia and Franz kissed and made up from their latest squabble...

Epilogue

The Satanic priestess caressed the cheek of her youngest follower. He was a pretty boy, a second son of a wealthy merchant and completely spoiled. He was no loss, merely joining the coven for the chance of behaving badly and rampant sex. She denied him a chance of joining her in her bed, knowing this spoiled brat would do anything she asked if she denied him her favors.

"I knew you would yield to me," he said, smiling and caressing her blond curls.

She stabbed him in the stomach with her stone knife. Her favorite servant, Nanette, appeared form a nearby alcove and looped a thick rope around the dying fool's ankles. Together they pulled the rope and smiled as the pulley raised the dying body above the open coffin in the center of the room.

The coffin was a simple wooden box lacking adornments with a shrouded skeleton visible beneath a heavy layer of dust. The blood from the dying young man splashed on the shroud, falling like a crimson rain upon the body beneath. Smoke rose from the skeleton and a gray mist formed over the coffin as the blood fell with increasing speed.

A body formed beneath, that of a man with long limbs, a deep chest, and a head of thick, dark hair. The body stirred and slowly sat upright, pulling the bloodstained shroud away from a handsome face. A pair of pale eyes stared up at the satanic priestess, who smiled upon the vampire.

"Welcome back from the dead, Count Stefan von Karnstein…"